Never Been Good

By Christi Barth

Bad Boys Gone Good
BAD FOR HER
NEVER BEEN GOOD

Coming Soon
GOT IT BAD

Naked Men
RISKING IT ALL
WANTING IT ALL
GIVING IT ALL
TRYING IT ALL

Shore Secrets
UP TO ME
ALL FOR YOU
BACK TO US

Aisle Bound
PLANNING FOR LOVE
A FINE ROMANCE
FRIENDS TO LOVERS
A MATCHLESS ROMANCE

Never Been Good

BAD BOYS GONE GOOD

CHRISTI BARTH

AVONIMPULSE
An Imprint of HarperCollins Publishers

Excerpt from *Got It Bad* copyright © 2018 by Christi Barth.

Digital Edition APRIL 2018 ISBN: 978-0-06-268565-0
Print Edition ISBN: 978-0-06-268566-7

Cover design by Nadine Badalaty

Cover photograph © Volodymyr Tverdokhlib / Shutterstock

Avon Impulse and the Avon Impulse logo are registered trademarks of HarperCollins Publishers in the United States of America.

Avon and HarperCollins are registered trademarks of HarperCollins Publishers in the United States of America and other countries.

FIRST EDITION

18 19 20 21 22   HDC   10 9 8 7 6 5 4 3 2 1

*To my beloved, darling husband who
is the very best man I know.*

Acknowledgments

THANK YOU, FIRST and foremost, to all the readers who fell in love with the Maguire brothers in *Bad For Her*! Massive thanks to my editor, Nicole Fischer, for patiently pointing out where I have to add things that I skipped just because they were hard. Thanks to my agent, Jessica Alvarez, for always having my back.

One of my readers, Mary Rogers, very kindly provided the name for the villain in this book—'Rick'. Eliza Knight and Misty Waters never stopped cheerleading me through the rough spots. Mary Vaughan provided me with write-ins that fueled my competitive spirit and got thousands of words out in record time. And endless hugs to my besties—Stephanie Dray, Laura Kaye and Lea Nolan—for, well, *everything*.

Prologue

Seven Months Earlier
Graceland Cemetery, Chicago
11:30 p.m., October 31

"THIS IS NICE." Frank Mullaney's brother nudged him, flashing a grin from behind the enormous fake white beard. "We haven't celebrated a Halloween together in years."

Yeah. His brother Ryan had lost his mind, no doubt about it. His brother, who happened to be currently dressed like Santa Claus. On freaking Halloween.

Not that it was any better than his own off-season costume. Frank had flat-out refused—at first—when Ryan laid the leprechaun costume across his bed. Until he pointed out the two best points of the costume. A big red beard and hat that would totally disguise Frank's features, and a fake pot of gold. *Aka* something that wouldn't look weird for him to be carrying, just like the bag good old Santa had draped over his shoulder.

Since it turned out that just under two million in cash couldn't be stuffed in your pockets.

Especially not when traipsing through a cemetery. On Halloween. At almost midnight, surrounded by drunken, screaming people on ghost tours.

"That's probably because we're grown-ass men. Trick-or-treating would be weird at our age." The thought of candy made Frank remember that he'd skipped lunch. And dinner. Because Ryan showed up at his front door with costumes and this crazy plan. "Although I wouldn't say no if you pulled a Snickers out of your pocket and tossed it my way."

Ignoring him, Ryan continued, his voice a little softer. "We haven't celebrated Halloween since Mom died."

Way to bring the mood back to serious-as-fuck. Grim enough to match the gravestones they were skirting. "You mean since she was *murdered*." Because Ryan had just shared that little bombshell with him. It was still rattling around in his head like a pinball. God knew it hadn't sunk in yet.

Ryan stopped at the edge of a replica of a Greek temple. He dropped his sack onto the concrete foundation of the tomb. Fisted his hands on the red velvet and padding near his waist. "Can we not talk about that right now? One thing at a time. Let's get through tonight. Through the next couple of weeks. Then, I promise, we'll sit down and hash everything out."

Classic Ryan. Solving problems. Staying focused on

the long game. It was exactly what he did as the right-hand man for the leader of the Chicago mob.

Did . . . past tense. Seeing as how today he and Frank had stolen all of the mob's cash. And then tomorrow, they'd watch their colleagues and friends get arrested in a sting—and hopefully the missing money would be attributed to the Feds' raid. After that, the Mullaney brothers would disappear forever, courtesy of the U.S. Marshals Service.

Frank shifted his weight from one foot to the other. The frostbitten grass made a crunching sound. Probably similar to the one his bones would make if this whole plan failed and the mob ever caught up with them.

"Are you going to talk to Kieran, too?" Because their little brother was out of the loop on all of it. He had no idea that his big brothers were even *in* the mob, let alone close to the top. He was balls deep in law school.

Until tomorrow.

Until they ripped that away from him.

Just to save Frank.

How was that *fair*? God. Frank swallowed so hard he swore he could hear his Adam's apple scraping against his throat.

Ryan's blue eyes shifted to the side. Easy enough to see his discomfort at being pinned down, with the whole place lit up with spotlights and luminarias along the paths and footlights edging the most famous tombs. "You and I will talk first. Then we'll decide, together, how far in to dial Kieran."

"You think he'll hate us?"

Ryan's mouth turned downward into a bitter smirk. "Since it was all my idea to put us into Witness Protection, yeah, I'm sure he'll hate me. For a while. Pretty sure that you will, too. Once our new reality hits."

"No way. Not possible." The only way they'd survived the death of their mom was by banding together as tight as stucco on drywall. Their dad dying . . . ah, no. Being *murdered* by McGinty, per the other surprise truth Ryan laid on him today. Their dad's death had made their bond more unshakeable. Strong enough to get them through their worst days. It made them strong enough to survive anything, as long as the three of them were together. He could never, *would* never hate Ryan.

"I'll check back in with you in a month, when you're jonesing for an MMA fight."

How many more surprises were coming? Frank shook his head. "I can't fight anymore?" The mixed martial arts training started as a way to prove that even though he sat behind a desk, he was just as tough as everyone else in McGinty's organization. Appearances mattered. Respect had to be earned.

Kicking ass in the ring went a long way to making sure people stopped calling him a pencil pusher. But Frank liked it, too. Liked teaching the skills to kids so they could defend themselves. A good fight worked out all his stress. And yeah, he'd cop to getting a thrill from winning the competitions, too.

"Keeping our noses clean is a pretty big requirement

in WITSEC. I think an underground fight club wouldn't go over—" Ryan broke off. Grabbed Frank by the neck and pulled him down behind the marble tomb.

"What?"

Ryan put his finger to his lips. Then he pointed at another tour group, coming at them from the edge of the lake. This one was full of shivering women in skimpy versions of superhero costumes, hanging on the arms of already drunk and stumbling men.

Classy. And definitely making enough noise to scare away any ghosts that were stupid enough to hang around. Chicago's most famous cemetery was full of tours on a regular day. On Halloween, it was as jam-packed as Wrigleyville during a Cubs home game.

Something else that they'd have to give up.

Shit.

Frank hadn't processed *any* of this yet. There'd been no time to think since Ryan burst in on him at breakfast. Told him McGinty was a lying son of a bitch who intended to send Frank to jail to cover his own ass.

Before Frank had time to even break into a cold sweat of panic, Ryan told him that he'd fixed it. That he'd gone to the Feds and offered to turn evidence against McGinty, and everyone else. That the Mullaney brothers would get a free ride and full protection as long as he lived up to the bargain and they played it straight.

Right after they socked away their "insurance" money.

Because neither of them fully trusted the Feds to keep them safe.

Yeah, that flop sweat was sure popping out now. It made the cheap polyester of his costume itch. Frank wasn't ready to give up his job, his clothes, his apartment, his fights, his *life*.

On the other hand, jail didn't sound much better.

His breath rasped out in little clouds. He realized how cold the marble was under his hands. Cold as death.

Jail—or a new life in the middle of nowhere—was definitely a step up from being cold in the ground. Which was undoubtedly McGinty's plan B if the Mullaneys pushed back at his making Frank the fall guy.

After the tour group went down the slope to the lake, Ryan asked, "You got a date for tonight?"

"No." He tugged at the cartoonishly wide lapel of his bright green jacket. "No chance I'll get one dressed like this, either."

"You should get one. Go to a bar. Hook up. Live it up."

Was he serious? Their lives were in the literal eye of a shitstorm right now. Frank could flirt half-asleep, half-drunk, only half-interested, and *still* score a girl. But tonight? His head wasn't in the game. Let alone his dick. "Not really in a pound-all-the-shots kind of mood, bro."

"Doesn't matter." Ryan stabbed a finger out toward the glow over the treetops indicating the bright lights of downtown. "You need to be visible. Hit the usual spots. Make sure at least a half dozen of our guys see you having the time of your life. It'll keep them from being suspicious after the raid goes down. Can you fake it?"

That was a funny question. That's all Frank did every day of his life.

He faked being okay with *not* being in on all the action. He faked being okay with not getting to choose his own damn college major, not being able to go to grad school. He'd convinced McGinty and the whole crew that he was fine with the choices made for him, the life they'd made and shoehorned him into.

Now he got to start over—and yet again, Frank still didn't get a say in it.

"Yeah. I can throw back some whiskey tonight, no problem." Probably the truest thing he'd said all day. The more he thought about it? The more getting shitfaced sounded like the only way to deal with all of this. No way he'd inflict himself and his weird-ass mood on a woman, though. "Want to grab one last deep-dish pepperoni at Lou Malnati's? Before we make the rounds of the clubs?"

"You bet."

Frank looked at his watch. The watch McGinty gave him the day he was promoted to vice president of the construction company. Damn. That promotion had been a way to keep Frank under his thumb all along. A way to keep a convenient patsy close by.

Turned out the job he'd worked his ass off for was basically the mob's version of a bench to be warmed. Just a placeholder in case McGinty needed someone who looked important enough—on paper, anyway—to take all the blame.

He planned to put this watch under the front tire of whatever government SUV drove them out of town. Crushing it, crushing the taint of its memory, would be his last official act in Chicago.

"We'll only make it if we wrap this up fast enough. Are we close, Ryan? Where are we stashing all this cash, anyway?"

"See that pyramid over there?"

Gray stone rose into a triangle of blocks, with a sphinx on one side of the doorway, an angel on the other. Talk about a weird combination. It was cool and creepy and Frank had no idea how they were supposed to get inside of it. "The one with the giant black padlock on the door?"

"It's modeled after an Egyptian tomb." Ryan stood, slinging the red velvet sack back over his shoulder. "You remember the thing about all those ancient pyramids?"

"There was always a secret way out." Okay, maybe tonight would be a little bit fun, after all. Sure, a slice of 'za from Malnati's always scored in the top ten ways to end a night in Chicago. But a crazy-ass adventure with his big brother sounded like an even better way to spend their last hours in their hometown. A story they'd tell over and over and over again through the years.

Crap.

They'd only tell it to each other. Since this all had to stay a secret. From everyone.

For the rest of their lives.

Luckily, Ryan seemed oblivious to how often Frank's

thoughts spiraled into near-panic. Gesturing for him to follow, his brother stalked in between the columns and zigzagged around a perimeter of six-foot-tall bushes. "Or, in our case, a way in. After this Schoenhofen guy died, his son-in-law took over the business. And he owed the mob a shit-ton of money. He ran the biggest brewery in Chicago back in the day. Thought he'd gotten so big that he could skip paying protection money."

That was just stupid, no matter what decade he was from. At least that stupidity erased the tiny bit of guilt Frank had been harboring about breaking into a tomb. "Let me guess. They took him out?"

"Drowned him in one of his own copper beer kettles." Ryan shot him a grin.

Frank couldn't help but smile back. It was kind of perfect. The Irish mob excelled at making their point in . . . creative ways. "Karma's a bitch."

"Whoever took over the business next wised up. He paid up. Fast. As a show of good faith, he offered this tomb as a place for us to hide . . . whatever we might need to keep out of sight. People. Money. Bodies. With Prohibition about to hit, we jumped at it. Settled his account right up. We used it for years. Nowadays a cemetery isn't so easy to go unnoticed in, so it just sits empty. I checked it out, oh, three years ago when I first learned about it. Nothing but cobwebs inside."

Suddenly, Frank didn't want to hear any more Chicago history. No matter how interesting. It just reminded him of the ticking clock hanging over his head. The one where he, Ryan, and Kieran were all leaving Chicago for good. As hard as he tried to ignore it? That fact only seemed to clear out of his head for about two minutes, before the weight of it crashed back down again.

Shit.

Ryan was jumping through all these hoops *for* him. To *save* him. No way could he let his brother see how freaked out he was. It wouldn't be fair to lay that on him. Frank caught up in a couple of long steps. "How did I never hear this story?"

"Because you kept your nose clean running the legit biz. You didn't spend every day hanging out, shooting the breeze with lowlifes like me."

"Look what good that did me," Frank mumbled. Great. His clear head had only lasted twenty seconds this time around.

Laying a hand on his arm to stop him, his brother asked, "What are you talking about?"

"Ryan, you're the fixer for the head of the Chicago mob. You've done more than your fair share of bad things."

The fingers on his arm tightened. "I take care of bad people. There's a difference. Whatever I do, I guarantee they've got it coming to them. It's justice, Frankie. No different than handing out parking tickets. Our way's just faster. More successful, too."

Frank gave a quick thought to the parking tickets filling his glove compartment. Well, at least he was off the hook for a couple hundred bucks there. Silver lining.

Get out of jail and get out of his tickets. Clearly, he owed Ryan a thank-you present. Something between a bottle of blue label Johnnie Walker and a boot to the balls.

He shook off Ryan's grip. Turned to face him. To bleed off some of the bitterness suddenly spurting up from his gut. "I toed the line. Ran the front. Paid taxes. Made sure all of you lowlifes had taxes and Medicare taken out of their paychecks. Health insurance. Made a construction company run even though half the people on the payroll never showed up to work. And yet *I'm* the one Danny McGinty wants to send to jail?"

"You're not going to jail," Ryan said fiercely. "That's the whole point of this. You will *not* see the inside of a cell, Frank. I've got that in writing from the U.S. Marshals. We turn evidence, we cooperate, we're free to go."

It was almost too good to be true. Nobody stood up to the mob and just walked away. "What if something goes wrong?"

Ryan put his head down, scanning the ground. Five graves down from the Schoenhofen pyramid the earth rose into a low bunker. Tombs with pointed roofs that came up maybe to his waist were built into it. At the first one, Ryan dropped to his knees. He pushed at the cornice of each of the eighth-sized columns. Then he put his fingers around the starburst carved in the middle and twisted. The entire front swung inward.

"That's why we stole all this money, isn't it? Best backup plan in the world. Plus, it gives you your one shot at finally being a bad guy to the core. I call that a win-win." Shoving his sack in front of him, Ryan hit the deck and shimmied inside.

Frank looked around at the shadows from the pine trees, the full moon overhead, and the stark lines of the tombs. This was a pretty epic way to end things here in Chicago. Belly-crawling into a century-old crypt on Halloween? Come on. Classic Ryan, thinking to hide the mob's stolen money *in their own hiding spot.*

So he'd have fun with this. No more sulking. No more freaking out. Maybe this new life was the best thing for all of them. They'd never intended to grow up to be criminals, after all.

Starting over would be good. Not just because it kept him out of jail.

And as long as he was with Ryan and Kieran, how bad could it really be?

Chapter One

FLYNN MAGUIRE HATED a lot of things. As he slowly, carefully drew a pint of Guinness, he counted them. Starting with his brother, Rafe, who had the dumber than dirt idea to throw them all into Witness Protection.

He also hated his new life.

They were on version five of it now, having been planted and then yanked from four other towns and jobs. Their personal marshal, Delaney Evans, had issued the warning—*aka* threat—that if this one didn't take, they were out of the program. He'd hate her a little, too, if he didn't respect that she was just doing her job. Of all people, Flynn sure as hell knew what that felt like. Seeing as how he'd spent five years running a construction company he didn't give two shits about. But he'd run it, and run it well.

For all the good it did.

He hated this quaint fucking seaside village of a town. On principle, anyway. Because it wasn't Chicago. None of the towns they'd moved to were anything like the Windy City. The food, the people, the action—none of it compared. Flynn hadn't realized how much he'd miss his hometown. Mostly because he hadn't had any time to think about it between being told they were leaving, and disappearing.

Top of the list? That had to be how much Flynn hated himself. Or at least the sad-sack version of himself he'd turned into since entering WITSEC.

"These should quiet down those thirsty backpackers. Thank you, Flynn," said a soft voice to his left. He whipped his head around to stare at the waitress as she picked up a tray of longnecks.

The *pretty* waitress.

The one thing in his life Flynn absolutely did *not* hate.

She was girl-next-door pretty. With long hair that fell in waves, the same dark brown as a good vanilla porter. Eyebrows that arched her face into a smile even when her lips didn't play along. Skinnier than his usual type back home, but it worked on her. She was small and fragile-looking. Made a guy want to be careful with her. Kiss her slowly. Thoroughly. Keep kissing her while taking off that blue shirt and finding out if her bra underneath matched . . .

The pretty waitress drove him crazy. Because Flynn wanted her. Had since his first shift here a month ago.

That was a hell of a long time to want a woman and not make a move on her.

But he was no good. No good for her, no good for any woman. Flynn was a morose son of a bitch who lied 24/7 to everyone but his two brothers and he wouldn't inflict himself on anyone, let alone someone as sweet as Sierra.

Sierra . . . huh. He didn't even know her last name. Not that it mattered. Because a name didn't tell you jack shit.

At least, he hoped his current name didn't tell anyone *anything* about him.

"Dude. My beer."

The outrage in Kellan's voice was enough to make Flynn tear his gaze away from Sierra and notice the foam pouring down the side of the glass. No wonder his little brother sounded pissed.

"Sorry, K." He flipped off the tap.

"You hear that sound?"

Flynn cocked his head. Since it was Sunday night, there was only the jukebox going instead of a live band. Only a handful of the less than two dozen tables were filled. The pool table wasn't being used in the back room. No darts going on, either. All in all, even for a Sunday night in June this bar was quiet. Which, to his mind, perfectly summed up this town of three thousand locals. "Hear what?"

"The sound of generations of our Irish ancestors rolling over in their graves." Kellan grabbed a stack of cocktail napkins and wiped off the glass. "Sure an' the fairies will punish you with bad dreams for wasting the mother's milk of our land," he said in a thick Irish accent.

"There's no fairies in Oregon."

Shaking a finger, Kellan gave him a look of disappointment. Something Flynn had gotten used to seeing from both him and Rafe, more and more often. "Is there no magic in your heart then, young Maguire?"

"No," he said shortly. Then Flynn remembered that Kellan had volunteered to leave the house tonight so Rafe and his girlfriend, Mollie, could have some privacy. *And* he'd sat here keeping Flynn's sorry ass company all night. So he ratcheted up the corners of his mouth to a smile. Well, something closer to a smile than his usual scowl. "But there's no bullet lodged in there, either, so I guess that's something."

"Jesus, Flynn." Kellan hunched his shoulders. Threw a lightning quick glance over each shoulder. "You can't say stuff like that. You know the rules. No discussing your old, um, *career* in public."

The only occupied tables were down by the doorway to the room with the pool table. Flynn could hear Carlos, the Gorse's manager, groaning over whatever baseball game he was listening to in his office. Sierra was still delivering that tray of drinks. He could've literally named every member of McGinty's crew and nobody would've heard a thing. Kellan was just overly paranoid.

Of course, Kellan hadn't been used to lying his whole life, like Flynn and Rafe. They hadn't come out and talked about being in the mob to their dates, but they also mostly hung out with women who knew the score. Whose families were involved, too. To everyone else they encountered—from doctors to bartenders to the kids he'd mentored—they'd stuck to their cover stories.

It'd been easier for Flynn, since he ran the legit business. The one they could launder money through whenever McGinty needed a fast influx of clean cash. The one that supplied paychecks on the up-and-up so that they all looked like tax-paying, law-abiding citizens, even if most of the organization only worked on Flynn's construction sites a couple of times a month.

He was used to how it felt to say one thing and know there were three more things deliberately being left unsaid. And he'd honed an instinct about when it was safe to reveal more.

Kellan didn't have the luxury of those years of training. He was still in the paranoid phase, assuming that everyone who crossed paths with the Maguire brothers could see right through them to their dirty-dealing histories.

Probably because that's all he saw when he looked at his brothers. They'd pulled Kellan from law school with only a semester to go after he'd worked his ass off to learn everything there was about justice. About being on the side of right and might.

Then he'd found out the rest of his family stood on the *other* side of that line.

"Relax." Flynn whipped his bar towel at Kellan's shoulder. "What did we tell you was rule number one?"

"Ever? Don't touch your shit without asking."

"Still true. But I meant the number one rule of this." He circled his hand to indicate not just the cranberry red walls of the Gorse, but the whole cranberry-crazy town.

"Nobody thinks you're guilty. Unless you give them a reason to." Kellan winced. "That's abominable grammar, by the way."

"There's no grades when it comes to what it takes to stay alive. You either do or you don't."

"Great pep talk. Thanks, bro."

Shit. Kellan was trying. But everything that used to get through to Flynn didn't work anymore. He didn't care about his clothes—and he used to buy every piece of workout gear between the covers of *GQ*. He didn't care about missing the fight club. He certainly didn't care about this bartending job that he'd been pushed into.

Instinctively, his gaze searched the room for Sierra. The one thing in this new life that made him feel . . . *anything*. Even if it was mostly frustration. Blue balls were no fucking fun. Working a whole shift with them? The worst. Just looking at Sierra, though, would soothe the frayed edges of guilt poking at his stomach for being a jerk to his brother. When he didn't find her, Flynn forced himself to look back at Kellan.

"Sorry. I'm being a dick." Add that to his list of things he hated. Because deep down, he really hated this fucking attitude that he couldn't shake. Now, though, it was comfortable. As easy to slip on as a pair of fleece pants.

Flynn worried that the day was coming—soon— when he'd lose the ability to ever take it off again.

"Oh, you mean tonight? Yeah. You've been a total dick. Pretty much every day for the past seven months, too? You bet." Kellan lifted his mug in a fake toast, then drained almost half of it.

Offering up as close as he could get to an olive branch, Flynn said, "This isn't as easy as we thought it'd be."

"Nope." Kellan cocked his head to the side. Those blue eyes, way lighter than his own, squinted at him. "Want to tell me what exactly you and Rafe were high on when you thought this might be easy?"

Drugs were for idiots. "You know we don't touch that stuff."

"Yet it's the only explanation I've got for you two thinking this would be a cakewalk."

Before he could defend himself, a loud shattering noise had Flynn jerking around just in time to see Sierra fall to the floor in a heap. Right next to a knocked-over table with a spray of broken glasses all around it. That she was lying in the middle of.

He didn't bother going down to the end of the bar and lifting the hatch. Every second he wasted was another moment that Sierra might put out her hand to lever up and cut herself. So Flynn just planted a palm in the middle of the bar and vaulted over it.

Crouching next to Sierra, he heard the crunch of

glass as Kellan rushed to his side. "Don't move," he cautioned her. Flynn put a hand lightly on her abdomen to drive the point home. Tried not to notice the way she tightened at his touch.

"It's hard to serve beers from the floor," she quipped. And those bluish-gray eyes that almost never looked at him head-on lifted to meet his. With what he'd swear to his dying day was an audible click.

Nah.

Had to be the crushed glass shifting.

Didn't it?

It was easy for Flynn to slip back into his take-charge mode. It was a mask he'd put on every day at the construction company and he knew exactly how much force to put into his voice to be sure people listened to him—and responded. "Where are you hurt?"

A self-deprecating smile ghosted at the edges of her pretty pink lips. "My pride's pretty well bruised."

"Sierra."

"My ankle." She sighed. "I landed on it and sort of twisted."

"Kellan, we'll need ice." His brother wordlessly left to carry out the order. Flynn splayed his fingers wider when he felt Sierra start to shift. "Does it hurt anywhere else? Are you cut?"

"No. Just sticky and wet from all this beer now on the floor."

Sticky and wet. If he didn't know better, he'd swear that the woman was trying to get a rise out of him.

But Flynn did know better. Because while Sierra was just about the only person he felt comfortable talking to, she sure as hell didn't *flirt* with him. Not ever. Only made bearable by the fact that she didn't flirt with anyone else, either.

"I'm going to pick you up," he announced. "Once you're vertical, put all your weight on me. Then I'll brush off the glass."

"Oh, you don't have to do that." Sierra spoke so quickly all the words merged together into one.

What the hell? Why did she sound . . . *scared* at the idea of him holding her?

Flynn put an arm beneath her knees and worked the other behind her neck and down her back. Glass nicked the back of his hand.

It didn't matter.

Because he was finally touching her. He might as well have been lifting a dandelion, she weighed so little. Even though he consciously held her away from his body because of the glass, Flynn noticed everything. The firm calf muscle against the back of his hand. The heat of her back through the sticky shirt. The way it pulled taut against her small breasts.

He watched to be sure she kept one foot off the floor, and then stood her up. Flynn grabbed the bar rag from where he'd stuffed it into his waistband and wrapped it around his hand for protection. Sierra white-knuckled his left arm.

Slowly, carefully, he brushed her off from shoulders to

ankles in long, sweeping motions. He kept an eye peeled for any dots of blood on her shirt that might indicate a nick. Instead, it was just the blood from the backs of his knuckles seeping through the towel. Flynn tried like hell to keep the whole thing professional. Medicinal. One co-worker performing a safety check of another.

Yeah. That angle sure as hell wasn't working for him.

When he finished her sides, Flynn came back around in front. Damn if her cheeks weren't pink. "I'm going to carry you into the back now."

"Oh, but Flynn, you—"

Whatever objection she was trying to get out he cut off by sweeping her back into his arms. This time, he did hold her close. Who knew when he'd ever have another chance? Flynn cradled her against his chest.

Holy hell. He almost stumbled in shock and decided that—if her ankle wasn't broken—this would now rank as his best day since they'd moved to this dot on the map. Maybe even his best day in the last four dots.

Holding Sierra was like holding sunlight. Her warmth shot through him, reminding him how good it felt to be alive. How good it felt to be a man. That maybe life wasn't a complete shitstorm after all.

Reminded him that no matter how hard he tried to be good and stay away from her . . . well, maybe he wasn't good *enough* to be that strong anymore.

This rush of goodness was the way he'd heard some of the mobsters talk about doing heroin. Flynn had no doubt that Sierra was even more addictive.

And dangerous. At least for him.

The trip around the bar and down the hallway to the manager's office took too little time. He had no excuse to keep holding her. No excuse to keep rubbing his cheek against Sierra's soft hair. No excuse for inhaling deeply and appreciating the clean, floral scent that spurted want and need and full-out lust straight down to his dick.

So Flynn placed her on the rolling wooden chair that Carlos pushed at him. Then he knelt in front of her and pulled her bad leg onto his knee.

Carlos put a hand on Sierra's shoulder. His thick eyebrows joined into a single dark line of concern. "*Dios mio.* What happened?"

"I was careless." She waved a hand, dismissing the whole thing. "A couple of the darts landed way off the board. I climbed onto a table to get them, but they were stuck into the wall so well that I lost my balance and fell."

"The drunk who threw them into my wall should've pulled them out," Carlos growled.

Sierra ducked her head. "It's no big deal. Really. I was just trying to be helpful. Instead, I've disrupted everyone and made a mess. I'm sorry."

The woman risked herself for stupid darts? Flynn's worry for her morphed into anger. "You're lucky you aren't cut from landing on all that glass. Why didn't you ask me to do it?"

In a low voice, not looking at him, she answered, "I didn't want to bother you."

A brick between the eyes would've hurt Flynn less. This was *his* fault. One hundred percent. He'd tried not to let his fucked-up darkness touch her in any way. She was his first friend here in Bandon—pretty much the only one he had besides Carlos. Something about Sierra's bone-deep sweetness made Flynn comfortable. Made him let down the guard he kept up around everyone else. She never pushed or asked hard questions. They just talked, and it was the most relaxed he was any given day.

But tonight he'd been wallowing in self-pity. *Again*. She must've picked up on his crap mood, and that made her unwilling to ask a man who topped her by at least six inches for a basic, work-related assist.

Flynn wanted to howl his frustration at his own idiocy. Actually, he really wanted to find a heavy bag and whale on it for a couple of hours until his knuckles ached, his lungs burned, and his muscles cried for mercy.

But now was the time to focus on Sierra. "I'm sorry. Sorry that you didn't feel comfortable asking me for help. For the future? I'll do whatever you need. No matter what I'm in the middle of. Got it?"

She nodded, long hair still shadowing her face.

Flynn unlaced her black sneaker. It was streaked with different colors of paint. It made him wonder what she did in her off-hours. Was she painting her house? Would she be climbing a ladder with a weak ankle? Would she let him help, or refuse his not-yet-made offer?

Even though he was careful easing the shoe off, Sierra's sharp intake of breath made her pain at the movement obvious. Which made Flynn's guilt stab into his gut even deeper.

Sierra's ankle was already swelling. He didn't even have to roll down her black-and-white polka-dotted socks to see that. Frankly, he didn't trust himself to touch her skin again. "Ice," he barked as soon as Kellan hustled into the room.

His brother handed over a dish towel bulging with cubes. "I'll go out and clean up while you two take care of her." He grabbed the broom and dustpan from the corner on his way out.

"Thanks, Kellan." Carlos barely spared him a glance as he fussed over Sierra with little pats and frowns. He was acting like a grandpa instead of a hard-ass covered in tats and a telltale curve to his nose indicating multiple breaks. "Do you want a drink, Sierra? A couple of shots to cut the pain?"

"Oh, no. I've got ibuprofen at home. I'd rather take that than make myself feel worse with a hangover."

Flynn pulled over the trash can, upended it, and rested her foot on it sideways, ice draped across. Then he noticed the sparkly glints of glass in her hair. "Do you have a brush?"

"No." She looked up at that to give him an amused half smile. "I'm not one of those women who reapplies their lipstick every twenty minutes."

He'd noticed. He'd noticed *everything* about her

look. Natural. Like hippy-natural. Which he found weirdly sexy. Weird because the women he'd dated in Chicago were all big boobs, loud makeup, and bigger hair. Sierra was just . . . herself. Which turned Flynn on more than he'd been willing to admit. Okay, hell. He'd admitted it. He'd just refused to act on it.

Until tonight.

Until seeing her crumpled on the floor of the bar. It had sent a primal surge of protectiveness through him that unlocked everything he'd kept tamped down for weeks now. All the interest. Lust. Attraction. Need.

Carlos produced a brush from his desk drawer. "Here. It's Madalena's." She was his sister who did the books for the Gorse. Flynn had only met her once, but appreciated her no-nonsense personality. "I'll go watch the bar for you, Flynn."

"Thanks." He carefully pulled Sierra's hair over her shoulders so it draped down her back. "This should be the quickest way to get the glass out."

"Oh, but you don't have to—"

That was the kicker. After spending years doing what people told him he *had* to, Flynn now did only the bare minimum. Sure, he could just hand her the brush. But this, helping Sierra, was a compulsion he couldn't resist. "I know I don't *have* to. I want to help. Let me."

"Okay." Her shoulders relaxed down at least an inch as she sighed. Then Sierra sighed again as the bristles made contact with her scalp. This one was different, though. It was pure feminine pleasure.

God, he couldn't wait to make her do it again.

Flynn made long, slow passes. A little more pressure against her head, because she seemed to like it, and then a pull through the long strands to shake out the glass. It was quiet. Intimate. Something he'd never done before for any other woman. The backs of his fingers grazed her neck as he gathered her hair in his hand.

Sierra shivered.

His dick throbbed at the sight. At her whole-body shiver, and at the view of her exposed nape. Right on the spot where, if he put his lips, Flynn *knew* he could tease another shiver out of her.

Then he noticed how her hair looked in his fist. He flashed ahead past a million impossibilities to a scene that he could never let happen. Sierra on her knees. Naked. Looking over her shoulder at him with that shy smile while he fisted her hair and drove into her.

The ice slid off her ankle, tinkling as it tumbled out of the towel onto the floor. The moment was gone.

Although Flynn knew he'd never be able to get *that* image out of his mind.

Carlos reappeared in the doorway. "Flynn, will you take her home?"

"I can get myself home," Sierra protested.

"Did you ride that bike of yours here?" At her nod, Carlos fished his keys out of his pocket and tossed them to Flynn. "Here. Take my truck. Load her bike into the back. I'll have Jeb drive me home once we close."

"That's really not necessary."

"And it's not up for discussion." Unbelievable. First of all, a bike? Seriously? Secondly, he had to prove to Sierra it was okay to let him help. Despite the stubbornly independent streak she had. "I'll grab my jacket and be right back."

Carlos shut the door to the office behind them, then rounded on Flynn. He brandished a stubby finger in his face. "Be careful with her."

What the hell? "I always am." He headed to his locker at the end of the hallway, right before the dry storage. Unfortunately, Carlos dogged his heels.

"No, you're polite. To everyone. That's not the same as being careful."

Damn it, he bent over backward to be *careful* with Sierra. Flynn spun the combination on his locker. He didn't really get into personal conversations these days. The easiest way to keep a life of lies straight was to say nothing at all. But he couldn't blow off his boss without a reason. "I won't give her the wrong idea."

"What? That you're a decent human being?"

"No. That I'm interested."

Carlos's swarthy features twisted into astonishment, and then humor. His laugh boomed out, echoing off the pans hanging from hooks above the prep counter. "Because you're God's gift to womankind? One smile and she'll lose her common sense, her good taste, and her ability to resist you?"

"Something like that."

"So far as I can tell, you've got exactly one strength.

Making up weird and wonderful cocktails. People go ape-shit for them. You know what they don't go nuts over? Your looks and barely noticeable charm. If you can squeeze out a smile, I promise that Sierra will be able to withstand it. She's strong."

"She's fragile."

"Doesn't mean she's not strong. People are often more than just what they look like." Carlos cocked his head to the side. "Guessing you already know that."

"What you see is what you get."

"A guy with a chip on his shoulder?"

"Yeah. That's it." That's all he was anymore. Flynn couldn't risk being anything but the empty shell of a man.

This move into WITSEC had hollowed him out. Hollowed out everything he thought he was, who he was. No point filling that back up. No point deciding on a new persona.

All Flynn believed now? Was that it wouldn't last long enough to matter. Because hope was a luxury he'd lost.

Chapter Two

SIERRA WILLIAMS KNEW that letting Flynn take her home was a huge mistake. No, it was several mistakes compounding into a gigantic one. Being alone with Flynn was . . . a horrible idea. Because Flynn was *gorgeous*. Chiseled, from his knife-sharp cheekbones to his ripped physique. Dark and sexy, with a quietly brooding bad boy vibe that pushed all her buttons.

Which was exactly what got her in trouble with her last boyfriend. Rick. Who then sucked her unknowingly into an art counterfeiting ring. And that led right into bad mistake number two. Letting Flynn know where she lived.

When you were on the run, trying to be incognito, you didn't invite someone over to your house.

Not that Flynn had waited to be invited. No, he'd just issued the edict that he was taking her home.

Which had been kind of hot, come to think of it. Rick's reasons for everything he said, did, and made Sierra do always came back to *himself*. Tonight, Flynn seemed hell-bent on helping Sierra. None of it benefitted him.

She'd made him lose tips by leaving early. Given his poor brother a mess to clean up. And now his evening was hijacked by taking her home. He got nothing out of it for himself. Less than nothing.

Probably why it felt so good that he insisted on helping her . . .

On to bad mistake number three. Letting herself get distracted by Flynn. Oh, Sierra *noticed* him all the time. How could any woman with a pulse not notice him? If she'd still been safely back in art school, all her friends would've been trying to get Flynn to model nude for their life drawing class.

The way he stood, with one hip canted forward as if he was about to command a Roman battalion to ride into battle. Powerful. In control of anything and everything within his sphere. Even though he rarely asserted that power, it rolled off of him. Gave him a sense of authority that sent shivers down Sierra's spine. On top of the stunning way his close-cropped, jet-black hair contrasted with his pale skin and almost navy blue eyes. Black Irish. That's how her art books would've characterized him as a portrait subject.

Just plain dreamy is how Sierra characterized him. Height that topped six feet and made her feel tiny and feminine. Muscles that bulged in all the right places. Forearms, with those long, thick blue veins running down them that popped out even more when he sliced the garnish fruit. Sierra had become an expert at rationalizing reasons to head over to the bar whenever she heard the knife snick against the cutting board. Just to watch. Ogle. Drool. All of the above.

But tonight she'd wallowed in Flynn on a deeper level. One not based in fantasies, but reality. The reality of his touch, his strength, his heat. It all almost, *almost* distracted her from the throbbing in her ankle. When he'd brushed her hair? It was the singular most erotic experience of her life.

Not that she'd had copious amount of legendary sex. Or even average amounts of average sex. Aside from a few hookups, Rick had been her first real boyfriend. But neither the hookups nor the ostensibly romantic sex with the man Sierra thought she maybe could love— eventually—came anywhere close to the near-orgasmic rush she'd gotten from having Flynn Maguire brush her hair.

"You're awfully quiet." Flynn's voice cut into her thoughts. Startled, her elbow slipped off where it'd been propped on the window. Because yes, she'd been half-hanging out of that open car window to keep from staring at Flynn. Watching the pine trees blur together seemed safer than indulging in stealing extra glances of him.

"So are you." Which was actually normal.

He didn't do small talk. Nor meaningless chitchat. Flynn was polite to customers. But he only said something above and beyond the bare minimum if it really *mattered*. Sierra liked that. That he didn't spout nonsense all day. Or try to schmooze everyone in his path like a bad car salesman. Like Rick used to. No, when Flynn spoke, you knew—whether big or small—it was the truth.

Flynn's truth was almost sexier than his forearms. Which was an extremely high bar.

In a low voice, he said, "I don't know what to say to you."

His honesty—although most people would probably interpret his words as an insult—merely intrigued Sierra with its strangeness. "Why not?"

"We work together. But now I'm driving you home. Like we're . . . something more. Which wouldn't be right."

Ouch. The truth of that stung. For probably a very different reason than he had, Sierra knew that they shouldn't expand beyond their friendship. Although Sierra didn't really want to be *just* Flynn's friend. Unless "friend" now also meant "person I'd like to take to bed and not surface again until we run out of condoms."

With equal parts defensiveness and wishful thinking, Sierra said, "We're already friendly."

"We're colleagues," he corrected. "I'm not used to being friendly with the people who work for me."

For him? Whoa.

Sierra darned well wouldn't let a man walk all over her. Not *again*, anyway. "I don't recall being supplied with an org chart when I got the job, but I'm pretty sure that I report to Carlos. As do you," she said pointedly.

"Sorry."

"That's it?" For once, Flynn's lack of elaboration bugged her. Maybe because this time it was personal.

"What more do you want?"

Sooo much more. Kisses. Tender touches. For Flynn to turn the same intensity that darkened his eyes when he invented a personalized cocktail on to *her*. To see him shirtless. To see him naked. Basically *everything*.

Everything that could lead to exposure and danger. So everything she couldn't let herself have.

Sierra shifted to look at him. He didn't sound exasperated. The eyebrow closest to her was arched up, as though Flynn genuinely wanted to know. She had nothing to lose by telling him. Well, not by telling him the naked thing. Just what more she wanted from his actual apology.

"Maybe an explanation of why you think I work *for* you, instead of with you. Sure, the customers wouldn't get the drinks if you didn't make them. But they also wouldn't get the drinks you made unless I delivered them. If anything, we work in a perfectly synchronous balance."

"I don't."

His clipped delivery could have shut her down. Sierra Williams was not known—in her other, real life, the life *before*—for pushing. For poking at people. No, she avoided uncomfortable situations and conflict as much as possible. Even more so now that she worked so hard to go unnoticed by everyone except this man, who seemed to be able to look straight into her.

Ergo, this *dangerous* man.

But if they were going to keep working together, Sierra wanted to know that Flynn valued her. At least as a colleague. "You don't think what we do has balance?"

"I don't think you work for me. It was a slip of the tongue." Flynn canted his head away from her. His wrist still hung loosely over the steering wheel, but every other muscle she could see in the bright moonlight was tensed to near steel. "I ran a company, before. I got used to thinking of myself in that role. Sometimes habit takes over. I speak before remembering that everything's changed."

"Everything?" Now Sierra was intrigued.

Her entire life had turned upside down. As she went through that topsy-turviness, she'd realized that it was indeed rare for absolutely *everything* to change all at once. Rare and hard. And lonely. And had she mentioned *hard*? It would certainly be nice to unload some of that onto someone who'd gone through the same thing.

Not that she could tell him. Not when keeping her secret might very well be the only thing keeping her alive.

"You know." He shrugged one massive, muscled wall

of a shoulder. "Different job. Different town. It's an adjustment."

At the Gorse, they chatted about their jobs. Joked about quirky/difficult customers. Talking to Flynn was a way to relax, to let go of her hunched-over shoulders and endless worries for a few minutes.

But they rarely revealed anything personal. Like there was an unspoken agreement not to talk about *themselves*. Now that Flynn had opened that door a crack? Sierra wanted to ask a million questions.

On the other hand, she absolutely did *not* want any of those questions volleyed back at her. Questions like why'd she moved here, why'd she left her old home, what life she'd left behind.

In the three months she'd been in Bandon, it had been excruciatingly hard to hide all of that. People here were friendly. Inquisitive. In a good way, but one that made it difficult to sidestep without being rude. So she kept her mouth shut. Kept to herself.

And Sierra was so very tired of it.

So lonely.

This conversation with Flynn was one of the longest non-work-related talks she'd had since moving here. Heck, since fleeing Wisconsin in the middle of the night seven months ago. Sierra *ached* to have long, deep conversations. Especially when she was off-the-clock.

So, darn it, she'd make Flynn keep talking to her.

Yes, about *himself,* for once. Because talking to someone who she'd had a painfully-going-nowhere crush on for weeks was the least she deserved.

Boldly, Sierra laid two fingers right at the crook of his elbow. And left them there. "Rumor has it that the best conversations happen in cars in the dark. Gotta start somewhere, right? That's part of putting down roots in a new place."

Flynn's head tilted backward to beat against the headrest. Twice. "Don't even start with that."

"You don't want to put down roots? You and your brothers aren't planning to stay?" Her fingers clamped down a little. Because Flynn leaving would be the worst. He and Carlos were the only people she really talked to in this town. And only at work. Her hours outside the Gorse were painfully lonely.

"We have a, ah, friend who keeps reminding us to put down roots. Delaney can lecture on the importance of it for a solid ten minutes straight."

It was hard to picture Flynn putting up with anyone telling him what to do. The authority that radiated off of him, the competence with which he did everything from changing kegs out to dealing with drunks did not indicate a man who sat still for a lecture. "I'm surprised you let her. Oh, turn right at the stop sign."

"Kellan's got the hots for her. It makes him happy to watch her lips move, so we throw the kid a bone."

Sierra giggled. It was such a silly, big brother thing

to say. Simultaneously, Flynn sucked in a sharp breath. "Hell, I'm sorry. That probably sounded sexist. Women are not objects. I know that."

"No worries." She patted his forearm this time, not just to reassure him, but to feel the crisp, dark hair that lightly covered the taut muscles and snaky blue veins that made her mouth water at their sheer masculinity. "See how easy that was? You're sharing *personal* things."

"About my little brother. Not the best topic."

"Okay. Stay to the left up there." She pointed at the fork in the road. "Well, you didn't answer my question about staying in Bandon."

"You've seen Rafe and Mollie together, right? He'd move to Siberia if it's where she lived. They're so in love it makes my teeth hurt. Mollie's planted here, so Rafe's staying here. Simple as that."

"You and Kellan want to stay near Rafe?"

"Yeah." Funny how . . . grim he sounded about it. "The Maguire brothers are a package deal. Family's important to us."

Sierra wanted to ask if he had any other family. But she didn't dare. Not without risking him asking about her family. And that conversation wouldn't be worth having.

#1biglie.

"You don't sound overjoyed. Do you not like Mollie? Or is it Bandon?"

"Doc Mollie's great." He chuffed out a laugh. "She's way out of Rafe's league. He doesn't deserve her."

"Bandon, then?"

Silence hung in the truck. It kept puffing up, all spiky and uncomfortable and pressing in on both of them, making it hard for Sierra to draw a deep breath. Finally, Flynn said, "It's . . . an adjustment."

"You said that already," she said in a singsong voice.

"Yeah, well, what about you?"

Uh-oh. Sierra straightened in her seat and looked out the window at the sprawling ranches and wide lawns they passed. "What about me?"

"Do you like it here?"

Ahhh. A softball question that required neither lies nor sidestepping. "I like it a lot. Living by the ocean is great. Watching the fog roll in, feeling the moisture in the air, watching the light and water change literally every time I look at it. Smelling the pines whenever I step outside. Cycling past the red blur of the cranberry bogs. It's all magical and beautiful."

"You should join the tourist board. Get paid for spouting off like that."

Sierra hadn't stayed long in many other places as she zigzagged across the country. A couple of big cities, like Houston and Phoenix. Lots of smaller ones, down to stops on the highway where she was able to wash dishes in a truck stop to earn a few days' worth of money. In a short amount of time, she'd sampled so many different parts of America.

Bandon was the first one that felt like home. Flynn didn't get to look down on her for that. It brought out a rarely utilized feistiness.

This time Sierra didn't tap his arm. Or almost-pet it. No, she flicked at that ropy vein. Hard. "Are you one of those people who thinks it's uncool to gush about something? To actually say what you're feeling?"

"I'm a guy. We don't even *think* about what we feel, let alone say it out loud."

"Now you do sound sexist. Men have feelings." Sierra had spent almost six years at art colleges. That had to be the epicenter of men who drooped around sighing their feelings even more dramatically than the women did.

"We try to ignore them." He pretend-scowled at her and rubbed his arm. "And ouch."

Sierra sassed right back. "I thought the twenty-first century was the age of the enlightened male. One in touch with his feelings."

"I'm in touch with mine. I just ignore them."

"That's a shame." Although the strong, silent type did *totally* work on him. "Turn right at the house with the mini-lighthouse in the yard." Bandon being right on the coast amped up lawn decorations. Rock grottos with mermaids lolling on the edge, piers that led to a duck pond, buoys around the mailboxes. It was artistic and silly and Sierra adored it all.

"You going to psychoanalyze me?"

Primly, she folded her hands in her lap. Mostly to keep from reaching over to touch Flynn again. "If you feel bad about something, it makes you appreciate the good that much more."

"Honey, I feel like shit about more things than I can count. Believe you me, they're not making me want to write poems about the beauty of a sunset."

"Well, that's a shame."

"You said that already," he said in a singsong voice, parroting her words back at her.

Maybe it wasn't the time to rant about her viewpoint on how to live life. But Sierra was so enjoying the luxury of a full-scale discussion that she couldn't resist. "I think there are a lot of gifts that people dismiss as ordinary. Yes, a sunset—which is actually an astronomical phenomenon that should blow your mind. Breathing deeply of salt-tinged air, instead of a lungful of smog. You get used to those everyday miracles and don't enjoy them. I think we should force ourselves to notice all the good—big and small. Feel the wonder. The joy."

He covered her mouth with his broad palm. It stopped her words. But his touch drummed her heart rate into rollicking gallop. "I wasn't wild about chewing the fat about my little brother. But fighting about feelings is even worse. Can we just talk about the weather?"

Sadly, his hand left her lips. "No."

"Are you sure? I have it on good authority that it's going to storm tomorrow."

Omigosh, that lightness in his voice. Was the always-stoic Flynn Maguire *teasing*? That was just about the sexiest thing Sierra had ever heard. "What good authority?"

"Mick's arthritis is acting up. He ordered two beers with dinner to counter it."

The retired colonel had been curt when ordering, so Sierra had gone out of her way to tease him out of the mood. That's when he'd revealed his pain. "You were listening? You didn't join in."

"I'm not an orthopedist. Nothing useful to add."

"Conversation doesn't have to be useful. It's just nice to have." Conversating with Flynn was always the best moment of her day, even if it was usually over in a matter of minutes. "Like a foot rub."

"Does your foot hurt a lot?"

Sierra lifted the mostly melted bag of ice from her ankle. "Nope. The ice numbed it up."

"Still, you shouldn't walk on it for a few days. Why do you ride a bike, anyway?"

Cars—even junkers—were out of her on-the-run budget. And they required paperwork. A paper trail was exactly what Sierra was avoiding. "Bandon's a small town. I like the exercise and being in nature."

"More of your appreciating every moment thing." He said it this time without any derision. Like he'd truly *heard* her. Wasn't that interesting?

"Yes." Because it was true. Sure, she'd like a car. Especially with all the ubiquitous Oregon rain. But biking to work wasn't a hardship. "Oh, pull in at that mailbox on the right."

Flynn slammed on the brakes only twenty yards down her long dirt drive. "What is that?"

"My house."

He rolled the rest of the way up to her white front door. "You can't possibly live in that oversized closet."

"It's a tiny house."

"No fucking kidding it's tiny. It only has two windows and a door."

Along with weathered blue shingled siding. A two-shelf vegetable growing box with a little awning to protect from the relentless rain. A sunroof right over the loft with her mattress. "There's a whole nationwide movement. Tiny houses are less than five hundred square feet. For people who want to live for themselves, rather than to accumulate things."

"I don't see where you'd have room to accumulate two rolls of toilet paper." He unbuckled her seat belt. Then, instead of going around to her door, Flynn just scooped her into his arms and pulled her across the bench seat. Sierra dropped the ice, she was so surprised.

Surprised and then turned on. Again. Because being cradled against Flynn's rock-hard body was a treat.

Talk about needing to take a minute to appreciate the simple things. The heat burning through his cotton shirt. The cording of the muscles in his neck as she looped an arm around it. Every single ripple of his abs against her hip and thigh.

Yes, Flynn was danger personified. Because he pushed every single one of her buttons. Because she could easily lose control at his touch. At even the attention and care he'd already shown her.

Sierra knew in her bones that her ex had messed with her. Made her weak. Needy. Yearning for someone to treat her well. Make her feel special. So that now she grabbed at even the smallest of gestures and pressed them into her heart the same way she pressed flowers to keep forever.

"Why do you live in a damn shoebox?" His breath whispered across her cheek and eyelashes. Even though it was warm, it chased shivers up Sierra's spine.

"One person doesn't need much space. If this was a studio apartment in Manhattan, you'd call it both roomy and a bargain."

"It's supposed to be a whole *house*. I call it crazy."

"The rent is affordable. I like being cozy."

The look he gave her was so close and searing, it felt like those dark blue eyes had just x-rayed her brain. "Just so you know, I don't believe any of that. And you fought pretty damn hard about letting me drive you home. If I didn't know better, I'd think you were hiding something."

How did he know? Then Sierra remembered what one of her foster parents had told her. A football coach, he'd always spoken in sports metaphors. Most of which went right over her head. But he'd insisted that the best defense was a good offense.

So she lifted her chin, met his gaze with what she hoped was cool confidence, and said, "You won't talk about yourself. Does that mean I should assume that *you're* hiding something?"

Surprisingly, his gaze flicked to the side immediately. Had she hit a nerve? Sierra wished she had more experience—with men, and with life in general—to be able to read him better. Because she had the feeling that Flynn's tiny tells probably revealed a lot about himself.

"Give me your keys."

She scrabbled in her purse and handed them over. Without another word, he unlocked the door and carried her inside. Where he stopped one step into the living room and just gaped. His mouth literally fell open.

Admittedly, Sierra had done the same thing when Madalena first showed her the place. The living room that flowed right into the galley kitchen was smaller than her old dorm room back at the Milwaukee Institute of Art & Design. That was pretty much the whole place, if you included the bathroom tucked into the corner and the bedroom loft. Windows on both sides let her pretend she was living in a magical forest. The potted palm at the foot of the stairs took up valuable room, but was a much-needed pop of color against the stark white walls.

Flynn set her down on the gray futon couch. It was the only seating besides the one-person bench that slid under the narrow table. "No way are you walking up those stairs tonight. Tell me what you need and I'll bring it down."

Not bothering to bite back her giggle, Sierra shook her head. "You won't fit up there."

"I can bend. You, on the other hand, are semi-broken."

Thank goodness years of living with dozens of foster families had ingrained into her the need to make her bed and not leave underwear lying around. Because the man was halfway up the stairs before she could open her mouth.

"My pajamas are on the hook."

A dull thud rang down the stairs. "Holy Mary Mother of God."

"Are you okay?"

"Yeah. I always wanted a dent in the middle of my skull. Then I won't need a sweatband when I work out. It'll all just pool in one spot."

Flynn's dry sense of humor always cracked her up.

He crab-walked down the steps, clutching her tulip-dotted cotton pajamas. "I almost killed myself getting around those stacks of books. Why do you have them all over the floor?"

Sierra deeply regretted leaving behind all her books when she ran. As an artist, she loved the tactile sensation of real books. The scent. The shiny embossing on the covers. The *whish* of each page turn. Once a week she cycled to the Goodwill store and brought back as many as five dollars would buy. It was all the splurge she'd allow herself, but with so many priced at a quarter, she'd accumulated, well, the stacks that had taken down Flynn.

"I don't have a bookcase."

"I'll build you one," he snarled. "This is dangerous. A nuisance. Hell, both." Taking her chin between his thumb and index finger, Flynn's gaze bored into hers with scant inches between them. "Your safety matters. I insist."

Oh, my.

Ever since he'd stroked those soft brush bristles down her scalp tonight, Sierra had been hoping for a kiss from Flynn.

This was better.

Almost.

Chapter Three

THERE WAS A big list of places Flynn didn't want to be. That third town that Marshal Evans dragged them to in East BumFuck, New Mexico. That observation deck on the ninety-fourth floor of the Hancock Building. He could do heights. He'd just rather have his feet on the damn ground.

Oh, and the back room at Billy Smoothboar's in the middle of the Bandon Chamber of Commerce meeting Rafe had dragged him to. Yeah, that topped the list at noon on this particular Tuesday.

The official, spiffy millennial word for it was *voluntold*. Or so he'd heard from Delaney as she bit back her laughter at the thought of the Maguire brothers helping with the town's annual Cranberry Festival. Community service was an important part of protectees integrating into their new location. Rafe was all up her ass being the most perfect protectee ever, because he fell in love with Mollie.

A mistake he'd never make.

So Flynn's ass was in the chair. He'd ordered a club sandwich to be ornery. To prove that Rafe couldn't tell him what to do, even though this place was supposed to have the best steak sandwich in the whole state. And he also couldn't force Flynn to pay attention to the idiot in the fishing cap droning on at the front of the room.

He pulled out his phone and thought about skimming baseball scores. But that reminded him he hadn't found a team to replace his beloved Cubs yet. The Mariners were closest. The Giants had a better record. Flynn just didn't give a shit about either of them.

He didn't give a shit about most things anymore. What was the point? After working hard and caring and trying and fucking bending over backward to be perfect for so many years, McGinty had turned on him. His whole life got yanked away. So, yeah, even picking a new baseball team seemed pointless.

Then his thumb slid over the message icon. One tap pulled up his most recent contact. And Flynn remembered that there'd been one thing he'd been unable to resist caring about since his first day in town. One person, anyway.

He'd put in Sierra's number last night. In case she did something stupid like climbing those stairs with no railings. What if her ankle gave out? Sure, her house was so small she'd probably be able to catch herself if she put her arms out and touched the walls.

Empty walls. That needed a bookcase.

He'd promised her.

Flynn got his thumbs working. Light or dark?

Sierra responded right away. What? Chicken? Are you hungry? Or . . . OMG. I'm an idiot. You mean beer, don't you?

F: My life doesn't revolve around pulling pints.

Especially since his "career" had only started six weeks ago. It was true this job sucked the least of all the ones the Marshals Service tried to make stick. Flynn had always been "that guy" at parties. The one who made up cocktails and hung by the bar all night. It happened to be an awesome way to pick up women. Now he still had fun making up the cocktails and listening to people. That was the trick of being a good bartender—not talking, just listening. Which made it right up Flynn's alley.

S: Oh. What does your life revolve around?

Being an insufferable bastard to his brothers? Yet another example of the truth not always being the best way to go. Did you get that question from an online quiz? I hate those things.

S: That makes two of us. Why should my chances of finding Mr. Right be determined by the first initial of my third grade teacher, whether I prefer chicken or fish, and if I can curl my tongue?

Flynn almost smiled. Almost. Can you?

S: What?

F: Curl your tongue. The rest is all crap. But tongue curling could definitely up your chances with a guy.

"Pay attention," Rafe muttered under his breath.

Uh, hell, no. Flynn shot him a dirty look for interrupting. "Isn't that why you're here? I'm just the warm body with the last name of Maguire, filling another chair."

"For fuck's sake." Rafe shoved back his chair. The squeak against the wooden floorboards had all heads in the room swiveling to stare at them. He dropped a kiss on the top of the head of the gorgeous brunette next to him. "I'll be right back, Mollie. Gotta show this guy where the bathroom is."

Mollie arched an eyebrow. "It's a bathroom, Rafe. Not a maze leading to the Wizard's Cup."

The jerk of his head—and the tight, white line of his lips—made Flynn follow Rafe around the corner. Some things were ingrained. When your older brother looked like he was about to pop a gasket, you fell in line.

That was the kind of thinking that had kept him safe in the Chicago mob for so long.

Until, suddenly, it didn't.

Rafe pushed through the bathroom door. And immediately turned on Flynn. Those blue eyes, two shades darker than his own, practically threw sparks like an old muffler dragging on asphalt. His voice was just as rough. "What the hell is going on with you?"

Flynn jerked past him to lean against the sink. Not like this was the first time big brother had tried to take him down a peg. It worked when they were little. Hell, it even worked when they were teenagers, after their mom and dad had been killed and Rafe tried his damnedest to parent Flynn and Kellan.

But it didn't work anymore.

He crossed his arms over his black tee shirt, meeting Rafe's hot stare with his own well-honed icy indifference. "What? I showed up, didn't I?"

"That's not enough." Rafe banged a fist into the tan metal support between the stalls. "You fucking promised me, Flynn. You stood on that beach with me three weeks ago, when we were deciding if we should quit WITSEC and run, or stay and trust the program. You, me, Kellan—we all agreed to stay. And you both promised to *try*. To make an effort to fit in. To find something to like about this town. To become a part of it."

Rafe was right. Guilt swamped him.

On the other hand, he'd been drowning in guilt ever since they left Chicago. Why bother surfacing when he'd gotten so damned used to feeling like he couldn't breathe?

Still. He had to throw his brother a bone. Not an

apology, but an acknowledgement. Of his ongoing status as a first-class jerk. "You're right. I did promise. I also promised to wash the dishes, and I think our coffee mugs from three days ago are still in the sink. Probably already sprouting moss in this rain freaking forest. Sometimes I need a reminder about things."

"Yeah? Kellan forgot to do the laundry for the third week in a row. I'm going commando over here."

Looked like Rafe was throwing him a bone, too. Flynn shrugged one shoulder. "He didn't forget. His master plan is to *pretend* to forget until you get fed up and do it yourself."

A dark eyebrow shot up practically to his hairline. "He thinks he can play me? A Goody Two-shoes almost-lawyer trying to go up against the Chicago mob's fixer? Unbelievable. The kid's got bigger balls than brains."

Flynn figured that Rafe was just pissed he hadn't thought of that strategy to get out of his trash duty. He tried to hide it, but Flynn knew his secret weakness. His big bro turned green and almost heaved at just the smell of a day-old banana peel. A full and reeking bag of trash was his kryptonite.

Flynn's acknowledgement might be enough for his brother, but it didn't give him any satisfaction. He didn't want Rafe to think he'd been a jerk without any provocation. Not when there was such an obvious target to take the blame of his lousy behavior. Because his mood had soured worse than month-old milk as soon as the meeting started.

So he jerked his chin toward the door and the twenty people gathered to discuss the Festival in already endless detail. "That guy in the hat's a self-important prick."

"No argument here." Rafe's boots thudded against the floor as he paced the small space. "From anyone, as a matter of fact. Way I see it, the whole town can't stand Floyd. But he does the job nobody else wants, so they all put up with him for twenty minutes once a month."

That actually made Flynn feel marginally better. "As long as everyone knows he's a first-class douchebag . . ."

"Ask Lucien and Mick."

Talk about proof. Lucien was the heir apparent to the Sunset Shoals Golf Resort that kept half the town in business. Mick was an old kook of a vet. He'd bet the two of them couldn't even agree on the color of the ocean. If they both thought Floyd was bad news, then Flynn could give the rest of the Chamber a chance, too.

"I will." Because Flynn had learned—the hard way— not to take anyone at face value.

Not to trust anyone's word.

No matter how small the issue. Not even the only family he had left in the world.

"What were you looking at on your phone, anyway? It'd better not be any site connected to Chicago."

"It's not," he said swiftly. But Flynn didn't shift fast enough to keep Rafe from grabbing the phone from his front pocket. His brother skimmed the still-live screen.

Damn it. Flynn needed to change the settings to have it hibernate faster. But it had been his one luxury.

Not having to hide work texts anymore. Not having to hide . . . anything on his phone anymore. Nothing in his new life was important enough to keep secret.

His old life? Well, that was so shrouded in mystery it might as well be the love child of Bigfoot and the Loch Ness Monster. *Aka* nonexistent.

Rafe's jaw dropped. With as much drama as the lead on a CW teen soap, he grabbed the top of the stall door for support. With his other hand he waved the phone at Flynn. "You're . . . flirting?"

"No." The answer popped out automatically. He didn't *flirt* with Sierra. Flynn didn't allow himself to do that. Or he hadn't, until last night. When he'd lost all common sense and restraint and just given in to the *fun* of being with her. But today was a new day, and his emotional walls were back in place.

He'd just been checking in on an injured colleague. Camaraderie. Playing nice, the way the marshal hounded him to all the time. No big deal.

At least, that's what Flynn kept telling himself.

"You're sexting, then. With a *woman*?"

"No, a highly literate and functional otter. Of course it's a woman." Not that he actually was sexting, either. God, that'd be more dangerous than flirting.

"Good for you." Rafe clapped him on the shoulder and handed back the phone.

"Don't be a condescending ass. I talk to women. I've probably slept with more of them than you have, seeing as how I'm the more handsome Maguire brother." It felt . . . normal to tease Rafe. Like Flynn always had. Before.

Before he became the reason that his brothers had to give up their lives.

Before he ruined everything.

"First of all, my left elbow is more good-looking than you are." Rafe used that elbow to shove him away from the sink. Then he looked in the mirror and tweaked his hair until it looked, yes, *exactly* the same as it had thirty seconds ago. "Secondly, you *used* to talk to women. You haven't in a while."

Flynn bristled. It wasn't like he was broken. Or, God for-fucking-bid, celibate. Shit went down. Literal life-changing shit that put dating on the back burner. "So what? None of us did once we left Chicago. Not until you met Mollie."

"I'm glad, is all."

He was shutting this shit down right now. Just because Rafe farted hearts and flowers every time Doc Mollie crossed his mind? Didn't mean Flynn had any intention of doing the same. "I'm not dating."

"Fine." Rafe made air quotes with his fingers. "Sexting."

"I'm not—" Flynn gave up. It wasn't worth continuing the fight over the stench of urinal cakes. "Can we get out of here now?"

Rafe took two big steps over the green speckled linoleum. "Who is she?"

No point lying. If he tried to hide it, Rafe would

probably go into crisis mode. Assume the worst—that he was in contact with someone from their old life—and alert the marshal. The last thing Flynn needed was a visit/lecture/yawnfest from Delaney to get to the bottom of what wasn't even a situation. "Just a waitress at the Gorse."

"Mariana? She's hot. Well-done." He held up a fist to bump.

Flynn refused to fist bump over texts that weren't anywhere close to flirting. Just . . . fun. "Not her. Sierra."

"The one who's so quiet I can hear the foam on my beer evaporate when she brings it over?"

The description made him bristle. Flynn didn't know why. Seeing as how it was true. Mariana served up her big personality and an easy sighting of her even bigger boobs with every mug of beer she dropped on a table. Sierra, on the other hand, rarely initiated a conversation with a customer.

But when pushed a little, she did engage and her whole face lit up. Sierra went out of her way to talk to the solo regulars like Mick and the wrinkly, cranky Georgie Minton. Anyone who looked lonely or lost or upset got extra attention from her. Sierra didn't need to be showy about it. She just made people feel better about themselves, about their day.

God knew every time he was around her, Flynn felt better. No, that wasn't it. He fucking *felt*. Something he hadn't let himself do in months. Sierra's quiet caring, the way she looked not just at him, but all the way into him on the rare occasions she met his eyes, it scraped off some of the cement he'd put around his emotions.

So Flynn's hackles rose when Rafe dismissed her as "quiet."

Not that he should care what Rafe thought. Because nothing was going on between him and Sierra. No need to jump to her defense.

Even though it felt—damn, there was that word again—necessary to make his brother see Sierra as more than a wordless waitress.

Frowning, Flynn said, "She's nice. She got hurt last night. I helped her get home. No big deal."

Rafe stared at him for a long minute. Then, wordlessly, he opened the door. Flynn didn't know what he'd said to effect his escape. Didn't care, either. He just walked out and looked back down at his phone.

Sierra had never answered his original question. It wasn't that he wanted to keep the text conversation going. Flynn simply needed to know so he could follow through on his promise. So he tapped his thumbs against the screen again. Light or dark wood? For the bookcase?

This time he had to wait for an answer. He noticed two families had the bad luck to be seated at the edge of their most-boring-ever meeting. They had a passel of ankle-biters that reminded him of the slightly older kids he used to mentor in Chicago.

The ones Flynn never let himself think about because he missed them so god damned much.

And yeah, he forced himself to tune in to the wind-bag discussing the float Flynn was supposed to build for the parade. The signature float that would carry the Cranberry Court. The one that would be on the town's brochure and website for the next year.

Whoopee.

The twerp in the hat approached Flynn's table. "What sort of float-building skills are on your résumé?"

"None." First of all, because his entire "résumé" was a damn fucking lie. But mostly because who the hell *would* put float building on a résumé?

Twerp's eyes bugged out. Further than a cartoon character who realized they'd stopped running seven steps off a cliff in mid-air. "Rafe, when you offered your brother's help on this vital part of the Festival, I assumed he had the necessary talent to pull it off."

Without bothering to look up from cutting his steak sandwich, Rafe said, "Flynn doesn't have a special skills section on his résumé. But he can build the shit out of a float. No worries."

HatTwerp clutched the clipboard to his chest—*why didn't he have an iPad like the rest of America?*—and drummed his fingers against the back of it. A red flush spread up from the collar of his madras shirt.

Flynn didn't want to do this guy any favors. But he also didn't want him to stroke out in the middle of lunch. Delaney always told them not to draw attention. Accidental manslaughter probably fell under that category. So he took a deep breath and put down his own sandwich. The one that didn't smell half as amazing as Rafe's, damn it.

From out of thin air, he snatched his cloak of professionalism and wriggled back into it. "I understand your concern. The Festival is your baby. A point of pride for the whole town."

"Exactly. The float is a symbol."

No point bothering to ask what the hell it was a symbol *for*. Flynn 1) didn't care and 2) figured it would only prolong the conversation. So he nodded. Hopefully that would signify that he both cared and agreed. "Let me assure you that I can, indeed, build things." His phone vibrated on the table, shaking his silverware. It was a perfectly timed reminder. "I'm building a bookcase for a friend right now."

"From IKEA? Or from scratch?"

Oh, he wanted to scratch HatTwerp, alright. "I'll be building it from the ground up. No instruction sheet necessary."

"So you think you can handle the float by yourself."

Fuck a drunken goat sideways, *yes* already. With his construction experience, Flynn could do this with half a toolbox and scraps, let alone all the money they'd crazily allocated for it.

Right then, a little kid raced past the U-shaped table setup. His sneakers had wheels and lights on the back, which explained why he fell on his ass as he cut tight around the corner to aim a bottle of silly string at HatTwerp. Flynn pegged him at about eight or nine.

Old enough to laugh hysterically instead of crying when he fell.

Seeing as how he got the shot off and covered Hat-Twerp's crotch in the sticky string, Flynn laughed, too.

Back in Chicago, he'd trained junior high kids in MMA and he'd been a part of the Big Brothers program, too, with some elementary-school boys. Boys that always made him belly laugh and remember just how much he'd lucked out with Rafe and Kellan as his family.

Flynn was keenly aware that not all kids got the same breaks in life. After all, both of his parents had been killed. Then the mob sucked him in before he knew any better. But his work with underprivileged youth wasn't about righting a personal wrong.

It was because the world would turn into a shit show if everyone didn't pitch in and help raise the next generation.

Flynn didn't exactly walk away empty-handed, either. Excitement, joy, fun—they were all contagious. And kids spread those things around faster than cold germs in December.

Hell, maybe that's why he hadn't stopped sulking. A job—let alone the fifth one that he didn't even get to pick—wasn't enough reason to get up every morning. He spent the bulk of his days sulking. Pissed that he'd spent years doing what everyone else expected and wanted and it got him nowhere.

Now?

Well, Flynn still didn't know what he wanted to do with the rest of his life. But now he had an idea of where to start.

"I *can* do it myself." *And could kick you in the nuts for doubting that for even two hot seconds*, he thought. "But children should be involved with building this float, too. It'll teach them community spirit. Strengthen their teamwork. Give them something constructive to do over the summer."

"You want to put power tools in the hands of children?"

Yes. Flynn *specifically* wanted to hand a nail gun to the kid who'd nailed HatTwerp in the crotch and let him rip. "Of course not. But they can design it, paint, decorate—there's plenty to do that doesn't involve an extension cord or a hacksaw."

A murmur ran around the table. From the smiles and nods, it looked like the majority agreed.

"Solid idea, Maguire." Mick lifted the Marine vet ballcap he wore 24/7 in a salute.

"Thanks."

Rafe banged his elbow into Flynn's biceps. That was the Maguire brothers' wordless, non-embarrassing code for "well done, bro." And Flynn didn't mind admitting that it felt damn fine to get that tap.

Mollie half raised her hand, then just spoke up. "My friend, Lily, runs a summer camp with Madalena."

"Carlos's sister that does the books for the Gorse?" Flynn hadn't bothered to think about it before. But in a town this small, some people probably did overlap jobs. Maybe he should've wondered what Madalena did the other four days of the week.

Maybe he should open his damn eyes and ears a little.

"Yes. I'm sure all the children in their program would like to help. One-stop shopping. And you'd be doing a favor by providing an activity."

HatTwerp looked . . . deflated that Flynn had come up with an idea not already on his sacred clipboard. But the undeniable approval running through the room didn't give him any room to say no. He *did* frown. "They'll need to have their parents sign safety waivers."

"Sure."

"They'll need up-to-date tetanus vaccines."

HatTwerp seemed convinced that injuries were a given, not an outside possibility. With an attitude like that, he probably carried an umbrella on July Fourth to protect from overly large hail. Numbnut.

Before Flynn could answer, Mollie waved her hand. "They need those to be in school, Floyd. Not a problem."

Flynn grabbed the clipboard. He printed his email in all caps on the bullet point agenda. "You send me a list of hoops to jump through. Then I'll stretch out, put on track pants and sneakers, and get started."

"Fine. You'll need to contact Lily as soon as possible."

"Just gotta finish my sandwich." He pulled the yellow flagged toothpick out of one half, then pointed it at Floyd. "If you'll let me start it?"

HatTwerp backed away. Flynn called that a win. Not

just because he was hungry. He grabbed his phone to scan the answer from Sierra.

S: I prefer whitewashed shelves. They make the colors of the book spines pop. But I'll be grateful for any color wood you can get. I can always paint it myself.

Flynn snorted so hard that his napkin flew off the opposite side of the table. What kind of a lazy jackass did she take him for? Or was this her stubborn refusal to ask for help again? The same one that almost had her biking home on a sprained ankle?

His thumbs flew.

F: I'm not giving you a half-done bookcase. I'm a full-service shop.

S: I get that feeling about you. That you can do anything you put your mind to. You're very competent, Flynn.

He'd been called a lot of things over the years. Everything from pansy-ass (by idiots who didn't know him) to a ballbuster (by people who *did*), McGinty's pawn (sadly true until last Halloween), and even crybaby (once, when tears of blood ran down his face after a left hook connected too well in the ring. He'd wiped the blood out of his eyes with the crook of his elbow and then took down the name-caller with a single round-house kick that brought all the fans to their feet).

But this just might be the *worst* thing Flynn had ever been called. *Competent? Can't even tell if I should be insulted or complimented. Is that like calling someone smart instead of pretty?*

Her answer took long enough to come that he got a bite of sandwich down. But then grabbed for the phone with greasy fingers the moment it vibrated.

S: I also get the feeling that you know exactly how 'pretty' you are.

Ha. She'd poked at him, which meant Sierra was finally letting down her guard. That's when the real fun began. Flynn wiped his hands on his jeans and noticed Rafe staring at him.

"Mind your own damn business."

"Minding you has become my business. I don't mind noticing you're having fun sexting that waitress."

Damn it, he wasn't sexting. Mostly because Flynn was trying to do the right thing and *not* flirt with her.

Anymore.

But they *were* friends. So he could blur the line. A *little*.

Nobody else could, though. "Tell Kellan and you're a dead man."

Rafe waved the threat away with one hand. "Scarier men than you have tried. And yet I'm still here."

"Yeah, but I know all your secrets. How you'd fall to pieces without your special lotion tissues when you're sick."

Rafe's eyes narrowed. "You've got a mean streak."

"Runs in the family, I hear." Then he shot his brother a grin. Something that felt . . . awkward and lopsided. But it also felt damn good.

Flirting—yeah, he'd admit it—with Sierra also felt damn good.

F: Bite your tongue. Men aren't pretty. I'll take devilishly handsome, though.

S: Handsome, yes. But not devilish. You're not a bad man.

Shit.

Flynn pushed the phone back. Ate in slow bites, putting off the inevitable. He even paid attention to the discussion about what percentage of Festival proceeds should go toward the sheriff's office. Wasn't that just a laugh and a half? The Maguire brothers *helping* fund the police.

Finally, when the meeting wrapped and Flynn couldn't come up with an excuse to wait any longer, he texted back.

Don't go making assumptions. You don't know me. At all, Sierra.

Chapter Four

SIERRA SCOOTED THE tall stool right up to the curved edge of the bar. Hunching over the laptop, she turned the web browser to incognito status. The icon of a man in a trench coat, fedora, and dark glasses always made her smile . . . and then sigh. Because she *barely* pulled off being undercover.

Sure, she was at the Gorse, using Carlos's computer to search for updates on her ex, Rick. Even her limited knowledge—all garnered from movies—made Sierra aware that if somebody did reverse-track her web browser, far better they end up at a bar than the side of her bed.

But she didn't know how to use the Dark Web. Or, really, what it even was. No clue how to piggyback from one router to another so that her search history would be untraceable.

For goodness sake, she was an art major. Computers were for ordering brushes online. For checking WebMD to see if splitting headaches were just from stress or inhaling too much turpentine. Most importantly, for always checking the news feed for Kensington Palace. Sierra was head over heels in love with little Prince George.

Wouldn't it be fun to move to England just to teach him how to paint with watercolors?

Not in a stalker, get-thrown-in-the-Tower way. Just because she adored all children. More than anything, she wanted to teach. But Sierra couldn't teach without a degree and she couldn't finish her master's without going back to the town where her crazy ex almost murdered someone in cold blood.

So yes, Sierra occasionally daydreamed about running away to the land of tea and scones and Gainsborough's blissfully dainty and detailed landscapes.

What was the harm? When she stopped daydreaming, she'd still be at the bar, in a large room that always faintly smelled of beer. She'd still be on the run. Constantly looking over her shoulder. Twitchy. Ridiculously scared of her own shadow.

"How are you doing?" Carlos hustled across the room, wearing his usual dark green bar apron over a black tee shirt and jeans.

A quick alt-tab with her thumb and forefinger switched screens. Hopefully he wouldn't notice the small motion. Because Carlos did *not* need to see her Google search for criminal records—hers or her ex's.

"I'm fine. Much better. Flynn took good care of me last night."

Carlos squatted down to stare at her barely swollen ankle. "Did he? Good."

"Thanks for having Jeb swing by and bring me in. It wasn't necessary, though." After a whole life where nobody *ever* looked out for her, the way Carlos fussed like a big brother was nice. Weird. Hard to get used to and completely impossible to know how to respond to—but nice.

"I'll make sure that Flynn or I take you home tonight, too."

Letting Flynn—well, nobody *let* Flynn Maguire anything. He was a quiet but super strong force all by himself. Like gravity. Anyway, letting Flynn see her house last night was bad enough. Against her basic safety protocol of staying a loner.

Bandon itself, without the massive influx of tourists, was a small town of only three thousand people. So it was impossible to kid herself that nobody knew where she lived. That her neighbors didn't recognize her after living here for three months. But Sierra took comfort in thinking that her whereabouts were secret. Just because she hadn't *told* anyone where she lived.

Sort of like an ostrich sticking its head in the sand to avoid seeing an oncoming attacker. Sierra recognized that hiding in plain sight . . . still kept you in plain sight. Which was why she'd gone ahead and shared her address with Flynn.

He was enough, though. Her non-secret didn't need to spread any further. Carlos was *not* taking her home tonight. Sierra smiled at him, hoping it looked more like gratitude and not the *you're freaking me out* grimace that she felt at the thought of him discovering her little hideaway.

"Really, you don't need to bother yourself."

Standing, Carlos slapped a palm on the cutting board next to the tub of limes waiting to be sliced into garnish. "I'm putting you at the bar tonight."

"To do what?" Because Sierra didn't know *drinks*. She'd spent six years straight with cash-strapped college students. Beer—or box wine—had been the sum total of her alcoholic knowledge until starting at the Gorse. She had no clue what most of the drinks were that she served.

"Pour drinks." He started unloading a dishwasher tray of beer mugs onto the shelf behind the bar.

That wouldn't go well. And then what if her screw-ups made Carlos fire her? Where would she go? Panic clogged her throat, so Sierra just shook her head back and forth for a few seconds. "I'm a waitress, not a bartender," she finally spit out.

"Tonight, you and Flynn are swapping jobs. That way you can sit on a stool most of the night and get the weight off of that ankle."

"That's ridiculous. I mean, overkill. Overly generous of you." Wow. Saying no to your boss was complicated.

Sierra cleared the browser history before closing the window.

"You're not even doing that much until you're cleared by a doctor."

Her mouth dropped open. Carlos had to know that money was a problem for her. He paid her under the table, after all. Sierra had discovered in her flight across the country that plenty of restaurants did the same. That asking to be paid in cash didn't raise even a teensy red flag with most managers.

Carlos had been slightly different. He'd stared at her, hard, for more than a minute. Then asked if she was in trouble.

Funny, that's what Sierra wanted to know. It was why she trawled the internet daily looking for her name to pop up in a police blotter. Not knowing who would come after her—the police or her ex—made it especially difficult to fall asleep most nights.

"Carlos, I can't afford to see a doctor."

"This visit will only cost me a bison burger with sweet potato fries." He curved his hand to beckon over a regular who Sierra recognized. Tall, with long, dark hair, Mollie grabbed lunch on the weekends with her nephew, and came in for girls' night every first Saturday. Sierra liked waiting on her table. Liked listening to the laughter and silly reminiscences of four lifelong girlfriends. Something else Sierra never had, thanks to moving so often in the foster system, but craved almost as much as she craved Flynn.

Flynn?

She craved Flynn?!? Where did that thought come from?

Not that it wasn't true.

Because . . . well, *look* at him. Sierra angled her neck to peek around Mollie. Flynn stood on a chair, arms overhead, changing out a light bulb. Faded jeans hung low on his hips. Muscular thighs strained the seams below a butt that Sierra was torn between wanting to both sketch and bite. Biceps bulged below the short sleeves of his burgundy Gorse tee. You could stack five of her art school friends together, and they still wouldn't pack half the testosterone as Flynn Maguire.

Oh, she'd *wanted* Flynn the first time she'd laid eyes on him. But craving? That was a whole different level. One that inferred her life couldn't be full until the craving was fulfilled. That she wanted him more than anything else.

Aha. Turned out that she *did* crave Flynn. That status change in her heart must've kicked in after last night, when their conversation finally stopped being stilted as he'd tucked her in blankets on her sofa. Or maybe it was during their text-a-thon at lunch today that had put a giggle not just in her face, but in her heart.

"Sierra? You're all flushed. Do you feel okay?" Mollie advanced with one hand out, as if to check her forehead temperature.

Sierra reared back so hard that she almost slid off the stool. "I'm fine, thanks." How many degrees did lust

add? Because she was burning up just staring at Flynn. If they ever touched again, she might just go up in flames. That would be great to paint. Just the outline of a female body, covered in red-orange flames that licked all the way up to a crown, the only other color her blue eyes locked on a male profile. All sinewy muscles, from the back.

"If you say so." Mollie turned in the direction of Sierra's gaze. Since that portion of the restaurant was empty aside from a frazzled-looking mother and her toddler in this post-lunch lull, it was easy for her to see Flynn the target. An amused smirk lifted her lips as she back around. "I get it. Those Maguire brothe visual punch, don't they?"

"Yes," was all Sierra could get out dry mouth.

"Carlos told me that you've go

"I twisted it, is all." Sierra w After icing it twice last nig swelling had mostly dis

But a tiny corner mode. What if it discovered it a lowed to wo

Her h of a hum

Yikes. The pening more ofte she put between hers

Sierra wanted them to stop. Wanted to stop jump[ing]
straight to the worst possible scenario. Wanted to st[op]
living in fear. But she worried that there was no way t[o]
surface from the depths of all this panic. That one day
she'd simply *not* find the strength to claw herself out of
it one more time.

Her phone buzzed on the bar. "Sorry," she said to
Mollie. Flipping it over, she saw a text from Flynn.

F: You okay?

Was he watching her? The same way she'd stared at
[h]im moments before? Too embarrassed to check, she
[jus]t popped off a response. I'm fine.

You look like you're ready to run out the door.
[t]hrow something. Your face is all red. Is Mollie
[both]ering you? I'll get her to back off.

watching. And that was . . . interesting.
[po]ssible that Flynn had noticed their connec-
[tha]t he was interested in her as a woman, and
[o]bligation that Carlos had foisted on him?
[t]hat her craving had a chance at being

[s]haking wrist bumped against the
[ ] Sierra of the stark truth that only
[ ]was on the run. That she lied to
[so] long, to keep herself safe.

Craving Flynn was one thing. Satisfying that craving *should* mean opening up to him, sharing with him. A relationship shouldn't, couldn't be based on lies.

Unless she only gave in to the physical part of her craving. Could she? Flynn seemed older than her own twenty-three years. Definitely more experienced. Having a meaningless fling didn't feel like her MO, though.

On the other hand, neither did going on the run. Maybe this new version of herself that Sierra had made up *could* do a fling with Flynn.

Geez, her cheeks were undoubtedly turning even more red. Sure enough, she looked up from the phone to find Mollie staring at her quizzically. Swiftly, she typed out a response.

Mollie's fine. After a second of consideration, Sierra decided to embrace her newly bold side. My face is red because I'm thinking about you.

There. Let him come to his own conclusions about what it meant. So what if it was far from the sexiest come-on ever? It was a step, a first step, a *big* step for Sierra.

"That was just a friend checking up on me. I guess that in a town this small, my sprained ankle is the biggest news since they announced the date for the Cranberry Queen tryouts."

"Annoying, I know. But also comforting." Mollie smiled and tapped her chest. "I think so, anyway. I hope you see it that way, too."

"Um, yes." Sierra liked that feeling of community. In theory. If only, in reality, she wasn't still living a lie and hoping against hope not to slip up and reveal anything about her old life.

"Let's get this over with, then." Mollie pulled over a chair from the closest table. "You know I'm a doctor, right?"

Sierra nodded. That tiny coil of fear unfurled like one of the giant tree ferns in the forest. If Mollie found something wrong, she could be out of a job. There weren't that many employment opportunities for a woman with no provable degree, no résumé, and only the special skill of being able to paint *anything.*

"May I?" Mollie had her hands down by Sierra's foot, clearly asking permission to pull it onto her lap to be examined.

It would only draw attention if she refused. Who, in their right mind, *would* refuse free medical care? Carlos was only looking out for her. It was hard to turn off the panic once it started flowing, though. Sierra lifted her head to gulp for some air. That's when she spotted Flynn again. At the opposite end of the bar.

Strength and surety radiated off of him, as easy to see as heat shimmering off asphalt on a July day. There was a man who did what he wanted. Who was in control. Who was oh-so-strong as he lifted the giant speaker on the small band stage and repositioned it with barely a flex.

Staring at him made Sierra stop imagining all the

horrible things that could happen if Mollie examined her. It helped all her muscles to unclench. Her breath came smoothly again, instead of in half gasps. Okay, her heart still raced, but now only from lust. When it came to panic, Flynn calmed her. With a bit of a jolt, Sierra realized how often in every shift she looked over at the bar to center herself on Flynn.

Right now, she kept staring at his broad shoulders flexing. She siphoned off a little of his strength for herself. Could almost see it coiling through the room toward her like a lifeline. And then she put her foot in Mollie's hands. Literally.

"We haven't gotten the chance to know each other yet. Which is a shame. Like you said, Bandon is small. A new woman under retirement age is a rarity." Mollie's chatter was slow but steady. Just like her hands pressing along both sides of Sierra's ankle, and then flexing it.

Sierra saw through the distraction, but appreciated it nonetheless. "I'm, um, shy. Meeting people isn't easy for me." Then she winced and hissed when Mollie poked on the sore spot.

"Tender, huh? Sorry."

Mustering up a weak smile, Sierra said, "Only when you press on it."

"Well, I'll avoid the oldest doctor joke in history and stop doing that." Mollie circled Sierra's foot both ways, then pulled her sock back up. "You've got good motion. Only minor tenderness. You'll be fine in a few days."

The last tendril of panic knotting her stomach

melted away. She could still work. She could stay here, in Bandon. At the Gorse.

Thank *goodness*.

Sierra just didn't have it in her to move again. The past eight months had worn her out. She didn't crave the new and exciting like other twenty-three-year-olds might. No, Sierra craved stability. A real home, for the first time in her life. Routine and friends and the familiar.

And if it wasn't too much to ask, maybe a certain tall, dark, and brooding man to keep her company.

"That's what I thought." Sierra leaned in and dropped her voice to a near-whisper. "Carlos and Flynn went way overboard worrying about this little twist."

Mollie looked over at Flynn—pointedly—wriggled her brown eyebrows over twinkling green eyes and then whispered back to Sierra. "Having a big strong man fuss over you isn't the worst thing in the world, is it?"

"Flynn doesn't fuss. He's more . . . intense than that." Even his texts were direct. No wasted words. No beating around the bush. After the flowery dramatics of everyone in art school, Sierra liked the contrast of his style. A lot.

"Focused hotness is the best kind. Especially in bed." As Sierra gasped and laughed, Mollie turned her back to Flynn. "You know, he hasn't taken his eyes off of you since I came over here."

"Really?" Sierra had to force herself not to look. Luckily, Carlos came over with Mollie's burger, providing a less embarrassing focal point.

Mollie grabbed a sweet potato fry before he set down the plate. "Yep. There's so many sparks flying between you two, it's amazing the bar hasn't caught fire."

"He hasn't made a move." Aside from the flirty texts. And the simmering stares. But the texts might just be an extension of the friendship they'd built up over the past month. The stares could be those of a concerned colleague who knew how much extra weight he'd be lifting with a waitress off the schedule. "I'm not sure that he sees me 'that way.'" Sierra made air quotes with her fingers.

"Oh, he sees you, alright. That man sees nothing *but* you. It's only a matter of time before he makes a move. Trust me on that."

"I'd like to . . ." Sierra got caught up in the sheer fun of sharing her *what-ifs* about Flynn. "I've learned not to get my hopes up."

"About men?"

"About life." Growing up in foster care, the biggest lesson learned was that dreams rarely came true. Sierra had gotten the miracle of a full ride scholarship to college. That probably used up all the luck and dreams-come-true allocated to her by Fate. "If you set a low bar on expectations, there's a better chance of not being disappointed."

Mollie frowned. Hard, with a wrinkled nose and brows almost touching. "You sound like a hardened fifty-year-old with three divorces in their rearview mirror. When, in fact, you're just at the start of a big adventure."

"I don't want a big adventure." There'd been enough

unintended *adventure* over the past year. Honestly, Sierra just wanted to be happy. Period.

Burger halfway to her mouth, Mollie froze. Her eyebrows arched upward in surprise. "Sounds like there's a story there. Maybe I can get it out of you if I ply you with liquor."

"There's no story. No need to get me drunk, either."

"Sure there is—just for the fun of it. I'm having a birthday party Wednesday night. Nothing outrageous. Just an excuse, really, to drink wine and eat cake with my girlfriends, guilt-free. I want you to come."

"I couldn't possibly intrude on your birthday. We basically just met."

"Please. You've asked me how I like my meal dozens of times. That makes us practically besties. And the point is that I *want* to get to know you better. This'll be the perfect opportunity for you to hang with all of us under-forty, unmarried peeps and have fun. In fact, as your doctor, that's my prescription. One night of fun. On me. Well, on my bestie whose family owns Sunset Shoals Resort. Because we're doing it at their spa. The warm water of a pedicure will soothe your stretched ligaments and muscles."

Sierra was torn. Mollie seemed awesome. From stealthy eavesdropping on their girls' nights, all her friends seemed great, too. Sierra hadn't indulged herself in forever. The invitation was an amazing gift. Maybe she could enjoy this one night and decide what to do next later.

Because Sierra couldn't just ignore the danger of making friends. Of getting comfortable and slipping up. Telling them things that could bring Rick and/or the police straight to her. That could bring danger into their circle. Or how she was supposed to keep lying to people that she could grow to care about. Like that mom with the toddler banging the spoon gleefully against the plate. What if Rick tracked her down, came into the Gorse, and did something unimaginable that might hurt that little tot?

Geez. She *wished* it was unimaginable. There she went, zipping right to the horrible again.

No. She wouldn't let panic steal her fun.

Her phone skittered away, buzzing repeatedly. Sierra ignored it for a moment, knowing that Mollie deserved a response to her generous offer. "I'd love to come and meet everyone officially." She stood, keeping most of her weight on one foot, and gave Mollie a swift hug. "Thank you so much."

Sierra limped around behind the bar to start cutting limes into wedges. It was one of the few bartender tasks she could do without thinking, and she wanted to bask in the possibility of new friends for a little bit. But her phone buzzed again and this time, she picked it up.

F: Did the doc say you'll live?

Sierra pushed through the swinging door to the back hallway with the staff lockers. It felt easier to text-talk with Flynn without seeing him across the room. Huh. I forgot to ask her that.

F: You think you're funny?

S: Occasionally.

She grabbed her half apron from her locker so her trip away from the bar looked necessary.

F: Doesn't matter what Mollie said. I'm still taking you home tonight.

Her heartbeat picked up the pace. Another car ride. More time alone. Time to get to know him even better. Everything she shouldn't want, but did.

S: Is that a threat or a promise?

F: It's me laying down the law. You're going to let me take care of you. End of discussion.

It was authoritative and demanding and thoughtful and downright hot.

Evidently Sierra's worry about the danger of getting close to Mollie and the girls? That danger wasn't the biggest risk in her new life, after all.

Flynn was way more dangerous.

To her heart, anyway.

Chapter Five

IGNORANCE IS BLISS.

Whoever said that had been a frickin' genius. Flynn could ask Kellan who said it. His brother knew tons of useless trivia. But then Kellan would give him a look that inferred he was stupider than dirt, and he'd need to beat him senseless for it. So Flynn would just offer up a salute to Mr. Nameless.

When he hadn't known how good Sierra smelled up close, how soft her skin was? Flynn had been a happy man. Okay, not at all true. He'd been a miserable son of a bitch. But he'd been content like that.

Now he *knew* all those things. Now the inside of his car smelled of her tropical-scented shampoo. The softness of her hand bumped against his where they shared the center console. And their conversation in the ten-minute ride from the Gorse to her house had been light and flirty like he used to have with women back in Chicago. Before his life imploded. Before he stopped talking and basically communicated in grunts and scowls.

So now? Flynn was miserable in a whole different way. Mad at himself for letting their friendship slip over that line in the sand. For having lost the strength to resist her ease and fun *for her own damn sake*. Succumbed, selfishly, to the temptation of her that he'd tried so hard to keep in the friend zone for weeks.

Also? Frustrated that he had to be guarded, to think before every response so that nothing about his old life slipped out. Pissed that he didn't have a shot in hell with this woman because she deserved two hundred percent more than he could possibly give. Sierra didn't deserve to be lied to day and night.

But then, because he was so weak and selfish, Flynn pushed all those thoughts to the side. This was the best car ride he'd had in months.

"This isn't Carlos's truck," Sierra said. She reached up to run her fingertips along the seam of the classic Camaro's T-tops.

"I brought my car tonight. In case you needed a ride home again." He'd had to negotiate for it. Now he'd have to make time tomorrow to detail the whole thing. Not to mention putting up with Rafe's ribbing about how Flynn needed a "coach" for his "lady." His brothers didn't buy that he was just being a good coworker, taking care of Sierra.

Probably because they'd known him for twenty-seven years.

And God knew Flynn sure as hell wasn't even fooling himself.

"Well, I didn't *need* a ride. But I do appreciate it. Why don't you drive to work every day?"

"I share the car with both my brothers. This is Rafe's baby."

"That's unusual."

"When we moved, it seemed stupid to bring all three cars to a town this small." Shit. Did that come off as an insult? Flynn was under strict orders from Delaney not to insult this zit of a zip code in front of anyone but his brothers. "I mean, a town this, ah, walkable. So we thought we'd make do with one while we got the lay of the land."

"How's that working out?"

"Crappy."

Sierra giggled. The sound tickled along his skin like the bubbles on top of a gin and tonic. Flynn could listen to that all day. "You're not a fan of walking?"

"On the beach with a beautiful woman tucked under my arm? Sure. When I'm jonesing for Doritos and want to make a fast run to the store? Hell, no."

"What flavor?"

Flynn gave her a cool glare for asking a question with such an obvious answer. "Cool Ranch. None of that new double-layered, jacked-up shit."

Another giggle. Damn if just the sound of it didn't

make him want to smile, too. "You're a purist, then," she said.

"I know what I like. I know what's right for me." And wasn't that the biggest load of bull that had ever come out of his mouth?

Yeah, Flynn knew what he liked in chips and clothes and movies. But he hadn't managed to pick a new baseball team yet.

More importantly, Flynn had no clue what was right as far as the whole rest of his life went. He'd always assumed sticking with his brothers was the best path no matter what. Now, though, Rafe had Mollie. Kellan seemed way past done with the attitude Flynn hadn't managed to shake.

Well, except for when he was around Sierra.

She gave a happy sigh. "Doritos are kind of a treat for me. Something not at all in my weekly grocery budget. So when I get a chance to gorge, it doesn't even matter the flavor."

That was rough. Flynn couldn't imagine being on a budget so tight that frickin' tortilla chips were special. He risked another look over at Sierra. What was her story, anyway? He knew there was one, since Carlos refused to tell him.

Flynn wanted to find out. Why she was scrimping so hard. He wanted to fix it, to make her life easier. Given her comment about the chips, her bike-riding made more sense now. Foot power was way cheaper than gasoline.

Why couldn't Sierra afford to drive? Talk about a

basic right that most of America took for granted. Shit. Was she in trouble?

Flynn parked in front of her stupidly tiny house. Once again, he didn't give her a chance to open her door. Just scooped his arms under her knees and behind her back and pulled her across the seat into his arms.

Sierra's arms curled around his neck. "Flynn, you don't need to carry me."

"You were on that ankle too much tonight. You should stay off it now."

That was what he said, anyway.

What he thought? Was that he'd take any chance to have her warmth tight against his chest. To cradle her soft curves. To breathe in the dick-hardening scent of coconut coming off of her hair. To stop thinking and bitching and worrying about everything else in his life.

Because when he held Sierra, it all melted away. There was only her. It had only happened twice so far, but that wasn't nearly enough.

"A girl could get used to this."

"A guy wouldn't object."

What the hell?

Flynn was seriously flirting with her. *Again*. Still. The thing he'd sworn to himself not to do, *again*. Because he was no good for her. Because she deserved better than a lying ex-mobster.

God knew he didn't deserve her sweetness.

Couldn't fucking seem to stop himself, though.

After a quick fumble with the keys, they were in.

Where Flynn promptly banged her foot against something. He was too busy ducking and angling to tell. "Sorry."

"It wasn't my sore foot. But you should probably put me down now. This place isn't to scale for grand acts of chivalry."

Flynn chuckled as he set her down on the couch. "What do you need? Ice? Are your pj's still down here?"

Her cheeks turned the pink of a Cosmopolitan. "You can't talk about my pajamas, Flynn. That's as bad as talking about my underwear."

"I never claimed to be good." Especially not thinking about the tank top and leggings covered with tulips the same color as her cheeks. Her in those pj's had been his first thought this morning, too. To wonder what Sierra looked like with the soft cotton hugging every inch, her hair all messy from sleep . . . or him . . .

Right about then was when Flynn vaulted out of bed and hit a very cold shower.

"Yes, I left everything down here. I really can take care of myself."

"I believe you. But you shouldn't have to. Nobody should, when they're sick or hurt." Flynn had no fucking idea where that came from, seeing as how McGinty didn't believe in sick days—they indicated weakness.

His brothers would open the front door to the delivery service if Flynn ordered soup. Maybe chuck a full tissue box through his doorway. But that was as far as their TLC extended.

Guess he remembered the old days, before his mom died. Not that there were many of those, since she'd died when he was only eleven. But he remembered that being sick was a free pass. No chores, no making the bed even after moving to the couch to play video games.

Looking down at Sierra, with her bottom lip caught in her teeth and a frown on her face as she rubbed her ankle, Flynn figured it out. He wanted to take care of her. He'd said it because *he* didn't want her to have to handle things by herself. Not because of what anyone else said or did. This was about her.

He wanted to press those frown lines away with his thumb. Rub her foot and her calf until Sierra relaxed into a purring lump of contentment.

He wanted to make things right for her.

"Geez. I'll just make some dinner and go to bed soon."

Was she insane? Did Sierra really think he'd walk out of here without making sure she was fed? Flynn wouldn't do that to a dog, let alone to this cotton candy-hearted swirl of a woman.

"No."

"No, what?" she asked absently as she folded her hoodie to put beneath her ankle. Because her couch didn't have any throw pillows on it. Flynn went to the freezer, filled a dish towel with ice, and carefully tucked it around her ankle.

"No, you're not making dinner. I'll do it." He headed right back to the kitchen—*right back* being all of two steps—and opened the fridge.

The contents were pathetic. And he was a bachelor, so Flynn's standards on what a fridge should contain were pretty damn low.

Milk, bread, butter, and a brown banana. Along with a jar of cranberry jam. Probably left there as a welcome present from whatever sadist rented Sierra this shoebox.

The locals were nutso for everything cranberry, which made sense, as the cranberry plant employed half the people in town. Rafe made a big fuss about hating the stuff. Flynn didn't mind it. He didn't think it was worth throwing a parade over, but he didn't *mind* it.

"Sierra, what do you eat? Is there a cupboard full of protein bars somewhere? A second fridge hidden under the floorboards packed with deli meat?"

"Carlos gives me a meal at the start of every shift. I only need breakfast most days."

Screw that. He grabbed everything and banged around in the search of a frying pan. And wondered again what her story was that had her scraping by on such a shoestring. "I'm not giving you breakfast for dinner. I can do better."

"Because you're secretly a great cook?"

"I'm a great take-out orderer. Bandon doesn't give me much chance to show off those skills, though. My brother Kellan's trying to learn to cook. He's the only one of us making the effort."

"Can he cook?"

God help them all, no. "Did you know it's possible to ruin frozen pizza? 'Cause I've got firsthand knowledge."

"And you say Kellan's a *better* cook than you? Now I'm worried." Sierra raised her voice over the commotion. "Is this payback for me doing your job tonight? Are you getting even for the drinks I screwed up that you had to come and redo?"

Christ on a stick, but the woman was bad behind the bar. She'd put a maraschino cherry in a dirty martini "because it made for a more pleasing visual aesthetic." Most of her mistakes had been with garnishes. Something about making the drinks look prettier.

He'd lay money on her choosing her sports team by the color of the jerseys.

Flynn sizzled the butter, then sliced in the banana. "I'm just trying to be a nice guy. Don't make a federal case out of it."

Ha. The irony of him saying that when he was scheduled to testify *in* a federal case would be lost on Sierra. But it'd make his brothers piss themselves with laughter when he told them later.

"Sorry about the drinks." Sierra sounded like she was apologizing for killing a cat. The woman had a heart three sizes bigger than fit her body. The regret in her voice absolutely slayed him. "I was trying to make them look fancy. Like the one you made for Norah's birthday."

Ah. He made specialty cocktails. Just for interested customers and the weekly specials board. If he tried to serve Mick anything but a Bud or a shot of Jameson, the old guy'd probably break his wrist.

Norah was Mollie's grandmother. She ran Coffee & 3 Leaves—which also dispensed pot. Nice lady. Even nicer when she came in a little high and ordered every appetizer on the menu.

He'd made her a tequila martini. Drew the shape of a pot leaf in the foam on top, and stuck a sugared lime wheel on the rim. Called it the Weed Eater, and she'd cackled with laughter before sucking down six.

The woman was ex-Navy and lived life full-out as if she wasn't missing a hand from a shipboard bombing.

Flynn flipped the bananas, now golden and crispy on one side. "How about I make you your very own cocktail? You tell me what color you want it to be. Which slices of fruit you want piled up to look pretty on the rim, and I'll make it taste good."

"Omigosh. What a sweet offer, Flynn!" Sierra's voice rose to a near silent squeal of excitement. Like a dog whistle in reverse.

Flynn got a kick out of her excitement. But it was oversized. Had he been a surly dick too long, and one simple gesture floored her? Or was it that Sierra wasn't used to nice gestures from anyone? Son of a bitch. He didn't like either option. "It's no big deal."

"But it is. That's . . . that's like you're making a personalized work of art for me."

He squeezed honey over the banana slices. Let that bubble up for a minute before scooping it onto bread smeared with peanut butter. Then he put the whole thing back in the pan to sizzle for a minute. "If it tastes good enough, it won't last as long as real art."

"Art can be about the beauty it captures in a moment. There's no use-by date."

Flynn liked the way she saw the world. It made him want to see it that way, too. Sierra's joy in life was contagious. And this from a woman with almost no food, and a house the size of his living room. Who regularly got soaked in the Oregon rain as she biked to work and still walked in with a smile on her face every day.

Yeah, he wanted to do everything in his power to keep that smile coming, and aimed right at him. Maybe that would burn through the thick scar tissue of ugly thoughts he'd kept bottled up since Chicago.

Nah. She didn't deserve to have any of his shit flake off onto her. Exactly why he'd kept her at arm's length.

Suddenly Flynn felt like he had T. rex arms. Short and useless.

Flynn sliced the golden brown sandwich, then dolloped cranberry jam in the middle of the plate for dipping. Paper towel draped over his arm like the snooty waiters at Morton's back home, Flynn presented the plate with a half bow. "Told you I could do better for dinner. Because I made you dessert, instead. Which always trumps dinner."

Grabbing it with both hands, Sierra inhaled deeply, closed her eyes, and then let out a tiny, honest-to-God moan. A moan that he *felt* in his dick, as sure as if she'd stroked it with her tongue.

Eyes the same pale blue as the stripes on the City of Chicago's flag finally fluttered back open. "This looks wonderful, Flynn. Any chance this means you share my sweet tooth?"

"Not enough to steal half that sandwich from you, but yeah. I'll take an apple fritter over eggs and bacon any day of the week."

Sierra looked up at him like he was chocolate cake dipped in fudge sauce topped with mocha ice cream. "A man as big and strong and tough-looking as you admits to craving donuts?"

She'd noticed his muscles? Flynn stood a little straighter. "I like bacon. Ideal situation is a donut with a side of bacon. As long as there's still pie with dinner."

"That's adorable." Sierra crunched down through the toast. Got another one of those practically orgasmic smiles on her face, then licked her lips. "And this is delicious. I don't know what's sweeter—you making me dinner, or how good this tastes."

"You don't get it, do you?"

"What?"

Shit. He'd have to tell her thoughts that were still barely formed in his brain. They were more of a gut reaction, an instinct. A need Flynn couldn't ignore. "I *want* to take care of you. It isn't a favor to you. Hell, you letting me help out is a favor to *me*."

"Why?" Those blue eyes squinted at him in confusion. Her nose scrunched up. Talk about adorable. "Why on earth do you want to go out of your way, after a long shift, to make more work for yourself?"

"Because it's *you*, Sierra. Bringing you home, making you dinner. It's the least I can do. Hell, it's all I want to do. Whatever puts a smile on your face."

It'd be better if *anybody* else in town took on that job, instead of him. Flynn was well aware—thanks to his brothers' constant reminders—that his attitude sucked on the best of days. He got plenty of reminders from the marshal that he was a criminal. Sure, the U.S. government wasn't pressing charges because of his testimony against McGinty. But every FBI agent, marshal, and lawyer who looked at his file then looked at him like he was shit tracked onto their shoe.

Or maybe Flynn just felt that way on the inside.

Bottom line, Sierra deserved someone better. Someone else.

Except . . . Sierra didn't seem to have anyone else. And Flynn couldn't make himself walk away. No matter how selfish.

She still looked confused. "You do make me smile, Flynn. All the time. You're patient with me. You never snap when I confuse a drink order. You stop whatever you're doing to open the kitchen door for me. Which kind of makes my heart explode because it feels like we're on a date even though we're just working. Even though you're way out of my league."

"Don't say that." He took the plate from her and set it

on the floor. Then Flynn knelt next to the sofa. "You've got the sweetest, biggest heart I've ever seen. So kind. Caring. And you're so beautiful that I have to bend over backward to ignore you so I can get work done."

"You think I'm beautiful?"

Did she really not know? Not know how much she affected him?

Fuck.

How could she when he'd never said a damn word about it? Never gave her a hint. Hell, almost never even acknowledged it to himself, because the thought of being with her was so impossible.

"Let me show you just how beautiful I think you are."

Flynn almost bracketed her face in his hands. But she angled back. It was barely noticeable, but he did. He noticed everything about Sierra. And she seemed skittish.

So he dropped his hands back down. Angled in to only touch her lips. It was a soft kiss. A brush, mouth against mouth, so light they barely touched. Just to see what Sierra would do.

She didn't pull back.

Flynn did it again. And again. Slow, teasing kisses that swept back and forth.

They practically killed him. Reining in his need was like having a fucking noose around his neck. Made it hard to breathe. Hard to think. But if Sierra needed him to go slow, that's what he'd do.

Finally, her lips parted just enough to let out a sigh.

It was all he needed. Flynn threaded his fingers through her long, dark hair. Took a split second to register that it was just as silky as he'd imagined. Then he tilted her head back and to the side to make the angle better. And then he *really* kissed her.

There was pressure this time but he didn't *go* for it. Didn't unleash all the want bottled up inside of him that he'd been resisting for weeks. But he did full-out kiss her.

Flynn stroked his pinkie along the nape of her neck and was gratified at the shiver that chased its way down her body. He licked the sticky sweetness of the honey from her. He pressed and shaped and fucking *learned* her mouth. Learned what she liked. Learned that her almost pouty lower lip was the perfect place to use his teeth, right in the center, to make that noise happen in the back of her throat.

Most of all, Flynn learned how mind-blowingly great it was to kiss Sierra. He could do it all night. Christ, he hadn't even gotten *inside* her mouth yet, and his dick was already threatening to bust through his jeans. She smelled like the beach, tasted like sugar, and felt like a dream.

Sierra kept shifting in his grasp, little moves that brought her closer against him. Little moves that rubbed her breasts against his chest, that made his hand on her waist slip down to the upper curve of her tight little ass.

He tongued along the seam of her lips, prompting her to finally, *finally* open to him. Flynn's tongue slipped in and swept up all that residual honey flavor that he swore had to be just her. He pressed her backward until she was lying on the couch and he could press his whole upper body against her. Their tongues swirled together, side to side and around in a dance that turned his dick to pure steel. And even with him lying on top of her, Sierra still arched up into his embrace with breathy little moans.

Easing back, he pushed the hair off her cheek with one finger. "Do you believe me now? When I say that you're beautiful? Can you tell how much you turn me on?"

Red flooded her face. "Yes. Those kisses—they clarified your point extremely well."

"You liked 'em?"

"A lot. They were very, very good." Her smile lit him up like a firecracker inside. "Even better than the sandwich."

How selfish was he, kissing her without letting the woman eat dinner after a long shift? Flynn practically dumped the plate back on her lap. "Sorry. Eat up. I'll get you some water."

Yeah, those kisses had been good—hell, *great*—and yet also very, very bad. Because they were *so* terrific. Because they made him fucking *feel* again, like he hadn't for all the months before coming to Bandon. Made him want to watch over her all night, feed her every day, and do anything in his power to bring out that smile again. He'd liked her for a month. Wanted her that whole time.

Now? Flynn *needed* her. That made what had just happened big, big trouble.

Forget that Flynn didn't deserve a woman like her. *Sierra* didn't deserve to be stuck with a guy figuring out who he was now, while living an elaborate lie.

But now that he'd had a taste of her?

He couldn't let her go.

Chapter Six

"EVERYONE HAVE ENOUGH cake?" Lucien asked, brandishing a long knife.

Sierra ducked as little bits of blue frosting flew off. The birthday cake was quirky and awesome—the doctor's symbol of a caduceus with a coiled snake, that apparently matched Mollie's tattoo—but she didn't want to *wear* it.

Considering he'd cut slabs of cake big enough to be a meal, everyone murmured they had enough.

Lucien was an amazing host. His family owned the super famous, super swanky golf resort/hotel/spa that employed the half of Bandon that didn't work at the cranberry plant. He'd shut the whole spa down for the evening and thrown Mollie's birthday party here.

It was the fanciest thing she'd ever been to in her entire life. They were all on lounge chairs with thick cream cushions. Soft fleece blankets the color of drift-wood lay across the bottoms, each embroidered with their names. Their *names*! Sierra had only been invited two days ago, and she still got a personalized party favor. It blew her away.

Bottles of champagne speared out of ice buckets on shiny gold stands. Trays and trays of appetizers lined the marble counter. Sierra didn't even know what most of them were. Besides utterly yummy, anyway. She sampled everything and then went back for seconds. Once they were finished with cake, technicians were coming in to give everyone manicures and pedicures. All six of them *at once*.

In addition to the birthday girl and the surfer-boy handsome Lucien, Mollie's friends Elena, Lily, and Karen were there. And *they* were amazing. Or maybe that was the third glass of champagne talking. Sierra was definitely tipsy at this point. But she truly did like everyone she'd met. Not just because she was so desperately starved for friends. No, she'd *connected* with them all.

As much as she could.

While deflecting every personal question they asked.

While lying about too many things.

She hated that.

Grabbing a bottle of champagne, Lucien topped off Mollie's glass. "If cake's over, then it's time for presents."

Her mouth dropped into a horrified O. "Cake is never over, Lucien. Only the first *round* is over."

"That's the dividing line between men and women." He continued around the circle of women, adding bubbly to their glasses and spreading some winks and smiles just as freely. Sierra had never witnessed a smoother customer. "We eat and move on. You circle back and nibble twenty times in an hour. Can't you just commit to stuffing your face?"

"Funny, hearing the word *commitment* come out of your mouth," Mollie sassed back. "I didn't think you knew what it meant."

"Are you kidding? I'm very committed." He winked at Sierra. "Committed to giving every pretty woman who crosses my path a full helping of this goodness." He swept an arm up and down his body.

Sierra giggled. And turned away. Lucien had flirted with her, in a friendly way, all night. It had been obvious from the start that it was just his style. He'd probably flirt with the potted ficus in the corner if a botanist told him it was female.

But she didn't want to flirt with him. Not even though he was hot. And rich. Charming. Easy to be with. Quick to fill in a conversational gap or make a quip.

Nope. It turned out that while she liked drop-dead hot, she didn't need charming and easy. Broody and difficult appeared to be what Sierra wanted on her man-menu. Flynn was by no means easy but that just meant when he did open up, offer a comment, share a smile, it *mattered*.

Sierra looked down at her phone, which was hot on the back because she hadn't stopped texting. Once she'd told Flynn where the party was, he'd demanded pictures of the secret inner sanctum. There might have been a little talk about wanting to see where women hung out in just towels and a need to see her in a towel.

In fact, she wanted to read that again. While Elena carried the gift bags over to Mollie, Sierra scrolled up in the message list.

F: If you're sitting around in just a towel, is there a window where I can come catch a peek?

S: There's a whole wall of windows, overlooking the third hole and the ocean. But I don't want you arrested for sneaking around, peering in windows.

F: If it meant seeing you in just a towel, it'd be worth it.

Flynn gave off an attitude of "I'll do what I want" and Sierra had no doubt that if he decided there was a strong chance to see her almost naked, he'd hightail it over.

Which was flattering in the extreme because he was . . . so sexy. Movie star sexy. Tall, dark, and more than a little mysterious. Older, self-assured, not caring what anyone thought, which was hot all by itself. He could get any woman in town without even crooking a finger. Just one of those half smiles of his was all it would take. Sierra was nowhere close to his league.

And yet he'd kissed her two nights ago. Over and over and over again. It had been amazing. And no, that was *not* the champagne talking. Flynn's kisses melted her from the inside out. They were drugging. Literally. They'd completely made her forget the pain in her ankle.

He'd kissed her yesterday, too. Showed up to drive her to work and kissed her right there on the tiny porch. Kissed her until her toes curled in her sneakers and her knees bobbled out from under her. Only Flynn's quick reflexes had kept her upright. And then they'd talked the whole way to the Gorse. Like friends, but . . . almost like a real couple?

To keep him out of trouble, Sierra texted him the truth. We're all wearing bathrobes that come down to our ankles. Probably not worth it.

F: Can we find a way to make the just-a-towel thing happen?

Sexting. That's what they were doing. And it absolutely delighted her. This man who was so serious all of the time was letting her inside his private thoughts, where it was considerably steamier than she'd expected. Who knew that texting about doing things to each other was almost, *almost* as fun as the real deal?

S: I'm open to suggestions. What did you have in mind?

F: You. Water dripping down your skin that I get
to lick off. Untucking the towel so I can get at your
breasts. Licking my way around your nipples until
they stand up and beg for me to bite them.

That's the point when Lucien had started passing
out cake. Fifteen minutes later, Sierra still hadn't fully
cooled down from the images Flynn had planted in her
head.

And she had no idea how to respond. Should she
offer to show up on his doorstep in a towel? Not that
she had the guts to actually follow through on an offer
like that. Because nothing that happened with Flynn
was planned. Things just kept . . . happening. With him
driving her to and from work, fixing her meals, texting
back and forth . . . it kind of felt like they'd accidentally
started dating.

How could she do that to him?

How could she get involved with him when she was
in so much trouble?

Flynn Maguire, though, was all kinds of irresistible.
Sierra hadn't done anything for herself—aside from
fleeing a criminal situation—in months. No splurges.
No movies, no hanging out with friends, no casual afternoon at the mall where she could make an impulse
purchase of a pretty pair of earrings. She'd stayed under
the radar. Stayed hidden.

Dating Flynn would not be a smart move. It would
open her up to the risk of blurting out the truth. It would

open her up to falling in love, when she might have to run away again at a moment's notice.

Yet Sierra couldn't stop herself from wanting him. Not when he was so good to her. Not with his wickedly teasing streak. His sly wit. The man was building her a bookcase, for heaven's sake.

Or maybe she was misreading the signs. The very sexy signs that could just be them speeding down the road to a casual fling. Which meant no entanglement. No—or less—worry about lying to him about who she really was. Very low risk, and a potentially sky-high reward.

Men were all for casual flings, right? It was only her emotions at stake?

Karen rapped a spoon against a crystal champagne glass to get everyone's attention. A stack of silver bangles slid down her wrist to clatter against the glass. "I'm all about celebrating Mollie, but I also want to get to that paraffin dip for my hands. Let's get this show on the road."

Mollie picked up a flat manila envelope. And then she gasped, her mouth opening in delight.

Sierra hadn't known how to wrap her gift, let alone want to blow money on an entire roll of wrapping paper and a card that she couldn't afford. So she'd gotten an envelope from the Gorse and decorated it with pastels. A blue box, with green and white ribbons curling in an elaborate bow. A row of three pink-frosted cupcakes with rainbow sprinkles. And a bouquet of white balloons floating out over the ocean. It had been fun to do this morning, out in the sun.

"This is fantastic. Did you do this yourself?"

"Yes." Sierra nodded, suddenly uncomfortable with the attention. She hadn't been trying to show off—just find some way to bring something special to the party. Something special enough to thank Mollie for including her.

Mollie held it up for everyone to look at, and a chorus of oohs and aahs filled the room. "I love it. I'll frame it and put it out every year during my birthday month."

Omigosh. Did Mollie think that was it? Sierra bit her lip, trying not to giggle. "That's just the wrapping. Your gift is *inside* the envelope."

Lucien handed over a knife so that she could slit it open. Mollie slowly drew out the piece of thick paper. It was a sketch of her and her boyfriend, Rafe, Flynn's brother.

They came into the Gorse together all the time. Sierra had noticed as soon as they started dating, because they were so *into* each other. When Rafe and Mollie looked at each other, they acted as though all the other people in the bar didn't exist. Like they were in a private bubble of love.

So she'd done a pencil sketch of them, just like that. With enough hints of furniture, jukebox, and a bar to show they were at the Gorse. But then, inside a shimmery, heart-shaped bubble, she'd drawn Mollie, with her chin in her hand staring at Rafe like he hung the moon in the sky. And Rafe kissing the knuckles of her other hand. His head was down but his eyes were up, fixed on Mollie and beaming with adoration.

"Sierra. My God, this is incredible." Mollie passed it to Elena and vaulted off the lounge chair. Two quick strides brought her over to Sierra's. Fat tears clung to her bottom lashes. She threw her arms around Sierra in a long, tight hug. "Thank you."

"You're welcome."

She sat back down, hand pressed together over her heart. "This is huge. We don't have any pictures together."

"Rafe's ridiculously camera shy. I don't know why, since he's so freaking gorgeous," Elena said, fanning herself dramatically.

Mollie's gaze shifted back and forth between the two, before her lips thinned, too. It was weird how she almost looked like she was trying to hide something. Did Rafe have a real phobia of cameras? Did he think he was a vampire and thus unable to be captured on film? Sierra bit her lip to keep from giggling.

"Anyway, this means a lot to me. Thank you, from the bottom of my heart."

Sierra dipped her head. "It means a lot that you invited me to your party."

Lily peered at her from behind pink cat's-eye glasses. "Sierra, you're so talented. Not like a hobby. This is art. The real deal."

"It's just a sketch. It only took half an hour."

"Did you learn how to do this in school?"

"Do you ever sell your work?" Questions popped at Sierra from every side of the room. The kind of questions she'd have to answer with lies. The kind of questions that had forced her, for months, to not engage with anyone.

Here she was, finally splurging in a few basic human connections, and after only an hour she'd been trapped. Trapped by well-meaning, interested people. Trapped by people who wanted to know more about her.

How could that be a bad thing?

How could she live her life avoiding that?

That question was a sucker punch from her brain straight to her stomach. Sierra bent forward, pulling a hand to her belly. Air became impossible to draw into her lungs. Because tonight had been wonderful. Between Flynn and this party, she felt more alive than she had in the past few months.

Attentive, caring people were staring at her. Waiting for an answer. Waiting for Sierra to share what *should* be the most basic information in the world. Instead, it was basically giving her a panic attack.

"I'll be right back. Which way's the bathroom?"

Lucien pointed at the furthest of five doors from her. Of course. Hoping that nobody noticed her fast, shallow, guppy-like gasps for air, Sierra hightailed it across the room as fast as the backless slippers would let her. She slid sideways through the door. When she turned to face front, she almost jumped out of her slippers.

Flynn stood right in front of her. He looked decidedly out of place in the driftwood and cream hallway that smelled of lavender. He wore black cargo shorts, a black tee, and flip-flops. Sierra was so used to seeing him in jeans that yes, her gaze dipped back down twice to take in the legs—or rather, *thickly muscled legs*—covered in dark hair.

"Oh. Wow, this is a surprise. Hi."

He didn't speak. Only bent down to brush his lips against hers. Once. Twice. Then Sierra gave up counting as he tunneled one hand through her hair to pull her even closer.

She surrendered to the dizzying, knee-melting sensation of being kissed senseless by Flynn. The way he started slow and then just consumed her with his passion that ignited even more of her own. It felt so good to be *wanted* so much. To hear the low growl that crawled up from his throat. To notice his growing hardness against her belly. To open her eyes and meet his fierce, burning blue stare.

Finally, Flynn eased back with one last kiss on the tip of her nose. "Hi."

"What are you doing here?"

"I'm hooked on the cucumber water. Can't get enough of it," he deadpanned.

Sierra didn't believe him for a second. Flynn's muscles and tan didn't give him the look of a man who came into the spa for a buff and polish. "Have you ever even tasted cucumber water?"

"God, no," he said with a shudder. "Cucumbers already taste like water. Why would anyone bother to combine the two?"

"Don't knock it until you try it." She started forward to the glass cooler filled with lemon-cucumber water. Flynn noticed her approach and grabbed her wrist, pulling her back flush against his chest.

"Don't punish me with that stuff when I've brought you a present."

Sierra didn't get presents. Her foster families never had cash to spare to celebrate birthdays or Christmas. Her friends in art school definitely couldn't afford to splurge on gifts. She rose onto her toes in excitement. "Really?"

"That's why I'm here." Flynn brought his other hand out from behind his back. He handed her a plastic grocery bag. "For you."

Surprised—and flustered, and caught off guard— that he'd stop by to bring her *anything*, Sierra dug into the bag. When her hands hit terry cloth, she started giggling. Her laughter grew as she pulled out a navy blue bath towel. It was funny and sexy and absolutely perfect.

"Why, thank you ever so much. I wonder what I should do with this?" She rubbed it against her cheek, trying to look innocent. No, trying to look sexy. In a shapeless spa robe and slippers. Probably not even a supermodel could pull that off.

"Anything you want. You could use it after your shower tomorrow. Or . . ." Flynn stroked his chin as if deep in thought. ". . . You could model it for me. Later."

Sierra was well acquainted with nude models—or life models, as they were called in artists' circles. She had zero problem staring *at* the naked human form.

But stripping down in front of Flynn? This paragon of masculinity and handsomeness? Who was 1) out of her league, 2) older, and thus undoubtedly 3) more experienced. It gave her . . . pause. Skittered nerves across her belly like ants marching across a gingham tablecloth. Sierra wasn't a virgin. Or a shrinking violet. She just didn't want to disappoint him. Turn him off. Do anything to stop all the fun they were suddenly having.

Life and Karma would undoubtedly pull the plug on it soon enough. She didn't want to hasten the process by screwing something up.

"Hey." Flynn took her empty hand and squeezed it. "You disappeared there for a second. I'm not trying to pressure you."

And just like that, her on-edge nerves smoothed out. Her breath whooshed in and out easily. His touch was all it took. Flynn grounded her. Calmed her. Made Sierra feel comfortably herself, instead of a panicked person she barely recognized.

"I know. Really." Sierra waved the towel in the air, letting it unfold. "I love it. Thank you. You made me laugh and feel sexy at the same time, which is a first."

His eyes opened wider. Surprise was an expression she hadn't seen on his face before. Like everything else on Flynn Maguire, it looked good. "That's a damn shame."

"Why?"

"Laughter and sex go together. If it isn't fun and funny at least some of the time, you aren't doing it right." Slowly, he trailed a finger from her chin, down her throat, all the way to the V where her bathrobe's fleece lapels met. He left a trail of goose bumps in his wake. "Or—and I'd put money on this being the case— you weren't doing it with the right person."

"I'm sure you're right." But Sierra couldn't imagine laughing during sex.

She thought back to the fast and altogether unexciting couplings with Rick. Sierra had stayed with him for the sense of belonging, the tenderness that had been there—at least, in the beginning. She'd always assumed that sex was like a summer blockbuster movie. Loud. Euphemistic penis measuring. Didn't come close to living up to all the hype.

Until Flynn.

Flynn made her believe in the flash and bang and romance and thrill of a big, old-school Hollywood ending that made you sigh and tingle down to your toes.

And that was just from kissing him.

Gently, he tightened her sash. "The towel can be just a towel."

"No. I want it to be more. I want it to be fun. Just . . . not quite yet."

"There's no rush, Sierra. Plenty of fun to be had along the way to towel-level adventures. I like to take my time." Flynn brushed another kiss across her lips.

"I don't want to keep you from your party any longer. See you tomorrow." He disappeared down the thickly carpeted hallway.

She'd come out here to catch her breath. Only now, Sierra was breathless for a whole different reason.

Flynn's gesture had changed everything. Or maybe, it just helped all the feelings within her burst out of the cocoon of fear in which she'd been living for so many months.

Turning in a circle, she looked for somewhere to sit. Barring that, something to steady her balance. Her ankle wasn't giving out, but the earth did feel like it was shifting beneath her.

On the counter, next to the water jug, was a stack of wet rolled hand towels. She grabbed one. Its coldness shocked her, along with the zingy peppermint scent. Sierra touched it to her forehead, inhaled deeply a few times, then laid it on the back of her neck. It turned out that major life revelations heated her up as much as a session on the couch with Flynn.

A burst of laughter teased out from behind the closed door. Her new friends were great. They cared. How could she have let a little thing like being *cared* for drive her out of the room in a near-panic attack?

Well, because she was exhausted. Tired of hiding who she really was. Worn-out from clamping down on thoughts and emotions and the basic truths of her life and who she was.

No more.

Not everyone was lucky enough to have the sound of crashing waves and seagulls as appropriate background music to a life-altering decision. Sierra cocked her head, listening. Taking a mental video of the moment when she put her foot down. Took a stand. Took her life back.

Finally.

Because as of this moment, she was done running. Rick—and his dangerous stupidity—forced her to give up so much. Her chance at finishing her graduate degree. Her home, no matter that it was just an RA suite in a dorm. Her sense of peace. Safety. Courage. She'd had exactly enough courage to run from her old life.

Now, though, Sierra vowed to find the courage to plant herself in a new life. For good. She liked these women, this town. She liked Flynn, too. More than was probably smart. So she'd stay put, right here in Bandon.

With her friends.

With her sort of boyfriend.

But how?

Chapter Seven

FLYNN ROLLED OUT butcher paper over a picnic table on the patio behind the Gorse. Each table had paper, a can full of markers, and a plate of cookies. He knew the importance of mid-afternoon snacks.

Not just for the kids, either.

"This looks good." Carlos clapped him on the back. "Lily and my sister should be by any minute with their students."

"I hope they have fun." Arts and crafts was a far cry from the self-defense and basic martial arts he'd taught children back in Chicago. But his mentor in the Big Brother program swore you only needed two rules to deal with children: keep 'em busy, and always listen.

Flynn could do both. He had a knack for talking to and listening to kids. Probably because the mobsters he'd overseen at the construction company didn't have much more maturity than a sixth-grader.

What he couldn't do was *draw*.

Not at all. He didn't even doodle in the sides of his textbooks during the most boring class ever—tenth-grade geometry. Why waste time doing something he sucked at? Nobody ever said *pay attention in art class because you'll need it to design a float for a Cranberry Festival when you're twenty-seven*.

How was he supposed to guide these kids in designing a fully decorated float?

"Carlos, can you draw?" he asked.

"Why? You want a tattoo?"

Flynn cocked an eyebrow. What was in Carlos's background that made a new tattoo a go-to, Thursday afternoon activity?

"I've got a tattoo," he said shortly. One he'd get rid of as soon as possible. When you joined McGinty's crew—*officially*—you got a tattoo. Proof you belonged. Proof you were permanently committed to the mob.

Good thing he'd learned nothing in this life was truly permanent. Including happiness.

"I know a guy. Up in North Bend. He can put something on your belly that moves when you breathe. Like eagle wings flapping."

More info than Flynn needed. "No more tattoos. Look, if you can draw, it'd be good if you could help with the kids."

Carlos let out a huge laugh. "Hell, no. To the drawing and especially to the kids. That's my sister's thing. I don't want 'em, don't need 'em, and sure as hell don't know how to deal with them. Why do you think I run a bar? Guaranteed kid-free zone."

He was missing out. Kids had a way of looking at the world that either made you think or pee yourself laughing. They reminded Flynn that not everyone was born cynical and greedy. They'd been his antidote to McGinty.

"But you're cool with them hanging out back here?"

"Sure. It's for the Festival. Everyone's gotta pitch in. Biggest weekend of the year."

Yeah, yeah. He'd heard it all before. This Cranberry Festival was like a religion to the Bandon locals. They threw a festival pretty much every other weekend in the summer. One for all the big holidays, a celebrate the dunes festival, a whale festival, and about a dozen more. But the Cranberry Festival mattered so much because more than half the town worked at harvesting and processing the fruit—and the other half knew someone who did. Pride in their jobs made it special.

Flynn hadn't felt that, well, *ever*.

He walked back inside and saw that Sierra was early for her shift. She always showed up early to noodle around on the computer.

Why did a twentysomething woman in the twenty-first century not have her own computer? She'd mentioned college a couple of times and you couldn't get through a degree without owning one. Flynn chalked it up to another mystery he wanted to figure out. And since she didn't reveal much about herself, he'd have to be sneaky about it.

Or maybe kiss it out of her.

Her whole face lit up when she noticed him. "Hi there."

"I thought you weren't on for another couple of hours? I'd have given you a ride."

"My ankle's fine. I came into town to look up something at the library, and thought I'd hang out here instead of going back home."

In other words, she'd wanted to use the computer some more. Flynn saw right through her. Why wouldn't she just tell him? He bent an elbow to lean on the bar. Got face to face, a breath away from her lips. "I'm glad you're here."

"Why?"

"I like looking at you." He swiped a kiss over her lips, and then another. "I like doing that, too."

"Nobody said you had to stop."

The woman really had no idea of how much she turned him on. Of how two kisses already had his dick as hard as steel. He lowered his voice to a quiet murmur. "If I keep going there won't be any stopping, and this bar will get used in a whole new X-rated way."

She giggled. The sound ran through his blood like soda bubbles. "It doesn't look comfortable to lie on."

"You wouldn't be lying on it. I sure as hell wouldn't

drive my knees into this thing. No, I picture you braced, bent over the end, on your tiptoes. Me behind you. Holding on to your hip with one hand and your breast with the other."

Sierra's sharp, indrawn breath was as loud as a bullet.

Flynn could hardly stand how much fun it'd be opening her eyes to all the possibilities of what they'd do together.

Because yeah, he'd lost the battle with himself to be good where she was concerned. It was no longer a question of *if*—just *when*. He had to have her. Had to get inside and fucking *bask* in the sunshine that was Sierra.

Was it selfish of him? Hell, yeah. Did she deserve a man who could do the basics, like tell her his real name? Yeah.

But he'd treat her well, that was for sure. Even when treating her right meant walking away before she lost her heart to a liar who'd always carry the filth of the Chicago mob with him.

He dropped his hand from where it'd somehow ended up on her cheek. It fell onto a napkin on the bar. But this one wasn't white. It was covered with pencil marks. Flynn pulled it closer. Sierra tried to grab for it. Weird. So he snatched it even faster and held it up.

It was a Gorse napkin, printed at the bottom corner with that big yellow bush that grew along every road in town. But the rest of it was filled with a pencil sketch. It was . . . him.

His face. Every bit as detailed as a photograph. But

with an expression on it Flynn hadn't seen in the mirror in a long time. What Kellan had always called his shit-eating grin. The one his brothers claimed that he wore when he'd scored more Snickers than Smarties trick-or-treating. When he walked across the stage at graduation and swung his tassel to the other side. When he and Rafe emerged from that tomb last Halloween.

It shook him to his core to see it so perfectly recreated. On a napkin, for fuck's sake!

Flynn waved it at Sierra. "How did you draw this?"

Her brows came together into a confused line. "Pencil. A pen would've ripped the napkin."

The absolutely adorable way Sierra's nose crinkled, the way he wanted to kiss away the vertical line on her forehead, distracted Flynn for a second. But kissing her at the bar would be a bad idea. One, because he wouldn't be able to stop until things got way past PG. Two, because it probably violated every frickin' health code in the book.

As bartender, he had standards. Yes, his responsibilities were two hundred percent less than when he'd managed an entire construction company. They still mattered. Flynn wouldn't half-ass his job *ever*.

Flynn waved the napkin again. "How the hell did you imagine me looking like this?"

"I didn't have to imagine it. Your face gets like that, all full of smug triumph every time we kiss."

After all these weeks of working together and talking, she'd gotten through his defenses and made him *happy*.

Son of a bitch.

How far gone did it say he was that it took a drawing to remind him of how it felt?

Flynn looked at it again. Looked beyond the obvious mirror image and took in the shading and talent. "This is great."

"Thanks. You should see what I can do on a paper tablecloth," she quipped.

"I'm serious."

The smile fell from her face faster than Mrs. Oblinsky had erased the dirty picture he drew on the board in sixth grade. Clutching his wrist, she begged, "Please don't be serious."

What the hell? Flynn patted her hand. "I'm complimenting you."

"I don't do it for compliments." Her tone sharpened. "Or for money, before you ask."

Seemed he'd touched one hell of a raw nerve. "If you don't want me to ask, I won't. Simple as that." Flynn could only hope that rule worked both ways, seeing as how he had an entire lifetime of things he couldn't tell her.

Sierra blew out a long breath. "Thank you."

Huh. There was a story there, no doubt about it. And Flynn figured it'd take more than a few kisses to sweet-talk it out of her, after a reaction that strong. There was a lot more to her than he'd originally thought. Definitely not just a waitress.

The not-knowing only made him want to know *more*. What could a sweet thing like her be hiding?

"This drawing is really good, though." He threw up his hands, palms out, before her hackles went up again. "No follow-up questions—just a statement of fact."

"There's so much great contrast to your face. Sharp cheekbones, a strong Roman nose. A five o'clock shadow that kicks in by three. That dimple in your chin, dead center. All that gloriously thick and tousled hair. You're a dream to draw, Flynn."

The familiar, happy burble came back into her voice the longer she talked. Normally Flynn wasn't thrilled with being the subject of conversation. But hell, he'd listen to Sierra count his eyelashes if it made her sound like that.

He gave a half bow. "Anything else I can do to make your dreams come true, just let me know."

A hunger kindled in her blue eyes that turned them darker than normal. An instant later, it was replaced by . . . sadness? Nah. That couldn't be right.

Sierra radiated more joy on her worst day than anyone he'd ever known. She got a genuine kick out of an extra fifty-cent tip. When he skewered three cherries and dropped them into her ginger ale. And if there was a baby on someone's lap in the restaurant, she damn near burst with bliss.

The thought of babies led him to think of children and a light bulb came on in his brain. "If I don't offer to pay you or compliment you anymore, would you do me a drawing-related favor?"

"Of course."

"I can't draw."

"As well as me? Few can." It didn't come off as bragging. More an indisputable fact. Like saying the sky was blue. Or that he wanted to have her.

Then Sierra threw him her own version of a shit-eating grin, and his heart flipped over. Moments like that, when she dropped the shyness and showed him her true self? It fucking humbled Flynn that she trusted him enough to drop her guard.

Evidently *she* could joke about her crazy huge talent and acknowledge it was real. She just didn't want a focus shined on it.

Well, Sierra was shit outta luck on that one, because all Flynn wanted to do was focus on her.

Later.

Right now, he had a more immediate need.

He pointed at the swinging door to the hallway. "There's a group of kids out on the back patio who are supposed to help me make a float."

Sierra's nose crinkled. Adorably. Again. Noses had never been a turn-on for him with any other woman. But nothing about Sierra was like any of the other women he'd dated. "A root beer float?"

If only.

"No. An honest-to-God truck bed, chicken-wire-and-paint float for the Cranberry Festival."

"Are you in trouble? Did you get community service for something?"

Flynn wanted to bang his head against the bar. As a matter of fact, yes.

Except that his 1) wasn't official through the sheriff, 2) being ordered to do community service by their marshal felt way more like punishment than the "road to community integration" Delaney labeled it, and 3) he couldn't tell Sierra about any of reasons one and two.

"Now that we've moved to Bandon, me and my brothers figured we should be involved. Be a real part of the town. The Cranberry Festival's the biggest thing going, so we all volunteered." That sounded believable, right?

Sierra cocked her head to the side and studied him as though she were making a sketch in her head. "You don't strike me as a joiner."

She had him there. Flynn had joined one thing in his life—the Chicago mob—and look how that turned out.

"I never said that we were buying-a-tee-shirt excited about it. Just seemed like the right thing to do. Get to know our neighbors. Work to put the Festival together, instead of just showing up that weekend and eating a lot."

"And you like to build floats?"

Hell if he knew. But how hard could it be? "I'm good with my hands."

"I've noticed." Then her cheeks suddenly blazed as red as a maraschino cherry.

Wasn't that fascinating as hell? Flynn carefully put the napkin sketch down on top of another one, for protection. Then he leaned an elbow on the bar. Threw her the look about two dozen Chicago blondes had labeled his "bedroom eyes." "Are you dirty-talking me?"

Sierra grabbed the sketch and put it in her bag. "You said my drawing talent was a statement of fact. This is no different. You, Flynn, happen to have talented hands."

"You can bet your life that we'll come back around to that later." He lifted her hand and kissed each long, slender finger from the knuckle down to the unpainted tips. By the time he finished with her pinkie, Sierra was looking at him with that hot stare that made Flynn want to rip off his shirt. "I want details."

The stare disappeared after her cheeks flushed again. Now she just looked flustered. One hand smoothed the buttons of her white shirt as if he'd copped a feel instead of just a glimpse. Her other hand brushed back hair that wasn't out of place—since he hadn't touched that, either.

Good to know that a couple of kisses made Sierra *feel* undressed. Flynn couldn't wait to pick up from where they had to leave off.

He looked back over his shoulder, relieved that they didn't have an audience aside from the table in the back corner full of tourists who'd set up a base camp two hours ago. The way they were slow-playing their beers— not to mention the deck of cards they were working— made Flynn think they wouldn't leave until last call. Not that there were many better options in town to hang and drink.

Flynn had to admit, the Gorse had grown on him. The bright red wall gave the place character. The surprise of the jukebox could be fun, as long as someone with crap taste didn't hog it too long.

He recognized regulars now. They nodded across the room when they came in. Called out his name when they wanted to threaten a friend acting like a dipwad. His insta-fame as a bouncer had come about after catching a burglar at Norah's shop last month.

When he clocked in for work, Flynn clocked out of worrying about the future. Stopped mentally thrashing himself for being the reason they were in this mess. This bartending job the marshals had foisted on him might actually be a good fit, the more he thought about it. Why hadn't he realized that until now?

Why hadn't he let himself feel good?

Flynn liked making up new drinks. Liked the routine of locals changed up by the summer tourist wave. He liked Carlos and Jeb and Mariana. He *really* liked Sierra. The Gorse was, maybe, starting to feel like it could be home. That felt . . . good.

Shit.

Not that he could get used to it.

Nothing was guaranteed until after they testified.

That thought ghosting in—like it did a couple of dozen times a week—straightened Flynn's spine. He needed to move before it snuffed out his good mood. "Look, will you help me or not?"

Sierra stood, stuffing her phone in her back pocket. A stern mask settled over her face, with her chin up and a purse to her kissable, bitable, lickable lips. "How do you plan to deal with the children out on the patio? Do you know how to talk to them? Children require active listening. Attention. Patience. Even a fun craft activity like this can be educational as well as a challenge for the adult."

Sierra on her high horse was—possibly—even sexier than when she was flustered. "I like kids. A lot. I mentored a bunch of them back . . . where I used to live."

He barely caught himself from saying "back home." Because he'd promised Rafe that he wouldn't pine for Chicago like it was the girl that got away.

Or at least *try* not to.

"You did?" Her tone was a fifty/fifty swirl cone of surprise and skepticism.

"Yeah." Flynn ushered her ahead of him down the hallway. "Kids are the future, you know? If we don't step up and put effort into teaching them to be good people, we're just throwing away our future."

Sierra stopped dead in her tracks right in between the bathroom doors and twisted around to goggle at him. "That's—wow, Flynn. That's not at all what I expected to hear."

"I can go back to the expected suggestive banter later." He gave her perfectly round ass a squeeze as punctuation.

"I'm serious. I'm impressed by your take on children."

"Well, both my parents died by the time I was thirteen. We had Rafe to keep us together, but it was still hard. I don't want any kid to feel lost and alone. Like they don't have somebody they can turn to."

Shit.

That . . . was not supposed to have come out.

Flynn didn't talk about his parents being gone. He never, *ever* talked about how hard it had been after that.

He sure as hell never expected it to slip out in front of a bathroom with a piece of driftwood as a door handle and Beyoncé blaring from the speakers overhead.

Sierra put her hand on his arm. Her big blue eyes puddled at the corners. "You were thirteen? But Rafe's not that much older than you, is he?"

"Three years." The words choked off. Flynn did not want to get into this. He *couldn't*. How did you explain that three kids—one not even a teenager—evaded Social Services thanks to shady strings being pulled by a mob boss?

If Sierra pushed him? Flynn didn't know what he'd say. He hadn't bothered to think up a lie to explain it, because he'd never planned on sharing that part of his history with *anyone*. Shutting her down would be confusing, hurtful to her.

Shit.

"Oh, Flynn. I'm so sorry." Sierra put her arms around him. Pressed herself against him, ankles to thighs to chests. It was a hug to end all hugs. Tight. Gentle. Comforting. "I lost my parents when I was three. I know exactly what you mean about being alone. Not having anyone to talk to. It's the worst."

He rested his chin on the top of her head and just enjoyed the moment. Enjoyed being soothed in a way he hadn't been since . . . he was fifteen. The memory slapped at his brain, out of the blue.

A hospital wasn't as easily stonewalled/bribed/whatever as Social Services. They'd required parental consent to do his emergency appendectomy. So McGinty's girlfriend-du-jour pretended to be his mom for three days. She'd held his hand, fluffed his pillows, and generally comforted him.

For a solid year after that, Flynn had wished for another hospital stay—a bad leg break, tonsillectomy, *anything*—just to feel that level of security and contentment again. Not just for the morphine, either.

But he'd stayed healthy. And toughened up.

Stopped wishing for what would never happen again.

Until now.

Until this very moment, when Sierra's touch and words and sensitivity slayed him and filled him up at the same time. Jesus, to think that she'd lost her parents at only three? It didn't sound like she'd had anyone to lean on like he had Kellan and Rafe. Yet here, she was much worse off and offering him sympathy. No questions. Just the hug he'd been needing for fucking years without even realizing it.

Special . . . caring . . . giving . . . these words didn't *begin* to describe Sierra Williams.

How on earth did he luck out like this?

After pressing a soft kiss right over his heart, Sierra stepped out of his embrace. Her eyes still glittered with wetness. Flynn swiped his thumb in a crescent under each one. Then they just looked at each other. No longer touching, but connected deeper than they were before coming down this hallway.

A tow-headed tough guy of about five barreled through the back door, then skidded to a stop in front of them. "Are you Mr. Maguire?"

"Depends." Flynn crouched on his haunches. "Does Mr. Maguire owe you any money?"

"No . . . I mean, maybe?" he said slyly. Then a series of big nods. "Yes. I'm pretty sure he owes me at least a dollar."

It took everything in Flynn not to laugh out loud at the brass balls on this one. He'd literally seen the kid start with the truth, and then the moment when the idea of scamming Flynn had marched across the freckles on his face.

"What's your name?"

"Brendan."

"Well, you tracked me down, Brendan. I'm Mr. Maguire. And this is Miss Williams. How about you shake her hand like a gentleman?"

Brendan stuck out his hand, and then flashed Sierra a smile sweeter than a jelly donut.

Shaking it, she said, "Wow. So grown-up. You must be at least, what, twenty?"

Giggles poured out of him. "No! Even my sister's not that old. And she can *drive*."

"Anyone can drive," Sierra said with a dismissive toss of her hair. "You know what I need in a man? Someone who can *help*."

"I'm a great helper. Momma says so all the time."

"Then I might just draft you to be my special helper, Brendan."

Flynn snapped and shot out both index fingers. "How about you help us out right now by telling us why you came looking for me?"

"'Cause we're all here. To make the float. I'm s'posed to get you to start."

"See? You're already a great helper." Sierra ruffled his hair. "Thanks, Brendan. Why don't you run back outside and tell everyone that we'll be right out?"

"'Kay." He got about four steps down the hallway before turning back around. "What about my dollar?"

Oh, he was a smart one. He'd be a challenge. Flynn frickin' *loved* those kids. He dug into his bar apron for a buck. Held it right in front of Brendan. "You can have the dollar. Or . . . you can have the oatmeal cookies I brought for a snack. See, if you take that dollar, you could buy your own cookies. You wouldn't need mine."

Brendan reached for the dollar. Then he pressed it against Flynn's chest and patted his hand. "You keep it." And he raced out the door.

Sierra put a hand on Flynn's arm as he stood. "I'm going to thank you ahead of time."

"For what? Dragging you into what could be a train wreck? Or, at best, will be loud and crazy and messy?"

"Exactly. It sounds like a perfect afternoon. I haven't had one like it in a long time. So thanks for asking me to help."

"Here I was, ready to bribe you."

Laughter burbled out of her throat. "You can't bribe me, I already said yes."

"That's too bad. I wanted to take you on a date. As a reward for helping out the greater good of the glorification of the Cranberry Festival."

"Funny, I heard Floyd use that very phrase when he was in here last night for a drink."

Flynn remembered. His usual was a Seabreeze. Cranberry and vodka. He wouldn't be surprised if the self-important chairman of the Festival had a comforter printed with a picture of the fruit. "Pretty sure he says it at least once a day, like a mantra."

She opened the door to the patio. Screams and laughter ricocheted off the high fence encircling the concrete patio. A few kids had already gotten into the buckets of sidewalk chalk. Smiling, she waved her arm at the scene. "I'm just doing my part as a good citizen."

"Aren't we a civic-minded bar staff? Carlos should make us shirts. *The Pride of Bandon*."

"I would, however, very much like to go on a date with you. Not as payment or reward. Just because it would make me happy."

Best. Reason. Ever.

Especially since Flynn was suddenly happy, too.

But no chance that'd last.

Not with his luck.

Chapter Eight

SIERRA TIPPED HER head back to catch more of the breeze from the open T-tops of Flynn's car. The rays of the early evening sun had lost their punch and felt relaxing on her forehead and shoulders. What a great way to start their date. Then she stretched her legs out all the way. "This car has amazing leg room."

"If Rafe were here, he'd counter by saying that this car has amazing *everything*. Then he'd proceed to explain that this 1970 Chevy Camaro, with its 'new Strato bucket seats,' along with a whole bunch of boring details about what's under the hood, is the best car ever made." Flynn shook his head.

"I take it you're not equally enamored of this classic car?"

He blew a big raspberry. "Some people say classic. I say old. I say, where are the automatic windows and

Bluetooth and a way to change the radio station without taking my hands off the wheel?"

"You're a technology lover, huh?"

"You bet. Why not take advantage of every advancement there is? Don't tell me George Washington wouldn't have given every set of his wooden teeth to have air-conditioning during those sticky summers at Mount Vernon. Or that Babe Ruth wouldn't get a kick out of watching his Yankees in HD."

He was a walking cliché of masculinity. It tickled Sierra to death. Flynn was the guy who'd upgrade to a new electric knife every Thanksgiving—and believe that there was a difference. He was the opposite of everyone back in her painting program, which made him twice as interesting to Sierra.

"So what kind of a car did you have before deciding to share one with your brothers? One with all the bells and whistles?"

Flynn opened his mouth as if to answer, then closed it again. Then he gave an almost imperceptible shake of his head before clearing his throat. "A Jeep Wrangler Sport. Leather seats, nine speaker system with an all-weather subwoofer and an overhead sound bar, SiriusXM radio. And yeah, seat warmers."

He sounded . . . wistful? It was a little hard to tell. Now that Flynn was finally opening up to her rather than just chatting, Sierra was hearing a lot of nuances for the first time from him. And she wanted to keep mining for more. Especially since he'd dropped that bombshell about both of his parents being dead. It gave them something deep and meaningful in common.

Not that she'd wish that particular experience on her worst enemy. But it wasn't easy to find people her own age who could begin to grasp just how *alone* she felt in the world. Flynn still had his brothers, but he had that "I am an island" shuttered look in his eyes that she felt deep in her soul so often.

She put her hand on his shoulder. "You must miss it."

"I do. Rafe deserves this old relic. He's wanted one his whole life. Loves to tinker with it. I'm glad he's living the dream. I just miss *my* car."

"How's the whole sharing thing working out?"

His jaw tightened until the side of his face looked as hard as a marble statue. "Not well."

"Because you're all grown, independent men not used to accommodating each other's schedules?"

"No. Because my brothers are asshats."

He said it so matter-of-factly, no different from stating that they all had black hair. Sierra laughed as she looked out the window. The wall of pine trees edging the Oregon Coast Highway blurred into a wavery, ombré wall of green, thanks to Flynn's heavy foot on the pedal. "Is that so?"

"It is. Well, some of the time. I guarantee they say the same about me. A car means freedom. Going your own way, doing your own thing. Without first being dragged through a ten-round negotiation and prioritization discussion."

Hmm. Flynn's schedule at the Gorse matched up with hers, most of the time. He never mentioned hiking or kayaking or windsurfing. On her days off, Sierra had started to go down to the boardwalk to draw. She didn't recall seeing him there, either. So she took a chance and pressed him. "To be fair, do you go anywhere besides the bar? Do *anything* that requires a car?"

One dark, thick eyebrow shot up as his neck slowly cranked around. In a low, threatening growl, he asked, "Are you taking Rafe's and Kellan's side?"

When they first met . . . well, who was she kidding? She'd been equal parts completely weak-kneed at his hotness and intimidated by his bad boy vibe. The wall of indifference and attitude that roiled off of him like steam off a mug of coffee had to make every woman within twenty miles want to be the one who broke through to him.

Sierra hadn't thought for a second that she had anything necessary to meet that challenge. But it hadn't stopped her from wondering what lay beneath that . . . *reserve*. Now that she knew about the big heart and caring tenderness, Flynn didn't intimidate her one bit. Not even when he tried his best to.

"I'm taking their side if you're going to be stupid about it. If you're, oh, I don't know, campaigning for your third of time even if you don't *need* to drive anywhere."

"Stop reading my mind," he ordered.

Giggling, she shifted in her seat to cross her legs. "I'm quite sure I've barely cracked the surface."

"You still hit the nail on the head," he grumbled. "But that's how it is with brothers. You have to keep on your guard, or they'll run roughshod over you. Next thing you know, your little brother 'forgets' to add your laundry when he runs a load. Then there's a whole complicated thing with reminding Kellan he's the youngest and he's got to show us a little respect."

Flynn talked about his brothers a lot and Sierra knew she'd never, ever get tired of hearing about them. Families—close families—absolutely fascinated her. "What does that entail?"

"Last week? It was a wrestling match in the sand that ended with Rafe dragging both of us into the ocean."

"At the same time? That's . . . impressive. I wish I'd seen it."

"Nah. I let him. Rafe hasn't been able to get the upper hand on me in at least five years."

That didn't sound boastful. Flynn said it as fact, which seemed unusual. From the times the Maguires had eaten together at the Gorse, Rafe seemed a bit taller than Flynn's six feet. "Really?"

"I can beat anyone in a fight." Another flat statement of fact. "I used to do that all the time."

Fighting was so far outside of Sierra's frame of reference. No artist would do anything that might risk injuring their fingers. "You were in actual fights with people?"

"In a ring. In competitions. Not over grabbing the last bag of peanuts at a ball game."

Wow. Big-time wow. Suddenly Sierra wanted to see

him in action. Wanted to watch the ripple of muscles and tendons and the utter grace she was positive flowed off of him like water. It would be beautiful. To her artistic eye. And incredibly arousing, as well. To all the parts of her that were on alert right now just from sharing a car ride with Flynn.

"And you always won?"

"Yeah. Yeah, I did. No point doing something unless you do it all the way." He huffed out a breath. Draped one wrist over the top of the steering wheel and pushed the other up his forehead and through his hair. "That used to be my motto."

"Used to be?" Flynn was dropping all sorts of crumbs of information. But Sierra had to push the conversational broom pretty hard to sweep them into a recognizable pile.

"New state, new motto."

That was it. He sighed, but said nothing more. Was Flynn really that oblivious to how hard she was trying here? With a tad less patience, she asked, "What is it now?"

Repeating the hand swipe over his head, he said, "I haven't figured that out yet." His voice sounded grim. Sierra didn't know anyone else who had a personal motto, so she wasn't sure why it mattered so much. But it obviously did to Flynn.

Now she regretted pushing. She still wanted to know—*everything*—about him. Every crumb he let fall showed Flynn to be that much more of an interesting and thoughtful person. But the last thing Sierra wanted to do was be the cause of that frown line between his eyebrows.

She scrambled to take his mind out of whatever emotional dark alley she'd accidentally sent him down. "I wish I could see you fight."

It did the trick. Flynn flashed her a smile, all full of cockiness and promise. "You want to see my muscles? I'll whip them out anytime you want."

"Yes. Yes, as a matter of fact, I think I do want to see your muscles."

Sliding his sunglasses down his nose to peer at her over the frames, he asked, "Which ones?"

Thanks to the required anatomy class at her under-grad, Sierra could literally name each one. Not all seven hundred in the body, but the correct name for each one that she wanted to see. It'd take too long, though. Not to mention seriously putting a damper on their flirting. "Would it be greedy to say all of them?"

"Not if you knew how badly I *want* you to see them. How badly I want you to touch them." Flynn grabbed her hand and put it just below the hem of his shorts. She felt the crispness of dark hairs covering the rock-hard rectus femoris and the diagonal sweep of the sartorius muscle. Then she gave herself a mental high five for re-membering the Latin names.

Then Sierra stopped thinking at all because Flynn squeezed her hand, curling his fingers around and mixing a sweet dollop of romance into the lust already pulsing right below her skin. "You'd be doing me a huge favor if you turned those gorgeous blue eyes of yours onto any of my muscles."

"I don't have a motto, like you, but now I've got a goal."

With a chuckle, Flynn let go and turned his attention back to the road as they bumped off the flat stretch and up onto the enormous bridge.

The green of the metal trusses almost matched the dull green of the Coquille River below. Sierra's fingers twitched with want for a paintbrush and canvas. "Someone at the Gorse said this is a lift bridge. I'd love to watch it go up and down, see a big ship go under it."

"Drawbridges are cool. Slow, though. I'd always start off excited to watch. Then after five minutes of idling, waiting for some dumb-ass weekend sailor to figure out how to get his boat in line, I'd be cussing and miserable."

This time, Sierra bit back the follow-up question literally *itching* on the tip of her tongue. Like where he got to see drawbridges all the time. One near miss of Flynn shutting down on her was enough. Especially since their date had barely begun.

No. *Especially* since she'd probably freak out if he pushed *her* to answer any personal questions. She'd take what he offered up. Not push for more. And hope against hope that Flynn extended the same courtesy.

"Are you planning to buy your own car soon?"

"Thinking about it. We agreed to try sharing one for, ah, about six months. You know, do our part for the environment. Bandon's so frickin' small. We can walk most places, no problem. Aside from getting rained on."

"I'm surprised your brothers let you take the car tonight, with so little notice."

"Are you kidding?" He drummed on the steering wheel. "A hot date takes priority over anything. Except a cold body in the trunk."

Just as Sierra began to laugh, Flynn sucked in air that almost sounded choked. "I'm sorry. I didn't mean—we don't actually cart around dead bodies."

"Of course not. That's why I'm laughing."

"You are, aren't you?" He turned his head to check on her once, and then again, like he couldn't believe it. "I've been told my humor's too dry—or morbid—for some people."

"That may be true. But you're not on a date with 'some people.' You're with me. And you make me laugh all the time."

He pulled into the Bullards Beach parking lot and gave her yet another long, appraising look. The kind that, if it came from anyone else, would make Sierra wonder if she had a spot on her shirt. But Flynn seemed to be having a whole internal conversation with himself as he looked at her.

Flynn pulled into a parking spot. "Then I'm a damn lucky man." As he got out of the car, he tossed out an order. "Don't move."

Weird. They'd clearly arrived at their destination and the parking lot was empty on this Thursday night.

It was in the middle of a state park, so there weren't any restaurants or services around. Just tawny sand, random bumps of bushes, and a still-bright blue sky overhead.

Then her door opened and Flynn extended a hand to help her out. His other gripped a backpack.

"I'm fine now. My ankle barely even twinges. You don't need to cart me around."

"I'm not carrying you. Unless you want me to," he said with a waggle of his eyebrows. "I'm opening the door for you because you're a lady and my mom would turn over in her grave if I didn't."

Now Sierra felt stupid. Younger than Flynn and like a country bumpkin. She should've known. He'd always treated her like a lady. He held open the kitchen pass-through for her all the time.

But she'd led a pretty sheltered life. Not a lot of high-brow manners, aside from what she read about in books. "How old are you?" she blurted as she got out of the car.

Flynn let out something in between a laugh and a snort. "You're carding me because I'm polite?"

"I've just been wondering. A lot of the time you seem deep and serious and older than your years."

He draped an arm around her shoulders and led her down the path leading to the beach. "I'm twenty-seven. Although if you factor in moodiness, 'cause I was on a bender with that for a while, my brothers would probably tell you I'm more like forty-seven."

"You *were* on a bender? Does that mean it's over now?" Because he had noticeably . . . *lightened* over the past few weeks. His smile flashed more often, he chatted more with the regulars at the Gorse. Flynn still had that strong and silent vibe on and off, but not nearly as often.

"Not over, no. But I'm clawing my way out of it. Or rather, you're pulling me up."

"Me?" Apprehension knotted Sierra's stomach. This was very, very bad. Every magazine she'd ever read said that men hated it when women changed them. "I haven't done anything. I didn't even know you wanted to be pulled somewhere." She spoke so quickly at the end that her words ran together.

"Simmer down." He pulled her in tighter against his side to drop a kiss on top of her head. "It's not an accusation. It's a compliment. I was in a dark head space for a while before moving here. You shined in all your bright, beautiful light. It reminded me that being happy is a hell of a lot better than the alternative."

That was . . . ironic. Because yes, Sierra excelled at finding joy in the little things. Living in the moment. Life in foster care taught you quickly to appreciate what you had, since it could be gone the next day.

But underneath that surface joy was constant worry. Anxiety. Dread. Exactly what Flynn had described—a dark head space. She went to sleep every night worried about Rick finding her, *hurting* her, and woke up every morning determined not to let that happen. The time she spent alone with Flynn was the safest she'd felt since leaving Milwaukee.

Sierra sure couldn't tell any of that to the big, strong,

sexy, and apparently *happy* man at her side. So yes, a little bit of hysterical laughter burst out of her. "Thanks."

"How old are you?" Flynn pulled a blanket from the backpack, spread it out on the sand, and put his shoes on the corners to hold it down. Sierra toed hers off and did the same.

"Almost twenty-four." Then that knot of panic came back because she'd answered Flynn without thinking. Without remembering that the age on the fake ID she'd purchased said she was twenty-six.

"Under twenty-five, huh? Then you might not be so thrilled with what I have planned for tonight." Flynn took her hand and started walking. A few seagulls and much smaller birds ran at breakneck speeds away from the crashing surf. "See that building up ahead?"

Squinting against the slowly dipping sun, she saw a squat white building with a brick-red stripe along the bottom. It was roundish, maybe octagonal, and almost at the tip of a wall of rocks that ended in a point right where the river frothed into the Pacific. A cupola was all glass, and tipped with a red roof that matched the bottom.

"It looks like a lighthouse—except its only about three stories tall?" As if a giant had stepped on a normal lighthouse, squishing it down to this miniature version.

"It's a lighthouse, alright. For guiding ships into the river. I guess that's why it doesn't have to be very tall. Abandoned now, but I thought it'd be a nice walk over to it, then out onto the rocks."

Sierra wanted to pull Flynn into a run. The need to

be closer, to look at it from all sides through her artist's eyes, jittered its way down into her feet. How could he just saunter? The water had to be six or seven shades of blue and green with the mixture between ocean and river. The stark contrast against the black rocks surrounding it, *and* the blue sky could be sketched from at least a half dozen angles. It should be painted at sunset. During a lightning storm. Under cloud cover.

Giving in to the urge, she tugged at his arm, trying to hurry him along. "It's beyond charming. It's postcard-perfect. I need to draw it. I *have* to draw it. Can we come back with my paints next time?"

Flynn chuckled. Then he patted her hand. "How about we see first if I bore you to tears tonight?"

She didn't understand. Not at all. "How on earth would you do that?"

"This—" he swept his arm to encompass the scenery, "—is the whole deal. We take a long walk on the beach, then go back and watch the sunset with the dinner I've got stashed in that backpack."

"Flynn, it sounds perfect." Or it would be, if he'd walk faster.

Or . . . maybe . . . she should focus on the handsome man next to her and save the painting mania for another trip. Sierra sucked in the salt-tinged air and reminded herself how lucky she was to be on the edge of the Pacific with such a wonderful guy. One who, miraculously, liked her. At least, the parts of herself that she *let* him know about.

She wouldn't ruin tonight by wondering what he'd think about her if he knew the truth.

The furrow in his brow said that Flynn wasn't convinced. "Does it sound okay? Or are you humoring me?"

"Why would I bother to humor you? If I didn't like this, if I didn't want to be with you, it'd just be a waste of a night."

They veered closer to the shoreline, where it was easier to walk on the packed sand. "Wouldn't you rather be in a club tossing back shots and dancing?"

"No." Sierra stopped. Using her big toe, she drew an outline of a bottle and two shot glasses. Put it in a circle and slashed a diagonal line across it. Flynn barked out a laugh. Then she bent down to unearth a half-buried strand of seaweed. The thick rubberiness of the leaves surprised her. "Is that what you did?"

Flynn took the seaweed and pressed on a bulb, squirting seawater at her. "I worked a lot. Did the fights. But I hit some clubs, too. Look, I know this date is pretty basic. But I don't know what sort of a good time to offer you here. This is all different to me. I'm off my game. Where I used to live there were more . . . options."

Where was that, exactly?

Oh, yeah. Her new dating rule: *don't ask any question you aren't willing to answer yourself.*

"Flynn. This is perfect. Truly, I don't need much to make me happy."

"What do you need?"

It was the kind of question that came up at two in the

morning—or on a deserted stretch of beach with only the crashing waves as background music. It deserved a thoughtful answer. A real one, as best she could share without revealing her secrets.

"A place to paint. Some . . . peace. Lots of honesty. No secrets or lies." It was one hundred percent hypocritical of her to wish for that. But Rick had lied to her for so long. The hurt and betrayal she'd felt when the truth unraveled was a feeling Sierra never wanted to experience again. So yes, it went on her wish list.

A girl could dream, couldn't she?

Flynn's fingers dug into the back of her hand all of a sudden, then just as quickly relaxed. He moved behind her so that they both faced the lighthouse, keeping the setting sun at their backs. Then he circled his arms around her in a loose embrace. "That's both simple and very specific."

"All I want is a simple life. I never dreamed of being rich or traveling the world." This moment, right here, with Flynn, was so much better than anything she'd ever dared to hope for. Because when you lived with nothing for so long, almost everything seemed out of reach and impossible to imagine. "I just want lots of happiness."

His head cozied up against hers, lips brushing the top rim of her ear. "How about lots of kisses, too?"

"Oh, geez. You're right. I don't know how those slipped my mind . . ." Sierra wound her hand around the back of his neck to make sure he didn't go anywhere. He clamped tighter the arm at her waist, pulling her back against a hard-on so impressive it made her gasp.

Flynn moved in on that gasp, capturing her mouth while it was still open. His tongue swooped in, tasting and licking and stroking the inside of her mouth.

But Sierra was ready. Ready for him. Primed by the happiness of being with him and the romance-drenched moment. So she shifted sideways and became the aggressor. Wrapped a leg around his like a vine up a marble column—because that's how solid Flynn's muscles felt—and *twined* to him with every possible appendage.

Her fingers wove through his hair. Her other hand boldly shot up his untucked black shirt to clutch at the warm skin of his back. *Her* tongue took over *his* mouth. It didn't matter what was in his backpack picnic. What Sierra hungered for right now could only be assuaged by more Flynn. More heat. More pressure. More moans that melded with the music of the waves.

Suddenly her other foot left the ground as Flynn lifted her and spun them in slow circles. She tipped her head back for a second. Then she blinked at the handsome man grinning down at her. "What are you doing?"

"Feels like the earth is moving?"

Sierra nodded, already dizzy and more than a little kiss-drunk. But she didn't want him to stop, either.

"I'm giving you a preview of what it'll feel like when we have sex."

She swallowed hard. "Oh."

Flynn carried her closer to the water. He stood with his feet submerged, turned so that spray hit her cheeks from the suddenly gusty wind. "It'll feel like this, too. Fierce. Inexorable."

Sexy and smart. Was there any better combination? Oh, well, yes. The icing on top of Flynn's mysterious bad boy vibe. "What kind of a person uses the word *inexorable*?" she murmured, not really expecting him to hear it over the surf.

"What kind of person knows what it means?" he whispered back even softer.

Was she supposed to have heard that? Did it mean that Flynn realized she wasn't telling him the whole truth about herself?

"Touché."

Chapter Nine

FLYNN DIDN'T MIND unloading the booze delivery. Hoisting kegs and cases full of bottles was a good workout. Well, a good *start* to a workout, anyway. The only gyms in Bandon were those women-friendly places that had circuits for weights and eight different kinds of dance classes. No free weights. No heavy bag. Flynn knew better than to go into a gym for weekend warriors if he wanted to avoid attention.

There was a rumor that Mollie was going to hook them up with memberships for the fully loaded gym at Lucien's resort. But he wasn't holding his breath. Flynn didn't doubt that Mollie would ask her BFF if it was possible to swing it without them paying the bazillion dollar membership fee for the entire resort.

He did doubt, however, that Lucien was inclined to do them any favors. He'd been skeptical of Rafe moving in on his best friend. And even though Flynn and Kellan hadn't so much as looked at Mollie sideways, he didn't seem willing to cut them any slack.

Until then, Flynn ran a lot on the beach. Sparred with his brothers. And tried to unload twice as much of the delivery as Carlos did.

"I'm sweatier than a camel's crotch." His boss took a faded red bandana out of his back pocket and wiped his forehead.

"Should I ask how you know that?" Carlos dropped comments—like this one—that added up oddly. Someone who'd been in the Middle East, knew how to fight, but didn't have the spit and polish of a vet. Walked with a hitch in his step at the end of a long shift that he refused to explain.

Not that Flynn would ever come out and *ask* him if he'd put his muscles and morals behind any cause that paid enough. Because that sounded waaaaay too much like his own choices with McGinty's crew. Last thing he needed was a mirror pointed his way.

Carlos rubbed the bandana across his eyes. "Once you've seen one, it's a sight you'll never forget."

Neither an acceptance nor a denial. Carlos was good. As someone who'd done the double-talk walk his whole life, Flynn appreciated the agility. He lifted the box of bourbon and put it on the top shelf of the storeroom. Without using the stepladder. Because that overhead push worked his lats and delts to a nice burn.

"Did you have a good time with Sierra last night?"

"Uh, yeah." Flynn had been genuinely trying—as he'd promised Rafe—to not walk around with a stick up his ass. To actually talk to people. So he'd pumped Carlos for ideas for his date. "Thanks for suggesting the lighthouse. It was a big hit."

Carlos moved a bunch of rum bottles to get to the back row, full of expensive imports he'd brought back from a Caribbean cruise. "I figured it would be, for someone who likes to draw as much as she does."

Pride surged in his chest. Sierra's talent was amazing. During their afternoon of brainstorming with the kids, she'd come up with a great new logo for the Cranberry Festival. Flynn intended to take it to Floyd himself and kiss as much of that flabby ass as necessary to get him to use it. "You've seen them, too? Her sketches?"

"Seen them?" Carlos batted away the question. "I asked her to paint *real* ones. I offered to hang them on the walls here. They'd probably all sell in less than a day. Good for her, and good for business."

It was a great idea. Except . . . he remembered the way Sierra's hackles went up when he first praised her drawing. The way she'd insisted that she didn't do it for money. Which was crazy, because Flynn was certain she could make serious bank with her talent. "Will she?"

"I'm not sure. She bobbed and weaved better than Floyd Mayweather, but never gave me a straight answer."

Flynn latched on to the name of the famous fighter. He hadn't had anyone to geek out over fighters with since leaving the MMA gym in Chicago.

He missed it. Missed hanging out over beer and brats to watch a prize fight. Missed talking trash about MMA versus boxers versus those pansy-ass WWE wrestlers. "You follow boxing?"

"Yeah. Doesn't go over well here, though, so I never have it on the TVs in the back room." Carlos started doing the usual pre-happy hour bottle pull: one of every clear and dark alcohol. Basically a Long Island Tea right here in the storeroom.

Sticking two of the bottles sideways under his arm, Flynn said, "I'm into it, too." Nonchalantly.

No big deal.

Not like he was fucking *jonesing* to talk about fighting worse than an addict in line at the methadone clinic.

"Boxing?"

Flynn bobbed his head. Figured he'd go for broke. Lay it all out. "And MMA. Big fan."

Carlos narrowed his eyes. "That's how you took down those punks who burglarized Coffee & 3 Leaves last month. You've got skills, don't you?"

"Some." And that was as far as he'd go. Going into detail was risky for a laundry list of reasons. The biggest being that Carlos might go nosing around the underground fight club boards to hunt up information on Flynn.

Not that he'd find anything.

Not as Flynn Maguire, anyway.

Safer to change the subject, though. Flynn hooked

the stepladder over his shoulder and backed out into the hallway. "You should poke at Sierra to make those paintings for the Gorse. I think she could use the money."

"Figured that out, huh?"

It didn't take Kellan's years of advanced learning to do the math. "The woman's only form of transportation is a bike. In a state where it rains approximately four hundred days a year. And she's far from stupid."

"Agreed." Carlos locked the door. Couldn't be too careful. People would do anything for a free drink—including liberating the alcohol themselves.

"She's happy, though. Even without a car. Which is a fucking mystery. I have to share my car, and it makes me grouchier than a grizzly." Flynn had heard Mick say that at lunch. It sounded . . . appropriate. He didn't know for sure if there were grizzlies or brown bears or if they fucking shit in a gold-plated cave in the woods together, but following Mick's lead was a safe bet. Flynn thought it made him sound like he fit in. Like he belonged here. Fake it 'til you make it, right? Delaney would be proud of him for the attempt.

So his mouth twisted viciously downward when Carlos laughed at him. "Why are you talking like a pioneer lumberjack?"

"Just trying on a local colloquialism for size."

"Take it from me, it doesn't fit you." Then he veered off to check the dishwashing sprayer.

Whatever. He'd tried. One small step for Flynn, one giant step for ex-mobsters in WITSEC everywhere . . .

His phone vibrated in his back pocket. Flynn stowed the bottles behind the bar and took it out.

S: Whatcha doing?

Flynn had to admit he liked getting that simple check-in from Sierra. It felt . . . normal. Nice. Something his life had been lacking for six months. Plus, it didn't suck to know that a pretty girl was thinking about him . . .

F: Came in early to help Carlos prep for the onslaught. Fishing tournament this weekend means this town's bursting at the seams. Your tips should be epic.

S: Here's hoping.

There was no emoji for a sigh but Flynn swore he heard one, anyway. He didn't like the thought of Sierra worrying about money. Of course, he didn't like that she lived in a shoebox, either. A good fart could blow in her front door, let alone a burglar. Or worse.

And Flynn knew there was a lot of "or worse" skulking around where you least expected 'em.

F: Are you on your way over?

S: Almost. I need to finish a sketch. But it's hard
to get right.

No way. With her talent she could probably draw the
inside of a cloud. Frowning, his thumbs raced over the
screen.

F: How come?

S: I'm trying to get down last night. The two of us
on the shore. You didn't keep your shirt off long
enough, though. I can't quite remember exactly if
your abs are a six-pack or an eight-pack.

He'd be damn happy to let her look at them as long
as she wanted. Hell, Sierra could do an old-school rubbing of them with charcoal, if it floated her boat. But an-
swering her question would be too easy. For *her*. Flynn
wanted to tip the scales back in his direction.

F: Well, I still don't know where you stand on the
T Swift/Katy Perry debate. Guess we've both got
some studying up to do . . .

S: When is class in session? I might need some
extra tutoring.

Was it too early to call a sick day? For both of
them, so he could race over to her? If this had been

any one of the last handful of towns where Delaney had—unsuccessfully—dropped them, Flynn would've pulled that stunt. Even after working for less than two months.

But those were places where he didn't give a shit. About the town. About the people.

Flynn wasn't willing to blow their chance of sticking in Bandon. The town was growing on him. He liked the people. Well, most of 'em. The ones he didn't like at least made it interesting.

He liked his job. So much that it surprised the fuck out of him. Liked his boss. And now he really, *really* liked Sierra. Would, in fact, do anything for her. Except for the one thing that would be best for her—keeping his sorry, dangerous self away from her.

F: We're gonna be in the weeds the whole weekend with this tournament. No chance to hang until Monday.

S: Guess I'll just have to hope that you're wearing a very, very tight shirt tonight.

Flynn dropped the phone like a searing hot potato.

Carlos opened the ice drawer. Gave its level a check. As Flynn tied his apron around his waist, he asked, "Would it be okay if I borrowed your truck? I need to pick up the supplies for the Cranberry Festival float."

With a clap on Flynn's back, Carlos answered, "Hey,

I'm a card-carrying proud citizen of Bandon. Anything you need for the Festival, I'm in."

"It might take more than one trip. I need to get the lumber and stain to make a bookcase I promised Sierra."

Carlos started mixing the pre-rush, single Jack and Coke he had every Friday night. "Same answer. Anything to make her life easier, I'm in."

That sounded . . . like Carlos *knew* something. Not just that she lived off her tips. Like Carlos knew for sure that Sierra had a rough life. Or at least one with a hell of a speed bump in it before she'd landed here.

Flynn grabbed a stack of napkins and started rolling silverware. "What's her story, anyway?"

Carlos stopped, mid-pour. Only after a couple of long beats did he finish filling the highball glass. And only after *that* did he slap a cool glance at Flynn that hit him with the strength of a six-foot wave. "Everyone's got a story. Not everyone wants to share it. Do you?"

"Hell, no." The words burst out of him. Probably way too fast to sound innocent or nonchalant or hell, *normal*.

And that's probably why Carlos pushed his drink to Flynn and made another for himself, chuckling the whole time.

Flynn chugged the first half of it like he was trying for a brain freeze. Why was it so damn hard to lie to everyone here? He'd been doing it in Chicago for half his life. Never bothered him there.

Of course, most of the people he knew back then

were in McGinty's crew. The guys he knew from the fight club were in gangs. Nobody there expected the truth. Or wanted it.

Shit. The realization spiked, much worse than a brain freeze. The truth had never mattered before. Not in the circles he ran in.

Now it did.

Now that he'd found a place he could settle. Make a new life, entirely of his choosing.

Unless things fell to shit when they went back to Chicago. And that was a pretty motherfucking big "if."

"Got a question for you."

Flynn made the shape of a gun with his thumb and finger. "Shoot."

"I heard you and your brothers talking about trying to find the best Oregon beer. Since you're not from here." Carlos held up one hand as he sipped his drink. "Don't worry, I won't ask where your old favorite local beer is from."

"So that first night we crossed the border, we had . . . I don't even know how to describe it." Flynn shuddered at the memory, only half for effect. "Some fruity shit show that probably didn't even have hops in it. But since Oregon's known for its beers, we decided to take the plunge. Risk our taste buds—and our manliness—and keep drinking until we found awesomeness."

Carlos shook the ice in his glass. "I own a bar. You could ask me for a recommendation or twelve."

"Where would the fun in that be?"

"Well, it'd be a lot more pain*less*."

"Like I said, where would the fun be? Making my brothers miserable is always a good night's work." The milky white bottle of Malibu behind Carlos caught Flynn's eye. He ignored it most of the time, seeing as how he wasn't a twenty-year-old coed looking to get drunk.

But it gave him an idea. A specialty cocktail for the Cranberry Festival. Mix it with cranberry juice, pineapple juice, and skewer some sugared cranberries for a garnish. It needed . . . something else. Good thing he had almost three months to work on it.

Carlos rubbed the back of his neck. "If that's your take on local beer, I'm not sure if I should ask my question."

"Sorry." Flynn shifted his attention back over. Looked like this was going to be something more serious than a shooting-the-breeze way to kill time until the first wave arrived. "I'm just pulling your leg. Ask away."

"There's a craft beer dinner next month. Up in Coquille. I thought you might want to come along. If you don't mind hanging out with the boss. Which, in a town as small as Bandon, can't really be a hang-up."

Flynn took a long, slow sip of his drink to cover his surprise. Hanging with the boss. Back in Chicago, that was a big deal. A private dinner with Danny McGinty—well, they were never *private*. But a dinner with just his inner circle was a big fucking deal.

Carlos was so different from McGinty. McGinty didn't ask—he issued commands. Whereas Carlos sweated gratitude out his pores every time Flynn refilled the ice or made a suggestion about the drink menu.

This invitation was a big deal. McGinty's invites always had an angle. This invite from Carlos was just . . . nice. He'd paid attention to some side chatter at the bar and acted on it. As a favor to Flynn, really.

And it was fucking nice. Thoughtful.

McGinty had *used* Flynn. He'd poured money into his college education—but not out of the kindness of his heart for a trio of orphans. No, he'd done it to ensure a loyal soldier running his side company. He'd valued Flynn as a commodity. As another way to rake in profits and keep his ass covered.

Carlos valued Flynn as a *person*.

It was very, very cool.

Flynn swallowed hard, because there was one hell of a lump in his throat. "That sounds great. Thanks for thinking of me."

"I'll send you a link to the Facebook event page." Carlos ambled back toward the kitchen. Flynn braced his hands on the bar—his domain, now, rather than a glass-topped executive desk—and took a fucking minute to accept this was his life now.

Or it could be.

Too bad that just made Flynn worry twice as much.

"Hey, F-man." Kellan waved as he sauntered in the door. He was in his jeans and red *Bandon Cooperative Cranberry Facility* shirt.

After a quick glance at the clock over the jukebox,

Flynn asked, "What are you doing here so early? It's only four."

"There's a barbecue on the beach tonight to kick off the fishing tournament. Half the plant's working it. Either schlepping food or drinks, playing in the band or pitching in with their personal boats for the day-fishers." Kellan toed out a stool and dropped onto it. "Instead of fighting it, they closed the plant early. I couldn't give a rat's ass about fishing, so I came here to drink with my favorite brother."

"Since when am I your favorite?"

"Ahh—since I know you could dropkick me halfway to the ocean with one foot?"

"Please. I could do that with just my big toe."

"And since you can pour me a Guinness without moving so much as a step."

Flynn took the hint and grabbed a glass mug with the gold and green harp logo. "You know I'm working tonight. We won't be able to drink together."

"Somebody will sit down next to me. If it's a guy, I'll drown my disappointment in beer and talk about the rumored new iPhone. If it's a woman—a hot one—I'll thank my lucky stars and start the ball rolling to the inevitable moment when I take her outside to make out."

"Good to know you've got a plan."

"I don't, really. But sitting here people watching won't suck. Better than summer TV. Watching you drool all over Sierra also promises to be prime entertainment."

Sierra. Yeah, it had been all of four minutes since

Flynn had thought about her. But she was another reason, the biggest reason, why he was happy and, at the same time, freaked the fuck out about how things were going for them here.

The faint clatter of pans from the kitchen wasn't enough noise to cover their conversation. So Flynn lifted the pass-through at the end of the bar. "I'm making you earn this draft. Come help me check the sound system."

As soon as they got to the small stage, Flynn crouched to fiddle with the wires coming out of the speaker. Or at least, make it *look* like that's what he was doing. "Kellan?"

"What?" His brother tapped on the microphone. "I don't think this is on."

"Get over here." Once Kellan knelt beside him, Flynn asked the question it'd been too risky to voice at the bar. "Do you ever worry about what happens next?"

"I told you, I'm hoping to lock lips with a luscious lady. Brunette, I think."

"I'm serious. Do you worry about getting settled here, making it home—and then it all gets yanked away after Rafe and I testify? If our identities are made public? Or worse, if McGinty's crew finds us before we go back?"

"Sure. All the time."

Thank God it wasn't just him. "It was easier before. When I didn't give two shits about anything except being mad. But I think I'm starting to care."

"About Sierra?" Kellan gave an exaggerated wink that drew up half of his face.

"Yeah, but not just her." She'd just wiped the bitter blinders from his eyes. The more Flynn though about it, he'd fit into Bandon from day one. He'd just ignored how easy, how comfortable it was out of habit. "About doing the right thing for everyone here. About doing a kick-ass job at the Gorse. Not letting Carlos down. Helping a great bunch of kids learn how to build a float."

His brother sniggered. "Do *you* know how to build a float?"

"Not the point." He knew how to Google. Choosing between the fun designs Sierra had helped the kids create—that was the hard part. "I think, after all their other epic bad choices, the Marshals Service did us a favor dropping us in this tiny, weird town. We could make lives here. Be happy. Rafe's already pretty well planted with Mollie. But as long as there's a chance it could disappear, isn't it stupid to let ourselves, well, *care*?"

Kellan dropped the funny face. Grabbed him by the shoulders, looked at him intently, and with utter somberness said, "YOLO."

Flynn jerked out of his grasp. "What the fuck is that supposed to mean?" Sure, Kellan was the jokester of the family. But Flynn didn't drop his guard very often. Not anymore. Couldn't K play along and be serious for five freaking minutes?

Kellan didn't seem phased by Flynn's flare of temper.

"YOLO—you only live once. Were we happy leaving Chicago? Hell, no. But when we were busy licking our wounds about that, we made ourselves even more miserable. And we fought like three fucking betta fish dumped into one bowl."

"It sucked." Being at odds with his brothers was the last thing Flynn had ever wanted. It was supposed to be the three of them against the world. For a while there, it felt like every man for himself.

Flynn didn't ever want to feel that way again. Even if a lot of it had been his own damn fault.

"It still does, sometimes. It's getting better. We're getting better. Worrying about what'll happen at the trial will only make every day until then a living hell. So live in the moment. Be the king of the bar tonight. Then go kiss your pretty girlfriend and call it a good night's work."

The kid was right. Flynn stood and ruffled his little brother's hair. "When did you get to be so smart?"

"Did you see the size of my law school textbooks? I know things now. Lots of things I'll never get to use. Doesn't matter. Law school was a different moment. I've moved on."

"Have you?" Because the mere fact that Kellan brought it up meant it was still a big fucking deal to K.

Flynn didn't care that he wasn't running the construction company anymore. It turned out he liked tending bar—making up drinks, the back-and-forth with regulars, helping people celebrate or wash away a bad day. Rafe had turned his hobby of working on cars into a job here. Kellan was the only one of them who still seemed to not have clue one as to what to do for a living.

Aside from the fact that he *hated* the cranberry plant.

"I'm working on it. Don't hassle me when you're the one so paranoid that you're whispering over a speaker."

Flynn plugged it in, then finally put his mouth right over the mic for a check. "Kellan Maguire is my favorite brother because he trusts that life is good. And he makes kick-ass egg salad." His announcement made the table in the corner turn and giggle. It made Kellan duck his head and stare at his feet.

"Can I have that beer now?"

"K, you just cleared out the cobwebs in my head. You can have all the beer you want tonight. On me."

Too bad it wasn't as easy to get back on even footing with Rafe. His *actual* favorite brother, not that he'd ever say so. A free beer wouldn't cut it. Not after he'd been such an asswipe to him. Flynn didn't have a clue in hell where to start with that.

Chapter Ten

SIERRA HITCHED HERSELF onto a stool to give her aching feet a ten-second break. It was almost midnight, so things were finally slowing down on this crazy busy Saturday. Not that she was complaining. It turned out that drunk fishermen were generous tippers.

"You're staying to close, right?" Mariana asked.

"To the bitter end."

"Take your fifteen now, then, so you get a rest in before I go. I'll do a sweep through your tables and make sure they're taken care of. If you know what I mean . . ." And then she gave an exaggerated wink and burst into a hearty laugh.

"Thanks." Mariana wasn't the kind of person she'd ever had as a friend before. Big and bold and unabashedly flirtatious. She didn't hold back on anything, and Sierra kind of loved that about her. Sierra hoped that she could learn to channel some of that brashness and come out of the shadows.

She'd spent all her years in foster care trying to be invisible. At both of her art schools, everyone did their own thing and barely noticed the other students. If Sierra was truly going to take a stand and declare that Bandon would be *her* home, her place to belong, then she needed to be a little more bold.

Flynn was a great place to start. Being bold with him got her lots of long, lusty kisses. She looked at his dark head, the gorgeously thick hair that she loved to thread her fingers through. It was bent in concentration on a line of four glasses in front of him. He wasn't working at his usual breakneck pace. He was just sort of . . . considering the drinks.

"Whatcha got going over there?"

"A surprise for you."

"I like the sound of that. But I haven't done anything to deserve a surprise."

"Sweetness, you don't give yourself enough credit. You've given me the best week I've had in months."

Sierra's first thought was how sad that made her. Gratified that she could make such a difference. But also sad that Flynn had been so unhappy that just spending time with her was such a treat.

On the other hand? When his words settled into her brain? She felt *exactly* the same way about him. Like she'd been just floating through life, and Flynn had finally anchored her safely. She wasn't scared all the time anymore. Opening up and being truly herself with him was a gift that had opened her heart back up. He listened to her as if every word truly mattered. Not to mention the connection that defied description. It was just an . . . ease. Knowing she'd say whatever was in her heart and he'd get it. He'd *get* her.

It made her realize how much Rick hadn't listened, hadn't gotten her. That he'd pretty much used her, kept dating her for his own profit. It made his betrayal of her a little easier to bear.

Just a little.

Sierra beamed at Flynn. Channeling Mariana's boldness, she said, "I feel exactly the same way about you. This week has been amazing, Flynn. I can't wait to see what happens next."

"Next is you trying your surprise." He beckoned her closer. Sierra shifted over two stools. "Realized something as I was thinking through a specialty cocktail for Elena."

She eyed the purply-pink drinks lined up on the bar. "Ooh, what are you making for her?"

"I'm working on a couple different options. But these aren't for her. They're for you."

"You're making me my very own drink?" Nobody had ever done anything like that for her before. No foster parent made her cookies when she was having a bad day or brought home a great report card. Nobody in art school drew her a picture. Sierra absolutely *loved* Flynn's surprise.

"Of course. I've got to make a Sierra Special. I'm honing in on the right recipe, but you should taste and vote."

"What are they?"

"You told me how much you like blackberries. I'm trying to make the ultimate Blackberry Pie Martini for you."

"Might as well just fill a glass with sugar cubes," Mick grumbled. He tugged at the brim of his USMC ball cap as he shoved his empty beer mug forward for a refill. "Only difference being that you couldn't upcharge the shit out of it."

The old vet's crotchetiness didn't do anything to still the flutter in Sierra's heart. Omigosh. She and Flynn had talked about the Cranberry Festival during their beach picnic, and she'd admitted that she preferred blackberries. And then had probably gone on a little too long about her favorite blackberry pie. The dining hall at the Milwaukee Institute of Art & Design had it through the beginning of October, and there wasn't a day that Sierra didn't snag a piece.

He'd *listened*. Not just let her words wash over him. No, Flynn had taken what she said to heart and then made an effort to do something special based on it.

What a wonderful man. He wasn't with her out of convenience because they worked at the same place. Or for a good time in bed. This was a thoughtful man who *cared*. A man who believed she mattered.

A man she could trust with her heart.

Bracing her elbows on the bar, Sierra boosted herself

over to kiss Flynn right on the lips. It wasn't the appropriate thing to do while they were both still on shift. But his gesture required a response. "Thank you. For paying attention most of all, *and* for the drinks."

Mick barked out a laugh, thwacking his palm against the bar. "I'll make you a drink if it gets me that kind of service."

"How about you get one just for being patient when I tended bar the other night?" Sierra gave him a peck on the cheek. Because she didn't have a grandfather. But there were many days when Mick's gruff concern made her feel special.

"Hey. Get your own girl, old-timer," Flynn threatened playfully. "Or I'll cut you off."

Mick put a fist to his chest. "You found my weak spot. My arthritis couldn't take the damp air without my medicinal hops."

Medicinal. He was adorable. Sierra beamed at the older man. Flynn just ignored him, touching her chin to bring her attention back to his creations.

"Don't thank me until you try them. I think I've narrowed it down to these two." Flynn pointed at the martini glass. "Blackberry vodka, vanilla schnapps, whipped cream, and a few drops of Chambord for color."

Sierra lifted it and took a small sip. Cautiously. Because she had very little experience with mixed drinks, and didn't want to embarrass herself by choking if it was super strong. "It's sweet." Surprisingly so. "Creamy. I think I could too easily drink quite a few of these."

"Hang on. No deciding until you try option two. It's a little more complicated, but probably worth it." He pushed a champagne flute toward her. "Muddled blackberries, lemon juice, simple syrup, gin, crème de cassis, and a splash of Cava."

"What's Cava?"

"Sparkling wine. Like champagne, except from Spain originally."

"I'm not fancy enough to merit sparkling wine."

His blue eyes squinted to slits of confusion. "Are you kidding? You're very sparkly. Every time you smile, every time you lavish attention on elderly customers who look alone and lonely. When you were helping the kids with the float, so many sparkles came off you it was like fairy dust filled the patio. Just try it."

Well. Sierra certainly *felt* sparkly after that flattering description. So she reached across the bar to take Flynn's hand. Gave it a long squeeze, and then kept holding it as she tried the second cocktail.

Wow. Holy crapballs of yummy deliciousness. Her gaze flashed up to his. "It's amazing. It's bursting with blackberry flavor. It tickles my tongue like . . . like stars twinkling."

"Funny you should say that." He took his own sip, turning the glass to drink from the same spot that Sierra had. And that tiny gesture set off supernovas exploding in her heart. "There's an old story that the monk who made champagne famous said he was tasting stars the first time he tried it. Not true, of course, but a fun legend."

Sierra took the glass from him to have another small sip. Mmmmm. "I'm very impressed that you're quoting a monk. You're so worldly."

Flynn cocked his head, as if considering. "I actually haven't seen much of the world. Never traveled much of anywhere before we, ah, moved." Then he looked down. Scrubbed his hand across his eyes as if trying to erase something. "I've seen a lot, though. Things I wouldn't want you to see. Or know. This little corner of the world's probably enough for me."

His voice had gone low and dark, like when storm clouds suddenly rolled in and turned the afternoon sky black. Whatever he *had* seen, it had left a shadow on him, that was for sure. Sierra didn't know what to do. Or say. How to pull him out of the bleakness that so swiftly had turned down his mouth and shuttered his eyes and stiffened his entire body.

A series of shouts followed by a big, loud thud had Sierra twisting around. Over by the jukebox, a woman, whose long red hair looked vaguely familiar, was slumping slowly down the wall. And a big man stood over her with a threatening scowl. But not still. No, he jittered a little, head to toe. Sierra had seen that before, too many times, at both her colleges. The man was high on *something*. Which made him dangerous, volatile, and probably not willing or even able to listen to reason.

"Flynn—"

"On it." As he rushed out from behind the bar, Sierra half stood on the stool to yell down the hallway for

Carlos. To her horror, the burly man in leather pants and the matching vest that she'd seen motorcyclists wear bent down to lift the woman just by her arm. It looked horribly painful. Then he pulled back his other arm as if about to smack her across the face.

Sierra gasped and held her breath. It sounded like everyone else in the Gorse did, too, because the crowded bar went extraordinarily silent. She could actually hear the crack of pool balls coming from the back room.

But before the man's hand connected, Flynn was there. He grabbed the wrist and gave it a twist that instantly unfisted his hand. "Let her go." It wasn't a low, scary growl. It was a simple command. Like Flynn was so certain of a response that he didn't need to put any threat behind it.

Leather Guy was the same height as Flynn, but with easily thirty pounds on him, mostly paunch. It scared her, how much bigger he was. What if Carlos didn't come out in time with his trusty baseball bat to help? The surrounding tables were mostly full, but no one was standing up to help. Admittedly, they were all pretty well toasted by this time of night.

He did let go of the woman, and Flynn dropped his hold. She immediately cradled one arm in the other. From her position, Sierra guessed that she'd cracked it hard on the jukebox when he'd thrown her into the wall.

Slowly, he shifted to face Flynn. "Who are you to tell me how to handle my woman?" A threat rolled off of him in waves, like heat coming off asphalt on a hot day.

He shifted constantly from one foot to the other. And one hand sort of shook. *Definitely* drugs. Probably got dragged here by friends for the fishing tournament, because this was not the usual clientele of the Gorse at all.

Ignoring him, Flynn looked at the redhead. "Are you hurt, Rosalie?"

"Not really. I mean, I think my arm is broken." At that, Mariana, who'd at some point joined Sierra and held on to her hand for dear life, whipped her phone out of her apron and dialed 911. After a brief sniff, Rosalie shook her head. "But don't make a fuss."

"No fuss." He smiled. Kindly at Rosalie, and then it transformed into more of an ugly, threatening sneer as he turned back to Leather Guy. "Just a reminder of a very simple rule here at the Gorse."

The bigger man crowded in on Flynn, shaking out his hands. "I don't have to follow your stupid bar's rules."

Carlos was on the other side of Sierra now. He held what he called his Bouncer Bat in both hands, but didn't move to join Flynn.

"Aren't you going to help him?" she whispered.

"Flynn doesn't need any help."

"I don't care who you are or where you come from. You walk in this door, you respect women. Period." As he said the last word, Flynn's arm shot out and up to punch Leather Guy in the chin. "You don't ever, *ever* raise a hand to them."

Sierra gasped again. He'd moved so fast. Leather Guy hadn't even had time to flinch or try to move out of the way. The dead quiet in the bar continued, so she could hear his embarrassingly high whimper.

Another lightning-fast punch, this time to the man's considerable gut. He staggered backward toward the door. Blood trickled down his face from a split lip. "If you don't treat the women of Bandon right, you'll answer to me." Then he grabbed the jerk's arm and half dragged him to the door. One kick opened it, and he flung the big man outside.

The whole room erupted in applause and cheers. Don and Jeremy, half of the band just packing up, hurried over with their extension cords. "Way to go, Flynn. We'll tie him up for you. Keep an eye on him until the police get here." A handful of other men crowded outside with him, echoing offers to keep him contained.

It didn't escape Sierra's notice that it looked like it was taking half a dozen men to clean up what Flynn had tidily handled all by himself.

Over his shoulder, Flynn called out, "Sierra, put some ice in a towel and come help Rosalie."

Sierra's hands now shook—just a little—as she filled a white bar towel with ice cubes. Seeing that kind of violence up close took her right back to the horrible events that sent her running across country.

But she couldn't get bogged down in the memory. That would just be letting Rick ruin her life more than he already had.

As she neared Flynn and the growing circle around Rosalie, she heard Carlos say, "Nice job." Sierra handed the ice off to a woman she knew was a nurse, and already fastening a sling. Then she stood next to Flynn. She needed the nearness. Needed to reassure herself that he was okay after that fight.

Even though he'd *totally* won it, hands down.

Flynn looked at his fingers and Sierra noticed the streak of blood across the knuckles. After wiping it on his jeans, he bent his fingers, and then shook them out. "I didn't pull my punches to teach the drugged-out piece of trash a lesson. Hopefully it'll stick."

"You're one hell of a bouncer." Carlos clapped him on the back of his shoulders twice. "I lucked out the day you came in looking for a job. You're just what this place needed."

"Actually?" Flynn turned to sweep his gaze over the buzzing bar. Almost absently, he tucked Sierra under his arm. "I think this place is just what I needed."

"You were incredible, Flynn." Heroic, really. The way he didn't wait for reinforcements. He just saw a wrong and stepped in to fix it. Flynn took charge. And it was unbelievably sexy. "The way you stood up for Rosalie was amazing."

"Thank you." He dropped a soft kiss on her crown. "But helping out one woman isn't enough. We get new strangers—strangers who drink too much—every week in season."

Carlos nodded enthusiastically. "If you're going where I think you're going with this, I like it."

"Well, I'd *like* to teach a self-defense class. I'm qualified in several martial arts."

"Your ability isn't in question. That's a lot to take on by yourself, though."

"You just don't want me sloughing off any of my shifts here." Flynn grinned. Sierra had never heard him tease Carlos before. From the astonishment blanking their boss's face, he hadn't, either.

"True . . ." his voice trailed off, eyes still pinched together a little.

Flynn let go of Sierra to tick off two fingers. "Rafe and Kellan aren't up to my speed, but they know their stuff. They could help out."

One of Sierra's tables, a big one full of couples, paused on their way out the door. "We left your tip on the table, but we want to give you something, too." A middle-aged woman with white-blonde hair tucked a folded bill into Flynn's palm.

"I can't accept payment for doing the right thing." Flynn tried to pass it back, but the woman closed his hand around it.

Her husband said, "Consider it blood money. We feel guilty as hell that we sat there, frozen in shock. Guilty that we didn't do anything to help. Thanks for being the good guy."

They filed out the door. Flynn unfolded the bill and his eyes bugged wide to see it was a hundred. "Those people need their heads examined," he muttered.

"You did a good thing, Flynn. Why won't you take the reward you deserve?" Sierra asked.

The hollowness of his laugh shocked her. "I don't deserve any reward. Trust me. I just want the opportunity to try to help more people. To make Bandon safer, so something like this doesn't happen again. Yeah—I need to do the class."

"I can help with logistics. Finding a place, getting the word out. I'll draw you one heck of a flyer."

"I'll bet you will. Just don't put me on it. No men at all. More like a Wonder Woman approach. How kick-ass a woman will feel after learning to defend herself."

That sounded about right. The less time and attention Sierra was giving to her fears, the better she was feeling.

Carlos cleared his throat. "Madalena would offer you a space at her school. Probably for free. Lemme talk to her."

Flynn pushed back from the offer with half-outstretched arms. "It doesn't have to be free—"

A sharply jabbed finger cut him off. "Yes, it does. Because the class itself should be free, so you can't have overhead to worry about."

"Okay. No overhead sounds good, especially if this is just a pipe dream that doesn't play out." Bending down a little, lowering his voice, Flynn asked, "Do you really think anyone would want to come?"

"I do." The forcefulness of Sierra's answer surprised her. "Can I be in it?"

"Of course. You're my number one priority to keep safe."

Sirens whooped outside. Red and blue lights arced through the window, painting colored shadows on Carlos's face. "We should go talk to them. Shouldn't take long. Fifty witnesses saw him manhandle Rosalie, even if she won't talk. You'll be in the clear, Flynn. I'll make sure of it."

"I'll be right back." One hand on her neck—the one with knuckles still oozing blood—Flynn pulled her close for a kiss. Then immediately arched back. "You okay? Your pulse is beating crazy fast."

Adrenaline from fear, shock, and then relief still coursed through her. Along with a little bit of excitement from the way Flynn used his body. It just gave Sierra chills. "I'm fine. Truly. I can't think of anyplace I'd feel safer."

On her way back to hold down the bar, Sierra mulled her oddly intense reaction to Flynn's idea. It had resonated down to her bones, like the vibrations when a giant church bell rang. A self-defense class sounded perfect. It'd be a perfect piece in her *take back her life* initiative.

She'd run from Rick because she'd had no idea how to defend herself. In hindsight, that was still probably the smartest course of action. But Sierra didn't like how it'd been her only option at the time. It wasn't just Rick, either. She'd been rolled more than a few times at foster homes, even in high school.

No more.

Sierra slapped her palm against the side of the cash register, just to hear the thump of affirmation. Okay, it was more of a sting than a sound, but it felt right.

No more caving to bullies. Watching Rosalie tonight try to dismiss what Leather Guy had done, how badly he'd treated her? That, she decided, was her tipping point. She'd let Rick make her a victim. Her fear kept her one. Her lies and secrecy had turned into their own weird little prison. Taking back her life meant breaking out.

That was it. Sierra wouldn't, *couldn't* keep the truth, her truth, from Flynn anymore. It'd be a big leap of faith. Especially since her last boyfriend hadn't turned out to be who she'd thought at all.

It wouldn't be that way with Flynn.

Trusting Flynn meant literally trusting him with her life. It was time. She hated lying to him, hated not revealing her true self. And if she couldn't do that, what good was it all? What point was there in running away?

It wasn't just about escaping a bad life.

It was about starting a good one.

Chapter Eleven

FLYNN HAD THOUGHT that going into WITSEC would keep him *out* of jail. But he'd logged more hours over the last seven months *inside* jails than he could begin to count. Sure, his black cargo shorts and sandals were better than wearing an orange jumpsuit and sneakers with no laces. Still weird, though.

"I don't get nervous anymore."

Kellan groaned. "If this is yet another retelling of how the Mighty Flynn Maguire coldcocked the scum of the earth two days ago with nary a shaking finger or loose bowel, I don't want to hear it."

"Loose . . . you mean being so scared he'd shit his pants?" Rafe unsuccessfully tried not to smile. Even wiped his palm across his mouth, but the stupid grin came back anyway. "Dude, that's insulting. Funny as hell, but still insulting."

Flynn kicked out a chair and sat down, hoping Delaney showed up soon so he wouldn't have to listen to Kellan bitch much longer. For God's sake, had *he* sounded as pissy at the world as Kellan did? Been as annoying? No wonder Rafe had ordered him to pull himself together.

Not that he could've even figured out where to begin without Sierra.

Kellan didn't have his own Sierra. Just an unending hard-on for their government handler. So Flynn would go easy on him. Calmly, he said, "Look, *I* haven't been the one boring you with the story. Don't blame me."

"No, just everyone else in this freaking town." Kellan paced the length of the conference room. At least, they were calling it that because they didn't deserve to be in an interrogation room. The door *was* unlocked. "The guys at the plant wouldn't stop talking about The Legend of Flynn Maguire. At Coffee & 3 Leaves, Norah was mentioning making a drink with your name."

"Nice. I hope it's a triple-shot espresso with a shake of cinnamon." Delaney couldn't pitch a hissy fit over that hint of notoriety. Could she? Maybe he'd ask Norah to just use his first name . . .

His brother's work boots drummed another path down the concrete floor. "It's like being in high school all over again. I'm left to trail in your glorious wakes. Being the third brother is not as glamorous and fun as I'd hoped."

Rafe half leaned, half sat on the edge of the table with

his arms crossed. He wore black jeans, a black tee, and a massive smirk. "Nothing about our lives is as glamorous or fun as you hoped. Hell, nothing *could* be. Did you want to be a celebrity attorney and get movie stars off with a warning when they're caught peeing in public? Hope to get some front row Bulls tickets out of it?"

Instead of mouthing off again, Kellan stilled. His voice dropped—along with his head. "I hoped I'd get the chance to forge my own path. I was starting to, anyway. But now we're all lumped together again, starting from square one. You and Flynn are freaking heroes to this town. You keep saving people."

Kellan may have chilled out, but his words lit a fire under Rafe. He popped off the table, rigid as if about to get a prostate exam. "Sorry that our kiboshing criminal acts is bugging you. Next time I see a burglar, I'll text you to hurry over, and then go grab a hot dog while I wait for you to show."

Now they were toe to toe. Both with bunched fists. Flynn was damned if he'd let his brothers start a fight *in* the jail that would automatically get them tossed behind bars.

Man, was this transition ever going to get easier? For all of them? At the same time?

Was that too much to fucking ask?

He pounded his fist on the table to get their attention. "Hey! Simmer down. Let's not mix it up with a sheriff ten feet away. Of *course* K's feeling left out. We told him that we've been doing this huge, secret thing behind his back for more than a dozen years. Of *course* he's upset. But can we put a pin in that for now, given where we are? Do the whole group therapy thing another day?"

His outburst turned Kellan's sullen sneer into a bona fide grin. "Flynn's being the calm and reasonable one? You dog, you slept with Sierra, didn't you?"

Yet another thing he refused to discuss inside a jail. Sierra was too innocent to even be brought up in conversation in this place.

Spreading his fingers wide as if grasping for calm, Flynn said, "To get back to my original point. I'm not nervous anymore. When I'm in *here*," he rushed through to the rest of it, gesturing at the one-way glass, "surrounded by handcuffs and cells and guys in uniforms that used to break me into a cold sweat. Now it seems . . . ordinary."

"Yeah." Rafe shifted back from Kellan. Crisis averted. He turned in a slow circle, hands tucked in his back pockets. "Not scary, either. For years we worried about getting dragged in to meet with cops. Now it's just a break in our routine."

"Does that mean we've turned into good guys?"

Rafe grunted his dismissal of the idea. "Not unless the floor dropped out of heaven and everyone better than us is suddenly down in hell."

"Can we get back to my question?" Kellan elbowed Flynn as he sat down next to him. "About sex?"

"Don't you ever think of anything else, Mr. Maguire?" Delaney's frown was the first thing Flynn saw. The rest of her body, dressed in a formfitting black dress that showed off all sorts of sexy, was just along for the ride. She looked pissed. Of course, she always looked that way when Kellan baited her. The only difference was that this time he hadn't known she was in the doorway.

Kellan rose from his seat. He always played the full gentleman card, even when stuck in a jail with their marshal. Or, more to the point, *especially* then. "I think about you all the time. But that's all wrapped up in thoughts of sex, so I guess the answer is no."

She closed the door behind her with a noticeable bang. Hard enough that the gust of air blew her blond hair into her face. Her eyes narrowed. "Maybe if you stimulated that big brain of yours, instead of just what's in your pants, you'd find a job that suits you better than the cranberry plant."

Man, that was *cold*.

Flynn's mouth dropped open. A quick glance at Rafe showed his older brother in the same slack-jawed position. Kellan and Delaney had their routine, their shtick. He flirted with her outrageously. She shot him down every damned time. Never tolerant, always annoyed. But never *mean*.

Silence bounced around the room, as loud as a shout. Kellan froze halfway between standing and sitting. Then, slowly, he shifted into the wooden chair. "They say the brain is the biggest sexual organ. Thanks for noticing that mine is . . . oversized."

Attaboy. They'd never had to get Kellan out of the

principal's office with a black eye. He always found a way to skewer with his words, and then get out. One sharp stab. Then he was gone before the other guy even figured out that Kellan had won.

Delaney, on the other hand, was definitely smart enough to know that he'd just turned her own words around on her. Before this escalated into a verbal blood-bath, Flynn figured he should step in.

"Marshal Evans. It's always a rip-roaring good time hanging with you. But if we keep being seen coming into the police station, it'll be suspicious. People will start to talk."

"Then make friends with the sheriff," she snarled. After pressing her palms flat to the door and taking a long breath, she pasted on a smile. "Apparently, Mateo paddle surfs. Wouldn't that be fun?"

Yeah, there was a whole lot to this West Coast life-style that still mystified Flynn. "I literally have no fuck-ing idea."

"Fine, then." She threw up her hands. Bright red nails this time. Delaney's cover for her trips to Bandon were "dates" with the sheriff. Her sexy outfits and full makeup were no hardship for the Maguire brothers. They were all grateful that their handler wasn't a buzz-cut Fed in an off-the-rack navy suit. Rafe and Flynn just kept their mouths shut about it. "Golf. Didn't I see in your files that you and Rafe golf?"

"We all do." Flynn missed playing it. Didn't love that the marshals knew their hobbies, though. "We also like deep-dish pizza, the playoffs of any and every sport, and hate nineties grunge music. Why do our files have random information that belongs on a dating profile?"

"Because Danny McGinty—and many of his high-level crew—participated in that charity golf tournament last summer."

Rafe made a two-handed snap/fist thump combo. "Whistling Straits Pro-Am. Can't believe we had to drag our asses past all those cows to Sheboygan for it. How'd that get on your radar?"

She sat down, across the table from them. "Because it's in Wisconsin. Someplace that McGinty did not control. Which meant we were able to bug the clubhouse and the golf carts."

Kellan perked up. All it *ever* took to get Kellan out of a funk was an interesting fact. "That's underhanded. Strategic. Impressive."

"Thank you, Counselor. So glad you approve of an investigation that took us five years, seven different agencies, and cost three undercover agents their lives."

Flynn's first thought was that he couldn't wait to tell Sierra all about this icy war erupting between their marshal and Kellan.

Quickly followed by his *second* thought—the remembrance that he could not, in fact, tell Sierra anything about this meeting.

Shit.

Kellan didn't snap back at Delaney's response. If anything, he relaxed a little more. He really would've been one hell of a trial lawyer. "It was a compliment. And an olive branch. The rules of polite society require that you accept it as both."

He needed popcorn for this. And maybe a beer. Watching his little brother put the marshal in her place was almost as fun as watching an MMA cage match.

Delaney lifted her hair off of the back of her neck. Then she shook her head a couple of times, as if trying to shake something off. "I'm sorry. I'm in a bad mood. Traffic down here from the Eugene Field Office was hideous. My air-conditioning's on the fritz. And this dress means I have to wear a thigh holster, which just isn't comfortable."

Flynn ground his heel into the top of Kellan's foot. Hard. Because he knew it'd take some serious pain to distract his little brother from making a joke about what *ought* to be between her thighs. "Let's make this quick, then. You can get on with your pretend date and start throwing back some icy margaritas."

"I can't drink. You know I have to drive back to Eugene tonight."

This time, Flynn landed a punch on Kellan's thigh. Because he knew, he fucking *knew* that idiot was about to offer to let Delaney spend the night in his bed instead. Aside from not telling anyone they were ex-mobsters? The number one rule was to stay on the good side of their handler. No way was he letting Kellan's blue balls ruin that.

"Sorry. But you brought your car trouble to the right

place. How about you let me tinker with it and see if I can't fix that air-conditioning while you're at dinner?"

Nice work, Rafe.

She slid her arms forward until she was almost half lying on the table. A big-ass smile slid onto her face, too. "Would you really? I'd pay you for it, of course. We can't accept gifts from our protectees."

"If you 'forget' your keys on the table when we're done, nobody's the wiser. I'll just find them in a few hours and leave 'em at the front desk. If your car works better? You can chalk it up to the magical ocean air."

Flynn cleared his throat. "What'd you haul us in for this time, Marshal? Because we've been on our best behavior. I'm building a float for the Cranberry Festival with a bunch of kids. It doesn't get more fucking wholesome than that."

"That sounds . . . I'm certain I should say it sounds lovely. But I'm having trouble forming that picture in my head."

"Forget imagining it. Come in person. You can watch a float-design session. Or just come to the Festival in September. Stuff your face with cranberry pie and wash it down with one hell of a cranberry cocktail I'm dreaming up."

Delaney shifted in her seat to face Rafe. "What's up with your brother? He's not being a stick in the mud. He's downright . . . friendly. Has he been sampling the medicinal wares at that coffee and marijuana shop? I warned you to steer clear of it."

Rafe held up his hands. "We only go for the coffee. Norah's promised that she won't ever 'spice up'—her words, not mine—anything the Maguires order. We're clean, Marshal."

"Flynn's high on life." Kellan made a heart with his hands and held it up to one eye to look at Delaney through. "Or love, to be more specific. He's got a girl."

Both of her eyebrows shot upward. "Is she aware of this development? And willing? You know, there are rules in this state about locking women in the basement."

"Very funny." Flynn had come clean with the government on a lot of the aspects of his life—right down to telling them what size boxer briefs to stock his drawer with in their first relocation house. But no way would he let the marshal weigh in on what he had going with Sierra. It was, officially, none of her damn business.

Delaney propped her elbows on the table and cradled her chin in her hands. "Ooh, I'm intrigued. Tell me all about her."

"Her name's Sierra. She's pretty great. And that's all you get."

Her arms fell to the scarred wood. "Sierra Williams?"

"Yeah." Uh-oh. Were they being bugged? Or followed? "How'd you know that?"

"Because she's in the police report as a witness to the event that brings me down here tonight."

Shit. "You came to talk to us about what happened at the Gorse on Saturday."

"No. Not 'what happened.'" Delaney made air quotes with her fingers. "More 'what you did.' A hailstorm *happens* to you. When you repeatedly punch and then toss a man out a door, that's a conscious choice."

Kellan's chair had barely scraped backward before he moved to the head of the table and lifted one upraised finger to hammer home his point. "Rosalie O'Hearn is the one who made a choice that night. She *chose* to put her faith in the wrong man. Flynn didn't make a choice. He had a *responsibility*—as a man, as a concerned citizen, and as the bar's official bouncer—to help her out of a tight spot. To prevent her from getting a worse injury than just her broken arm."

Pride puffed out Flynn's chest. There was nothing like watching Kellan on a tear. Law school might've honed Kellan's abilities to argue his point. Most of it, though, was raw talent. Rafe and Flynn had always called his current stance the *takedown* position. Once Kellan stood that way, whoever he argued against— for an extra bag of Cheetos or for class president—was going down. Period.

The kid was magnificent. Most of all because he was standing up for Flynn.

Even Delaney gave him a brief nod. But then she was right back into it. "While I appreciate your vociferous defense of your brother, I need to hear from Flynn himself." Palms up, she placed one hand on top of the other and laid that icy cool stare straight across the table. "What was your intent that night? Did you have any prior interactions with Mr. Neal before bloodying his face?"

Kellan's speech had given Flynn just enough time to think this through. If they were really in trouble, there wouldn't have been this time lag. Black SUVs would've pulled up to their house by 2:00 a.m. after the fight and disappeared the Maguires yet again.

They had a history of fighting in their previous towns. Not to mention his own string of underground fights in Chicago that the FBI and marshals were well aware of. Delaney was only doing her due diligence, questioning him in person.

No need for panic or pissyness on his part.

"Look, as far as I can remember, I'd never seen Gil Neal in the Gorse before Saturday night. We'd definitely never spoken before. Until he pushed Rosalie into the wall, I hadn't even noticed him. My intent? To get his strung-out ass out of there. And, to be one hundred percent honest, to teach him a lesson about the right and wrong way to treat women. If that broken nose makes him think twice before laying his hands on a woman again, then I don't regret any of it."

The sound of Delaney's skirt rustling as she crossed her legs was as loud as a burp in church. "Mr. Neal's not pressing charges against you. Or claiming undue harassment. Are you sure that you want to admit to a federal agent that you were teaching him a lesson?"

"I do. Because I'm being up-front." Because earning her trust was better than just expecting it. The marshal didn't have to like them or respect them. But she did. She'd fought for them, to give them this one last shot at staying in the program. Flynn needed her to know that it hadn't been a mistake. "I didn't get in a fight because I was jonesing for one. Hell, if you've reviewed the tapes of my MMA fights, it should be obvious that he easily could've been in much worse shape than how I left him. Out of respect for our town, for the promises we made to keep our noses clean, I took it easy on the scumbag."

"There is a part of me, the part that likes it when a date opens my door and believes in fairy-tale endings, that applauds your actions." Delaney stood. Crossed her arms and paced down to Kellan's end of the room. "The part of me that puts on a badge every morning, however, wonders when you'll stop looking for trouble."

"It's the other way 'round," Rafe insisted. His voice got louder. Lower. Rough like he'd run a cheese grater over the words. "We're laying low, living our lives. Period. Trouble finds us."

"Is that so? Because the weak link in that assumption is that the only one of you who never dirtied his hands with the mob still seems to be clean as a whistle. Kellan, has Lady Trouble found you yet?"

"I don't know." He gave a slow, exaggerated wink. "I've got blinders on to any woman who isn't you."

Flynn leaned back. Crossed his ankles, as loose as if he was in seats just behind the dugout at Wrigley Field. "Your office hooked me up with the interview at the Gorse, Marshal. The job listing is in your files. Go back and look at it. *Bouncer* is a job responsibility. You don't just bounce drunks. You bounce trouble, before it spreads. That's all I did."

"Agreed." With a sigh, she said, "You made the right call. I had to hear it from your lips, though. Look you in the eye and be sure that you weren't enjoying flexing your muscles again. That this wasn't the start of a slow, backward slide. Anger and resentment are dangerous. They're like tinder, just waiting for a single spark to set them off. I've seen a lot of both in you over the past few months."

"Fair enough." He curled his lip up into the smile Sierra had captured on that cocktail napkin. "See any in me now?"

"No. Which is a relief. Because as long as I'm here, I need to update you on McGinty's trial. A date's been set. The first week in October."

"Right after the Cranberry Festival," Flynn murmured. Good that they wouldn't miss it. It'd look weird, no, *suspicious* if they weren't around that weekend after spending all these months prepping for it.

"We'll have a technician swing by your house next week to give you a secure phone line. He'll look like he's installing a satellite dish."

Rafe shook his head. "Nobody has those around here. Cable works fine."

"Exactly. That's how we can slide him in. Since you're new to the area, you'll bring in this highfalutin technology without realizing you don't need it. Then, in a few months, you can get rid of the dish, admit it was a dumb idea, and nobody will realize what he was really doing in your house."

"Highfalutin?" Yeah, it felt a little weird. But Flynn was compelled to defend the town. "We're not pioneer folk in the eighteen hundreds. Bandon is a fully operational, modern city."

"It doesn't have a Starbucks. Or a Dunkin."

"Not a hardship," Flynn shot back. "Norah's coffee is pretty kick-ass."

"No, thank you. I don't want a contact high along with my mocha." Delaney looked at her watch. "I'd better wrap this up. The secure line is for you to rehearse your testimony with the prosecution lawyers back in Chicago. We can't risk flying you out there to prep. Every extra day you spend in that city multiplies your danger. You'll do weekly calls to go through it."

Rafe tugged at his hair. Kinda looked like he wanted to pull it all out with one massive yank of frustration. "We've been through it. No less than a hundred times already."

"You exaggerate."

"I really fucking don't," he growled.

"You gave us your sworn testimony, but you haven't walked through all the possible ways the defense will attack. There can't be any slipups when you're on the witness stand."

Itchy underneath his skin, five-cups-of-coffee jittery, Flynn shoved his chair back. Started jiggling his leg. "We know the facts. I turned over the books. The passwords. You have the proof of the money laundering.

There's no wiggle room."

"You'd be surprised." Delaney sauntered closer to look down her nose at him. Condescension dripped off of her as thickly as rain off of pine needles. "Why should we trust anything you say, Flynn? You voluntarily swore your allegiance to a mobster. Danny McGinty paid for your education, your clothes, box seats at Bulls and Bears games. Your entire life was funded by and revolved around the mob. That means that a certain flexibility with the truth is to be expected from you."

The way she put it . . . it wasn't how it happened.

Flynn didn't have a choice. There were explanations for all of it.

"You're twisting it all around."

"You better believe I am. And what the lawyers for the other side will do to you makes this little example look like child's play. That's why you have to get ready. Because if this doesn't work? If McGinty goes free? He'll rebuild in a matter of months. And if we don't get a conviction on any of the charges? It'll be almost impossible to justify keeping your whole family in the program."

"Is that a threat or a promise?"

"It's motivation. You've had a break, boys. Gotten comfortable. Seen how good things *can* be here. Now you've got to do the work to earn this new life." She walked out without another word.

So much for Flynn's calm. A hornet's nest inside his head would be an improvement from his current condition. Stirred up didn't begin to describe it. They'd had a rocky road getting here. He'd hated the idea of McGinty sending him to jail as a fall guy. But he'd hated going into WITSEC just as much.

Now they were finally settled in a decent place. With weird but decent people. Their house was too small for all of them to share, but Rafe was planning to move in with Mollie after the trial. That'd help.

If they got to stay. Delaney's speech brought home just how delicate their position was. How it could all disappear in a flash.

Damn it, they'd been suckered by a bait and switch. Shown the good life. The now really fucking good life, being with Sierra. With his new friends. With having a purpose that didn't embarrass and shame him anymore. And it had all been a setup. A bribe. A carrot to dangle, before being ass-fucked with the stick of reality.

How dare they?

How dare they finally give Flynn the chance to be happy again, and then remind him that it could spoil faster than mayo in the desert?

He headed for the door.

"Where are you going?" Kellan asked. "I thought we were grabbing tacos?"

Flynn white-knuckled the doorknob. "I need air. I

need to walk this off before I punch someone. And since you two are within arm's length of me, it'd be in your best interest to let me go."

And then he slammed the door shut behind him, with no idea of where to go besides *away*.

Chapter Twelve

A TINY BREEZE rustled through the trees, which was why Sierra had put in her earbuds. The breeze made her think of the beach and Flynn, and those thoughts made it very difficult to focus on the painting in front of her. So she'd dialed up some Bach—peaceful, but boring enough that she wouldn't get caught up in it— and promised herself that this time, her painting would be perfect.

The light on her porch was perfect. Diffused but bright. The temperature at six thirty had cooled down just enough to be perfectly comfortable. Just in case it was true that an artist's mood seeped through the paint and onto the canvas? Well, her happiness reservoir was finally back up at a level not seen since before leaving grad school. Every possible condition was perfect.

This one would be right. Would be good enough.

Would be perfect. Then she could send it to Miriam Newberry as an apology.

It wouldn't be enough of a gesture. But it was all Sierra could think of to do. She dabbed a tiny bit of Winsor Lemon on her brush. Swirled it with Winsor Yellow on the palette and hoped that it would finally match the perfect yellow of Mrs. Newberry's prized orchid.

Flynn ran to a stop right in front of her.

Sierra yelped, dropped her brush and was pretty sure her heart had skipped a beat or three in surprise. He took the three stairs up to the porch in one leap. Flynn's arms were outstretched, his face twisted in anger.

She lunged off her chair, earbuds slipping out. Except her feet got twisted in the rungs at the bottom and the whole thing tipped over. Sierra barely managed to stay upright. But it only took two steps to come up against the porch railing on two sides and the house wall on the other.

She was stuck. Scared.

This time, Sierra couldn't run.

So she lifted her wooden palette—still miraculously in her left hand—and tried to bash the side of his head.

Flynn simultaneously grabbed it and sent it flying like a Frisbee. "What the hell is wrong with you?"

"Why were you coming at me?" Why was he still looming over her? Sierra's teeth clenched so tightly her jaw ached. Her stomach knotted up, almost cutting off her diaphragm from moving her lungs.

"You looked surprised. Like I'd snuck up on you. I was trying to hug you to apologize."

Oh, *crap*. He'd been doing the sweet, normal boyfriend thing and her anxiety had blown it totally out of proportion. It made sense.

But the knee-jerk cascade of fear wasn't easy to shake.

"You looked so angry," she murmured. Her arms drew around her sides into a hug. Sierra needed the comfort, even if it was just from herself. The edge of the rail dug into her lower back, but Flynn still wasn't giving her an inch of space. "You scared me."

His jaw dropped open. Flynn took two steps back, all the way to the opposite railing. Then he put up his hands, palms out. "Sierra. Look at me. I'm not going to hurt you."

After two deep breaths, Sierra calmed enough to process the pieces. Flynn might be mad, but it wasn't directed at her. He hadn't tried to attack her. This was a full-blown panic attack on her part over nothing. Her arms slid down her sides.

In a very small voice, she said, "Okay."

"Can I come closer?"

"Yes."

Flynn shuffled back across the narrow space. When she didn't flinch this time, he put his arms around her waist. It felt reassuring. Comforting.

Who was she kidding? It felt amazing. Better than crawling under an electric blanket during a snowstorm.

Sierra's hands moved up to rest on his chest. The feel of it moving up and down with each breath, the quiet thump of his heart, also soothed her. Beat back the panic one long, slow breath at a time.

"Sierra." Flynn rested his cheek on the top of her head. "Sweetness, don't you know that you don't ever need to be scared of me? I'll never hurt you. I'll do everything in my power to protect you."

"Don't make promises you can't keep. But I appreciate the thought behind it."

"Sweetness." In one fluid motion, Flynn picked her up and set her down on the top step. He settled next to her, lightly rubbing her back in slow circles. "What happened to you? Why are you reacting like this?"

There really was no better segue. If she was ever going to tell him, this was the moment.

Sierra had spent the last three days waffling about sharing her secret with Flynn after her initial, hasty decision to do so. Bottom line? It was a selfish impulse. To burden him with that knowledge. Was it fair of her to put that on him?

No. Not exactly. But it was a lot *less* fair to keep lying to him. There had to be trust between them. There couldn't be any more forward motion without trust. Without admitting who she really was. Why she was out here.

Why she'd tried to clock him with a piece of wood just for trying to hug her.

Clearly, there wasn't a choice to be made. They'd passed that point.

Flynn had to know.

"It's kind of a long story. And you may not like me as much by the time I'm finished."

"Not possible."

It was nice that he said it. Sierra wasn't so sure she believed his easy reassurance, though. And she cannonballed into the story. "When I was little, a teacher gave me a box of crayons as a reward for something. It was the best gift of my life. I drew all the time. I'd draw in the dirt with sticks. I'd draw in the snow."

Flynn bumped her shoulder with his. "Also with sticks?"

"What can I say? They're an all-season tool. When I drew, when I painted, I could make beautiful things. Different worlds, different settings. Places that were prettier, happier, nicer. Art was my escape from living in foster care. Which, some of the time, was harsh. Not pretty at all. Crowded and dirty, full of yelling and fighting."

"God, it sounds awful."

"Not everyone fosters because of their love of kids. Lots of people just do it for the money. Money they're in no hurry to spend on their foster children. I landed in a few good situations. They never lasted, though."

His hand tightened to knead the suddenly rock-hard muscles along the ridge of her shoulder. "I'm so sorry you went through that."

"I'm giving you the short version. I mean, I still had food and clothing and got to go to school. I wasn't living on the streets. I wasn't getting beat up—much. Lots of kids had it way worse." That used to be Sierra's mantra. That she was lucky. That she at least had her art.

"Don't diminish how far you've come. How you managed to bloom into an amazing woman out of a dung heap of a beginning."

"I'd hold off on giving me too much credit until I finish."

Flynn leaned against the post to the railing and pulled her back against him. "Go on."

"I got a scholarship to art college. A full ride, but money was still tight."

"I'll bet a scholarship doesn't cover clothing and Q-tips."

"Nope. So I worked two jobs, too. The thing is, an undergrad degree from an art college doesn't give you many options after graduation. It was supposed to be my ticket to freedom. But with nobody to fall back on, it wasn't enough."

"What was your major?"

"Painting and art ed." It felt so good to answer a normal question, without any hesitation.

"Someone should've warned you there is no guaranteed weekly paycheck with benefits if you major in that."

No kidding. "In retrospect, I agree with you. Not sure I would've listened, though. I loved painting, and this college was literally paying me to show up every day and learn how to do that better. What was your major in college?"

After a weirdly long pause, Flynn said, "Business."

Smart guy. Although now they were both working in the same bar, so what did it truly matter? "Well, a teacher with only a bachelor's can't get hired. I earned a scholarship to grad school. Got my own room in the dorm as an RA and still worked at a diner, too. It was enough to live on. It *wasn't* enough to sock money away for the down payment on an apartment, for after graduation."

"Even if you got hired as a teacher right away, school wouldn't start for three months. You'd have to save up a ton to cover that gap."

Exactly what had kept her awake and worried the whole summer before starting grad school. It kept her working double shifts whenever she could grab them, too. "Out of the blue, one of my regulars at the diner asked me if I'd paint a birthday present for his mom. A replica of a Maxfield Parrish landscape that was her favorite. We'd gotten friendly. I'd told him how I taught myself to paint by copying famous works, over and over again."

"That's the trick? I spent at least a month when I was ten trying to draw the frog on the Honey Smacks box. How come I could never get it down?"

Sierra loved that Flynn kept trying to lighten the mood. It showed that he realized how hard this was for her. Even though he had no idea what was coming. "Copying isn't a magic shortcut. It was just the path that worked for me. I've got a knack for it. Better than doing my own original stuff."

"Did you make a replica?"

"Yes. Rick paid me a hundred dollars, plus supplies. He paid me a lot of compliments, too, and we started going out. Then he said his grandma was jealous of his mom's present, and wanted one of her own. Of course I whipped out another."

"I feel like we can skip ahead to where obviously Rick is the biggest schmuck in the universe. He's gotta be, to not move heaven and earth to make you happy and keep you next to him."

Sierra clasped her hands so tightly that her fingers turned chalk-white. "Rick conned me into doing a lot of replicas. Not just the Parrish landscape, but others, too. I was desperate for the cash. Desperate to please him. Then I discovered that he actually sold them to a man who ran a huge counterfeiting ring. Wayne Kornieck."

"Wait. Hang on. What?" Flynn's body went absolutely rigid behind her.

This is the part where Sierra felt utterly stupid. Stupid that she'd ever believed Rick liked her. Stupid that she hadn't wondered what he was doing with all the paintings.

So her words came out in a rush. "He took me along to meet a business associate. I was thrilled, because Rick never talked about his work. All he said was that he was in acquisitions. That it was business that'd be over my head. It'd bore me. Finally including me felt special. Instead, it turned out he was just tired of pretending to be my boyfriend."

"God damn, Sierra. I can't believe it." Flynn's voice held shock, but not judgment.

Not yet, anyway.

"It gets worse." She turned her cheek to press against the rock-solid warmth of his shoulder. His strength would help her get through this. "The meeting was so that Wayne could lay out exactly what he expected me to do going forward. I refused, of course. I was horrified when I found out that Rick and Wayne had been selling my knockoffs as the real thing."

"Did you tell anyone? Try to get help?"

"Wayne said that if I told anyone, he'd tip off the police that I was selling counterfeits. That he'd put the blame on me. Since it truly *was* my work, that'd be easy to prove. They'd send me to jail for something I both did and didn't do."

"Not the worst threat ever. Impossible to prove, though. I think if the police looked at the head of a counterfeit ring and you, they'd figure out pretty quick who to believe." Flynn stroked his hands up and down her arms. "But that's hindsight. Makes sense that at the time, his threat threw you for a loop."

At the time? How about every time nightmares woke her up in the middle of the night? "I drove myself crazy trying to figure out the next step. I didn't have the money to hire a lawyer. If I got arrested, my life would be over. No way out. For a solid week, I skipped classes and tried to come up with a solution."

"You're here now, so you must've come up with something."

Sierra licked her dry lips. Wished violently for a glass of water, but she refused to stop until it was all out in the open between them. "Rick called me up, said he felt bad about how upset I was, and asked me to meet him to talk. Except we didn't. He drove me to a mansion. His plan was to steal the original that I'd copied already. Replace it with my copy and sell the original himself. He'd been scheming for it since he saw a story about this woman with crazy famous works of art just hanging in her house. 'Easy pickings,' he said. It was his big plan to retire to a Caribbean island by thirty."

"There are so many things wrong with that as a retirement plan, I don't even know where to start."

"The painting was hanging in the hall. It had already been authenticated. Nobody would inspect it again until the owner died. The theft part he'd thought through pretty well. What came after . . ."

Sierra's voice trembled as she broke off. She'd never told anyone this story. Never shared the details of what transpired that night. Reliving it in her mind was hard enough but saying it out loud was ten times worse.

Flynn moved her into the crook of his arm, looking at her with eyes darkening to indigo. "You don't have to keep going. Not now, not ever. I can't stand how torn up you look."

"No, I do. I have to tell you everything." She stood, taking the steps down to the ground. Shook out her trembling hands as she walked in a circle. Stomped her feet hard against the packed dirt to feel the zing of pain through her sneakers. "He made me go with him, to be the lookout. Rick picked the lock like a pro."

"He probably was."

"Well, he got us in, and up the stairs. But when he tried to lift the painting down, the screws came right out of the wall." Sierra closed her eyes, playing it back like a movie. "It threw off his balance, and he banged against the balcony rail. The owner, Mrs. Newberry, came out to see what was going on. She had a big old rotary phone in her hand, and she tried to hit Rick in the head with it."

"Where were you?"

"Behind her. Watching. Frozen. Rick had sworn nobody was home, not even the live-in servants. He grabbed the phone and bashed her skull. Then she fell down the stairs. She just lay there, crumpled, in a pool of blood growing across the parquet floor."

Sierra opened her eyes, drinking in the sight of the sun-dappled grass and the sparrow chirping by the poppies around the mailbox. It grounded her here, in this place, today. Far from violence and criminals and fear.

Flynn leapt to his feet. Then he took her in his arms and just held her. "Breathe. You're safe here. Just breathe."

Huh. She *had* forgotten to breathe. That explained the burning tightness in her chest. Sierra pulled in one long, deep, shuddering breath. Then another. But the oxygen didn't fix her nearly as much as Flynn's steadiness did. Being enveloped in his arms pushed everything away so that she *could* breathe.

Cheek nestled below his collarbone, Sierra said, "I ran. Not that very moment. I didn't want to make Rick suspicious. He freaked out. Wouldn't let me call an ambulance, not even from a pay phone. He took me back to his place, hid my cell and his keys, then slammed five shots of tequila and passed out. I didn't sleep all night. Was she dead? Would she have lived if we'd called for help? I was sick to my stomach."

Hands moving to her shoulders, Flynn pushed her away so that he could meet her eyes. "Sierra, the man basically kidnapped you." His tone was firm, allowing for zero wiggle room. Like a teacher reminding you that homework was mandatory to your grade. "There was nothing you could've done. He didn't get the painting?"

"No. There was no time to go back for it. Rick was worried that she'd hit a panic button on an alarm system or called 911."

"What happened next?" Flynn led her back to the porch. He sat, then pulled her onto his lap.

All the touching helped steady her. A lot. Enough.

"The next morning he dropped me off at class, and said he'd pick me up after to go over our story. I went back to the dorm, packed my bag full of art supplies and my backpack with clothes. Then I hitched a ride to the place where all the undergrads went to get fake IDs to hit the bars."

"It takes time to make a fake ID. They don't spit them out of a computer."

Spoken like a man who must've gotten his own for some freshman year beer runs. "True. They said it'd take a day. So I went to a casino."

Flynn burst out laughing. So loudly that three birds erupted out of the treetops, squawking their displeasure at the interruption of their night. "That's a fucking brilliant place to hide."

Since she'd never told this story before, she had no idea if her choices had been stupid, desperate, or smart. His praise meant the world to Sierra. "I'd never been to the Potawatomi Casino. Rick wouldn't have thought to look for me there. They've got a huge bingo hall, with yellow and green chairs, filled with senior citizens. It felt almost safe."

"Did you win?"

He was making this as easy as possible on her. "A couple of times. Which just made me feel guiltier. I gave everything I won to the grandmother sitting next to me. The next day, I got my new ID and got on a bus out of town."

"Where did you go?" He closed his eyes and shook his head. "Hell, where did you start from? When did this all go down?"

"I was in my final year of the graduate program at the Milwaukee Institute of Art & Design. I went on the run in October of last year. Switched directions a few times in case Rick was looking for me. Chicago for a week, then down to Tennessee. Stayed there a month before going over to Lawton, Oklahoma. I figured if I went any more south, my lack of an accent would make me stick out."

"Where'd you get the money to do that? You spent all your savings?"

It felt that way. Untouchable was just as bad as spent, in her case. "It's mostly in the bank still. I couldn't get much of it from the ATM, and I couldn't risk withdrawing it at all once I left Milwaukee. But after Rick passed out that night, I took his money. Well, my money, really. After talking to Wayne when he laid out what he expected of me, I realized he paid Rick lots more than I ever saw for my paintings. So I searched his apartment and found a stack of cash in a cereal box." Sierra bit her lip, still ashamed of her middle-of-the-night skulduggery.

Flynn used the side of his broad thumb to tease her lip back out. "For Christ's sake, the man was an attempted murderer who fleeced you for the work you did. Don't you dare feel bad about that for a second. You were in survival mode." He switched to brushing the back of his knuckle along the outline of both lips. "I'm so damn glad that you got out of there."

"Bandon's the end of the road for me. I have to stop running eventually. I like it here. And I can't keep being the scared, cowardly girl, always looking over her shoulder waiting for the bad man to grab her."

"You're not a coward. You're beyond strong. Brave. People who aren't running for their lives have trouble moving two towns over. Someone should turn you into a movie of the week."

"Oh, no. I truly just want peace and quiet. After I make things right with Mrs. Newberry."

"She's alive?"

"Yes, thank goodness. Lots of broken bones and some internal damage, but from the news reports I could find online, she's out of rehab and back home." Sierra scooted off his lap to go and turn the easel toward Flynn. To show him her version of the yellow and purple orchids that Miriam Newberry placed with in flower shows all across the country. She'd scoured the web compulsively for info on the woman. "This painting? I've started and restarted it for months. It's a gift for her. It isn't enough of an apology, but it's all I can do right now. I just need it to be perfect before I figure out how to get it to her."

"You don't have to apologize. You didn't do anything."

The tender reassurance in Flynn's voice—for once—did not help at all. "That's just it. I didn't *do* anything. Don't you see? I didn't stop Rick. I didn't call an ambulance. I might not have technically done anything wrong, but I sure didn't do anything right."

Flynn just stared at her for a minute, his face hardened into an unreadable mask. The silence lasted so long that Sierra noticed her fast, almost pants of breath. She noticed the early screech of an owl.

Most of all, she noticed that now that she'd admitted the very worst, most shameful part of her story, Flynn had stopped reassuring her. Stopped praising her. Stopped . . . everything.

Abruptly, he got up. Crossed to her in two long steps and gripped her biceps tightly.

"Don't. You hear me, Sierra? Just don't. Don't value your very survival as any less important than someone else's. What happened was fucking awful. To her—and to you. This Rick dipshit may have ruined your old life, but don't let him taint your new one."

Relief turned her knees to jelly. Good thing this amazing, understanding man had a hold of her. "Okay."

"Focus on the good. Here and now. What do you like about Bandon?"

As a kid from the Midwest, it was easy to pop out the first answer. "The ocean. I don't think I'll ever stop being in awe of it. I like working with the kids on the float. I like how our regulars at the Gorse tell me about their lives. I like the friends I'm making."

"Anything else?"

The intensity of his gaze pulled the words out of her. Ones Sierra hadn't known she was ready to say out loud.

"I like *you*, Flynn. I didn't want to drag you into my messed-up life. But you're irresistible. You're incredible. You make me feel more myself than I ever have before. You're the best thing about Bandon."

Then Sierra held her breath. Hadn't she dumped enough on him already for one night? Why, *why* had she gone and dumped her feelings onto him, too?

What would he think?

Would the truth of her heart be more upsetting to him than the truth of her accidental criminal past? And if it was, if he shied away from what she felt, it would prove Sierra to be, officially, the worst judge of boy-friends *ever*.

Chapter Thirteen

FLYNN DIDN'T TALK about his feelings. Losing both your parents before you could shave made a guy shut down. Working for the mob and having to hide it from everyone at college? Running a real company, interacting with the real world while hiding his true ties to the seedy underbelly of Chicago? Those things gave him plenty of reasons to keep his lips zipped.

It also added up to years of casually dating. Of never letting anyone get too close.

Until Sierra.

He'd tried *not* to let her get to him. But her big eyes and even bigger heart were exactly what she'd just said—impossible to resist. Sierra made him want to tell her how she made him feel.

She made him want to tell her *everything*.

Which was dangerous as fuck.

But . . . he could still *show* her how he felt. Show her, no, lavish her with feelings. Turn Sierra into a quivering, satisfied mass of feeling. Then she'd know what was in his head and his heart without him using any words at all.

It was a solid plan.

Flynn pulled her in to him, latching on to her mouth like it was the last kiss two people on earth would ever share. This kiss would let Sierra know his intent for the next, oh, six to eight hours.

Pleasuring her.

Making her scream his name.

Making her beg him to keep going.

Giving her literally everything she could take.

Flynn devoured her mouth. He poured his heart into it, pulling breathy little moans out of her. His tongue circled. Teeth nipped and bit. Sucked and licked. Treasured and claimed. It was an unending stream of every kind of kiss he'd ever given. All completely different here, now, as he gave them to Sierra.

As he gave himself to Sierra.

Whether she fully realized it or not.

Now that she had his shirt clutched in her fists, Flynn let go of her arms. Instead, he moved to cup her face with his palms. Slid her ears in between his fingers. From the gasp that pulsed out of her mouth, he could tell they were sensitive. Flynn filed that under *get to later*. Sex would come, but now was about this kiss. It was his promise, his vow, his heart, all poured into her.

So he gentled his approach, turning from lustful to tender. He gave her tongue long, slow strokes exactly like he'd do between her legs later. Tickled his pinkie along her neck that immediately brought up goose bumps beneath his touch.

But mostly he drank in her moans, her gasps, the heat she gave back to him by meeting his every kiss with an urgent need of her own. All the outward proof of her lust fueled his. Every response from her, every sigh and sound and flutter of her lashes sizzled just beneath his skin like a hot wire.

Sierra matched him, stroke for lick for bite. Her hips swung back and forth, grinding her belly against his dick. The shyness, the hesitancy from the first time he'd kissed her was gone. There was just a woman, no, *his* woman, who showed him right back how badly she wanted this.

Flynn's eyes popped open. Maybe it was stupid. Maybe it was over-the-top mushy. But he wanted to look at everything around him. Take a mental picture of it to always remember this exact moment.

Because there was no guarantee he'd make it back from the trial in Chicago to have lots more of these moments.

Life didn't care if you lubed up before it fucked you. He'd learned that the hard way.

Put him on the front of a god damned card with a heart and a flower and a puppy—the whole works. Flynn Maguire was memorizing this moment. The one where he and Sierra had sex for the first time.

Because it *mattered*.

So, yeah, he opened his eyes to see the pine trees mixed with whatever the other ones were with fat, green leaves. The brown and white speckled birds pecking in the dirt. The gray clouds skidding across the sky like the tumbleweeds he'd watched during their brief stint in Utah. Flynn filed away the damp breeze lifting his hair, the distant rumble of thunder.

The crazy spectacular beauty of Sierra's painting right in front of him. The orchids that looked so dainty but stood tall with an impossible curve, weighed down by the purple and yellow blossoms. Just like Sierra. Small, delicate even, but ten times stronger than he was.

Thunder didn't just rumble. It crashed this time. "We'd better go in," Flynn said.

"Good. That's where the bed is." Sierra unwound herself from him, then took his hand.

"Wait a sec." Flynn tugged free. He picked up the painting and the wooden board with paint daubed all over it. Only then did he let her lead him inside. Sierra took her supplies from him. She tucked them into a little closet next to the front door, and propped the painting below.

"Thanks for remembering the painting."

"It's important to you. So it's important to me."

"You make this all so . . . easy for me, Flynn. I didn't expect that."

"Because I'm such a complicated guy?"

"You seemed that way, when I first met you. Closed

off and, um, secretive. No, haunted. Unapproachable. But also amazingly hot and interesting and kind."

Man, she nailed that description of him. That observant artist's eye thing she had going didn't miss a single thing. "Glad you came around to hot. That'll make what happens next easier, too."

"Actually, ridiculously good-looking, I believe, was the first thing I registered about you. Tall, dark, and brooding. No woman can resist that."

"I don't care about other women."

Sierra took a whopping three steps past the couch to the stairs and pulled off her light blue tee shirt printed with the letters MIAD stacked into a fat block. It gave him a jolt to realize it must be the logo for her college. To know her secret, and be able to put the pieces together.

Then he stopped thinking about her holy-shit-complicated past—another *get to that later*—because she was standing there in just a white lace bra and shorts.

It was simple. Not that fancy, expensive stuff the women in Chicago dolled up in. But the lace cradled breasts that he fucking yearned to touch. And pink showed through the lace from her nipples, poking straight out. Her breasts called to him. Flynn could spend all night with his mouth on them.

As he moved toward her, his leg brushed against the handle of a mug on the end table and sent it crashing to the floor. Flynn spared it a quick glance. Couple big pieces. Nothing that couldn't wait, since it looked to have been empty. "I'll buy you an even dozen to replace it if you just keep standing there."

"Here? I thought I'd head up to bed, actually." After tossing him a teasing smile, she moved up two more steps.

A hamster could've caught up with her in a house this small. Flynn didn't bother to even lunge. He just leaned out a little and grabbed for her shorts as he made it onto the first step. Except that motion connected his shoulder with a shelf, and his head with the one above it. A picture frame tumbled off and onto the couch. A plant clocked him right above the eyebrow.

Flynn threw out the opposite arm to catch himself . . . just in time to remember the stupidly steep staircase didn't have a bannister.

"For being so tiny, this house is one giant cock block," he grumbled.

Sierra's hand flew to her mouth. "You're bleeding."

He thumbed off the couple of drops beading along his eyebrow. After all the hits he'd taken in the ring, a simple clay pot to the head wouldn't slow him down one damn bit. "Doesn't matter. I'll clean all this up later. Myself included. I need you *now*, Sierra."

At the top step she dropped to her knees. The sight of her crawling onto that mattress would stay with him for the rest of his life. Her tight little ass twitched beneath the denim. Long legs straightened then bent again, just like they would when he was between them. Those just-big-enough breasts hung down, swinging a little from side to side in a way that dried his mouth out. Hell. It was the sexiest god damned thing Flynn had ever seen. Punctuated by the look—half-lidded eyes, one cocked brow, pink lips parted just a little—that might as well be her hand around his dick pulling him forward.

Flynn took what was left of the staircase at a combination crawl and climb.

Then his knee hit the brass rail that kept the mattress from falling out of the loft space. A space he couldn't even kneel in without hitting his head.

"No. No way. This isn't going to work."

"You mean because of what I told you tonight?"

"I mean because your house wouldn't even fit a hobbit." Flynn was pretty sure he got that right. Hobbits, elves, dwarves—all creatures with a shit-ton of hair in movies he'd mostly slept through. But he thought he remembered a round door that had intrigued him in a house where the human-sized wizard couldn't stand up straight.

He looked over the railing. Assessed his options. They'd make this work here, tonight, if he had to stand on one leg in the shower to make it happen.

If there was a shower.

"Back downstairs. I've got a plan."

"Should I take off the rest of my clothes first?"

"Don't you dare. That fun's all for me." But Flynn did yank his own shirt over his head. He pressed on the cut to soak up whatever blood was still there so that it wouldn't scare Sierra, or give her a reason to worry.

Her head needed to be focused on one thing, and one thing only.

By the time he tossed the shirt onto the mattress and crab-walked back down the stairs, Sierra stood in the middle of the living space, arms loosely at her sides. Flynn dropped to his knees. Unbuttoned her shorts, but left them hanging at her hips.

He feathered a line of kisses where the waist gaped open. That creamy skin soaked up each kiss. Her fingers dug into his skull.

"*That's* where you're starting?" Sierra said on a half laugh, half gasp.

"We started weeks ago, when we met. This is where I'm finishing it. Now. Here." Flynn tipped his head back to watch a smile bloom across her face. "If that's okay with you."

Sierra nodded so hard that her hair fell over her face. Kind of hiding behind it, she said in a very small voice, "I, um, don't have any condoms. They seemed like an unnecessary expense. Until recently, that is."

Now that Flynn knew the depth of her struggles and her journey? The reason behind why she couldn't spare the cash for a six-pack of condoms flayed him. The woman had had one hell of a tough road. One that would've broken other people. But no way would he let her feel bad for not splurging on a rubber.

"No worries." He tossed her a wink as he dug a foil packet out of his wallet. "A man who doesn't always carry a condom is a man without hope."

Her soft giggles proved that he'd taken the right tack.

Flynn stood to toss the condom onto the kitchen counter. Then he crowded up close behind her, with his balls nestled right at the top of her sweet, tight little ass. He tucked his arms around hers to squeeze those lace-covered white mounds. Looking over her shoulder at them, his dick jerked against his zipper painfully. She was perfect. She was everything good and bright and beautiful and so damned kissable.

Flynn circled her nipples with his thumbs, knowing the rasp of the lace would make them even more sensitive. Sierra jolted back against him, then reached up to hang on to his forearms. Using his chin, he moved her hair out of the way to get at her neck. His tongue traced the tendon standing out sharply on the side of it. At her earlobe, he flicked it fast before taking it in his teeth and tugging.

Sure enough, her breath ratcheted up into pants. The woman responded to wherever, however he touched her. And that response filled Flynn with such satisfaction. Drove his need painfully high, too.

But his didn't matter. Not yet.

Flynn popped open her bra with one hand. Immediately, she shrugged it off her shoulders and shimmied it to the floor. Which treated him to one hell of a view of jiggling, pink-crested breasts. "God, you're beautiful, Sierra."

"No." She whirled in his arms. When her breasts connected with his bare chest, they both inhaled sharply.

"I'm average. You're . . . you're like a statue of a Greek god."

"Don't contradict me. Out of the two of us, I'd say I'm the expert on assessing a woman's beauty."

"I'll bet." Her face fell.

What had he said? "What's wrong?"

"I just . . . I figure you're much more experienced than me. I don't want to disappoint you."

How badly had he screwed this up? Did she really not know? "My experience will make you feel good. What we did with other people doesn't matter. What we do together, you and me, that's what matters. There's only here and now. And I'm going to fucking worship your body. If that's okay."

Another almost frantic series of nods.

Flynn skimmed his hands down her spine, over to her narrow rib cage. Her skin was smoother than butter. He flipped his hands so his knuckles dragged back up her sides, along the curve of her breasts. Her shorts would have to stay on until the very last second to keep him in check. Because he was practically ready to come just from touching her.

He laved his tongue in a wide circle around her nipple. Then another one, slightly smaller. Another that just touched the row of tiny pink bumps right at its edge. When he finally closed his lips on the erect nub, Sierra mewled. Like a kitten when you rubbed its belly, but a hundred times sexier. The sound curled through his balls before spiking desire straight to the tip of his dick.

"Do you like that?"

Another nod.

"Honey, I need you to talk to me. This only works if you let me know what does and doesn't get you off."

"Everything you do is good. But . . ."

"But what?" Flynn moved his ear closer to her mouth to hear over the sharp drill of the rain against the roof.

"I want to touch you, too," she murmured.

"You don't ever need to ask. Trust me when I say there's nothing I want more in the world right now than your hands on me."

Sierra brushed those long, delicate artist's fingers along the edge of his collarbone. Lightly, so light it almost tickled.

Except that it didn't.

That light caress fired him up more than his last blow job. It was the *way* she touched him. With so much tenderness and care. And then her nails scraped down the center of his chest to the start of the line of dark hair that went beneath his waistband. That wasn't tenderness.

Flynn saw the teasing, sultry glint in her eyes, the half upturn to her lips. That was lust. That was heat matching heat.

God, his dick throbbed with wanting her.

"Sweetness, can we take turns later? We've got all night. But I want you too damn much to wait."

"That might be the absolute best thing you've ever

said to me." A vertical line formed between her eyebrows. "But if you can't fit on the bed, what are we going
to do?"

A laugh burst out of Flynn. "We don't need a bed."

"Sure we do." She turned in a slow circle, eyes dart-
ing about the tiny space. "Um, the couch unfolds flat to
sort of an extra bed."

Flynn eyed it skeptically. Maybe a half-inch foam
cushion, at best. Might as well kneel right on the damn
floor. This entire house was a giant chastity belt. "Do you
remember when I told you at the Gorse how I wanted to
take you? On the bar. Braced, bent over the end, on your
tiptoes. Me behind you. Holding on to your hip with
one hand and your breast with the other."

Her cheeks turned the same pink as her nipples. "Of
course I remember that. Every single word."

"Ever since I got that picture of you in my mind, I
knew I needed to make it come true. Replaying it in my
head's no good. We've got to do it for real."

"Standing up?"

"Yeah." He'd have to crouch over her, surrounding
her. It'd be so damn hot.

"Are you sure it'll work?"

Flynn fished his wallet from his back pocket and
dropped it on the floor between them. "I'll put all my
money on it."

"Okay. I really like the idea of my first time with you
being another first, too."

Fuck. So did he. Flynn was no seventeenth-century

knight jonesing for a virgin. Talk about no fun and too much pressure. But he loved the idea of opening Sierra's eyes to something new. Of being the one to show her a new way to experience pleasure.

He wondered how many other firsts he'd get to have with her. However long the list turned out to be, he didn't intend to leave a single one undone.

"C'mere." With one finger, he beckoned her to join him at the counter. Flynn unzipped her shorts the rest of the way and shoved them to her ankles. Then he lifted her up and sat her on the counter.

Sierra kicked her clothes off onto the floor. "What are we doing? This isn't bent over."

"I'm indulging in a sweet treat, first." Flynn dropped to his knees. Wedged her legs apart with his shoulders and saw the triangle of . . . blond? . . . hair. As he looked up at her in surprise, Sierra tugged at the dark hair lying across her breast.

"I'm on the run, remember? I dyed my hair as soon as I hit Chicago."

"You're full of surprises today." Then he leaned in to blow gently on the patch of fine blond hair.

Sierra jumped. "You are, too. Wow." She patted with more than a little force on the back of his head. "Do it again."

"You bet." He blew a little harder this time, and enjoyed the hell out of her corresponding wriggle. Then he took both his thumbs and opened her up wide. His tongue lapped a long, slow stroke the length of her hot, sweet crease. Sierra tasted fantastic. Like he could eat her all night and never want to move on.

And yet, the ache to be inside her was so strong his balls were practically cramping. Yeah, this first time had to be fast and fucking soon to take the edge off. Then he'd take his time with her. To learn her. To learn her tells and what every sigh meant—faster, or stay right there, or if she just couldn't hold on another minute.

Flynn eased one finger inside of her, just to the first knuckle, as his tongue flickered over her clit. Sierra was bouncing on the counter now, arching up to meet him in a fast circle. She was so tight, and he didn't want to hurt her. So he swallowed hard and counted backward from forty to force himself to take his time.

The noises coming from her throat were that mix of adorable and sexy that fucking drove him right to the edge. One finger all the way in now, Flynn added another. Sierra went wild. Her ankles locked around his back. More sweet moisture gathered on his tongue.

"Flynn. Oh, Flynn, I . . . I don't want to without you."

Still pumping two fingers inside of her, crooked just enough to hit her G-spot, Flynn licked his lips to look at her flushed and beautiful face. "Let yourself go. Let me make you feel good. Please, let me take care of you, Sierra."

Then he scraped his teeth across her clit before sucking hard. Sierra shattered, with one, long high scream as her thighs trembled violently on his shoulders. It was the hottest thing he'd ever seen.

With little licks and kisses, he eased her down a bit before removing his fingers. Flynn stood up and he loved that she didn't move. Just kept her legs splayed wide and that lazy smile of satisfaction on her lips. Flynn suddenly wished he could draw as well as Sierra, to be able to put that utterly feminine and boneless look of pure pleasure down on paper forever.

"Now can it be your turn?"

This woman and her selflessness. How did he get so lucky? "Now it's *our* turn." He started to unbutton his shorts, but her fingers got there first. Nimbly, they undid him in record time. Flynn ripped open the foil packet with his teeth. And practically inhaled it when Sierra cupped his balls in her talented fingers before squeezing his entire length.

"Christ almighty, I have to get inside you."

"Good."

He helped her off the counter, then turned her around. For someone who didn't seem convinced this position would work, she braced her elbows without any prompting. The sight of her waist flaring out to hips perfectly shaped for his palms made Flynn impossibly harder. Then she wiggled her ass for good measure. Like he'd needed any more visuals to pop him off in two seconds.

Condom on, he pushed inside of her. Just the tip. Just enough for them both to know this was happening. He got the impression that sex had been blander than tap water for her in the past. Flynn intended to make her see stars.

"Stop me if it's uncomfortable."

"I'm uncomfortable that you've stopped," she said tartly.

A woman who sassed him and made him laugh in the middle of sex? Nothing better, as far as Flynn was concerned. Slowly, and then slower still because of her obvious tightness, Flynn eased in the rest of the way. It drew guttural moans out of both of them.

"Sierra, you're beyond my wildest dreams. I want to stay in you all night. But I also want to come right the fuck now, it's so good."

"Do it," she urged. "I won't be able to again."

"The hell you won't," he growled. "Insults don't count as foreplay, babe. Have a little faith."

"In you? I've got nothing but faith."

The sweetness of her words almost did it. But Flynn gritted his teeth and held on. He reached around to squeeze her nipple, which made her squeal. Twice more, after that response, before moving down to palm right above where they were joined. Sierra immediately stiffened and rose to her toes.

Yeah? He could do better. Hands on her hips, he shifted her angle just a little to drive even deeper. Then Flynn lifted, taking her feet off the floor, and let himself go. Fast, hard strokes that had her alternating whimpers with a babbled repeat of his name. At least, he thought it was his name. The two ounces of blood that weren't in his dick were pounding in his ears.

Sierra slapped her palm against the counter and

threw her head back on a scream. At the same moment, Flynn plunged even deeper and jerked his hips against hers as he came so hard his vision blacked out. Or did his eyes shut? However it happened, the orgasm fucking decimated him in the best possible way.

When his ears stopped ringing, Flynn heard their ragged breaths fall into sync. He pulled out, lifted her into his arms, and then dropped onto the couch. Sierra curled up, hands right over his heart, face tucked against his collarbone.

"I was wrong," she murmured sleepily. "Sex does live up to the hype."

"I'm not sure I was in on the first part of that conversation, but I'm damn glad to hear it."

"I meant what I said. Before. About having faith in you."

"Goes both ways, babe."

Sierra lifted her head. A single tear glistened in the corner of each eye. "Knowing I can trust you means *everything*. I didn't believe I ever would again. You don't just physically make me feel safe. I trust you to keep my heart safe, too." Then she tucked her head back down.

Flynn was gutted by her statement. Once he'd watched a fisherman on the shore run his knife up the white underbelly of . . . well, some kind of fish. All the bloody entrails tumbled out.

Yeah. That was *exactly* what he felt like. This woman who life had bitch slapped, over and over again, hadn't lost faith. No, she'd put it all in the man who lied to her about who he was every single damn day.

And that's what made Flynn realize he was pretty sure he was falling in love with her.

What the hell was he supposed to do about that?

Chapter Fourteen

SIERRA SPRAWLED ON the floor of the elementary school gym, breathing hard. Her elbow stung where it'd knocked the floor. Her head ached a little from where Karen had accidentally yanked at her hair before they'd both lost balance and toppled over.

She felt *great*.

Who knew that a self-defense class would make her feel that way? On a bunch of levels?

First of all, she was proud of Flynn for how quickly he'd pulled it together. He'd only come up with the idea eight days ago, and here they were finishing the first class with ten people in it.

She was proud of herself for drawing the brochure. She'd sketched Wonder Woman in a bunch of kicking, fighting, awesome poses, but with the faces of Mollie, Norah, and Lily. Anyone who drank coffee, went to the doctor or had a kid in school would recognize them. This week she planned to draw something to pull the tourists in. Because after today, she knew that even attending just one class would make a difference to a woman's safety.

Sierra felt great for *attending* the class, not wimping out in fear of a few bumps and bruises. Which she'd definitely garnered. As had everyone else. But it was fun and empowering as all get-out to realize that, thanks to gravity and physics and a little centuries-old Eastern martial arts mysticism, a woman *could* take down a man a foot taller than her. Or at least put him out of commission long enough to run for safety, screaming at the top of her lungs.

Even the screaming had felt great. Primal. It came from deep in her belly, and seemed to have released some of the tension and fear and, yes, anger about her situation that she'd carried around like a turtle lugging a backward shell.

And, truth be told, she tingled just about everywhere after watching her muscled boyfriend demonstrate moves barefoot, in just a tank and gym shorts. That body was her playground, now. It had been for a week. Sierra still could barely believe it. Could hardly believe all the different *ways* they'd explored and enjoyed each other.

She couldn't get enough of him. Not just Flynn's body, but *being* with him. Hanging out, walking on the beach, laughing over dinner with his brothers before watching a movie. Ordinary dating stuff that felt extraordinary.

Flynn laced his hands together behind his back and then straightened his arms. "This will open up your chest muscles. Every move has a counter move; every muscle has a set of muscles that balance it. You've got to be sure to stretch so you don't stiffen up."

Sierra tried to mimic him. She got her fingers laced, but her elbows stayed bent. Glancing around the room, the other women were having the same problem.

When Flynn noticed some grimaces, he unpretzeled himself and held up one hand. "Don't force it. You can only do what you can do. Take ownership of that. Be proud of your achievements. Don't focus on your limitations. Not just in this class, but in life." Then he shook his head. An almost . . . flustered look had his lids flashing down, and his lips pursing. "Sorry. I'm used to teaching kids. You guys probably don't want a side helping of a life lecture with your self-defense."

Karen blew a raspberry. "Don't censor yourself, Sensei." She'd also teased him with the titles of Karate-San and Master Yoda. "I'll take a giant scoop of whatever you dish out."

"Ewww—" Jackie, who worked at the salon and always ordered fries with a double dip of cheese to go with her Diet Coke, frowned at Karen,"—and yes, she's right. What you're teaching isn't just physical. It's about self-confidence, right? I don't know about the rest of you, but I run low on that most days."

Sierra nodded fiercely. "It's so easy to assume that everyone else is better than me, more together. But deep down, on the inside? They're probably as messed up in their own way as I am. It's good to be reminded that I am *enough*."

Immediately, she worried that she shouldn't have spoken up. But one glance at the pride beaming from Flynn's blue eyes told Sierra he appreciated that she got it.

Fluidly, he bent over and touched his toes. The women were much better at this move, with almost everyone trailing their fingertips on the floor. "You don't get better without pushing yourself. But take breaks. Set reasonable expectations. Don't book a flight to Hollywood and try to take down the Rock tomorrow with one rolled shoulder to the gut."

"Worth it, if he's naked," Karen quipped.

Sierra bit back a giggle. Maybe it was true that exercise gave you a natural high. Because Karen was sure, um, *loose*.

"You're all strong. And you did good work today. Give yourselves a hand." Flynn clapped, and everyone joined in with matching grins. "Spread the word, too. Same time next weekend."

Sierra headed for the wall where all their shoes and socks were lined up. A handful of women came with her, but the other handful fluttered around Flynn. It reminded Sierra of the end of class in art school. Kids would flock to the professor, jostling to eke out some praise for their work.

She didn't mind one bit. Because Sierra knew he was hers, even if they hadn't talked it through. She knew it from the tenderly possessive way Flynn cupped her face when he kissed her. The way bags of Doritos kept mysteriously showing up in her locker at the Gorse. The way he completely dropped his guard and gave those rolling, deep belly laughs she was so tickled to wring out of him.

"This was fun." Karen screwed up her button nose as she tightened her messy ponytail. "I mean, I'll be cursing your guy tomorrow when I'm too stiff to roll out of bed, but I'm glad I came."

"Yeah. Some aches are *good* aches." And Sierra meant *all* of the ones that Flynn had given her in the last week from their vigorously awesome sex. The look of satisfaction that she was responsible for putting on his face each and every time was even more empowering than learning how to take down an attacker.

"Are you being proactive? Or are you working out old demons?"

Okay. So *maybe* she'd visualized Rick's face when flipping Karen over her shoulder with a satisfying grunt. Sierra didn't want to give a dismissive lie out of the habit of protecting her secret. This class was a big gift Flynn gave them, and it was probably helping people banish bad memories. Choosing her words carefully, she said, "Um, both? I've been in situations I wish I could've gotten out of better."

"Me, too. More than once. I'm not proud of not doing anything to help myself, either. That's why I liked what Flynn said at the end. Not beating myself up about what I *didn't* do a decade ago is a hard pill to swallow."

It was like Karen was pulling words—and feelings—straight from Sierra's head. So she'd take a chance and share a thought that had occurred to her mid-class. "What if we turn it around? Instead of trying to ignore that humiliation from not being able to save ourselves, we accept it as a stepping-stone. One that brought us to this class. That the bad feelings were the kick in the pants we needed to force ourselves to do better, be stronger."

Karen bit her lip, considering. Her expression morphed from thoughtful to hopeful with arched eyebrows and wide brown eyes. "That's very wise."

"Only if it works. We both have to promise to try believing it." Sierra stuck out her hand, with just the little finger extended. "Pinkie swear."

"You got it." They shook, and Sierra felt about twenty pounds lighter. She'd never be able to fully remove the weight of her secret past. But she wasn't letting the fear of it control her anymore.

Yep, this new life of hers in Bandon was pretty great.

And as she savored that thought, melting into her brain with the sweetness of a chocolate truffle melting on her tongue, Sierra felt a kiss on the top of her head. Excellent. It had been a whole hour since they'd last kissed, and she was *desperate* for Flynn's lips.

She didn't even finish the bow on her shoelaces before swiveling around. Sierra looped her arms around his neck and pulled him down into a deep kiss. Well, it started out as just a kiss, but their tongues were magnetized or something, because they just twined around each other at every single chance.

Karen gave a soft tug on her ponytail. "Hey, lovebirds, this is an elementary school. Keep it clean."

Flynn straightened up, arms in the air. "Not my doing. The woman's insatiable for me."

Oh, he'd pay for that later. Because she'd discovered last night that the big MMA fighter was particularly ticklish on the soles of his feet. Her vengeance would be *brutal*. Sierra whacked Flynn lightly across his shin before standing. "Hey, don't throw me under the bus. You kissed me back!"

He ran the back of his knuckles lightly along her jaw. And paired the motion with an utterly heart-melting smile that crinkled the corners of his oh-so-blue eyes. "That's because I'm equally insatiable for you."

"Ugh." Karen scrunched up her face and shook her head, like she was clearing an Etch A Sketch. "This undiluted romance is harder to watch than the PDA."

"Sorry. We'll take it in the hall." Flynn grabbed her hand and pulled Sierra at an almost jog toward the door. "That wasn't a kiss. That was a *taste*. A tease. I need more."

Laughing, she tried to slow him down, pointing back at his sneakers. "What about your shoes?"

He took her other hand, too. Pressed swift kisses along each of her knuckles. "I don't need shoes to kiss you, beautiful girl." He pushed against the horizontal metal bar that opened the door with one hip. Flynn didn't bother to turn around the last few steps. His eyes were locked on Sierra's, with a single-minded focus that she *loved*.

Flynn's hands ripped from Sierra's. "What the fuck?" Except the last word was more of a whooshed exclamation, as he fell sideways and hit the floor, hard.

A child in ridiculously huge football pads clutched his belly and laughed. Sierra couldn't believe that he'd run out of nowhere just to take Flynn out at the knees. Well nobody, not even a nine-year-old, would get away with taking out her man.

Sierra bent over, bracing her hands on her knees. She didn't yell, but she did use her stern voice. She'd babysat for extra money for almost a decade. A good, stern voice could be wonderfully effective in producing both guilt and confessions in anyone younger than a teenager.

"Why did you deliberately run into Mr. Maguire and push him over?"

The voice did the trick. His laughter cut off. And he started shifting his weight from one foot to the other. "To test the teacher. Mommy took his class while Braden and me practiced our throws outside. If he was good enough to teach Mommy this stuff, then he should be ready for the element of surprise."

"You know what? That's an excellent point. If we were still in class, it would've been a good thing to try. But now that class is over, you just knocked him down for no reason."

He didn't need any prompting. After tugging a few times to get his helmet off, he turned to Flynn, now sitting with his knees raised and arms circling them. "I'm sorry. I didn't mean to hurt you. I just want to be sure you were a good teacher."

Flynn nodded slowly, his lips pursed and squeezed to the side in an overly dramatic "thinking" look. He sized up the kid slowly, from the jet-black hair sticking up to the grass sticking out from his cleats.

Finally, he sucked in a long, loud breath. "You're looking out for your mom. I get that. We're square. Knuckles." The two bumped fists, the sides of their hands, and then fake-spit. "What's your name?"

"Matthew Tanaka."

Sierra wanted to make friends with him, too. Just without the spitting. "What grade are you in?"

"I'm gonna be in fourth when we start back."

She pointed at his pads under a Seahawks jersey that almost hung to his knees. "You're going to be on the football team?"

"Yeah. Just like Braden." Those black eyes sparkled with obvious hero worship of what she assumed was his big brother. "He's teaching me to throw a spiral. I'm not good at it yet."

Flynn blew a raspberry. An unnecessarily wet one that sprayed everywhere and brought the smile back that had slipped from Matthew's face. "Dude, it's not even the Fourth of July. You've got time. You just keep practicing." Then he cocked his arm back and mimed a throw.

"That's what Mommy said." He shuffled closer to Flynn, and looked between him and Sierra. "But what if Braden's not teaching me right? What if he knows as soon as I learn, I'll be better than him?"

"Brothers are sometimes sneaky like that. How much older is he?"

"Five years. He's in *high school*." The awe conveyed in those two hushed words was eight kinds of adorable.

Flynn scrubbed a hand across his mouth. "My big brother's only three years ahead of me. He can be bossy and a pain in the butt."

"Yeah." A big, long-suffering sigh. "That's Braden."

Sierra would've given anything to be able to hop in a time machine, go back about fifteen years and watch the younger versions of Flynn and Rafe hassle each other. It was probably hysterical. She'd also bet that Flynn held his own from whatever point their height differential disappeared.

She'd also bet that despite the bossiness, Matthew and Braden loved each other fiercely, just like the Maguires. "But if Braden's that many grades ahead of you, you two would never be on the same team. So I'll bet that he's teaching you right."

"Tell you what. I'm more of a baseball guy, but I can throw a football. What if I come out and toss it around with you two, just to be sure he's on the up-and-up?"

"Really? That'd be great."

"Go ask your mom for permission."

Sierra seized at the opportunity to make a new

friend. She'd only met Beth Tanaka today. "Tell her that I'll hang out and wait with her."

Flynn went flat on his back, then rolled his knees up to his belly, planted his feet and magically rose to his feet without using his hands at all. Sierra had seen the move in about a zillion vampire shows, but always assumed the actors were helped with wires. Omigod, it was sexy. "Give me ten minutes to scoot my class out the door, and I'll meet you outside."

"Thanks, Mr. Maguire." He only made it one step over the threshold before Sierra stopped him.

"Hey, Matthew." Before he finished turning around, she drilled her fingers into his ribs, dissolving him into giggles. "You have to learn the same lesson as everyone else did today. Be prepared for that surprise attack."

Once he raced off, Sierra slid her arm around Flynn's waist. "I can't believe he got the drop on you."

"Me, neither. For a good cause, though." He swiped his hand from his forehead down to his neck, and then back over. "I was exactly his age when my mom died."

Oh, no. She hadn't realized their mother had been gone for so long. Sierra's heart broke all over again for him. For all the Maguires. She circled her other arm around his stomach and leaned in to squeeze him tightly. "That's so young for such a loss."

"Yeah. I remember how I spent weeks wondering what I could've done to protect her."

"How did she die?" At that age, it was probably either cancer or a drunk driver. Both equally horrible.

The door opened and closed twice, women walking out with a wave and thanks, before Flynn answered. "She died from a gunshot wound."

There simply was no response to that. So Sierra just pressed her face against his chest and listened to the overly fast, hard thump of his heart. Was it wrong that she felt lucky for not having memories of her parents? For not having that pain of someone so integral being ripped from your life? Obviously the wound had scarred over by now for him. But it was fresh for Sierra, and she ached to comfort him, to figure out a way to make it better.

He stroked her arm, back and forth. "They said it was an accident. Wrong place, wrong time. But that's too hard for a kid to process, you know? Too random. So I worked through a million scenarios where I could've protected her. Including a bunch of superhero stuff, be-cause . . . *nine*."

The age right before you went from believing in magic to scoffing at it. Sierra would bet he'd stopped be-lieving faster than was fair, or right. "Of course."

"But when I got a little older, I wondered if some-thing I did could've changed everything. The butterfly effect, they call it. If I hadn't whined about taking the trash out, her whole day would've been two minutes ahead, and maybe it wouldn't have happened."

Sierra angled her head up to look at him. His thick hair was uncharacteristically mussed. His eyes looked almost as dark blue as Rafe's, deepened with pain and ghosts. "Please tell me that now that you're even older, you know that's not true. That there's absolutely nothing you could've done."

His back teeth audibly clicked together. "Yeah. That's been made abundantly clear to me. The only people responsible are the asshole who pulled the trigger, and the fucking violent dirtbag who gave the order."

What? "You mean it *wasn't* an accident?"

His whole body jerked. "No. Just . . . you know, gang rules, right? Somebody orders a hit, for retaliation or initiation into the gang, and suddenly there's a whole bunch of people caught in the cross fire. Accidents happen. I'm glad Matthew's looking out for his mom, is all."

Sierra didn't think that was all.

Not one bit.

But she'd take the gift of vulnerability and pain that Flynn had shared, and not push for more. One step at a time. They'd been friends for a month. More than friends for a week while they figured out where to go next. And now they'd been lovers for one whole, glorious week.

They'd get there. Men weren't great about opening up about their feelings. She knew his feelings on chip flavors, grunge music, women who wore cowboy boots nowhere *near* horses, and even politics after a spirited 2:00 a.m. discussion about how different countries handled medical insurance.

The rest would come. Especially since Flynn couldn't possibly have a deep, dark secret like Sierra's.

What were the odds?

Chapter Fifteen

SIERRA WATCHED AS Flynn tucked his change into the tip jar at Coffee & 3 Leaves. Then he opened his wallet again to add a few more bills.

He snagged her gaze, then flashed an almost guilty smile. Like he'd been stealing cookies instead of rewarding hard workers. "Should've probably tossed in another twenty for the hell of it. The people here deal with caffeine-deprived monsters all morning. They deserve every cent in my wallet."

"Thank you, but you don't have to buy my coffee." Sierra went up on tiptoe to kiss his cheek.

"It's been three weeks since the first time I tasted your lips. What makes you think it's okay to just give me a peck?"

A hand at her waist prevented her heels from touching the ground again as he took her lips in a long, slow kiss. No tongue, not with all the people around them in the coffeeshop. Didn't make it any less thorough, though. Not to mention arousing.

Visibly, on his part. Sierra could tell as she slid back down his body. Giggling, she pointed at the arousal tenting his cargo shorts. "Sorry about that."

"Do not ever, *ever* apologize for turning me on. But do feel free to say the feeling is mutual."

"Let's just say I should've ordered an iced coffee to cool me down. Thank you again for treating me."

Flynn widened his stance and pulled Sierra in between his legs to hide what she did to him. "You don't have a coffee maker in that matchbox-sized house of yours. Buying you coffee is a matter of survival. Because I need it. And I don't want to let you go yet."

"I could buy a jar of instant—"

He cut her off with a palm over her mouth. "Don't finish that sentence. We've got a good thing going right now. But if you suggest I drink freeze-dried flakes, I'll have to assume you hate me. Or are trying to murder me. Or both."

Over the last few weeks, most of his guardedness had slipped away and this teasing side of him came in its place. Sierra absolutely adored this newer side of Flynn. And she loved volleying it right back at him. A nip at his fingers got her mouth free. "Is that because you're so much older than me? You need coffee to keep up with my youthful vigor?"

"I need coffee to rejuvenate after you drain my manhood twice a night." Flynn pulled her more snugly against him and the still rock-hard erection. Then he ran his knuckles down her cheek in a casual caress. One that thrilled her and almost felt like a stamp of possession in the crowded shop. That he was letting everyone know they were together.

Which was absolutely fine with Sierra.

Poking an elbow into his ribs, she asked, "Did you really just use the word *manhood*? Like you're a Knight of the Round Table?"

"It's nine in the morning. And there's a ton of people around. I'm being discreet."

"I'm not sure that's possible. You're too arrestingly handsome to be discreet."

Behind her, he stiffened. And not in a good way. That perma-erection vanished in a heartbeat. All she'd done was offer him a well-deserved compliment.

"Let's not imagine a scenario where I get arrested." Drumming his fingers on the iron back of a stool, Flynn asked, "Do you miss the snow?"

Weird. Talk about an obvious topic change. One about as smooth as a rubber eraser dragging over hand-made paper. Sierra turned to face him, trying to see what was going on behind the utterly unreadable flat compression of his lips and that distracted glance over her shoulder.

"It'll be July in one day. So, no. I'm happy to be wearing shorts. More to the point, I'm happy that you're wearing shorts so I can do this." Sierra rubbed her thigh against his. Maybe good, old-fashioned feminine wiles would pull Flynn back into the moment.

She just wished she knew what had catapulted him *out* of it.

"I mean from . . . before." He shrugged one shoulder. "From the other place."

Sierra whipped her head left and right. They were around the corner of the counter, by the front window with its old-fashioned glass jars full of crumbled herbs. Okay, one particular herb in many different varieties. But there weren't any people next to them. Most were at tables, or clustered in the back around Lorena Hunley's six-week-old on her first official outing.

In a harsh whisper, she asked, "What are you doing?"

"Wondering how weird and difficult this—" he circled his hand in the air, "—all is for you."

Didn't Flynn realize that her secret was not to be discussed in public? How was she supposed to hide if he dropped nuggets of information in front of half the town?

Flynn took her hand. Brought it to his lips and tenderly kissed each of her knuckles in turn. "Don't be so jumpy. Think about what I said. The words themselves, not the depth of meaning and history you know are behind them. Everyone here knows you're from somewhere else, because you only appeared four months ago. What I asked wouldn't set off alarm bells, *if* anyone happened to overhear. Which they didn't."

"You're right. I'm sorry. I'm . . . a little paranoid

about someone else knowing about me. Not because I don't trust you. I do. Completely. I'm just going through a mental adjustment."

"I'm careful, Sierra. I wouldn't do or say anything to put you in danger. Not ever." An urgency infused his voice. "Please say you believe me."

"I do," she stated, without any hesitation or second-guessing. Which was still a kick in the pants to Sierra. She'd assumed that after Rick's astounding betrayal that the right thing, the smart thing to do was not trust men again.

But his sudden intensity made her wonder what the heck else was going on in his head.

"One large black, and one frozen blueberry with extra whip." Norah set the paper cups on the stylized counter painted with a giant marijuana plant. "Now don't you skedaddle off yet. I need to ask you a favor."

"I'll stay." Flynn popped off the plastic lid and held up one finger. "As long as I can drink this while I listen."

"Slurp away. Remember that specialty cocktail you made for me?"

"Of course." Sierra nudged him as a reminder that Carlos wanted him to follow up with Norah about that. Flynn winced, then scratched at his temple. "Oh, yeah. I'm supposed to ask about your birthday."

Norah rolled her eyes at Sierra. Then she turned a scathing look on Flynn. "Didn't your mother teach you never to discuss birthdays with women over a certain age?"

"My mother's dead. And my dad."

Sierra's heart dropped down into her stomach at his cool statement. She never went back—inexcusably—to ask Flynn for details about his dad's death after he'd told her about his mom. She'd gotten caught up in the whole *don't ask questions you can't answer yourself* habit. Living in the now.

How self-centered of her.

On the other hand, Flynn sort of . . . *paused* whenever she asked about his past. Maybe it was too painful for him to discuss? What had happened to him? How had the Maguire brothers survived, being so young when their second parent's death turned them into orphans? Flynn said they were alone, but there must've been a grandparent or uncle or someone who took care of them.

It explained why he lived with his brothers, now. A way of banding together after . . . what had to be tragedy?

Norah, however, just barreled right along. "If that was an excuse for not having manners, Prince William wouldn't be so darn suave." But then her tone gentled, and she patted his wrist. "I am sorry, though."

Flynn gulped at his coffee and sucked in a breath between his teeth as he probably burned the entire length of his esophagus. "Look, Carlos wants to put all the special cocktails I make on the menu permanently in rotation. Yours would be up the month of your birthday."

"Isn't that nice!" Norah positively beamed.

Sierra loved knowing that Flynn had made the veteran feel special. Especially since it had been Flynn's idea—not Carlos's—to highlight the locals in this way. But he also wanted neither the credit for the idea, nor the responsibility of tracking down the birthdays. Her guy sure liked to fly under the radar.

Norah took back his cup and scrawled her name and the number eleven after it. "The month's November. I'll tell you the date if you promise to give me a free drink on it."

"Fair enough." Flynn leaned over. Dropped his voice to a conspiratorial stage whisper. "Don't tell anyone else, though."

Norah tapped her index finger against her chin. "The thing is . . . I need you to make up two more."

"Why? You don't like the flavor? Because I think I watched you suck down three of them last Tuesday."

"Love it. I'm going to make you a very special coffee as turnabout."

Flynn reared back dramatically, waving his hands. "No. I've heard what you put in your 'special' coffees. I want to be able to pass a drug test after my morning jolt."

"Most of what I sell is purely medicinal." She winked broadly. "Especially if the State Board is the one asking."

"Of course." Flynn took a much more cautious sip of his coffee.

"In the meantime, I want you to make Mollie and Rafe their own drinks. For their engagement party."

Flynn did an actual spit take. It was sort of amazing how much of a mess one little mouthful of coffee made as it sprayed onto the counter. And onto Sierra's drink. And the cranberry muffin that just got plated. As awkward as Sierra felt letting Flynn pay for her, she'd feel no guilt in asking him to replace that muffin for her.

"No. No freaking way. Rafe's not engaged."

His shock would be funny if his tone wasn't so adamant. Oddly adamant, given that Sierra had watched Rafe and Mollie interact quite a bit at the Gorse. They weren't just into each other. They were seriously head over heels, ignore the rest of the world *gone*. How could his own brother not see that?

With a roll of her eyes, Norah whipped a towel off a magnet shaped like an anchor on the side of the enormous espresso machine. "You and your commitment phobia are a menace to my establishment, Flynn."

With a wince, he said, "Sorry." His apologetic grimace encompassed Sierra, too. "This isn't me playing the man card. Rafe has no plan for getting engaged. No offense to Mollie. It's that it's only been a few months."

Odd how the more he explained that it wasn't about Mollie or a fear of commitment, the more that was *exactly* what it sounded like. A few weeks ago, knowing Flynn didn't want a relationship would've thrilled Sierra.

Now it made her sad. For him, as well as for herself. Curious, too, to know what was behind his strong stance.

"They're established adults who know their own minds. It's obvious they love each other." Norah waved the metal pincer prosthesis that stood in for her missing hand in the air. "Life's short. If you ever take that for granted, just look at me. Or what's left of me. When you realize what makes it good, what makes it worth getting up each morning, you embrace it. No matter what the timing or rules or any little life complication that might stand in the way."

Norah's words resonated right through to Sierra's heart. It was why she'd decided to take a stand and stay in Bandon. Why she'd risked telling Flynn the truth. Being here, being with him—that definitely made it worth getting up in the morning.

Norah's words seem to have struck a chord with Flynn, too. Because he stared at her prosthesis—no, *through* it, his gaze fixed on the window behind her. Was he happily imagining standing next to Rafe in a tuxedo?

Or imagining that with dread in his heart?

FUCK A DUCK *backward*.

Trouble had found the Maguire brothers . . . *again*.

Flynn's heart raced like it'd been juiced up with a shot of adrenaline mixed with five shots of espresso. Patrick O'Connor stood just across the street. Patrick O'Connor, a loud, brutal, mean-spirited soldier in Danny McGinty's crew.

The Chicago mob was here. They'd found the Maguire brothers.

"Flynn? Do you want a muffin, too?" Sierra's question dragged his gaze off the mobster and back to the sweet, wonderful, beautiful woman at his side.

The woman he refused to let be touched by any of the filth of his past life. The one he'd fucking defend to his death.

He needed to get away from Sierra. Right now. He couldn't risk Patrick even catching a glimpse of them together.

Flynn whipped out his phone as though it had vibrated. "You know what? I'm sorry, I have to bail on breakfast. Forgot that I promised to help Rafe with something for the Festival. I'm late already, and he's pissed." He waved the phone as if a pissy text burned up the screen. "You stay here and enjoy yours. Enjoy your night off. Norah, I'm sorry about the mess." He dropped another ten to cover the replacement drink for Sierra. Kissed his girl on the cheek as if he'd see her again tomorrow, no problems.

He was on his way out of the café and in the front of the store before Sierra could even respond. He angled himself behind some big-ass smoking-related thing with eight long tubes coming out of it. Kept an eye on Patrick while texting Rafe to meet him behind the shop *now*.

And not to get out of his car.

Then Flynn added a shamrock emoji. It was their

warning signal. The unofficial symbol of McGinty's crew, the one every man got tattooed upon full membership, was a mashup. The pale blue stripes of the Chicago flag, but instead of the red stars, in between were three shamrocks. A reminder that you were in the *Irish* mob.

Flynn's sat just below his waistband, by his right hip. Smaller than everyone else's, because McGinty knew that as the face of the "legit" business, Flynn's couldn't be obvious. Doing business in Chicago meant being out on a boat in trunks during the summer, sharing a locker room at a golf club. His tattoo had to be discreet.

God, he wished it was gone. The moment the trial was over, he was getting that thing burned off. The first step in his official mob-free life.

If he got to have one.

Patrick went into the bait shop and Flynn took the opportunity to walk out. He immediately cut right, putting his back to the shop, in case he came right back out. Then he stopped just around the edge of the building. Flynn scanned the street. Not too busy, this early in the morning and the crowd was thin enough that it was easy for him to scan. No other Chicago faces popped out at him.

Yet.

But Pat was in a bait shop. That meant fishing. Was everyone else on a boat? Were they doing the tourist thing during the day as a cover, before coming to take out the Maguires at night? From his hiding place, all

Flynn could see were the tops of some masts down at the marina. No way to tell without going down there and searching all the boats.

The silver lining to not seeing anyone meant that nobody had seen *him* with Sierra, either. As long as she stayed safe, Flynn could handle whatever came at him.

Footsteps crunched over the mix of gravel and crushed oyster shells of the back parking lot. Flynn didn't bother turning around. If it was a bullet to the back of the head, he didn't need to see the face of the coward pulling the trigger. Otherwise, it was Rafe.

"Tell me your finger slipped." His brother's voice was harsh and low. "That you meant to send me a flaming shit emoji, and not the shamrock."

"Although they're one and the same in my book now, no." Flynn met Rafe's worried gaze head-on. Let him read the certainty in his own expression. "No mistake."

Rafe's hands fisted at his sides. "They're here?"

"One is. Built like a fireplug. Red hair. Nose broken so many times it looks like that famous curvy street in San Fran."

With a double snap of his fingers, Rafe said, "Pat O'Connor."

"That's the guy. I saw him through the window of Norah's shop. Hightailed it out of there." Flynn held up a hand to cut off the next obvious question. "He didn't see me. I'm positive."

As Rafe flexed his fingers, he gave a nod of agreement. "Pat's big on muscles and temper. Massively lacking in the brains and patience departments, though. If he'd seen you, there'd already be blood on the ground. Where is he now?"

Flynn looked around the corner again. "Bait shop. Easy to spot, too. He's wearing a Hawaiian-type shirt covered with sharks."

"Such a douchebag. Some things never change." Rafe put a hand on Flynn's shoulder, leaned over and eyeballed the street. "You see anyone else?"

"No."

"Could mean we're in the clear. That it's just a hell of an unlucky coincidence."

Once the panic stopped icing over his neurons, the same thought had occurred to Flynn. "You remember Pat ever talking about fishing? You hung out with him. I only saw him a couple of times a year at parties."

"The city's backyard is Lake Michigan. Everyone swore they'd retire and fish at every great watering hole. Never noticed it happening. Nobody retires. No real vacations, either. How often did you and I leave Chicago for the hell of it?"

They'd taken Kellan on a three-day trip to celebrate his high school graduation. Boat ride to Ellis Island, a Broadway show, a game at Yankee Stadium just so they could boo them, and some of the best steaks they'd ever had—not that they'd admit to it back in Chi-town. That was it for vacations.

Wonder what they'd do now for a vacation? If they made it past the trial?

Damn, Flynn was starting to wonder, to care about that a lot more.

He squinted against the morning sun. "Should we call Kellan?"

"Not yet. Shit." Rafe slammed the flat of his hand against the brick building. "I fucking hate that we have to tell him at all."

Yeah. But that was nonnegotiable. It didn't matter that Rafe was the eldest. Flynn would insist on dialing Kellan in or he'd never trust the two of them again. "We promised. No more secrets. No more lies."

"I know, I know." This time he kicked at the gravel. "I just hate it."

"Me, too." Without saying anything, they alternated quick looks around the corner. "Does this mean we're having another war council?"

"Hell, no. We're not sliding backward." Rafe stabbed an index finger, pointing at both of them in turn. "You and me, we're not those people anymore."

Funny, since Flynn had *never* felt like one of those people. He'd always felt out of sync with the rest of McGinty's crew. That's what came of straddling the line between legal and not.

For now, though? Flynn would jump to whatever side of the line was necessary to protect Kellan and Mollie and Sierra and everyone else in this town who never asked to have mobsters fucking infiltrate them.

"That means killing him's out?"

"For fuck's sake, Flynn, you and I have never killed

anyone." Rafe fisted Flynn's forest green tee at the neck and yanked his brother close enough to see the darkening flecks of navy and black in his eyes. "We're not starting now that we're *out* of the mob!"

Flynn shook his head. Rafe's intimidation didn't scare him one bit. A Chicago mobster possibly hunting them down—*that* scared him. "Didn't say I wanted to. I do want to be certain that we're strategic about this. Smart. That we pro/con every option that exists and choose the best one."

"You and your damned lists. No war council, and no PowerPoint, bullet point list." Rafe let go to pace in a circle. "Let's just think for a second. I'm telling you right now that running's off the table. I won't leave Mollie."

Maybe Norah hadn't been as off the mark with that engagement talk as he'd thought. Even though they'd all sworn to not plan for any kind of a future until the trial was over. "So that's how it is?"

"Yeah."

"See, I was going to say the opposite." Another quick glance. No movement. How the hell long did it take to buy a bag of worms? "That if we have to run to keep Mollie, or say . . . Sierra safe, then we should."

Rafe smirked. "So that's how it is?"

"Shut up. How about we start with a little reconnaissance? Tail him. Figure out why he's here."

"That's what my gut says to do. But what if he's not alone?"

"We'll figure that out by tailing him, won't we? If he

rode in on a shitstorm of a coincidence? If he's really just here to catch whatthefuckever is lying in wait out there in the ocean?" Flynn hooked a thumb in the direction of his workplace. "Chances are good that he'll end up at the Gorse tonight."

"Where he'd definitely spot you. Then all hell would break loose. So whatever we do has to be wrapped up before your shift starts at what—four?"

"I'll follow him."

"Amateur." Rafe rolled his eyes. "The only person you've ever followed is me. In everything."

They were both scared spitless at the possibilities represented by the redheaded son of a bitch across the street. So Flynn would let that one go. Give his brother a pass this once. Good thing Kellan wasn't here to see it happen. "I'm the one with the free day. You need to stay at the garage. Stick to your routine."

"Flynn, this isn't a game. Pat could spot a bad tail."

"He's in a bait shop. Chances are good that means he's buying bait and heading out on a boat. If anyone else from Chicago is out here, they'll be on that boat, too. Once I find that out, I'll call Delaney."

"Fine." Rafe jogged to his car and came back with a baseball cap. "Wear this. Stay at least a block behind him. Whatever happens, do not engage."

"Funny you should use that word. I'll tell you why later. When K's around to mock you, too."

"As soon as you see his car, text me the plates and the location."

After checking out the yellow Oregon Ducks logo above the bill, Flynn settled the green cap on his head. "Why?"

"If we want him out of our hair, we need to give the police a reason to discover his rap sheet, right? Couple of broken taillights should be a good start. And I haven't had any fun with a crowbar in a long time."

"What happened to not turning into a mobster again?"

Rafe flashed an angelic smile. "Hey, I'm aiding and abetting the law on this one. Pat O'Connor's a dangerous man. With at least fifty unpaid parking tickets he bragged about a year ago. Bet its twice that high now. Pretty sure there's an outstanding warrant for him in Indiana, too. I'm just using my talent and experience to keep the streets of Bandon safe."

Flynn wanted that. But keeping Bandon safe wasn't at the top of his list. Keeping Sierra safe was.

That's why he was going to spend his day skulking behind a known criminal with a hair-trigger temper who undoubtedly wanted to get revenge on all the Maguire brothers for breaking up his crew.

It was the most romantic thing he could do for her. Chivalrous, like a knight defending his lady in her teeny tiny castle.

Too bad she'd never know . . .

Chapter Sixteen

SIERRA SLICED THE crusty, golden loaf of garlic bread. "Lily, you never explained what the occasion is? Why we're all together at your house on a Thursday night?"

The strawberry blonde shoved her shag cut behind her ears. Steam from the pasta pot billowed around her face. "Because you have to work on Saturday nights."

"No, seriously," she said with a roll of her eyes. Like they'd really bump their long-standing GNO tradition for *her*.

Lily fisted her hands on her hips, still clutching the bright red pot holders. "I'm dead serious."

It . . . it was too much. They were all too sweet. Aside from Mollie's birthday party, Elena, Karen, and Lily had only bumped into her in town a few times. She didn't have the long history that the four of them shared. "You moved Girls' Night? Just for me?"

Elena cocked her head to the side. The quizzical look crinkling her nose pretty much said that Sierra had lost her mind to even ask. "Of course. You're one of the girls now."

"Although we really ought to update and feminize that term." Karen scowled as she set the salad bowl on the red farm table. "It's too militantly 1950s, *get me a cup of coffee, doll.*"

After a loud scrape against the burner—*did Lily actually know how to cook?* Sierra wondered—she lifted the pot and upended it. Lifting her voice over the whoosh of water, she said, "Dr. Vickers, what is your professional opinion on the gender politics of the phrase *Girls' Night*?"

Mollie pulled the cork out of the bottle of red and flipped it end over end, considering. "I guess we could change it to Women's Wine Night, but that's both too long and excludes our awesome margarita binges."

"Elena? Where do you stand?"

A few deft twists of her wrists had her long dark hair up in a bun that Elena secured with a chopstick from the jar of utensils on the counter. "This isn't your kindergarten class, Lily. You don't have to call on each one of us."

The sharp tone made Lily's eyebrows raise above her pink frames. "If you're going to be snippy, I won't call on you at all."

Sierra felt the tension rising in the air, like fog creeping its way up the beach. This was the problem with not knowing people well, not knowing their histories. Would this be a big blowout of a fight? Should she leave the room and let them work it out? God, she hated feeling like she was on the outskirts even when in the cheerful white and red shininess of Lily's home.

This was just more proof that her decision to stay, to put down roots, was the correct one. By the end of the night, she'd make sure that she knew something uniquely personal about each of these women. Something that proved they were friends and not just acquaintances.

And Sierra would share something about herself, too. No matter how much the very thought made the olives and cheese she'd nibbled on sit like lead in her stomach.

"Sorry." A quick one-armed hug from Elena cleared the air instantly. Lily hip-checked her back with a grin. That was it? Wow. They were so easy with each other. Sierra's art school friends had been either loudly dramatic or dramatically shy. These women were just . . . *fun.* "I'm a grump. Alan texted that he isn't coming down this weekend."

"Alan?" Karen tapped her index finger to her lips. "The city manager up in Bend?"

"Mmm-hmm."

Mollie poured the wine. She looked as skeptical as Karen. Adorable, in her black leggings and a royal blue cold-shoulder top, but still skeptical. "The city manager who *also* has a girlfriend stashed in Portland and another in Vancouver?"

Uh-oh. Sierra took in Elena's perfectly bronzed skin, hourglass figure, and a smile that was powerful enough to almost make her curious about playing for the other team. Well, pinch-hitting, maybe. How could any man cheat on a woman like that?

"We're not exclusive." Defensiveness wafted around Elena like a fresh squirt of perfume. "He's got that hot nerd thing going for him. And Alan says he's going to take me to stay at the Bellagio in Vegas."

Lily poked a wooden spoon in her direction. "How long has he been stringing you along with that?"

"We're both busy, okay?" Elena shrugged and shifted her gaze away. "Coordinating our calendars isn't easy."

Yep, Elena was in denial. This was a semisecret that Sierra wasn't thrilled to know. But she could start repaying the friendship she'd been offered with a hard-learned truth.

Sierra set the basket of bread on the table and then crossed her arms. Looking at Elena dead-on, she stated flatly, "You deserve better."

Another telltale, timid shrug from a woman who usually radiated confidence and brashness. "We're just having fun."

"Are you, though? Because it doesn't sound like fun to me. It sounds like he's putting out the minimal effort required to keep you interested. If this guy truly cared about you, truly appreciated you for the strong, sexy, fun woman that you are, then he'd bend over backward to squeeze you into his schedule. That's what a real man would do."

Whoops. Too late, Sierra realized the volume of her rant had risen considerably. Probably . . . no, *definitely* louder than was polite in Lily's home.

Slowly, Elena picked up a glass and took a sip. Her deep brown lipstick left a perfect semicircle below the rim. "Is this about me and Alan? Or about you and an ex?"

Sierra paused. "Yes. To both. But that doesn't diminish its message."

Swirling her wine, Elena raised a single dark slash of an impeccably groomed eyebrow. Sierra had never had hers done. Would she need to wax things now? All sorts of . . . things and places? To keep Flynn happy?

After another sip, Elena asked, "Because your ex penciled you in too infrequently, I'm supposed to stop seeing a real catch?"

Alan sounded more like a real louse than a real catch to Sierra. But hey, she'd dated a skeezy criminal/almost murderer, so who was she to judge? Elena's cool challenge almost had her backing down.

But that wasn't the new and improved, Bandon version of Sierra. Bandon Sierra didn't run away. Didn't back down from sticking up for herself or her friends— even *to* said friends.

She did, however, grab the full glass Mollie had pushed in front of her and took a sip of something red and strong. "I didn't say that. What you do need to do is make sure that he starts *truly* seeing who you are and what you need."

Lily clapped three times, bouncing on her toes. "Ooh, that's good. I mean really good, Sierra. Because when you care about someone else, their needs should be at least as important as your own."

Which made Sierra wonder what Flynn's needs were. He had this core of . . . something that she was well aware might as well require a retinal scanner to open its vault. His eyes shuttered over. Quiet descended over him, although far less often, like a moody cloak. When it happened, he sure didn't look happy. Or content.

How could she push into that secret darkness, whatever it was? How could she make him feel better? How could she possibly give him everything he needed when she didn't even know what that *was*?

Another quick sip of the wine added concrete to Sierra's already semi-stiffened spine. Whatever it was? She'd find out and find a way to give it to him. Because Flynn had given her so much already.

"Hmm." Elena clicked toward Sierra on her strappy black sandals, then bent to give her a firm hug. "Why weren't you around to be this perceptive when I started dating this loser?"

Sierra smiled against the dark mass of Elena's hair. This hug was everything. Proof that she hadn't pushed too hard. Proof that she'd been right to venture outside of her comfort zone. "I was off learning life lessons to impart to you."

Everyone scraped out chairs and sat down. Happy chatter filled the room as they passed the bread, salad, and the heaping bowl of pasta with vodka sauce and sausage. As over-the-top luxurious as their party at the spa had been, to Sierra, this was better. This night—like everything about Elena's outfit, from the red bandage top to the black leather cropped pants and choker—was perfect.

Maybe she could ask Elena for fashion advice. In approximately a year, when she finally had enough money *after* saving for a car and putting aside a lot for . . . whatever she ended up doing with her life. Then Sierra could let herself splurge on a new outfit. One to make Flynn's eyes pop out of his skull.

If they were still together in a year.

Because they hadn't talked about their relationship and where it was going. Reveling in the moment was more their jam right now. After all, they'd only been together just under a month. Sierra absolutely couldn't, *shouldn't* rush into anything after her last debacle. The mere fact that she'd opened herself up to dating Flynn was a miracle.

But what *if*?

What if he cared about her as much as she cared about him? What if Flynn stopped sharing a house with his brothers and started sharing one with her?

She'd have to move. That much was clear. Her cozy little tiny house was not built for a man of Flynn's considerable—and considerably sexy—height. Or breadth. His shoulders barely made it into the bathroom.

Wow. Thinking about all the possibilities in front of her—good ones, finally—made Sierra a little bit dizzy.

Or maybe it was all those sips of the wine she kept taking.

"Want to tell us about the jerk who let you down?" Mollie asked.

"Maybe someday. Not right now." Not just because it still wasn't safe to let the cat out of the bag. More that Sierra didn't want to turn the fun evening into a pity party over her clueless idiocy.

Rick and his horrible, illegal scheme had forced her to abandon *everything*. He'd put a dark splotch on her life. One that Sierra couldn't erase.

She could paint over it, though. Like the old masters, hiding some original elements in their paintings with *pentimenti*. Obscuring what was with a different viewpoint. A different truth. A different, new, final version of what they wanted the world to see.

Sierra wanted the world to see her as a woman with kick-ass friends and a sunny disposition. A woman who deserved a man as awesome as Flynn. A woman who simply wouldn't allow the darkness to spread onto another inch of the canvas of her life.

Setting her fork down, she turned to Lily. Because there was no better time to start sketching out her new future than right now.

Well, there probably was a better time. A time when she hadn't guzzled wine before leaping into a potentially risky discussion. A time when she'd done research and prepared a multipoint reasoning.

Waiting simply wasn't an option any longer, though. Sierra knew, firsthand, how quickly plans could turn on a dime. How life could spin you around as recklessly as a car doing donuts in an icy parking lot.

Not to mention that waiting would give her the chance to change her mind. To chicken out.

Her empty hand inched toward the wineglass. Before it hit the stem and the liquid courage it represented, Sierra blurted out, "Are there any openings at your school for the fall? Ideally an art teacher, of course, but I'd take anything. Kindergarten. Classroom assistant. Chief cook and bottle washer—as long as you don't actually expect me to cook."

"I didn't realize you wanted to teach?" Lily's voice rose at the end, a verbal mirror of the question on everybody's faces. The obvious one, of course, being why she was waitressing. The more burning question, of course, being why she hadn't mentioned it until now.

"More than anything. I'm qualified. I have a degree." *Might as well go for broke,* she thought. "Two, almost. I can't prove it, but I do."

Mollie reached across the table to rest her hand on Sierra's. "Are you in trouble?"

Sierra almost gurgled out a laugh. Yes. Definitely. She just refused to let that be the defining element of her life anymore. "Trying to get away from it, is more like it."

Karen's hand landed on Sierra's other arm. The tinkle of her dozen gold bangles soothed Sierra. Like they were personal wind chimes. "Do you need help?"

Her heart swelled. Tears pricked against her lids. "I need a job. A better job than waitressing."

Elena snorted. "Since when is teaching a better job than one where you get an extra ten percent in tips from Joe Fujisawa every time you hike up your hemline?"

The pragmatism of the questions settled Sierra. For an orphan who'd teetered on the edge of poverty her whole life? Living comfortably was an almost unreachable goal. One that definitely landed below being happy and fulfilled on her life priority list. "I adore children. Art is my passion. The logical way to combine those two things is to teach. I think, I *know* I'd be good at it."

Pursing her lips, Lily said, "The kids all raved about you after the day they spent working on the float design with you and Flynn."

Sierra grabbed on to that mention. The vote of confidence was enough to give her the strength to keep going, on to the part that might make her friends regret being so supportive. Not wanting to wait and see if they pulled back, if the reassuring touches disappeared, Sierra slid her chair back to fold her arms in front of her plate.

"I realize that my lack of transcripts could be a sticking point. I can't provide them. It's too dangerous to try." Getting new ones was out of the question, too. She didn't have the portfolio required to get another full ride scholarship. Sierra simply couldn't afford the time or the money to go back and spend another four years getting a degree under her new name.

The sound of the jazz playlist Lily had dialed up filled the room because nobody was making so much as a peep. Was it that the word *danger*—one she'd chosen oh, so carefully, to give them as close to as much honesty as they deserved—had indeed scared them silent?

Finally, Elena asked, "Have you met Mateo yet? Not very tall, but *very* handsome in a swarthy, muscled way?"

"Um, I'm not sure?" A lot of people came into the Gorse. And Sierra didn't really notice the handsome men, because she only had eyes for Flynn. Just thinking about him almost, *almost* made it difficult to focus on her friend's reaction to her big revelation.

Karen rolled her eyes. "Oh, for God's sake, Elena. Not everyone can be described like a dating profile."

"But I *did* date him. Well, more of a fling. I think." She tapped a bright red nail against her cheek. "How many orgasms does it take before you cross the line from fling to dating?"

That question—one that Sierra rather wanted to know the answer to herself—netted another eye roll from Karen. She did that a lot to Elena. "Mateo's the sheriff. Aside from Elena's rating, he's also nice and very trustworthy. If you need help? Don't hesitate to talk to him. I mean, you can always talk to us. We can offer hugs and wine and emotional support. But Mateo might be able to *truly* help you."

"Thanks. I don't think he can, but I'll keep it in mind." And by that, Sierra meant avoiding the sheriff at all cost. The last thing she wanted was Mateo nosing into her past. Figuring out that she was on the run, an accessory—no matter how innocent—to an attempted murder. Attempted involuntary manslaughter? Sierra had been, and remained, too terrified to look up the difference.

"This is crazy. And I'm guessing we don't even know the half of it?" Lily waited until Sierra slowly nodded to continue. "Now I'm worried about you. What can we do?"

"Help me figure out how to do this. How I can work with kids with no degree. I was hoping that if you vouched for me, that would be enough, but . . ." Her voice trailed off as Lily frowned.

"Especially with funding cuts, things like the arts get short shrift in schools. What if we thought outside the box? You could do an after-school class. Or maybe a weekend thing at a church? Something that wouldn't require accreditation."

Sierra couldn't believe she hadn't thought of that. Of course, she'd been so mired in what *wasn't* possible any longer that she hadn't spent any time contemplating what *was*.

Karen waved a slice of bread. "That's a good idea. It needs execution by someone who knows all the players in town. Lily, you should look into that." Clearly her accountant's brain liked to line up life to fit into tidy spreadsheets of to-dos. And her matter-of-fact approach signaled everyone to tuck back into their food.

"I think I've got an idea," Mollie offered, a few bites later. "One you could do to augment teaching. You should paint for the tourists on the pier."

"I don't paint for other people for money." Her words slashed across the room, sharper and faster than an arrow. "Not anymore. Only for myself." Sierra couldn't explain the why to them. Not ever. Hopefully her tone alone got the point across.

"If you did it to make money, the end result *would* be for you."

Karen rubbed her thumb and fingers together. "Do you even realize how much you could make? Tourists love any sort of beach-centric crap. You could take appointments to do family portraits, or just churn out fast seascapes while they wait. It could be a gold mine."

"It sounds idyllic. Doing what you love, in a beautiful setting." Lily chimed in, her whole face bright with enthusiasm. "I'll bet some of the restaurants along the boardwalk would hang your paintings and let you sell them, too."

Elena sipped her wine. Slid her a sideways glance that Sierra *knew* meant she was coming in for the kill. "Or do you want to keep schlepping beers and burgers past midnight every night? Sore feet, sore arms, sticky shoes—is there really a choice to be made?"

Logically? No.

But emotions, guilt . . . they weren't logical. Nor was the frustration burning through Sierra. She couldn't screen tourists. *Nobody from Milwaukee, please. I don't want you taking home something that might be recognized.* Even though the chances of that were slim. One in a gajillion.

Was it worth the risk?

Her life hadn't been full of luck up to this point. On the other hand, things seemed to have turned around spectacularly since moving to Bandon.

What if she gave it a try?

Or what if all the stars aligned in a very, very bad way and that led to Rick finding her? Or the police . . . if they were even looking for her?

Sierra shoveled in an enormous forkful of pasta.

Maybe she'd ask Flynn for his opinion. Flynn, who only wanted what was best for her and made her happy.

Flynn, who didn't deserve to carry the weight of making that decision for her. Flynn, who didn't even deserve to have to carry around what she'd already dumped on him.

Crap. It was her life. Her mess of a life. Whether she flipped a coin, used a Ouija board or asked Flynn for his take on the whole thing, the ultimate decision rested with Sierra.

Adulting was hard. Even with the best wine she'd ever had. Why hadn't *that* been on any of her grad school syllabuses?

Chapter Seventeen

FLYNN CHECKED THE clock on the dashboard, then stepped on the gas. Sierra had texted that the party was breaking up so that Lily could watch whatever vampire or time travel show was popular. He didn't watch and he didn't care. He only cared that Sierra wouldn't bike home, in the dark, with Patrick O'Connor and who freaking knew else running around Bandon.

"If you get a speeding ticket, Delaney will be all over your ass," Rafe said from the passenger seat of his beloved Camaro.

"So what?"

"I'm just saying, the woman's scary when she's pissed off. I don't know what Kellan sees in her."

Flynn rested his elbow on the open window. He had to admit that summer nights on the Oregon coast beat the sticky, sweltering goop that filled the air in Chicago all to hell. It felt good to have the cool wind ruffling his hair from the T-tops. Okay, it actually felt like he was in a movie of somebody else's life, but it was still *nice*.

"Yeah, you do. Delaney's hotter than a firework and just as dangerous. It's an irresistible combination to a guy who's stuck to the straight and narrow his whole life."

Rafe switched the radio station. Even though they'd always had a rule about the driver picking the music. Guess he wasn't thrilled with riding shotgun in his own car. "The opposites attract thing?"

"You ended up with a whip-smart doctor who happens to be kind and funny and beautiful. Can't think of anything more opposite from you, bro." Flynn bit back a grin.

A punch—with a fucking *lot* of heat behind it—landed just below his shoulder. "Seriously? You think just because you're driving I won't take you down?"

"Yep." Flynn didn't even flinch. He knew better. "You wouldn't do anything to endanger this car."

"You're lucky that's true."

"Thanks again for letting me borrow it."

"I'm more than cool being forced to spend the night with Mollie. Easy enough to walk to her house from here. And Kellan—" Rafe drummed his fingers on the center console. "Where the hell is Kellan?"

"Dunno." Flynn sucked in the pine-scented air. He'd worried, their first day here, that the whole place would smell like the air fresheners that car washes hung from mirrors. But it took less than a day to enjoy it. To stop comparing it to the thousand different smells of Chicago and just enjoy the simplicity and pureness of *one*. Okay, two if you got close to the ocean. "We never bothered to get that chip implanted that'd tell us where he is. Because Kellan's not a fucking labradoodle."

"He's been gone more than he's been home lately."

"How would you know? You're at the hospital with Mollie more than *you're* home."

"What can I say? The hospital's got all those beds, sitting empty most of the time. I'm just being a good citizen, making sure they get used."

"For *sex*."

"Used is used. Don't nitpick like Kellan."

Flynn racked his brain. Tried to think of the last time they'd stared at each other, bleary-eyed, over cereal.

But he'd been grabbing breakfast with Sierra for at least the past two weeks. It was his way of making sure she ate. She wouldn't let him help any other way. Definitely not with money to get her out of that matchbox of a house. Sharing his place with his brothers didn't exactly make it believable that he had extra cash to throw her direction.

They'd turned into a neighborhood that would be perfect for Sierra. Mostly condos. That translated to lots of neighbors. Well lit. Safe. Too bad she was too stubborn to be coerced into moving. Not to mention too broke. How was he supposed to fix that without revealing their steady WITSEC paycheck? Not to mention their hidden stash of millions, back in Chicago?

Thoughts of Chicago brought Flynn right back

around to his brother. His mostly MIA brother. "I think you're right. Something's going on with Kellan."

Rafe startled, bouncing against the leather seat a little. "I didn't say anything was going on. Just that he's more or less disappeared."

"Man, you've really let your mob-honed instincts go. You and I are the only two people Kellan can confide in, and *we* don't know what he's up to. That means something's going on."

"We need to find him. We haven't even told him about O'Connor being in town," Rafe said in a much lower, more serious voice.

"You said O'Connor went on that overnight deep-sea fishing trip up the coast."

"Yeah. Bragged about it so much I think people up in Portland got the news flash. You need to be at the dock in the morning to pick up the tail."

Flynn nodded as he parked in front of a building identical to those around it. He noted a couple of trees, but no clumps of bushes where somebody could hide between him and the front door. "No problem. I'll talk to Kellan, too. About our problematic visitor *and* our plan to involve Delaney once we know more."

"Christ, save that for last. One mention of the marshal and he'll be trying to tail O'Connor himself just so he can report to her sooner." Rafe worked his phone into the pocket of his jeans as he got out of the car.

Flynn hurried around the trunk to ask quietly, "Are you packing any heat?"

O'Connor showing up in town changed everything. They'd agreed to check in with each other every time they changed locations. And for once, a condom wasn't the only protection Rafe had with him at all times.

Rafe stuck out his foot and wiggled it. "I've got a knife. Strapped to my calf. Why do you think I'm wearing long pants at the end of June? What about you?"

"No weapon." Flynn wasn't ignoring the potential danger. Or being cocky. His MMA skills, along with Krav Maga and other martial arts techniques, were enough. "Just my fists. And my feet. That makes me more lethal than your knife by a long shot."

"You're probably right. Remember, the number one thing is to protect yourself. If anything feels off, do what you gotta do. We'll work out the rest later."

"Number one is to protect Sierra."

"Fair enough." Rafe started to walk up the flower-lined path to the front door, but paused after just a step. "She's good for you. You were a pain in the ass when we moved here. Now you're getting back to being the brother I knew. The brother I've missed."

"She's amazing. But—" Flynn broke off, trying to figure out what to say without breaking Sierra's trust. Although, in a perfect world, he'd convince her to let him dial Rafe in to her trouble. No doubt Chicago's most notorious fixer would be an asset in figuring out how to clean up her situation. God knew Flynn didn't intend to let the status quo remain. Sierra couldn't live with that dark shadow over her life. "—it's complicated."

Laughter rolled out of Rafe. So much that he bent over and braced himself on his thighs. When the hilarity finally ran its course he looked up at Flynn, gasping a little. "You thought falling in love would be easy?"

"Shut up." He hated it when Rafe pulled the wise older brother routine. Especially when Kellan wasn't around to bounce it down onto.

"You're a moron, Flynn. Seriously. Love's complicated. Like . . . a hundred times more complicated than reconfiguring your fantasy football team when your star QB gets injured game one."

Flynn *knew* that. Just like he'd *known* that leaving everything behind in Chicago would be hard. Shitty. But knowing something didn't come anywhere close to *experiencing* it. Kind of like having sex. The description fell about eight miles short of the reality.

Rafe clapped him on the shoulder. "Let's go get our women."

SIERRA PUT HER hand on top of Flynn's where it rested on the gear shift. Such a normal, coupley gesture, but one that absolutely thrilled her. "It was very sweet of you to pick me up. Totally unnecessary, but sweet."

"Wrong. Making sure you don't bike across town in the dark is very necessary. Girlfriend Safety 101."

Geez. This wasn't Manhattan. Or even Milwaukee. There weren't roving gangs outside. Unless you counted gangs of crickets. Cicadas? Whatever nighttime, noise-making bug called Oregon home. Flynn was being massively overprotective.

And wasn't that just adorable?

"I feel like I'm in a poodle skirt being escorted home after milkshakes at the diner."

Flynn snorted. "If by milkshakes you mean several vats of Chianti, then yeah, it's just like that."

"Don't judge." How many bottles were in a vat? Was it possible he wasn't judging but actually *knew* in some weird numbers way? Like how some people actually *knew* the metric system?

Or was it possible she'd had a *teensy* bit too much wine and shouldn't be paying any attention to the babble in her brain?

"If you hadn't carried out the trash for Lily, you'd have no idea how many bottles of wine we went through. We're all still vertical, and putting consonants in all the right places in mostly the right words."

Flynn gave her a fast glance before turning his attention back to the utterly dark road. No streetlights along this stretch. "You're not vertical. You're sitting down."

"But I'm sitting vertically. Straight up. Like your penis."

Yep. That was a check mark in the column of too much wine.

"Let's not talk about my penis." Flipping his hand over, Flynn lifted hers to his mouth and dropped a soft, wet, kiss right in the center of her palm. It sent tingles . . . *everywhere*. "Since I have to go right back to work after dropping you at home, it's pointless to get yourself all worked up and needy for it."

"Somebody's got a big head. Oh, wait. That was my original point." Then Sierra dissolved into giggles.

He put his elbow on the window frame and curled his hand onto the roof. Boy, that was sexy. James Dean plus Channing Tatum sexy. A bare forearm was apparently all she needed to see of Flynn Maguire to get all lusty. Hot. Squirmy.

Okay, maybe thinking about his penis contributed to her squirminess, too.

"I'm starting to wonder if I should turn this car around and have you spend the night with Lily. Are you okay to be on your own?"

"Always." His question sobered her up faster than an entire vat—however big that actually was—of espresso. "I've always been on my own. Alone. I might not have finished my MFA, but I've earned a PhD in life skills at being alone."

"Sierra. Stop." Flynn's tone was as harsh as the bed of broken shells just beyond the shoreline. "You're not alone. Not anymore. Not ever again."

There he went again, being so sweet that her heart melted faster than a mouthful of cotton candy. And like that cotton candy, his words disappeared just as quickly. They vanished into the air, blown away by the wind streaming in through the open T-tops. Which was a good reminder that it wouldn't last.

"Don't make a promise you can't keep," she said

dully. Because she'd always been alone. Before Bandon. Maybe it was the wine giving her such an emotional flip-flop, but her history proved that any time something good came her way, something bad snatched it away, sooner or later.

"Sierra, listen—"

"No, Flynn. You listen to me." Sierra kept her eyes on the dark blur of pine trees out the window. Looking at him would make this too hard. "There is *nothing* you can do to guarantee I'll get to stay here. You can't promise that trouble won't come looking for me. If that happens? If the whole town finds out what I did? They'd never look at me the same. Staying or going, I'd still be alone. Even you might change your mind about me."

She'd spiraled, fast and deep, into a super dark place. Sharing even a tiny bit of her story with the girls tonight was supposed to have been freeing. Another chunk of mortar and brick in her foundation here in Bandon. It had absolutely felt that way, as the delicious food filled her up every bit as much as the wine and laughter and hugs.

Then Flynn—albeit unwittingly—had reminded her of her true status in the world. An orphan. *Alone.* A woman on the run, living a secret life. All the good things about being here were an illusion. A house of cards predicated on a lie that could fall apart at any second. When she didn't have anything in her life, it'd been easier. Having things, having people just gave you something to worry about losing.

Sierra was well aware she'd spend the rest of her life

lying to those she cared about. And how deep, how real, how lasting could any relationship be when she couldn't be truthful about who she was? Where she came from?

And why did it feel like an elephant had just parked his big, hairy behind on her chest? Why was it so darned hard to pull in a full breath?

The car stopped abruptly, tires crunching over gravel onto grass along the side of the road. Then she heard the car door open. It sounded like Flynn jogged around the front of the car. Sierra wasn't sure because her eyes were squeezed shut as she tried to will her lungs and diaphragm to work normally. What was wrong with her? She was so scared.

That was it.

She was *scared*.

Her door opened and Sierra felt Flynn grab her ankles, turning her until her feet were hanging out of the car. Then he tugged her thighs forward so that the bottoms of her sneakers rested on the spongy grass.

"You're safe, Sierra. Feel the ground underneath you? You're planted here now. Right here. In Bandon. And in my heart."

"That's why I'm so scared," she managed to gasp out. "Now that I have such a great life with so many people in it, I don't want to lose them. I don't want to lose you, Flynn." Then, to her utter mortification, the tears came. Sierra leaned forward, clutched at the bright yellow logo of the Gorse on his tee, and dropped her head onto his shoulder.

Sierra hadn't cried before. She hadn't cried over leaving her potential career behind, not finishing her degree, or even the shocking fear that had spasmed through every muscle in her body as Miriam Newberry tumbled down the stairs. As she'd been forced to flee with a man that she was suddenly aware was more than willing to kill to get what he wanted.

So it all came out now. Because she trusted Flynn to hold her, to keep her safe. Sierra trusted everything about him. And trusted that, even though *she* was embarrassed by the breakdown, Flynn would take it in stride and not think less of her.

The tears stopped as suddenly as they'd begun, just like the semi-daily rainstorms that deluged the afternoons here. After a quick swipe beneath her eyes, Sierra pushed herself up, off of the comforting wall of heat that was his chest.

Flynn took her chin between his thumb and first finger. Looking her right in the eye, he asked, "What the hell was in that wine?"

The laughter that burbled out of her sealed off any further self-pity. "Maybe you should call Rafe to check if Mollie broke into ridiculous tears on their way home, too."

Tapping his index finger against her lips, Flynn frowned. "Not ridiculous. I'm guessing they were necessary."

"Yeah. I think they were." Sierra could acknowledge that much. That it was healthy to unbottle her feelings—

especially the ones she'd worked so hard to ignore. "It still feels dumb to indulge like that."

"Do you feel better?"

Her heart wasn't racing anymore. The giant invisible elephant had shifted off her chest, so she could breathe normally. And the jumbled knot of fearful thoughts that had ping-ponged around her brain sat quietly, barely noticeable. "I do."

"Then it wasn't dumb." Flynn rocked off his knees back onto his heels. Then he sort of zoned out, looking over her shoulder with a soft focus that made Sierra think he wasn't seeing the forest or the road at all. "You know, I, uh, hit a rough patch. About something I've been going through with my brothers."

Now? Oh, no. Had she missed some warning signs? Not taken care of Flynn the way he took care of her? "Are you okay?"

"Getting there." He slowly stroked the backs of his knuckles down her cheek. "Thanks to you, mostly. But I have a feeling that if I'd let it all out months ago, like you just did, I wouldn't have been a grouchy, miserable bastard for so long."

Ohhhh. This was about the dark and moody quietness when he first started at the Gorse. Or maybe even before that. Sierra raked her gaze from his boots, up his jeans to the flare out of the magnificent muscles of his chest and shoulders, ending at the dark stubble and sharp cheekbones that gave him a thoroughly dangerous look. "You don't seem like the type to get refreshed by a good cry."

"Ah, no." His knees cracked as he stood. Flynn gently lifted her feet back in and shut the door. Once he'd slid behind the wheel and belted in, he winked at her. "Whatever the masculine version is—that's what I should've done."

"Lots of swearing?"

Flynn eased them back onto the road. "Could be a good way to express bad feelings, right?"

He sounded like he was joking. But Sierra genuinely hurt for him that there was any tension with his brothers. To her, family was a sparkling gift to be treasured. Any tarnish on it had to be removed right away. "I'm so sorry if you're still having a hard time with Kellan and Rafe."

Hooking his wrist over the top of the steering wheel, Flynn said, "It's better now. Family stuff gets messy and complicated. Under all that tension, I know I'm damn lucky to have them."

Good. But *better* didn't sound entirely *resolved*. Which meant she still needed to help him get the rest of the way. Sierra put her hand on his thigh. And even with the serious vibe inside the classic car, a part of her thrilled to the thick muscle, bunched and wider than the span of her fingers. "I'm available to listen. I promise nothing you say would shock me."

A harsh laugh erupted from Flynn. Then he sucked in a long breath between his teeth that grated like sandpaper. "Don't bet on it."

Wait . . . what was *that* about? His entire demeanor

had changed. It was too dark to see much, but Sierra could tell that he'd stiffened from head to toe. She could hear the shift, the rustle of fabric against the leather of the seat. Um, weren't they sharing? Being open and honest—*both* of them?

Well, Sierra had experience dealing with Flynn in a snit. He'd been that way—although never directed at her—from the day he started at the Gorse. A little snarl wouldn't deter her. "I'm just saying—you were patient and kind to me just now. I want to do the same for you."

"Are you kidding? It was an honor to hold you. To know that you felt safe enough with me to let go. It was a fucking gift, Sierra, to be there to help you again." He turned onto the gravel drive to her tiny house, then parked right in front of the porch.

Well. That had to be the loveliest thing any man had ever said to her. Sierra literally did not have the level of experience to know how to respond. Because, although fast, this thing with Flynn was definitely the most serious, most deep she'd ever been with a man. Time wasn't the only measure to a relationship. Quality mattered far, far more, she'd learned.

"Call me if you get scared tonight. By anything." He rubbed her thigh. "Even if there's just a branch tapping on the window."

"I'm fine. Honestly." One moment of weakness. That was all it was.

Probably.

Deep down, Sierra knew she'd lie awake tonight, dissecting those fears that had surfaced. Would she *ever* stop having to worry and second-guess and wonder if the past would ruin her future?

"You're the strongest woman I've ever known." Flynn squeezed her hand, then kissed the back of it. "Of course you're fine. That doesn't mean you can't call me if you get spooked."

"Spooked? By a branch? Like the boogeyman would try to break into my teensy, tiny house?" she teased.

"You never know." Flynn got out of the car. Pointedly looked around the yard, then did a fast circuit around the entire house. By the time he finished, Sierra had climbed out and hefted her bag onto her shoulder.

"Are you trying to scare me?"

"Maybe a little. You're isolated out here. Off the main road. No neighbors within shouting distance. Maybe it'd be good to be a little uneasy, to keep your guard up."

That's something she'd never have to do with Flynn. With the man she loved.

Omigosh.

She *loved* him?

The feeling didn't hit her like a return of that elephant. It was more like being cocooned in a warm blanket, but from the inside out. Sierra loved this man. It didn't matter that there were still so many things she didn't know about him. She loved what she *did* know. Couldn't wait to fall in love with more of him every day as he revealed himself.

She *loved* him.

Guess there was one more reason to lie awake tonight. Because what was she supposed to do with this feeling? Tell him? Wait for Flynn to tell her he felt the same way? What was the appropriate number of days to wait after having a panic attack to tell him that he's *loved* by an emotional mess?

Did *Cosmo* cover that in any of their quizzes?

Flynn took the keys and unlocked the front door. "In you go. I've got to head back before Carlos is ready to kill me. So no trying to lure me inside with your kisses."

That was probably for the best. If he came inside, and if they started making out with this whole *love* thing all fresh and swirly in her heart, there was a chance she'd blurt it out. Sierra needed this night apart from Flynn to wallow in the sweetness—and immediately lock it down.

"Fine. Be a responsible employee. But expect a whole ton of kisses when I meet you for breakfast."

"Oh." He rubbed the back of his neck while his head dipped down. "I, uh, can't. Meet you for breakfast. I have a bunch of things to do, starting early."

"Okay." That was disappointing. But entirely reasonable that the man wouldn't be glommed on to her 24/7 every day of the week.

"I'll see you at the Gorse tomorrow night for our shift." Flynn tipped her chin up. "I meant what I said, Sierra. You're stuck with me now. This alone nonsense

is over. No matter what I have to do to make sure of it."
With a swift kiss on her forehead, he was gone.

No matter what? What did that mean? Was it good? Because the words sounded good, but the tone sounded . . . grim.

Now Sierra had three reasons to lie awake all night.

Chapter Eighteen

TRAFFIC WAS LIGHT this early in the morning, even on Bandon's main drag. Of course, to Flynn, compared to Chicago *everything* had light traffic. It meant he needed to stop stalling and start talking to his little brother before their walk ended. "Look, I don't really need you to help me pick out a car."

"Sure you do." Kellan's flip-flops slapped against the sidewalk. "You finally want to cash in on all the money you spent on my law school. Use my mad skillz—with a *Z*—at negotiating to force Rafe to give you a massive discount."

He had a point. "Okay, maybe I do need you there. But it's not why I asked you to come with me to see Rafe. I have to tell you something."

"Is this where you finally admit I'm smarter than you? More handsome? Better at basketball?"

"We all suck at basketball." Flynn banged his elbow against Kellan's. "Remember when we changed HORSE to DEER so we'd get done faster?"

Kellan's head did a fast left-right-left, as if checking before changing lanes. His voice dropped to a whisper. His shoulders hunched in. "Is this mob stuff?"

Yup, baby bro saw right through his forced teasing. "Yeah. First of all, you're safe."

"That's not as reassuring as you probably intended it to be."

They turned the corner, away from houses and onto a busier street that led to the harbor. No other pedestrians yet—just random seagulls every so often coming in hot toward the toast in Flynn's hand—so it was safe to spill. "There's a guy in town. Patrick O'Connor. Doing all the tourist crap. Obviously just here on vacation. But he's in McGinty's crew."

Kellan's arms flew out from his sides. "Holy shit!"

Way to attract all the wrong kinds of attention. Good thing none of the shops topped with weathered gray shingles were open yet. "Can you find a middle ground between skulking cartoon spy and overly dramatic and just listen like a normal fucking person?"

"I don't think so. Does O'Connor know you're here? Has he seen you guys? Are we leaving town? Will Delaney stash us in a safe house until he's gone?"

The stream of questions irritated Flynn. Until he remembered that Kellan had zero context, and zero experience. Only the knowledge that if McGinty tracked down his brothers, their lives would be forfeit. And maybe his own, too, out of spite and revenge.

God, he hated putting Kellan through this. Exposing him to it. This was everything he and Rafe had tried to prevent. Guilt churned his stomach, sending acid up his throat. He backed up until the edge of a wooden bench bit into his legs, and he flopped down on it. Dropped his damned toast, too. If this was even one percent of what Sierra felt like during her panic attacks? He didn't know how she stood them.

Flynn jerked his chin so Kellan would sit, too. "Rafe and I are following O'Connor. Have been since yesterday. That's how we know what he's been up to. You gotta believe me when I say everything points to this being a shitty coincidence, nothing more."

Surprisingly, after a sharp double nod, Kellan calmed way the hell down. "Okay. I trust you. This is your wheelhouse, after all. What's Delaney's plan?"

"Not her plan. Ours."

"You haven't told her yet?"

"Hell, we hadn't even told you." Talk about a golden opportunity to drive a point home. Flynn narrowed his eyes. "Because we didn't know where you were. We never know where you are anymore."

That defensive jut to Kellan's chin said *fuck off* louder than a neon sign. "Isn't the whole point of our stay here to get integrated? Make friends, make a life?"

"Yeah. But we're your brothers. We're supposed to still be looped *in* to that life you're making."

"Hell, you weren't this much of a nag when I was in high school."

"The mob wasn't hell-bent on finding and killing us back then." Evasion duly noted. Flynn would file it under *what the hell was the kid hiding* and tell Rafe later. "Look, we're following O'Connor for a day to make sure that he isn't here on reconnaissance for a hit. Then we'll dial in the marshal. You want her to yank us out of some knee-jerk protective reflex? Pull us out of Bandon when all we have to do is stay off this goon's radar for a couple of days?"

The sound of his brother's sigh was even louder than the seagull trio fighting over a shard of waffle cone in the street. "No."

Kellan stood. Offered a hand to help Flynn to his feet. Flynn gave in to instinct and pulled him into a bear hug. They started walking again.

"Then just stay cool. Don't go near the waterfront," Flynn cautioned. "And remember that Rafe and I would literally give our lives to keep you safe."

"See, that's what I'd like to avoid."

A deep laugh rolled out of Flynn. "Fuck, K. Me, too."

THE STEEL DOOR to the service bay at Wick's Garage was still down and locked up tight at nine in the morning, even though it was normally wide open to catch the breeze as well as new customers. Flynn knew it had to be Rafe taking extra security precautions with O'Connor in town.

"Wonder how he's justifying the lockdown to Frieda?" he muttered to Kellan. "I swear that woman would bend over to pick up a penny if she was in a full body cast."

His little brother shoved his hands deep into the pockets of his orange shorts. "Rafe managed to keep his involvement in the Chicago mob a secret from me for more than half his life. I'm guessing that coming up with a cover story for a closed door won't tax his mental faculties."

"You don't get paid by the word, dude." He bumped Kellan's shoulder. Just for fun. Just to razz him like he used to all the time. "Would it have killed you to just say Rafe's a good liar?"

"That'd be a waste of the one hundred and fifty thousand bucks you guys spent on my almost-law degree." Kellan stopped walking. Jaw slack with . . . surprise? . . . confusion? . . . he asked, "Jesus Christ, was my education financed by the mob?"

A car at the end of the block honked, laying on the horn in one long, unending blast. Because Kellan had stopped dead in the center of the street. The garage wasn't on the main drag, but there were enough people around to notice. Which was the very *last* thing the Maguire brothers needed.

Flynn put an arm around Kellan's shoulders and pushed him the rest of the way to the sidewalk. Then he kept his arm tight while he whispered in Kellan's ear. "Remember how we can't risk O'Connor accidentally finding us? You getting run over—how much attention do you think that would attract?"

"A metric shit-ton of attention. Especially if I got taken to the hospital and Mollie saw me in my briefs and decided to leave Rafe for my obviously bigger, ah, attributes."

Classic Kellan. The kid could be serious as a heart attack—for about a minute. Then the jokes and charm rebounded, twice as strong. He would've kicked butt as a trial lawyer. Kept the other side on their toes and jumping to keep up.

"Ugh." Flynn let go and made a show of wiping his hands on his jeans. Jeans, so he'd be able to wear his steel-toed boots without looking like a guy who was both prepared and willing to kick someone's teeth in. "Don't talk about your attributes while I'm touching you. That's just wrong."

"Sorry. For stopping like that, I mean." He scrunched up his face and ran a hand through his short, dark hair. "The thought hit and sort of sucked the air right out of me."

"If you wanted to know, why didn't you ask before now?"

"You guys hate to talk about it."

"About you going to law school? Rafe and I couldn't be prouder that you made it into Northwestern."

"No. You don't talk about anything to do with Chicago in general, let alone what you did for the mob. At first, we weren't supposed to talk about it. Delaney's whole *you can't focus on the future if you're dwelling on the past* rule."

The rule made sense. Flynn just hadn't been able to follow it for shit.

All he could think about was his old life. Every single step and decision and action that led to them abandoning everything. That always led to running through the laundry list of what each of them had given up. Big things, like Kellan's JD, and little things like Rafe's Valentine's Day tradition. He'd put on a suit, walk to what used to be the address where the infamous St. Valentine's Day massacre of Irish mobsters took place in 1929, and drink a shot of whiskey.

Sure, that had been a tradition Danny McGinty dragged Rafe along on initially, but it came to mean something to him. This year on Valentine's Day Rafe had quietly and methodically gotten drunk off his ass—but on tequila.

"We told you to ask whatever questions you had."

"Yeah, but every time I do ask something, you and Rafe look at each other." Kellan squinted. "Like you're having a whole private conversation, figuring out the equation of how much you want to tell me vs. how much I really need to know divided by how upset the truth might make me."

Well, Flynn couldn't deny a single word. Because he and Rafe had agreed, back on Halloween, that *lying* to Kellan was entirely different from *omitting* things from the truth that they shared with their little brother.

They'd wanted to protect him from the ugliness of the full truth. Hell, it was their job in life.

And a fucking hard habit to break. Hard to remember, no, *acknowledge* that Kellan was now twenty-five. That if they hadn't screwed with his life, he'd already be trying cases that could decide the course of other people's lives. They didn't give him enough credit.

Great. *Another* punch to the gut of how Flynn had fucked up.

Again.

Flynn looked up and down the street. Then he nudged Kellan into the nook created by the garage door and the brick wall. "Your education—every red cent—was paid for by me and Rafe."

"You didn't let McGinty pay?"

Kellan still looked skeptical. Probably because the amount of trust they'd rebuilt with him wasn't strong enough to hold up belly button lint. "We never let McGinty near anything to do with you. That was always the deal. Rafe and I were in it to the end, but only as long as he kept the hell away from you."

"Guess you two were worth it to him."

"Maybe. Honestly? We were worried that once you got your law degree, he'd find a way to drag you in." Lawyers on the mob payroll were handy. Rafe and Flynn spent way too many nights sitting on the roof deck of the North Avenue beach house arguing about it. About if they should tell Kellan, warn him that McGinty might try to use him. Or if he'd be so disgusted by the choices his brothers had made that he'd turn away from them forever.

Guess they knew the answer to that, now.

"How'd you afford it, even with the loans?"

Still skeptical. Looked like he'd have to spill another secret that he and Rafe had sworn to keep. "Well, we used the life insurance money from Mom and Dad. We saved it all for you."

"Oh. Shit." Kellan's eyes widened. "I can't believe you saved it all for me. That's . . . that was solid of you guys. Thanks." He clasped Flynn's forearm.

They hadn't done it expecting thanks. In fact, they'd hidden it from Kellan so he wouldn't feel guilty about taking all of what, legally, was split between them evenly. But he'd sure as hell make sure to tell Rafe how much Kellan appreciated the gesture.

Gulping hard past the lump in his throat, Flynn said, "Hey, the bright side of disappearing? All our debts got wiped out. That includes what was still one hell of a hefty balance due on your schooling."

"Get what you pay for, huh? Seeing as how Northwestern doesn't get their money and I didn't get my degree. Some would call that a karmic balance."

That comment, right there? Made Flynn want to drive his fist so hard into McGinty's face that the crushed nasal bones would trickle down his spine. For two seconds, he clenched his fist, tempted to bash it into the bricks. "Some would call that pure bullshit."

"Maybe I just need to get laid." With a jerk of his

shoulder, Kellan led the way over to the smaller door to the office of Wick's Garage. "It's sure worked wonders for you." He barely got the door open before Flynn slammed it shut again, then kept his hand braced on the peeling red paint of the wood.

Leaning in, he growled, "Don't talk about Sierra like that."

"Like what?" Kellan shrugged, palms up at his waist. "Like I'm thrilled that she's turned you from a snarling zombie back into a fair-to-middling copy of my brother?"

Shit. He'd overreacted to what turned out to be a compliment. Kellan really was the best of them. Bighearted and cheerful and . . . well . . . *nice*. In a way he and Rafe often didn't take the time to be.

Still, Flynn had a point to make. "Like this thing with her is just about sex."

The knowing smirk formed on Kellan's face at a glacial pace. "Oh, reaaaaally? What is it about, then?"

"It's about time we got on with the day. I've got a mobster to tail, remember?" Flynn opened the door with a flourish and a half bow that hopefully would smooth over the flare-up of bad temper.

Rafe looked up from the pile of receipts in his hands. "What's wrong?"

"Nothing." For now. Which was a fucking relief. Every moment that the status quo stayed normal was another weight on the side of their theory that O'Connor wasn't here to carry out a hit on them. "I brought K up to speed. He's cool."

Rafe's gaze ping-ponged slowly between Flynn and Kellan. Then back again, skewering Kellan with a suspicious glare. "Then why aren't you at your shift at the cranberry plant?"

Kellan toed out the crooked wooden chair and lounged into it, hands crossed behind his neck. "Can't brothers just hang out?" He appeared unfazed by the man whose menacing scowl had made grown men all over Chicago pee in their pants. He just angled sideways to prop his feet on the corner of the desk. Yeah, he was baiting Rafe for the shits and giggles of it, no doubt.

Flynn leaned against the file cabinet. "It was my idea for him to call in sick. Told him I needed his help." Which had been an idea that hit in the middle of his drive back from Sierra's. This whole car sharing thing needed to end. And asking for his brother's help with that was the perfect excuse to yank him out of work for the morning. "I didn't want K to feel rushed as we talked through the O'Connor situation."

"Oh. Okay." Rafe pushed Kellan's feet to the floor as he sat back down. "So now that you know, you're hanging out with Flynn because . . . you don't feel comfortable by yourself? Scared of O'Connor?"

"What?" Kellan surged to his feet. He paced the ten steps to the connecting door to the service bay. "Christ, Rafe, I'm not the little kid who used to wake you up when I had nightmares. I may not be able to dropkick a superhero like Flynn here, but I can defend myself. And I'm not going looking for trouble, either. I came along with Flynn because he asked for my help and I thought it'd be fun."

"Tailing a dangerous criminal?"

"Nah." Flynn poured himself a cup of coffee. This day would require a nonstop stream of caffeine. "I did that before Kellan even woke up. Pat got off the boat just after sunrise. He was green and sweating and clutching a puke bag. Guess he never found his sea legs." It didn't suck one bit, thinking of the miserable night Pat must've spent heaving over the rail into the ocean. "He's staying up at Lucien's resort. I followed him there. Heard him ask the front desk clerk for Pepto, ginger ale, and a wake-up call to make his one o'clock tee time."

"So he's contained for a few hours."

"Yep."

"If you follow him on the front nine, I'll take the back. That should sync up pretty well with our work schedules." Rafe opened the desk drawer, then thumped a big leather case onto the desk. "You'll need these."

"What?"

"Binoculars. I found 'em a few weeks ago. Guess Frieda's husband is into bird-watching."

They sure didn't look like the tiny, powerful scopes Rafe used to bring home "from work" whenever they went to a game. "Geez. Are they from the prospectors on the original Oregon Trail? I'll have to hide behind two trees to keep something this big from being spotted. Can you text Mollie and ask her if I have to worry about ticks out here?"

"No. Because then she'd ask *why* you're spending the afternoon skulking in trees, and I won't lie to her."

"You can leave out the skulking part," Kellan pointed out.

"And Flynn can do a damn Google search." He handed over the case. "So why *are* you two here?"

Suddenly Flynn felt awkward. Rafe's nerves were obviously stretched as tight as his own with O'Connor in town. Maybe this was the wrong time to change up their situation.

Or maybe it was the perfect time. He'd worried on the drive last night that one car wouldn't be enough if, God forbid, O'Connor did mean danger had found them. The car could get the Maguire brothers out of Dodge. But not Mollie and Sierra, too.

Kellan elbowed Flynn's biceps. "Flynn wants to buy one of those junkers you've got in the lot out back. I'm gonna make sure you don't scalp him raw in the negotiations."

Rafe stood. Slowly, this time, but it was still obvious that it wasn't a casual stretch. "You want to buy a car?"

"Yeah."

A couple of steps forward brought Rafe to the front door, which he locked. Great. Added privacy meant a guaranteed fight. "I thought we agreed to share a car— and a house—until after the trial."

Flynn shifted his weight from one foot to the other. Because, damn it, Rafe was right. "We didn't swear in blood. We agreed because it made sense at the time. It no longer makes as much sense. Not with Mollie and Sierra in the picture."

"My take?" Kellan raised one hand in the air, wiggling his fingers. "I'd say that Flynn needs a place to screw his sweetheart, but he already threatened me once this morning about putting 'Sierra' and 'sex' in the same sentence. Even though it's obvious they're doing it. Having all the sex."

"Shut up," Flynn ordered. He didn't need Kellan's back-assward help. He could fight his own battles.

"We made the decision to share a car under Delaney's guidance. This isn't a smart move."

Was it the end of the fucking world that he wanted to be able to drive his girlfriend home every night so she wouldn't have to ride her bike?

Flynn tried to keep his voice level, not let his temper slip out. "Our rent is paid for by WITSEC. They give us a living allowance. I'm banking my whole payroll. I can afford to buy a used car. Or, here's a thought. I can put it on a credit card. Buy a freaking Beemer and pay it off once we retrieve the millions we hid in Chicago after the trial."

Rafe's eyes turned from dark blue to black with fury at Flynn's suggestion. "That's to pay for an emergency, and you damn well know it. It's to keep us alive if we have to go on the run. Not to blow on a hot sports car because you miss spending money."

Really? Rafe thought this was about Flynn missing buying trendy gym clothes, or dropping a hundred on lunch without blinking? Did his brother really see him as that shallow?

That accusation pushed Flynn over the edge. Pushed him to the point of blurting out what he'd been holding in for so many years.

"I'd say I miss making my own decisions, but I never really got to do that, did I?"

Kellan sucked in a short, sharp breath. Flynn swore he almost, *almost* heard the grind of his eyeballs shifting to glare at his big brother.

After enough beats that Flynn could barely inhale through the thickening tension, Rafe tunneled a hand through his dark hair. "The money isn't why we're sharing a vehicle. It keeps us close. Safe. Able to keep tabs on each other."

"You can text, can't you?" Rafe's attempt to calmly de-escalate the situation pissed Flynn off even more. "Or is your thumb so far up your ass that you can't manage it?"

Rafe smashed his palm against the wall. "Why have you been so fucking angry at me since we left Chicago?"

"I'm not," Flynn shouted. "I'm mad at myself. And that's a hundred times worse."

Fuck.

That tense silence a minute ago? It was flannel-covered puppy nuzzles compared to the atmosphere filling up the room now. Dark. Choking.

Not that Flynn wanted to let one more word force its way up and out of his throat.

"Why?" Rafe finally shook his head. "I don't like it, but at least I get why you've been mad at *me* all these months. I made the decision to put us into WITSEC. But you're saying that's not it?"

Flynn fisted his hands around the collar of his green tee shirt. "Hell, no. You saved our family. You did what you've always done. When McGinty warned you he'd make me take the fall and go to jail for a crime *I didn't even know went down*, you fixed it. You got us out of trouble and kept us together. Of course I'm not mad at you for that."

"I'm really trying here, Flynn, but you're not making any sense."

What didn't make sense was how Rafe had thought Flynn was worth the sacrifice for all of them. Worth throwing his whole life, *and* Kellan's aside just to keep Flynn's ass from sitting behind bars for a few years. Yeah, it would've sucked. But it only would've been his burden, not one thrust upon all three of them.

The guilt for his brothers' abandoned lives weighed on him every day. That guilt had grown into the wall between them over the past few months. It had dried out his heart. Guilt had kept Flynn from enjoying anything, from using his senses for anything beyond the basics to stay alive. Guilt filled him with misery every damn day. Its heavy blackness had muffled the rest of the world to him. It even hid itself—so he felt so numb he almost forgot about the cause.

Until Sierra.

Until her light got through to him.

"This—" he broke off to turn in a circle with his arms outstretched, to indicate the entire town, their entire lives, "—this is all *my* fucking fault. I'm the reason we disappeared. I'm the reason why we only have a single picture of Mom and Dad left that I smuggled out in the sole of my boot. Why Kellan had to give up his career. Why we go to sleep every night wondering if there's someone in the Marshals Service on McGinty's payroll. Someone who'll share our new identities and lead a hit man straight to us. I'm the reason we lost fucking *everything*."

Flynn let his arms drop to his sides. Okay, they just sort of flopped there. Because he was spent. Letting out his feelings was harder than a day spent hammering and lifting at a construction site.

Kellan shoved a chair behind him. Flynn's knees took the suggestion and gave up the ghost. Rafe took some slow, dragging steps to get back around the desk. The chair squeaked as he sat down. Kellan stood next to him, wearing identical frowns of concern. Moments like these Flynn noticed how very similar the three of them looked, from the dark hair that Rafe wore the longest, to the blue eyes, each a shade lighter than the older one, to the stubborn jut of the jaw.

Their mom would've been tickled to see them like this. Well, not like *this*. Not the two of them staring at Flynn like he should be carted off to a mental hospital. But the three of them, all grown-up and still together.

Still leaning on each other. Still wanting to be involved in each other's lives. Not out of habit or guilt or necessity, but because the Maguire brothers were a single unit, first and foremost.

That was what they'd always sworn to each other.

Flynn just hadn't realized that by swearing that, he'd sentenced his brothers to a possible life on the run. That he'd maybe given them a reason to hate him forever.

He absolutely couldn't take that. So he'd shut himself off from them before they could do it.

Would they now?

Rafe folded his hands together, then rested his chin on them. "I could candy coat this. Ease into it. But that's not how we roll. So . . ." He slammed his hands down onto the desk, making the stack of papers flutter a little in the air. "You're a fucking idiot, Flynn."

"Thanks. I feel much better now."

"You want a hug and beer? You've got a girlfriend for that. You come to us when you want the truth laid out. And the stone-cold truth is that we didn't lose everything. More to the point, we didn't lose *anything*. Not anything that really mattered. So stop with this martyr shit."

No way. Rafe couldn't let him off the hook that easily.

Flynn white-knuckled the wooden arms of the chair. "This isn't a coffee commercial on Christmas morning about life's moments being special. This is for real. We could be found and killed. We could go testify and be killed. That's *my* fault. You put us in this position to save me. Do you know how fucking hard that is to live with?"

"I do now." Rafe wiped his hand across his mouth, his cheek, and then down off of his chin. "Wish you'd told me before."

Kellan nodded. "It would've explained that perma-scowl hanging off your ugly mug."

What the hell? "You get that I'm serious as fucking syphilis, don't you?"

"We do. Can you see how equally serious we are that the three of us being together is what matters most?"

Feeling pricked back through Flynn. Similar to rolling off an arm after sleeping on it for too long. Relief, calm, a release of the blackness that had still filled the parts of him Sierra's sunshine hadn't yet melted.

Kellan thumped his chest. "I'm the brains—and charm—of this group. Rafe's the brawn. But hell, Flynn, you used to be the heart. You were always the glue for us. You're the one who makes us work. As brothers. That's why we *haven't* been working since we left Chicago. Not because I left law school and Rafe left his criminal scumbag lifestyle. We haven't worked because you haven't been *you*. You're all we need." He straightened up. Threw his arm out and pointed a finger at Flynn. "So stop trying to take all the sucky credit. It turns you into an asshat."

Laughter rolled out of him. "Is that the technical, legal term, Counselor?"

"You could also go down as an assclown. Douche canoe. Twittlefuck."

Rafe snorted. "Come on. That last one isn't even real."

"Look it up," Kellan taunted, throwing back the command Rafe used to give him as a kid when a big word went over his head.

Flynn kept laughing in sheer joy. They were back. They were fine. And god damn it, if he hadn't been an idiot for not admitting sooner to them how he felt.

"Although . . ." Rafe shifted. His gaze bopped around between the file cabinets and the doors and a shelf of wipers and headlight bulbs. "If it's okay with you guys, I'd like to add Mollie to that list of things that matter, too."

Kellan grinned and clapped him on the shoulder. "Fine by me."

"That's the other problem." Rafe's eyebrows shot up. Flynn hurried to clarify. "I mean, yeah, Mollie's one of us. Definitely. But I think I feel that way about Sierra." *Be honest with them, idiot!* "No, I know I do. But I'm scared that Sierra won't be with me. Because of, well, all the lying."

Without even blinking, Kellan said, "Go ahead. Take the leap."

That was fast. The way Flynn's luck was turning today, he should buy a lottery ticket on the way to the Gorse.

Or just be fucking grateful that he'd already won at life by having such kick-ass brothers. "Yeah? You're sure? It could lead to trouble."

After a grunt, Rafe said, "Trouble lingers around us closer than a fart in an elevator. Coming clean with Sierra won't make things any worse. Officially, anyway."

"Dude, you haven't really done anything for yourself, from what I hear, for your whole life. Start this new one right." Kellan opened the door to the service bay. "Now let's go pick out some god-awful clunker of a chariot for you and your lady."

Flynn was on a roll. He'd buy a car, tail Pat O'Connor's smelly ass then spend his shift behind the bar figuring out how to tell Sierra that she wasn't the only one of them leading a double life.

What could possibly go wrong?

Chapter Nineteen

Sierra was grateful that the post office provided mailing supplies. Super happy that she didn't have to drop any money at Target to get the heavy-duty packing tape to properly seal her finished canvas inside layers of paper, bubble wrap, and cardboard.

But after five minutes of struggle that felt like twenty, she was ready to march across the street to the bait and tackle shop and ask for a spool of fishing line to wrap around the box oh, eight thousand times. *Why* did the tape keep resticking to itself? On the roll. On the handle of the tape gun. Was this a secret skill she would've learned if she'd stuck around for the final semester of grad school?

"I think you need a bag."

The low murmur in her ear had Sierra whipping around. "What?"

Yup. She was still super jumpy. Even though it had

been seven months of time and space between her and Rick. Even though the voice was a woman's, and now that she'd turned around, recognized that it belonged to Norah, Mollie's grandmother.

Norah rummaged in her sack, tie-dyed in shades of green, then held out a crumpled brown paper bag that looked like it had held sub sandwiches. "Here."

"Thanks, but my painting won't fit in there."

"Of course not. The bag's to breathe into. You're so worked up that you're hyperventilating." She rubbed her hand in a light circle on Sierra's back. "Or, if you'd prefer, I could give you a peanut butter cookie with white chocolate and coconut. They're very calming."

Sierra *loved* peanut butter cookies. But she knew better than to go near Norah's cookies. Because the secret ingredient wasn't love—it was marijuana. "Thanks, but I've got to be on my toes to handle the Saturday crowd at the Gorse tonight. No cookies for me."

"Then at least get some air with me." Norah handed the box—with its flaps still open—to the woman with hot pink dreadlocks behind the counter. "Rosie, fix this up and hold it until we come back."

Before Sierra could protest, Norah had her outside, sitting on the red metal bench next to a matching trash can repurposed as a planter, exploding with orange and yellow blooms. "Just sit for a minute and breathe."

"I'm fine. I'm not actually hyperventilating, I promise." Sierra was frustrated to the max, but not out of control. "I'll cop to having a bad morning."

Norah opened and closed the pincer attachment to her prosthesis. Flexed her wrist. "After I lost my hand, everything was . . . *hard*. But I didn't complain. The only point in complaining is when you expect something to change. You complain about cold soup, and the waiter brings you another bowl. You complain about global warming, and start recycling. My hand was gone. It wasn't ever coming back. So I kept my frustrations to myself. I didn't want to be a downer, or bother anyone."

That was incredibly brave. Going it alone was hard. Sierra knew that down to the bone. "I'm sure your friends would've understood."

"Well, they did. Eventually. What they didn't understand was why I kept my problems to myself for so long. Why it took me losing it in line at the grocery store when I got my prosthesis stuck in the side of the cart. I yanked and pulled and finally unstrapped the damn thing from my arm. That's when it came loose. So I chucked it across the aisle where it knocked down an entire pyramid display of Triscuit boxes."

Sierra giggled. Then her hand flew to cover her mouth. What sort of horrible person was she to laugh at a story about a missing hand? And then she heard Norah laughing softly next to her, and knew it was okay. "Sounds like a rough day."

"Rougher than the waves around Cape Horn in winter. And that's saying a lot. Talk about a pukefest. Anyway." Norah grimaced, and then patted Sierra's thigh. "Holding your frustration inside is no good. Talk to somebody. Mollie—who thinks you're sweeter than a strawberry daiquiri. That good-looking hunk of a boyfriend you've got. Or, if it's easier to unburden to a person who barely knows you, talk to me."

Sierra had gone it alone her whole life. Literally. Until Flynn. Until he'd shown her that leaning on someone didn't make you weaker. It made you twice as strong.

Everything had gone wrong this morning. She'd tripped turning sideways to get out of the tiny shower. Looked everywhere for her red tee shirt before finding it in the laundry hamper. Only found her keys by stepping on them in her bare feet. Ever since the night before, when she'd decided to proclaim the orchid painting finished and send it to Miriam Newberry, her mind had been doing somersaults. Clearly, *making* the decision wasn't the same as being *okay* with the decision.

She'd been brave enough to share with the girls at dinner on Thursday. Sure, it'd led to one heck of a panic attack. Sierra just chalked that up to growing pains. Two steps forward, one step back. As long as the end result was forward motion, she had to keep pushing herself.

Why *not* talk to Norah? Sierra had never had a real mother/aunt/grandmother figure in her life. No mentor to turn to for the wisdom that came with extra years of living.

Now seemed like a good time to start.

"I've been keeping a secret for a while. Out of guilt, but mostly out of fear." Sierra's hand slid around to the back pocket of her denim shorts. To the envelope with her apology to Miriam Newberry. The one she hadn't decided whether or not to include with the painting.

"That must be hard on you."

"It is." Funny how being on the run, scrabbling for every dollar, worrying about having enough to eat—none of that had been half as difficult as struggling with the fear/guilt combo that kept her awake so many nights.

Amazing how Norah had zoned right in on that. Guess there really was something to being older and wiser. Not that she'd say that out loud. Norah kept her brown hair dark with monthly trips to the Beach Hair Don't Care salon and definitely looked more like Mollie's aunt than her grandmother. Well-traveled and wiser? Was that a safe way to put it, with Norah's trips all over the globe in the Navy?

"There are lots of reasons to keep secrets. Some good, some bad. Some cowardly, some heartbreakingly brave. You want to know my secret du jour?"

"Um, yes. Of course."

"I'm sad that Mollie's in love with Rafe." Norah dropped her hand into her lap and sucked in a long, deep breath. "Sad that it means she'll move out soon. That she won't be around as much to help with Jesse. Sad that after all the years she spent away learning to be a doctor, that I don't get her back, under my wing, as much as I'd hoped. I want her to be happy. To be strong and independent and with a man she adores. I just also want her five steps down the hall."

Completely understandable. Sierra stared at the gray shingled roof of a building, to avoid rolling her eyes at Norah and her winner for *most obvious reveal ever.* "I'm not sure that's really a secret. You raised Mollie. Of course you want to spend time with her."

"But I can't admit it. I can't let out so much as a peep of wistfulness. You know why? Mollie would hunker down and stay at my house longer. Out of pity. Respect. Love. All of the above."

Norah's obvious adoration of the woman she'd raised gave Sierra a lump in her throat. It was the usual unresolved longing for her own lack of a mother figure, which she didn't let herself notice much . . . *anymore.* On the plus side, Sierra got the feeling that Mollie and her friends could turn into sisters of the heart for her.

She put an arm around the older woman and squeezed her shoulders. "That just means Mollie loves you enough to want to fix whatever's making you sad."

"Exactly. Which would be a huge mistake." Norah shook her head, lips scrunched together into a tight line. "If I told her, she'd adjust her life to make me feel better. So revealing my secret would be pretty darned selfish. It would make *me* feel better. But it would make Mollie feel a hundred times worse." Norah tapped the tip of her prosthesis against the red slat of the bench between them. "Will revealing this secret make someone else feel better? Or just you?"

Why, that wily woman. She'd circled back from what Sierra thought was a totally innocuous comparison to hit the nail right on the head. Without even asking for the details. Without passing any judgment of her own.

Norah was a freaking *genius* at this motherly advice thing.

Sierra stood. Paced a half circle around the trash can planter, and back. Then all the way around the bench. Cars whizzed by, but they weren't moving nearly as fast as her thoughts. The note to Miriam in her back pocket didn't reveal Sierra's involvement. She wasn't that careless in her quest to relieve a tiny portion of her guilt. It simply said, *I'm sorry for the pain you suffered. Hopefully these orchids will give you some measure of peace.*

Or she could send just the painting. No note. Simply a beautiful gift that wouldn't set off any alarm bells, given Miriam's well-publicized love of the flower and all the shows she entered.

The note could be a trigger. Maybe Miriam had just gotten to the point where she didn't jump at noises. Didn't relive that fall down the stairs in her nightmares anymore. Would this note bring it all rushing back?

It could.

Then Sierra would be responsible for causing a whole new level of pain. Just to ease her own conscience infinitesimally.

Talk about selfish.

She bent her arm, pulled out the envelope, and ripped it in half before walking over to the real trash can at the door to the post office. With a little spring in her step, she returned to Norah. "Can I buy you a cup of coffee?

After I mail my package? I think you just saved me from doing something stupid and quite possibly hurtful."

Norah laughed as she stood. "I run a coffeeshop. You don't have to spend your hard-earned money caffein-ating me. But I'd love to take you back to Coffee & 3 Leaves and linger over a blueberry latte with you. That's our specialty today."

"I'd like that." If Sierra couldn't pay for her coffee, she could at least give the gift of honesty. "I don't have any family. I'm not used to having anyone to ask for advice," she admitted.

Walking back into the post office, Norah said, "You came to the right place. Bandon's one big, weird family. Once we suck you in, there's no getting out."

It sounded like heaven.

"Truly, thank you, Norah. You made this easy for me." Sierra pulled her into a long hug.

"Think you could give my grandson a testimonial to that effect? Getting Jesse to open up and talk to me isn't going so well. On the bright side, he ignores Mollie's opinions and mine equally."

"He doesn't know what he's missing out on," Sierra said fiercely. A thought popped into her head. A po-tentially stellar way to pay back Norah for the advice. "Mollie mentioned that Jesse's working at Wick's Garage, but he must have some spare time, since it's summer vacation. Do you think he'd be willing to help out with the float for the Cranberry Festival? Another set of hands wrangling all those kids would be appreciated. I guarantee I'll slide in a mention of how smart you are at least once a week."

"For that, I'll give you a blueberry latte *and* a scone."

The clerk hefted the box back onto the counter as Sierra stepped up. "You ready to move forward with this?"

With a grin, Sierra said firmly, "You bet."

She could hardly wait to tell Flynn.

FLYNN SPOTTED DELANEY crossing the jam-packed Starbucks lot in Bunker Hill. He'd seen her in boring, *please don't notice me* suits for the Marshals Service, all sexed up for pretend dates with Bandon's sheriff, but today's look felt like the first time he was seeing the real Delaney Evans.

Her long blond hair was in a messy ponytail. A pale pink tank top tucked into jeans shorts, and she wore hiking boots. Not to mention what appeared to be a fully loaded backpack, from the way it drooped off her shoulders.

Huh. He'd never really thought about their marshal as a person. Only as a necessary annoyance—and the person Kellan annoyed more than life itself. Which was often entertaining, even when Flynn had been eight hundred miles from able—or willing—to crack a smile.

Leaning across the cabin of his new-to-him used truck, he popped the door for her. Delaney handed over two tall paper cups. Unzipped the top of her backpack, stowed it in the foot well, and sat down.

"Hey, thanks." Flynn popped the lid to note that she'd added milk. Impressive that she remembered that small detail about him. Was it from memorizing his file or just being observant? "You didn't have to buy me a coffee."

She cocked her head to the side, giving him a look like he'd just told her the sun was green. "I did, actually. That's how this whole undercover thing works. If I meet someone at a coffeeshop and want to go unnoticed, I buy a couple of coffees."

"Oh. Right." Here he'd thought Delaney was just being nice. Guess that was a side effect of living in Bandon. That whole small-town, help-your-neighbor vibe was becoming second nature to him.

Well, not *second* nature. Maybe fifth nature, if there was such a thing. He wasn't volunteering to go out fishing at dawn with Rafe and the colonel in a giant kumbaya sunrise moment. Didn't want to bother running against the Chamber of Commerce president to unseat the giant, annoying douchebag.

But Flynn *had* refused to pocket the donations his self-defense class offered him. Instead, he collected the cash to put toward buying supplies for it, like a strike shield and a body opponent bag. And now that he had a truck, he planned to offer to help Elena take the leftover flowers every Sunday from the big events at the resort over to the senior center to spruce it up. Sierra had mentioned that it took her friend a bunch of trips in her tiny Volkswagen.

Did that mean he'd finally turned the corner from *pretend* good guy to a real one?

Delaney removed her lid and took a big swig. "It amazes me how you mobsters stayed out of trouble for so long if you can't even follow the logic of a damn latte in my hands right now."

"You know I never pulled any of that illegal stuff. I didn't need to be sneaky to run a construction company." Flynn dialed back his knee-jerk temper. He'd sure as hell never skulked around with a tire iron threatening people. Unless you counted threatening McGinty's crew to file their god damned taxes.

"Ah, that's right. You're the mobster *poser* brother." Delaney made air quotes around the word *mobster*.

"There's nothing halfway about belonging to the Chicago mob. And what's with the bitchy insult?" Usually the marshal—unless being baited by Kellan—was nothing but professional. Blunt as a butter knife, but she'd never passed judgment or been mean to them about their past affiliation.

"Sorry. Honestly?" Another slurp, as if to buy time while debating what to say. Which was not the marshal's MO at all. "I'm kind of annoyed that you called me for help. Which is the right thing to do, and you deserve a ticker tape parade for following protocol, yada yada yada. But it's Saturday morning of Fourth of July weekend. I've got plans."

Her whole different look suddenly made a whole lot of sense. "A date? Or just a three-day binge at the shooting range?" he teased. "You got a gun in there?" Flynn surged to the side, grabbing for the zipper of her open pack. It gaped wider, giving him a glimpse of the shiny metal of a barrel, right on top. "Jesus Christ, you do."

"I'm a U.S. Marshal. I'm meeting with my protectee, who is at known risk from past associates. Of *course* I'm carrying."

"We're at risk? Did you hear something about McGinty?"

"No. This is protocol, nothing more. Didn't mean to freak you out." Delaney twisted to lean back against the window. She gave him an appraising look that raked him from head to toe. "You're usually the calm one. The one who doesn't seem to give a shit about anything."

"Well, now I do."

"Good. Can I hope it's the result of my frequent and pointed pep talks?"

"Nah."

"Hmm. The love of a good woman?" she joked on a laugh.

Love. That wasn't a joke at all. Not if he could be sure that Sierra loved him back. Which would be the next hurdle he'd tackle after securing Delaney's help. Because they couldn't get on with their life together until he got the elephant of her past off her back.

"Still, I saw you white-knuckle that cup." She pointed to the drops of coffee he'd made overflow the lid when he squeezed it in alarm. "Something's got you jumpy. Is that why we're here today?"

"That's part of it."

He'd volunteered to make the trip to tell Delaney about O'Connor. They'd tailed him for two full days without seeing any sign that he knew the Maguire brothers lived there, let alone that he was out to put a hit on them. Better yet, he looked to be traveling with a brother-in-law. Nobody from McGinty's crew. Kellan had typed it all up last night to be presented to Delaney.

People ran into old high school friends in airports, on vacation in other countries, all the time. It was a small world, and while their town was small, it *was* a tourist mecca. O'Connor's presence was a random co-incidence. A Facebook-worthy mention, if they'd been normal people, but not dangerous.

Still, giving Delaney the intel was important. In the past, Rafe had handled all the official business with the Marshals Service. He'd looked thrilled that his middle brother was picking up the slack today.

What Flynn hadn't mentioned to either of his brothers was *why* he'd volunteered. Because he wanted to ask their marshal a very personal favor.

"Color me intrigued." Delaney dug underneath the gun to come up with a small notebook and a pen. "Anything I can do to help you succeed in your placement, I will."

That was the very fine line Flynn needed to balance on. Because the favor, technically, wasn't for him. "You keep telling us that for our new lives to work, we need to find reasons to be happy."

"Yessssss." She drew the word out longer than the Cubs catcher took to signal the pitcher at the bottom of the ninth with the bases loaded. "Why do I think that my own words are about to bite me in the ass?"

"Did I really ruin your date?"

She looked at the sturdy runner's watch with three dials and a whole bunch of buttons on her wrist. "Right now, it's only postponed. We'll see how this conversation turns out before I decide."

Flynn had rehearsed his approach three different ways on the drive. But now, looking at her squinted blue eyes so full of suspicion? None of them were good enough to break through her multiple layers of adhesion to rules and policy and every damned quintuple-checked loose end.

He had to use the big guns. He had to shoot from the heart.

"I need your help. Me, personally. Nothing to do with the case. Nothing to do with my brothers. I'm asking because this matters to me. Because this *person* matters to me." Asking Delaney for help fixing Sierra's situation had been a hard decision to make. Especially without getting Sierra's approval first. But this whole damn thing was a chicken and the egg. Did he explain first *why* he had an in with the Marshals Service? Or did he line up the cooperation of said marshal first?

"Oh, Flynn." Her voice softened to the consistency of a flannel sheet, straight out of the dryer. "You went and fell in love, didn't you?"

"Yeah. And I've never felt so helpless in my entire life."

Delaney laughed. Clapped her hand over her mouth as soon as it escaped, and then shook her head. "Wow. I mean, for a man restarting his life for the fifth time in Witness Protection gearing up to go back and testify against the mob . . . that's saying something."

Way to state the obvious. Flynn gripped the steering wheel and stared across the busy parking lot. Because she could have her laugh. Hell, she could ask him to boogie all around the lot with his underwear on his head and he'd do it. *As long as she came through for Sierra.*

"I'll do anything for this favor." Flynn slid his gaze sideways. "It's not one-sided. It'll end up being a favor to you, too."

"Aside from keeping your idiot younger brother in line, there's really nothing you could do to help me, Flynn. And those of us on the government dime tend not to bargain with semi-illicit felon-types."

Hell, did she think he was trying to bribe her? "I get it. Don't worry. This has nothing to do with the mob, or our case. But I do have information that, if you move on it, could make you come off as a rock star of a marshal."

"Withholding evidence is a crime." The words snapped out.

"I'm not withholding. And it's not my evidence to share. This is all hearsay. You have to do a *little* bit of the work yourself."

"Fine." Delaney waved a hand dismissively in the air

above the gear shift. "But let's stop talking in what-ifs and get right to this amazing font of info you're going to drop on me like a surprise Beyoncé album."

"I need a guarantee there won't be prosecution for this hypothetical person I'm about to discuss."

She blew a raspberry. "I'm not some naive rookie, falling all over myself at your earnest pleas. I can't promise anything until I hear the details, let alone guarantee an ADA would fall in line."

Damn. Had it been this difficult for Rafe when he'd struck the original deal to bring down McGinty's crew?

Flynn grabbed her forearm. Stared into those unblinking, icy blue eyes. "Give me your word, Delaney. That's good enough for me, seeing as how it's kept us Maguires alive this long. I promise you'll be helping someone who needs it."

Toying with the ends of her ponytail, Delaney asked quietly, "Does this person deserve to be prosecuted?"

"No. I swear on my mother's grave. She's an innocent. Just got accidentally pulled into something nasty. If anything, she wants to help you catch the bad guys. She just doesn't know it's possible."

A heavy bass beat coming from a motorcycle on their right rattled the windows. Flynn watched Delaney turn, almost absently, and check out the noise. He'd bet that she could give a full description of the bike, its driver, and the passenger from that three-second perusal.

She rapped the backs of her knuckles against the glass twice. "Okay."

Flynn let out the tail end of a breath he didn't know he'd been holding. This could really happen. He could save Sierra, banish the fear that kept her tossing and turning at night. No matter what did or didn't happen to him at the trial, *her* life would be good. Safe. Everything he'd gone through since entering Witness Protection was worth it if it all led up to a U.S. Marshal guaranteeing to help Sierra.

Feeling lighter already, he picked up his coffee and slugged back half of it. "How would you like to bust a counterfeit art ring wide open?"

"Well. What do you know?" A slow, sly grin spread across her face. "Kellan should take lessons from you, Flynn, because it turns out that you know just which one of my buttons to push."

Chapter Twenty

GROWING UP ALONE, in the often bleak Midwest, Sierra didn't have too many days that she counted as over-the-top fantastic. There were plenty of good days. Some even great. But few, if any in her life, that she'd deem worthy of being immortalized in a scene in a movie.

Until today.

This date today was *perfect*. And she had a sneaking suspicion that this feeling of perfection would repeat itself the more days she spent with Flynn.

She tipped her head back to enjoy the warmth of the bright sun on her cheeks. Sierra didn't care if her nose burned. Heck, she'd relish the peeling as a souvenir of this moment. The one with a salt-tinged breeze whipping through her hair. The one with other couples, also holding hands, walking toward them on the coastal path. The moment where she got to spend the entire day with the man she *trusted* with her whole heart.

Those suckers who bought lottery tickets? Even if they won, they wouldn't come close to the joy bursting out of Sierra's heart today.

"I love that you have your own truck now."

Flynn gave her a quizzical, sideways look as they tromped along the asphalt. "We're not in it now. And when you got out, you said your legs were stiff from sitting for the two-hour drive."

"I know. They *were* stiff, especially after that crazy shift last night." The Gorse always cranked up to standing room only on Saturday night. A holiday weekend with perfect weather meant Sierra's legs felt as if she'd walked the entire length and width of Oregon last night. All while loaded down with trays of beer and burgers and then *more* beers. "But that doesn't trump how thrilled I am that we *got* to make a two-hour drive north. That we get to have this fun day without any worry about rushing back so your brothers won't be stranded."

"Pretty sure you worried about them more than I did the past few weeks. The world wouldn't have ended if they had to walk to work one day."

Men. They always pretended not to care. Why did they think that made them cool? Especially when it was so easy to see right through it. To see Flynn start checking his watch, even though he didn't say anything, when it got close to the time to pick Kellan up from the cranberry plant. Or how he'd take a cold shower instead of waiting for the water to heat up again so that he could get the car back in time for Rafe to go to work.

"There you go again. Playing tough. But I know that inside you're just a big ball of Marshmallow Fluff. Especially when it comes to the two of them."

"I hate marshmallows. They're like dipping a Pixy Stix in glue. Can my insides be something else?" Flynn pointed to the towering spruces that fenced in the path. "How about the clump of moss? It looks soft."

The way he danced away from admitting how important they were to him? *Adorable.* So she'd play along. "Sure. You've got a heart of moss when it comes to Rafe and Kellan."

"And you. Don't forget you." The smile Flynn flashed at her was so tender and adoring that Sierra stopped walking. The force of that smile squeezed her heart in a new and breathtaking way.

Oh, yes. She definitely loved this man. And felt pretty darned sure that he'd admit he felt the same way on their date today.

Life just didn't get any better than this.

Flynn pulled her over to the railing where the walkway crossed a deep chasm in the black volcanic rocks below. Cars whizzed by behind then. Nevertheless, the roiling water was loud enough to be heard churning and thrashing. He pointed at a jagged assortment of those black rocks lining the shore. Just beyond was a. . . . well, Sierra wasn't sure *what* it was. A circle of black rocks had water flooding over the edge with every surge of tide and wave.

But . . . it was a *complete* circle. The water crested over the rock and dropped down. Straight down. Like there was a deep well, or a drain right at the start of the ocean. It was beyond disconcerting. It was beyond beautiful. It seemed otherworldly, a natural feature that would lie outside the red spot of Jupiter.

"What is that?" Sierra breathed in awe.

"Thor's Well."

Okay. She could picture its falls poised underneath the rainbow bridge of Asgard, too.

"That's why I got you up so early," he said with an apologetic caress of her shoulder. "We needed to be here at high tide to see it best."

"It's . . . magnificent."

"See how it looks like the water endlessly drains into it? Like it never fills up?" Flynn moved behind Sierra, locking his arms around her waist. "That's how I felt. Before we got together. I was empty, no matter what the world threw at me."

Sierra looked back at the water streaming down the rocks, on endless repeat. "I'm so sorry, Flynn. That must've been miserable."

"I was miserable. Too miserable to do anything about it. Or too stubborn. Didn't see the point in trying. Until you came along."

"I'm nothing special."

"Sierra. You are *completely* special. You're stronger than those rocks out there. Not giving up no matter how battered life makes you. Sweeter than anyone I've ever met. Most of all, you make *me* feel special."

"*That*, I'll cop to."

Flynn pointed at the Well. "They think it's a collapsed sea cave. The water only drops down about twenty feet. The tide sends it surging back up, through holes in the cave walls, as waves come over the top of the rocks. See, instead of draining to nowhere? The water's actually filling up that hole, over and over and over again."

"You're saying that you *thought* you were an empty cave. Except that you're actually all filled up and just sexy and powerful as all get-out?"

His low chuckle rumbled heat against her ear. "Not the words I would've chosen. But yeah. I didn't know exactly how to explain to you what I went through. Figured that showing you might get the point across better. Getting called sexy and powerful is just a bonus. Go ahead and call me that anytime."

Feeling reckless—and more than a little sexy and powerful herself—Sierra said, "How about I say it to you when we're both naked?"

"That'll work, too."

She twisted in his embrace to look up at those knife-sharp cheekbones that pointed down to the full lips she found so darn kissable. "All kidding aside, you sound like you were in a very bad place. But you've never told me what put you there?"

"That's a story for later." Flynn slid his hands along

her neck as he leaned his forehead against hers. "For now, know that you're the ocean to me. You're what keeps filling me up. I can't thank you enough. Hopefully, today's a start."

"You've got to stop. Every time you thank me, I'm compelled to come right back and thank *you*. For helping me work past my fear to embrace my life here. For showing me how strong you see me, which gives me the courage to feel it, too."

Flynn stopped her from saying anything more by taking her lips. Right there, in the bright sunlight with a solid row of other sightseers crowded elbow to elbow with them along the railing. He kissed her long and hard and just this side of way too much tongue for a state park.

"That'll be our punishment. The next one of us to thank the other will get kissed. Relentlessly."

She giggled and tried to pull him back into another kiss. "Is this reverse psychology? Because I kind of can't think of anything better."

"Wait. Hopefully this will be better. I brought you a present." He shrugged his backpack off. Flynn jutted his chin to indicate they should cross the highway as he dug in it. "Let's get away from this crowd so you can open it."

"Flynn, this whole day is already a present."

"That sounded suspiciously like you were circling toward a thank you. Are you looking to be kissed again?"

"Most definitely."

Grabbing her hand as he slung the pack back up,

Flynn jogged the rest of the way. Kept jogging, in fact, as he stepped off the marked trail and just pushed through the waist-high ferns and bushes. They were immediately swallowed up by the thick forest.

"Where are we going?"

"Someplace more private."

That would sound delightful, if they weren't in the middle of a national forest they both knew less than nothing about. "Let me rephrase that question. Do you actually know where we're going?"

"Nah. But this is a protected scenic area. I'm sure it's safe. We're just heading away from all the people."

"What do you have in mind once it's just us and the spruce trees?"

"Depends on how well my present goes over."

Laughing, Sierra took the lead, jumping over fallen logs thick with moss. A zigzag pattern removed them quickly from any sounds or sights of the trails. Sun broke through the canopy above, but only in indiscriminate spears of golden haze. Layer upon layer of green surrounded them.

Flynn pressed her against the springy, mossy bark of a tree. Spiky orange blossoms ringed the base of it. "This is good." He held up a small box, tied with a blue ribbon. "Open it."

She didn't need to be asked twice. Greedily, Sierra snatched the box away, curiosity burning through her. And yet she took her time removing the ribbon, rolling it up, and stuffing it into the pocket of her shorts. Because no matter what was *inside* the box, she was touched by the gesture alone, of Flynn going to the trouble to search out a sparkly blue ribbon. For her. That ribbon would be saved for the rest of her life.

Sierra popped the lid. Inside was a journal covered in teal leather stamped in gold with the words *DREAM BELIEVE DO REPEAT*. She stroked her index finger over the embossing of each word.

"You told me that you pressed flowers as souvenirs of good memories. I was thinking you could start doing that for memories of the two of us." He reached down to pull off a stem with multiple orange flowers spiking from it. "Here's one to start. Not exactly fireworks for the Fourth, but it's as bright as a sparkler, that's for sure."

It was unutterably sweet. Touching. Sierra knew she should wait. Both to protect her heart and to not put Flynn on the spot. But this gift . . . it filled her heart so darned much that she couldn't hold it in any longer.

Looking up at him, Sierra said swiftly, "I love you."

Flynn jolted. Visibly. Like a live wire got shoved into his chest and head to toe, he stiffened. Then he took a step backward.

Uh-oh.

She'd blown it. Freaked him out. Pressured him too soon.

They'd known each other, been friends for two months, but only dated for one. Sierra felt closer to Flynn in four weeks than she had to Rick after more than three times that. But they were *her* feelings. Ones that Flynn wasn't required to reciprocate.

At least, that was the *first* wave of thoughts that crashed through her brain. As he took a second step backward, a whole new flurry of thoughts barraged Sierra. They were in a relationship. Relationships were built on honesty, on trust. At least this one was. So she shouldn't *have* to keep her feelings a secret. Or be worried about sharing them.

Flynn could do whatever he wanted with her statement. The only way to be true to herself as well as their deepening . . . entanglement . . . was to be open. No different than telling him if she had a stomachache, or worried about paying her rent. So he'd darn well better stand there and take it like a man.

Sheesh. Sierra hadn't realized that declaring her love would bring out her feistiness.

She snatched the flower out of his hand. Opened the cover, carefully teased each petal flat, and then slammed the journal shut.

The sound must've jolted Flynn out of his coma of panic. He sort of jerked once more, then he set his shoulders. Great. Guess they were both bracing for a fight.

"I was going to give you more time," he murmured softly. His eyes were a little unfocused. Stunned, even. "Get you to come around to seeing that your heart would be safe with me. I should've remembered that you're by far the braver of the two of us."

Her heart leapt into overdrive, like she'd just run a

mile around the track. "What are you trying to say?" Because what Sierra *thought* Flynn was circling around to seemed too good to be true.

"That I love you, too. I didn't want to be selfish. Didn't want to tell you how much I need you before you were ready to hear it."

Wow. Now her heart was pretty much thumping as fast as a hummingbird's wings. "I'm ready. In fact, I think I'd like you to say it again."

Flynn framed her face in his hands. One thumb traced the curve of her lips as her smile grew. "I love you, Sierra Williams."

"Just Sierra," she whispered. "The other name isn't really mine."

"It's a good stopgap. Until, maybe, you think about trying on a new one. Something from the middle of the alphabet."

Omigosh. Could he really . . . did he really mean . . . Sierra squeezed her eyes shut. "Don't tease me."

"I'm not." He planted the softest, lightest kisses in the world at the outer corners of her eyes, his cheeks brushing her lashes. "I'm talking through what's in my heart. No strings, no ticking clock. Just a guy telling the prettiest, sweetest woman in the world how he feels. And how he hopes their future might shape up."

This man. This wonderful man was blowing her mind. Exploding her heart into little confetti-like shards of pure joy. It was everything she'd always wanted, yet never dreamed of achieving.

Almost.

Her eyes popped open. Because if they were really even skating close to talking about this, Sierra had to lay something on the table.

"I've got a nonnegotiable plan for my future."

One of Flynn's eyebrows shot up. But he looked amused, not challenged. He dropped his arms and made a beckoning wave of his hand. "Lay it on me."

"I want to foster children. I want to give a home to kids who need one. I want to keep as many children from feeling alone as I possibly can."

"You mean as *we* possibly can."

The sharp bite of bark against her back was the only thing convincing Sierra that this wasn't a dream. "Don't promise me the moon, Flynn, if you don't have one heck of a long tow rope to pull it down here and set it in front of me."

"My parents were both gone before I learned to drive. I know that feeling of loneliness, at least in part." He spread his arms wide, palms up. "I'm completely on board with fostering."

"No rearranging our lives while we're still getting used to intertwining them. I just wanted to lay it out there. As part of my future." Sierra looked down at her journal. A place where she could start making lists of dreams that Flynn would help her to make come true.

He eased the book from her tight grasp and set it on the ground. "How about we cement this unofficial officialness of our future by celebrating the present?"

"What does that mean?"

Flynn braced his arms on the tree trunk, caging her in. Which was exactly where she wanted to be. "It means I want you."

"Oh. Well, I want you, too."

"See? We're great together. On the same page for all the important stuff." Flynn captured her mouth. His tongue immediately probed, sweeping and sucking and tangling with hers. "This is going to have to be fast. We don't want to push our luck too much with not being discovered by other hikers."

"Fast is good. If it's with you. However we do it is always fantastic."

Flynn pulled a foil packet from a cargo pocket and unzipped his shorts. Rolled on a condom. "I feel like there should be romance to go with saying *I love you* for the first time. You deserve candles and flowers."

"You gave me a flower," Sierra reminded him, nudging the journal with the toe of her sneaker. "This entire date is the most romantic thing that's ever happened to me." She pushed her shorts to her ankles and stepped out of them. Pushed her man to the ground, then straddled him. "The only thing I deserve is a toe-curling orgasm."

"You've got to start giving yourself more credit, sweetness. I say you deserve two."

His hands settled on her waist before suddenly lifting her like she weighed no more than a feather. Flynn settled her right on top of his face. His mouth, to be precise. And precision is exactly what she got as his tongue gave two long licks before strumming across her clitoris.

Sierra fell forward onto her hands. Flynn was making the earth spin. Shudder. Or maybe that was just her. She only knew that her knees barely held her up as pleasure spiraled through her with intense speed. Her nails scrabbled past the leaves into the dirt. Then, when Flynn scraped his teeth along the path of his tongue, she screamed as she came. It had taken no time at all, but the results were as mind-blowingly spectacular as ever.

Again, Flynn's strength surprised her when he moved her back down his body. With aftershocks still pulsing through her, Flynn entered in one fast thrust. And he just kept going.

He set a relentless pace, not giving her time to catch her breath or help or even rearrange her legs. Flynn just kept his hands on her hips and controlled her movement for her, lifting and turning Sierra a little as he pounded that long, thick, amazing cock into her.

"Fall forward," he urged.

She put her hands on the ground just above his shoulders. Flynn surged up, capturing her left breast in his mouth. A yank of his teeth pushed her top and bra below it. Once her nipple was wet, he blew cool air across it. Goose bumps—what felt like both inside and outside—raced along her entire body.

"That's cheating," she panted. "It doesn't count as two orgasms if you just prolong and build upon the first one."

"How about we argue semantics after you scream my name?"

So cocky. Sure, he was a certifiable sex god, but Sierra still had some moves of her own. "How about we do it after you scream *mine*?" She sat back up to skim both of her palms in light circles over his nipples.

First he groaned, a deep and throaty sound that seemed eminently fitting for the middle of the forest. Then Flynn tilted her hips, readjusting so that his penis hit a spot that spiraled her right back toward orgasm. He picked up the pace, to where she couldn't tell where one stroke stopped and the next started. It was just a sensory overload of being filled and exploding at the same time.

"Let's do it together, Sierra. 'Cause I can't hold out any—"

Simultaneously, he groaned again, longer and louder, and she let out a high-pitched scream before falling onto his chest. It heaved up and down as Flynn gulped for air.

It took a few minutes before the sounds of birds and rustling ferns could finally be heard over their labored breathing. The whole thing had lasted less than five minutes, but Sierra felt as boneless and satisfied as if it had taken an hour. Whatever fireworks display Bandon ended up shooting up off the coast wouldn't come close to the brightness and heat of what they'd just shared.

Knowing it was the smart thing to do—since getting arrested for public indecency was not on her to-do list for the weekend—Sierra rolled off to tug her shorts back on.

"Is all . . . that . . . going to happen every time we say *I love you*?"

Flynn laughed. A long, rolling laugh that gave her a glimpse of what he must've looked like ten years ago. Completely open and happy and so young and carefree. "God, I hope so."

"Then we'd better not risk saying it until we get back to the car."

"There's no rush. I've got snacks to last us through a hike, since we're here." Flynn shoved her journal back into his pack.

Sierra carefully looped the ribbon around her fingers before stuffing it into her pocket. Then she grabbed his hand and swung it playfully as they walked down the path, underneath the towering spruces. "You really did plan the perfect day."

"Don't say that. Perfection's dangerous. It implies it can't ever be topped. Or it's just looking for trouble from that bitch Karma. You know, Turkish rug makers weave an imperfection into every rug, so as not to offend Allah."

Fat chance. "I don't think we have to worry about one hundred percent perfection being achieved. I've got an attempted murderer who may or may not be searching for me for the rest of my life. I'll never stop worrying."

Flynn's steps slowed. "What if . . . that wasn't the case?"

"I know, I should meditate or something to remind

myself that it does no good to worry about what's outside of my control. But meditation's boring. I'm not desperate enough to go for it, I guess. Or finding peace in Norah's special brownies."

"No." Flynn tugged her hand to stop them next to a tiny stream. He rolled his lips together, and then took a deep breath. "I mean, what if dealing with Rick *was* in your control?"

And here she'd thought forest floor sex was the biggest surprise of the day.

Chapter Twenty-one

FLYNN HAD BEEN nervous only a handful of times in his life. At his mom's funeral, worried that he'd cry and his classmates would never let him live it down. At the initiation ceremony for McGinty's crew. Rafe had sworn it wasn't like a street gang—he wouldn't be required to shoot anyone. But when Danny McGinty came toward him holding a big-ass dagger with an Irish cross on the hilt, he'd worried.

And, of course, the day he sat in a large conference room with a state-provided lawyer, two FBI agents, three U.S. Marshals, two Secret Service, and a video camera recording his testimony.

Those times had all sucked.

This moment, right now, staring into the confused eyes of the woman he loved? It was a hundred times more nerve-racking.

"Do you trust me, Sierra?" Man, wasn't that question just a fucking double-edged sword? Because he wanted her to say yes. Needed her to say yes. All the while knowing he was about to shatter that trust like a car window taking a hit from a Louisville Slugger.

But it was the only way. He'd thought about it. Had the long-ass talk with Delaney. Talked—well, more in circles than in specifics—to his brothers and gotten what Flynn took as a thumbs-up. Fixing Sierra's problem was the only way he saw clear to the future.

Even if her future didn't have him in it after today.

"Of course I trust you. It's funny how sure I was that I'd take years to trust anyone again. How I thought Rick had messed me up so badly that I'd be second-guessing every man I got close to, looking for their secret agenda. Not with you, though." She reached up to stroke his cheek, the softness of her palm making him close his eyes to savor the moment. "You make me feel so safe, Flynn, so, gosh, *treasured*."

"I love you, Sierra. There's nothing I want more than to keep you happy and safe." He captured her palm and placed a kiss in the center of it. "Which is why we're having this conversation. Because I need you to trust me when I say that I can get you out of this mess. For good."

Laughing, she asked, "Is this when you tell me you've got an uncle who's a private investigator? One who'll track Rick down and put the fear of God into him?"

"No. No uncle. No family at all except for Rafe and Kellan. That's the God's honest truth."

"For goodness sake, Flynn, I was just teasing." Her brows knitted together in concern. "Why are you so serious all of a sudden?"

"Because I need you to believe me. Believe every word that's about to come out of my mouth."

"Always."

Shit. He could barely take the undiluted love and unqualified trust shining like diamonds in her blue eyes. In case it was his last chance, Flynn kissed her. Hard, at first, with all the intensity of the passion he felt for her coming through, before he gentled his lips and tongue to give Sierra the tenderness fucking *aching* in his heart.

"I can help you deal with Rick. I have a connection to a U.S. Marshal. One who'd love nothing better than to get your testimony to shut down that counterfeit ring. To put him away in jail for attempted murder, put Wayne away, and make sure they'd never find you."

Her hand fisted at her heart. "I . . . I don't want to go to jail."

"No, sweetness, you wouldn't. I promise you. I have her word."

"Whose?"

"The marshal."

A little of that absolute trust leached out of her gaze. Disbelief—the first of what he figured might be a metric shit-ton by the time he got done—seeped in to replace it. "Why would a marshal make you a promise like that for a person she's never met and has no reason to trust?"

"Because she believed me when I vouched for your

innocence." *Here we go*, he thought. "Because she's my handler."

"What does that mean?"

"She's the marshal assigned to protect me. All three of us, actually." Damn it, he was easing into it like a ninety-year-old inching into a bathtub. Flynn stalked in a small circle. Shook out his hands like he used to before each fight to loosen up and get ready. "I'm in WITSEC. The United States Federal Witness Security Program."

"Oh, no. You witnessed a crime? You were a victim of a crime? Or Rafe, or Kellan was? Are you safe?"

Her obvious concern for his well-being, first and foremost, just showed how big a heart Sierra had. Flynn hoped he didn't break it with what came next.

"We're safe. The U.S. government has invested considerable time, money, and resources to make damn sure of that." Flynn even believed that a lot of the time.

Well, no, he'd give credit where it was due. He believed they'd done their due diligence. Made sure to stick the Maguires in a town where the Irish mob would *never* think to look for them. Made certain their fake IDs, cover stories, and pretty damn intricate online trails all rang true.

What he didn't believe in was people.

People could be bought. Bribed, blackmailed, threatened, promised . . . you name it, Danny McGinty found a way to twist people to do what he wanted. And Flynn had no doubt that, even with his organization all but dissolved, his reputation shattered, his health disintegrating and his family under constant surveillance, that Danny McGinty wanted his revenge on the men who'd toppled his empire.

Sierra gestured at his torso. "I don't . . . you have scars on your body, but nothing that looks like you survived an attack. Why are they protecting you?"

"Because Rafe and I are helping them to bring down the Irish mob in Chicago."

She gaped at him. "You're from Chicago?"

Funny how she'd zeroed in on that. Guess the little stuff was easier to tackle first. "Yeah. The Cubs, deep-dish pizza, and a deep-seated belief that anyone who gets scared to drive in anything less than full-out named blizzard is a pansy-ass."

Sierra shook her head, the tail of her brown hair slapping at her cheeks. "Why . . . how . . . are you bringing down the mob?"

"Because we used to be in it."

Aaaaand there it was. Sierra physically recoiled. No, not just recoiled. She skittered back several steps like a frightened forest creature.

Not that Flynn blamed her in the least.

"You're a bad guy?"

"No." Damn it, he'd never been altogether good, but he wasn't bad, either. "Sierra, I promise you're safe with me. Hear me out. Please. Don't run, don't cut me off, don't do anything until I tell you the whole story."

She pulled her phone out of her pocket. Punched in two numbers. "I've started to dial 911. You give me any reason, any weird eye twitch, and I'm calling the police."

Didn't she realize that just made him love her more? That strength and bravery that Sierra never gave herself credit for, but made her a freaking Atlas compared to some of the hardened criminals he knew? "Smart girl."

"No sweet-talking, either. Just the facts."

Flynn shoved his hands deep into his pockets. "Our father was in the mob. I didn't know it, but Rafe did. Dad sucked Rafe right into it when he was just a kid. And by kid, I mean he was seven when they started him running errands."

Eyes as big as the plates for the Nachos Supreme at the Gorse, Sierra breathed, "That's appalling."

"Our mom died, and then Dad not too long after. Danny McGinty, he ran the Chicago mob. He made sure that we were taken care of, that we didn't get split up and put into foster homes."

"What do you mean, 'taken care of'?"

"I mean he gave us money, doctored the paperwork, used his people on the inside, and Social Services never came around."

A long double blink went by before she spoke again. "So you and your brothers lived by yourselves?"

"Yeah. They made Rafe quit high school and run with the crew full-time. I got a full ride to college. The only catch was that I had to take the courses, do the major that McGinty picked. This wasn't out of compassion. And it sure as hell wasn't out of guilt for killing our parents. He was grooming me to run one of his businesses."

"Guilt for wait . . . what?"

Rage had him fisting his hands in his pockets. He'd only lived with this knowledge since Halloween, and it still burned like fresh acid in his throat. "Our mom was collateral damage in a mob shoot-out. That's the phrase that got used by the Feds. But McGinty himself killed Dad. Rafe discovered the evidence when he cased McGinty's office right before he went to the Marshals. It was a punch to the gut. This man who'd been a father figure to him, raised him to be his right hand in the organization, murdered our real father."

"And you didn't know? Didn't have any clue?" The hand brandishing her cell phone as a potential weapon dropped down to her hip.

Flynn hoped that small gesture meant she was less scared. Because he hated the thought that he was causing her even a few bad moments as he spilled his guts.

"I wasn't happy about being in the mob. I wasn't thrilled with having my life planned out by him. But I was fucking grateful every day that Danny took such good care of us after our parents died. Grateful beyond words that working for him made us able to be around to get Kellan through high school and all the way to law school. But no, we didn't have a clue."

Sierra held up a hand, like he'd hit her stopping point for absorbing info. Too bad Flynn still had a lot to share. "Kellan's a lawyer? Kellan, who works at the cranberry plant?"

"He's *almost* a lawyer. Can't bring anything from your original life into WITSEC, though, so he doesn't get to finish. He's trying to find a job that'll let him use his giant brain. We just haven't figured it out yet."

Sierra paced a tight circle. When she finally faced Flynn again, all the warmth had left her expression. Clearly the facts of his past life were settling in—and she didn't like them one damn bit. "So you were a mobster."

"Yes . . . and no. I swore the oath." Flynn patted his hip. "You've seen the tattoo. But I didn't do, ah, mobster things. McGinty paid for my degree so I could run his legit business. A construction company with books that could be safely audited. The one that supplied his whole crew with paychecks on the up-and-up so that they all looked like law-abiding, tax-paying citizens. My job in the mob was to *not* break the law."

"You ran a whole company? Aren't you a little young for that?" More disbelief. But Flynn appreciated that she challenged him.

With a shrug, he answered, "Yes and no. I worked the construction business every summer, high school and college. I knew it inside and out. Add to that my business degree, and let's just say I was a hell of a lot more qualified to run it than the last guy who did."

"But you didn't *want* to get a business degree?"

Ah, she was paying attention. Clueing in to the little

things he said as well as the big ones. "I wanted to do something in science. Chemistry. I started mixing chemicals, making them explode or change colors with my mom back in elementary school. But McGinty said no."

"Can you do it now?"

"Go back for another four-year degree, that'll probably take six while I also hold down a full-time job? No way. And McGinty laid down the law—do it his way or no degree. Then, once I had it, I wanted to keep going and get my MBA. Make myself more marketable. The day I went to ask him if he'd pay for grad school is the day Danny laid out the plan for me to come work for him full-time. And no, there wasn't a *thanks, but no thanks* box to check. Not if we wanted to keep Kellan completely clean."

"This man turned you into an indentured servant."

Flynn loved that she got it. Knew he wasn't blameless, though, and would cop to that, too. "He'd sucked me in slowly, with tickets to Bears games and gifts. McGinty was like a favorite uncle. Always there to bail us out of trouble. Always giving presents. And a whole bunch of friends who always hung out with him. It seemed awesome."

"Until?"

"Until I knew there was no way out. Until I learned what he did to come up with the cash he used to fund my education."

Her whole face crinkled in confusion. "You were a mobster . . . in name only?"

"More or less. Did some stuff when I was a teen-ager that bordered on sketchy, just to help Danny out, I thought. But once I graduated, he needed me to keep my hands completely clean. To be the legit and honest face of the construction company."

"If you didn't, you know . . ." Sierra punched the air, her face screwed into a grimace.

"Kneecap people?"

"If you just kept your head down and your nose clean, how did you get here?"

Like Flynn hadn't asked himself that every single day since Halloween. "McGinty had an operation that went badly. He decided he'd throw me to the wolves for cover. Let the cops pin the whole thing on me and he'd walk away with clean hands. The man had such a fucking God complex that he went to Rafe. Gave him the heads-up that he planned to make me take the fall. Thanked him in advance for 'his family's service to the organization.'"

"But you didn't go to jail?"

"No. Rafe made a deal with the Feds. Got them to put all three of us in Witness Protection. Rafe was the fixer, McGinty's right-hand man. He knew where the bodies were buried. Literally, in a couple of cases. Me, I knew about the second set of books. I had proof of the money laundering, the tax evasion—between the two of us, we knew enough to implode it."

Sierra gaped at him. Again. Then fury burned a hot flash in her eyes. "*Rafe* made a deal? He didn't come to you first and ask how you felt about it?"

The fact that she'd zeroed in on what had stung him the most when it happened just proved how perfect Sierra was for him. If only she'd stick around long enough for him to point it out.

"You caught that, huh? Yeah, it was a done deal before he dialed me in. I had a day's notice to secure evidence and tie up loose ends. Then we went into government sequestration. From there, we moved on to our new lives."

"So . . . who are you? *Really?* A mobster? Or a bartender?" This time the challenge in her voice was a little sharper.

Now probably wasn't the best time to mention the four other starter-lives they'd attempted to live before landing in Bandon. The ones that had fit worse than shoes four sizes too small. Sierra's question was a good one, though. It hit at the heart of what he was trying to get across to her.

Flynn shrugged. Looked down at the scuffed-up dirt. "I don't know."

"That's not good enough," she shot back.

Okay, okay. If there was ever a time to dig deep and connect with his innermost feelings, today was probably it. He owed Sierra that much.

"Being in the mob is a part of who I am. The guys in McGinty's crew—they're not that different than me. Okay, some are way worse. Violent scum that should spend the rest of their lives behind bars. But some were just making a living the only way they knew how. Same as I did to put Kellan through school."

Sierra jabbed a finger in the air between them, swirling with dust motes in the filtered sunlight. "But *you* didn't engage in criminal acts."

"Not really. And I was grateful for that." The words, the bitterness he'd hidden for so long choked out of him. "I did hate the mob. I hated that I didn't feel like I had any choice but to join. Hated that all my choices were taken away from me. Now the government's made *more* choices for me. And I'm pissed about it. Pissed my brothers are suffering for my sake. Pissed that I got dropped here. God, Sierra, I was mad at the world."

"Was?" she challenged.

"Until you. How you just enjoy what happens in a day. Then I started to realize that I liked my days, now, too. I liked that every shift is both the same and completely different. I liked the fun of figuring out new cocktails. I liked shooting the shit with Carlos. You woke me up. Made me see that it's okay to live this new life."

Color pinked up her cheeks. "Flynn, I can't take credit for something that huge."

"Tough." He stroked a hand down her arm, needing to touch her, needing to physically connect in gratitude if only for a second. "Your caring got under my skin. In all the best ways. Look, I faked who I was for years. I showed up to a job I didn't want. Made friends with guys who I knew I didn't respect on a certain level. I did what I was told. But that's over."

"What do you mean?"

"The man you've fallen in love with? That's the new

Flynn Maguire." He jabbed his fingers against his sternum. "New name, new life, new person inside. You're seeing the real me—as soon as I figure out who the hell that is."

Another long silence fell. Birds chirped overhead. Something small and brown raced under a fallen log. Sierra pressed her lips together. Anger, no, *disappointment* hardened every line of her face. And when she spoke, it was an indictment. "You've been lying to me."

Was she closing the door between them? With swift desperation, Flynn said, "Sweetness, I've been lying to everyone. WITSEC has strict rules. We aren't supposed to tell anyone who we really are. Ever."

Those big blue eyes got impossibly wide and round. Sierra's lips parted. "Are you going to be in trouble for telling me?"

Look at her caring shining through her obvious and justified temper. God, he didn't deserve a heart as big as hers. "Hopefully you won't email Danny McGinty telling him where he can come looking for his revenge. It'd be nice if you don't tell the U.S. Marshals that you know the truth about the Maguire brothers, too."

"Flynn. I would never put you or your brothers at risk."

"I can promise you I don't want trouble. I don't want to go back to any part of that life, or bring it here to Bandon."

"You're done with being a bad guy?" Doubt coated her words thicker than the frothy head of a Guinness.

Flynn might not be sure of a lot about his future—including if he'd even have one once he went back to Chicago to testify—but he was sure about that. "Yes. I swear. Relieved as hell about it being over . . . on top of feeling guilty."

"That's a lot to carry," she said, almost cautiously. Like she wasn't entirely sure of how to react or what to say next.

"I've been sitting with it for a while. It's time to get over it. Put all of it—including the feeling shitty parts—behind me. My brothers helped by not giving up on me. Time helped. This place, the people in it, helped. All of that opened a door. Falling for you pulled me through it."

"To what? What's your big plan?" Sierra's eyes narrowed to slits. "Who is Flynn Maguire?"

He caught her hand and brought it over his heart. "The man who loves you. That's the God's honest truth."

"Those are pretty words. Ones I'm not sure I should believe."

Desperation jacked up his heart rate. She was pulling away, literally and emotionally. "I hated lying to you. A good relationship can't be built on lies. But I would've kept lying to you forever, knowing that it would keep you safe."

"Looks like you just blew that." She yanked her hand back. Everything about her rigid stance told him not to try touching her again.

"No. Sierra, I told you all this so you'd trust me when I told you that I could fix your problem with Rick. My handler. Marshal Delaney Evans. I trust her with my life. Literally every day. She's, ah, gone to bat for us more than once. Let's just say that we weren't the most by-the-book protectees she'd ever been assigned."

A faint smile, the kind he wasn't sure he'd ever see aimed at him again, ghosted across Sierra's lips. "That's not hard to believe at all."

"If you tell Delaney what went down in Milwaukee, she'll bring down Wayne's counterfeit ring. And she'll keep you safe, keep your identity and whereabouts protected."

"I'm so mad at you." Then a single tear tracked down the center of her cheek.

"Aww, don't cry." Flynn tried to put his arms around her. Sierra shook her head and shuffled back a few steps, hugging herself.

"No. Don't . . . don't touch me."

"Sierra. I won't hurt you. I swear. That's not who I am."

"You've already hurt me. After everything I went through with Rick and Wayne, I promised myself I'd never so much as jaywalk again. I don't want to be with anyone on the wrong side of the law. I don't want to be with someone who'd file their taxes a day late. I *hate* that you pulled me back into a criminal association, even secondhand."

"I'm so sorry." He thumped his fist against his sternum. "I swear I'm not that man anymore. I'm not a criminal."

Her head jerked up as she flung the words at him. "Don't you see, Flynn? I don't know who you are. I only have your word to go on. And right now, your word's not worth very much, is it?"

"I'll spend months, years working to convince you how much I love you, if you'll let me."

"I'm not sure that's an option anymore." Hand across her mouth, Sierra's chest rose and fell a few times, and he could tell she'd stopped reacting and begun processing the ramifications of everything he'd blurted out. "The mob, Flynn. The omigosh *mob*. Dangerous, unlawful people who profit off of others. Just like Wayne. How on earth am I supposed to be okay with reconciling that man with the one standing in front of me?"

Shit. Shitshitshitshit. Seeing the pain he'd caused her made him want to howl. He'd fucked up. Again. Just like with Rafe and Kellan. It was his fault she was miserable.

It was breaking his heart.

When would he stop hurting the people he cared about the most?

"I get it. I do."

Another fast shake of her head. "But the fact that you'd put your own safety on the line to give me mine? That's huge. To be fair, that has to carry some weight, too. I'm so confused about how to feel. It's so much to take in. I can't . . . I feel sick."

"Trust, if nothing else, that I want you to be safe. To be happy. Do you believe that much?"

She backhanded a few more fat tears from beneath her eyes. "Yes."

"Then talk to Delaney. Not for me. For yourself. So that you can sleep at night. So the bad guy gets punished. So nobody else gets scammed."

Sierra licked her lips. "If I do, what about us?"

"That's up to you." If he had to give her up, give up her love to guarantee her safety, that's the way it'd be.

"I'm so very, very mad at you." She looked down. Then away. Flynn could almost hear a door slam between them.

"I know."

"I'd like to go home now. I think I'd like you not to text me. Or call me. Or talk to me outside work."

That was too fucking fast. Wouldn't she at least take the time to absorb it, try to see it from all sides?

Heart lodged up in his throat, Flynn growled, "You're breaking up with me?"

"No. You just did that." Her words grew louder, hurling at him like bullets. "By telling me I've been dating another man without knowing it." Sierra waved a hand up and down his body. "This nameless man with a shady past who lied to me. *That's* who just broke up with *me*. Cause and effect, Flynn. What you did brought us to this point. I only wanted to care for you. But I don't know that I can risk my heart now that I know you're really a criminal."

Flynn had thought nothing could hurt more than the time he powered through to finish a fight with a dislocated shoulder.

He'd been wrong.

Chapter Twenty-two

SIERRA TIED THE laces of her shoes with exact precision. She'd painted the white canvas sneakers with yellow polka dots because it looked perky. And because what was the good of having one and three-quarters art degrees if you couldn't use them to jazz up your clothes? But now, she reconsidered the flirty fashion. Because it didn't look . . . serious, no matter how tight and straight she yanked the bows.

In fact, her whole outfit looked . . . silly. If you could call tan capris and a yellow tank top an outfit. Which you probably couldn't.

Sierra sighed. Her clothes all came from Goodwill. Scoring this outfit had cost her less than four dollars. *That's* what made it work. But would the marshal take one look and dismiss her as frivolous? Naive? Untrustworthy?

What the heck was the dress code for confessing your stupidity to a government official?

The urge rose to text Flynn, to ask him what he'd worn that first day he sat in the marshal's office. But she couldn't. That would be selfish and unfair, seeing as how Sierra had been the one to ask him not to talk to her. In the moment, brimming over with betrayal and anger and . . . why sugarcoat it? *Emotional devastation.* That's what she'd been riding on when she cut Flynn out of her life.

That was probably an even dumber move than this outfit.

How come self-preservation made her feel so lousy? How come it had been exactly twenty-four hours and Sierra ached as though she'd been separated from Flynn for weeks?

It'd be great to talk over this huge upset in her life with her new, awesome girlfriends. Except that she couldn't share what she was going through with a single person. Which also meant Sierra couldn't beg advice from a single person. With her thumb and first finger, she worried the hem of her top.

Was this a turning point in her life? If she pushed Flynn away for good, would it harden her heart against ever trusting a man again? Would it be cutting off her nose to spite her face?

Until yesterday, she'd thought Flynn to be . . . well, not *perfect*. But perfect for her. She'd told him those three little words that felt like the biggest thing ever.

Had started brainstorming ideas for what she could paint as a birthday present for him.

Not that Sierra knew when Flynn's *real* birthday was.

Which was the problem. Her not knowing what was and wasn't real about him. Especially the big factor of if he was really a bad guy, deep down. Someone that might too easily fall back into that way of life, and drag her with him.

Did he even have the same birthday he'd grown up with? Or was that a lie, too?

"Ms. Williams?" A woman with long blond hair came around from the back of her tiny house. She wore a teal unstructured tank over jeans with to-die-for flat teal sandals. Sierra would assume it was someone who was very, very lost—there being no road at the back of her house—except that she'd spoken her name.

"You aren't . . . you can't be Marshal Evans?" Sierra whispered the name, in case she was wrong.

"I am." She stuck out a tanned arm and gave a firm handshake.

A good quarter of Sierra's nerves died down. Because this woman looked younger than Mollie. Like they were going to hang out on the grass and just soak up the sun. "You're not dressed very, um, officially."

"I was led to believe that you wanted this visit to go unnoticed." The marshal hooked a thumb over her shoulder toward the forest she'd come from. "I'm blending in."

"How did you get here?"

"I parked about a quarter mile away, then cut through the trees. Again, keeping a low profile."

"That's amazing." It sounded like a little thing. But that level of attention to detail, the way she'd respected and followed Sierra's wishes without any proof this meeting would be worth her while? That professionalism instantly calmed Sierra the rest of the way.

Marshal Evans slid her backpack down one shoulder into her hand. "I'm no superhero. It's not a hardship to rock a pair of shorts on a holiday weekend on the rarity of an Oregon full-sun day."

"Are you from here?" If Sierra could glean even a scrap of personal info on the marshal, it'd make it easier, more fair when she had to spill her deeply personal secret to the woman.

"I go where the job takes me. Right now, that's your porch. May I?" After Sierra nodded, the marshal climbed the stairs. She kept one hand on the wooden rail as they faced off. "I can tell you're nervous."

"Not at all. Terrified, yes. Nervous, not so much, now that I've met you."

"There's no reason to be scared. But I get that me saying that doesn't make the clenched belly go away. We can stay out here and chat first, if that's easier for you. But I don't think skating through small talk will diminish your nerves. How about you just tell me what was the first reproduction painting of yours that Rick passed off as the real thing?"

The answer popped right out, easier than spitting

out a watermelon seed. "*Daybreak*, by Maxfield Parrish."

It was that simple. Because, as the words flooded out of her, Sierra realized she *wanted* to tell the story. She wanted someone to be outraged on her behalf. Like Flynn had been . . .

No. Flynn wasn't a part of her life, her narrative anymore. So maybe if her brain could stop circling back to him every three minutes, that'd be great, 'kay?

Sierra wanted to tell the story to someone who could make a difference. Who could stop Wayne. Stop Rick. Fear had kept her small, curled into an emotional and physical ball for all these months.

Speaking up made Sierra feel ten feet tall.

And Flynn was the one who'd given her the opportunity to do so. Damn it.

After Sierra had run out of details and names and dates and yes, more than a few choice expletives, she sagged against the siding of her tiny house. Running a 5k sounded infinitely less exhausting than revealing her biggest secret to a woman with the power to toss her in jail for being an accessory—no matter how unwittingly.

"Am I safe?" she finally asked in a low voice.

"From Rick?" Delaney flipped shut the notebook she'd been scribbling in and shook her head. "No way of knowing until I verify his whereabouts. I'm going to put out a BOLO for him. Just to keep tabs and make sure he doesn't bolt out of Milwaukee. We want to know exactly where to find him once we get some warrants and are ready to move on this art ring."

Wow. That sounded like it would come together *fast*. She'd only been talking for half an hour, and now there was suddenly a whole operation planned out in Delaney's head. Sierra grabbed a brush from the edge of her easel. Running it back and forth through her fingers gave her something to do besides squeezing her hands together so hard her nails could draw blood.

"No. Not from Rick. Am I safe from you, Marshal? Safe from prosecution?"

Delaney's honey-blond brows knitted together. "Why, yes. Your cooperation is conditional on total immunity. I was told that was nonnegotiable."

"Oh. Yes. Right." It was one thing to hear Flynn *say* it. He'd said a lot of things since they met. Many—most—*who knew*—of which Sierra now guessed were straight-up lies. So yes, it was altogether a different and better thing to hear the marshal stipulate and agree to the terms.

Putting a hand on Sierra's shoulder, Delaney leaned in and asked, "You are okay with moving forward on this, aren't you?"

"Yes." Firmly, resolutely, and with a nod so sharp her neck cracked, Sierra said, "Yes, I am."

Still pinning her with that blue gaze cooler and sharper than Antarctic icebergs, Delaney pressed once more. "Sierra, why'd you decide to come forward now? Did someone talk you into it? Did you hear a story from someone about how the Marshals Service can protect a witness?"

Omigosh. She was being subtly interrogated. About *Flynn*. The pretty blonde with the super cut arms was trying to find out if Flynn had told Sierra about his other life. About the Maguire brothers being in WITSEC.

This was her chance. If she admitted Flynn had told her the truth, his cover would be blown. They'd move him. Out of Bandon. Give him a new name and a new life somewhere else.

Sierra wouldn't have to look at him every day, wanting to touch him but not trusting him enough to do so. She could be free of the reminder of how gullible she'd been to fall *yet again* for a man who lied to her up one side and down the other. Free of criminals, even those with six degrees of separation. She could be rid of her second biggest mistake.

But that would be horrible. For a whole slew of reasons.

Rafe and Mollie would have to break up. Or did Mollie know the big secret? All three of the brothers would not only have to leave their current jobs—which Rafe and Flynn seemed to enjoy—but switch to new ones in no way connected. Yes, she'd spent quite a bit of the night Googling everything she'd never known that she'd want to know about WITSEC.

Mostly, it would be horrible because Flynn wouldn't be in her life anymore.

After a light chuckle, Sierra said, "All I know about

the marshals I learned from watching *The Fugitive* and *The Untouchables*."

"Even bald and at sixty, Sean Connery was smoking hot in that movie." Delany fanned herself and fluttered her lashes.

Sierra dug the toe of her sneaker into the tiny gap between the planks of the porch. "I came forward because a friend called me brave. He sees me quite differently than I see myself. I decided it was time for me to become the person he thinks I am. The person who could deserve a man as strong and caring and sweet as—"

Her voice trailed off. Because she needed to gulp back the tears already thickening her throat. The ones running down her cheeks were a lost cause.

She loved Flynn. Despite the lies. Despite how after he knew about her horrible mix-up with the criminal element, Flynn had continued to lie to her. To hide so many things about himself. Especially what he had to know was the most important—that he'd broken the law, too.

The marshal rubbed a small circle on Sierra's back. Tentatively. Like you'd pat a hissing cat you were worried might hork up a furball in your face. Touchy-feely clearly wasn't her jam.

"Are you okay? Do you need to take a break from the hard stuff and talk about something else?"

"The only other thing I want to talk about is ten times as hard." She sniffed. Twice. Then worried that her mascara was streaking down her cheeks. Talk about a look even less serious than dotted sneakers.

"I'm a good listener," Delaney offered. "Not as a marshal—just as a friend. Because it seems like you need one right now."

That's when it hit her. She *could* talk to the marshal. It'd be like confessing to a priest. Sort of. Delaney was required by law to keep her secrets, and would immediately be leaving town anyway.

Sierra hitched herself up to sit on the railing. Let her feet dangle. "I'm attracted to a man who is all wrong for me."

Delaney sat on the corner opposite her. And gave an exaggerated wince. "Ah, the classic bad boy. Those are hard to resist."

"I fell for him thinking he was a moody, quiet bad boy. But now I think he might be *actually* bad. Reformed, but without any guarantee it'll stick. Especially because he just hurt me pretty badly. As I'm sure you guess from the whole Rick story, I've got some baggage. Scars on my heart. Why should I metaphorically open my shirt, hand over a knife, and give this guy a chance to stab me some more?"

Yup. That rant about summed it up. Sierra was just plain scared.

Delaney's nose crinkled. Her mouth twitched to the side as if she was deciding between two responses and had no idea which one to spit out. She rubbed at the thin bracelet on her left wrist. A silver key and a heart-shaped lock dangled from it. "Can I tell you something? A little nugget of wisdom I've gleaned not just from dating, but from the complicated work life I've got going?"

Oh, thank goodness. Because she really and truly had no idea what to do about Flynn. Flynn-the-freaking-ex-mobster. Except, Sierra reminded herself, that wasn't Flynn. Flynn was the man who opened the door for her and gave her foot rubs. The ex-mobster was someone else. Someone she didn't know.

The real questions was whether or not Flynn saw himself as two different people. The old bad guy, and the new-and-improved good guy. Should it make a difference that he'd sort of fallen into it? That he'd balanced on the legal side of the fence—albeit while knowing full well what was going on with the rest of his organization?

Didn't knowing about the criminal activities and yet not reporting them make him complicit?

On the other hand . . . she'd never picked up the phone and reported Rick or Wayne to the police. She'd skipped that obligation out of pure selfishness, to keep herself safe. Flynn had the added responsibility of keeping his secret to keep Kellan safe.

So no, Sierra didn't have a leg to stand on in the Self-Righteously Aggrieved Territory. It just left her as Empress of Cowardly and Petrified Land.

A growing headache throbbed behind her right eye. "Of course. I'll take any advice you want to toss my way. I'll even pay you for it, with a sketch, if you want."

"Thanks, but this'll be free. I'm not supposed to accept presents from witnesses." A tiny smile lifted the corners of Delaney's lips as she played with the intricate key. "Bad boys aren't always as bad as they seem on the outside. In fact, they can be pretty darned wonderful on the inside."

Sierra recognized that type of smile. The googly eyes. The unfocused gaze. It was an over-the-moon-for-a-guy smile. Clearly this so-called advice was colored by a serious case of lust. No wonder it was weak. "That's not advice. Advice is a black-and-white line between the right choice and the wrong one."

Delaney steepled her hands in front of her nose. Sucked in a long, deep breath. Then, as if imparting the secret of the universe, she said in a near-whisper, "Life isn't black-and-white."

Seriously? What was next—a marine biologist stopping by to tell them that water wasn't wet?

"That's an odd thing for a law enforcement official to say."

Her hands dropped back to her sides. Her face fell, too. "Trust me—I'm getting slapped with the confusing dichotomy of that with growing regularity. It's very difficult to balance your heart—and your hormones—against what you think is right."

"Adulting is so darned *hard*." Sierra wrapped her arm around the post and leaned against it. Wishing it was Flynn. How pathetic was it when even a splintery support for the roof made her miss him? "I don't know what to think. All I'm doing is feeling. And all I'm feeling is miserable."

"When you're with your bad boy who's all wrong for you?"

Sticking out her tongue, Sierra replied, "No. I'm miserable because I broke up with him."

"Would you feel better if he was here, right now, holding your hand?"

Yes. A thousand times yes. But would she wonder about every gesture, every word he uttered? Wonder what was true? Wonder if he'd hurt her again?

"I'd feel better if I had a drink of water," she said lightly and brightly. *Aka* it probably came out sounding more high-pitched and fake than the time she'd told her last good foster mom that her hot dish casserole was delicious, and didn't cop to it being a flavorless, gluey disaster. "Come on inside."

If the marshal saw through her less-than-subtle topic change, she didn't say anything. Until she got two steps through the door. Then gasped and muttered, "Wow."

Sierra turned with a glass in each hand. Charcoal sketches covered the couch, the table, and the stairs. "Oh, I'm sorry. My place isn't usually this much of a mess. I was, um, sprint sketching against a stopwatch, so I just kept flinging papers everywhere as I finished."

"You timed yourself drawing these?"

She filled the glasses, hoping Delaney wouldn't mind tap water with no ice. Her tiny house didn't have room for a freezer. "A friend suggested that I do sketches for people on the boardwalk. And I definitely need money.

But if I'm going to do it, I need to be able to finish in less than ten minutes. Today was a test to see if I could."

"You did all these in ten minutes?" Delaney stooped to pick up a sketch of Elena, all sex and attitude. Then Norah, shoving at her hair with her prosthesis. Mick with his grump face on underneath the USMC cap he always wore. Carlos, grinning like a fool as he totaled the nightly receipts.

"Most were faster. I'm headed down there this afternoon to see how it goes. I just have to figure out how much to charge."

"I'll give you fifty dollars."

Um, *wow*. "You don't even know these people."

"I don't want one of them. I want you to draw the person I'm going to describe to you." Delaney snapped her fingers, then pointed at Sierra. "Can you draw Wayne? Something we can run through facial recognition, add to the BOLO?"

"I don't have to." Sierra took the stairs two at a time. When she came back down, it was brandishing a handful of papers. "I did these the day I ran away. While everything was fresh in my mind. Wayne, his house, Mrs. Newberry, Rick, the nameless muscle-guy who stayed in the room with Wayne. I've got it all."

Shuffling through them, Delaney's mouth dropped open. "These are terrific."

"I had a lot of alone time, being on the run. Gave me the opportunity to polish each one." Sierra grabbed her pad. It sounded crazy. But fifty dollars was more than enough to make her not question it. "Let me set the timer."

"No need. I just want the finished product. However long it takes." Delaney stacked the sketches and sat on the couch. Then she started reeling off characteristics.

Sierra sat cross-legged on the floor and just listened for a bit. Then she held up a hand, stopping the flow of information, and started to draw. They went back and forth like that enough times that Sierra lost count.

Finally, Delaney leaned forward and just stared at the paper. "That's good."

"Great. I captured the spirit of your imaginary friend," she joked.

Delaney went outside, retrieved her pack, and pulled out her wallet. She handed Sierra a small laminated photo from it. "That's who you drew. My father."

It looked . . . well, not exact, by any means. But Sierra would give herself a pat on the back for getting darned close. Close enough that the resemblance was super obvious. "If you have a photo, why'd you put me through that little exercise?"

"You're fast. You're intuitive. I think you have the makings of a good law enforcement sketch artist."

Random. But just the idea sent a thrill of excitement racing up her spine. "For the police, you mean?"

"The police, the Marshals, the FBI, you name it." Delaney carefully tucked the photo back away. Then she propped her elbows on her knees. "There isn't formal training for this job. You just need to have the skills.

It would only be sporadic. You'd need to travel up to Eugene and Portland, for sure. But it'd be a way of using that education you gave up, and a way of helping us put criminals away. Plus, not to be too blunt, but it looks like you'd welcome the cash."

Talk about a way to make her feel strong again. Using her talent for *good*. That would go a long way to restoring her karmic balance over all the replica paintings she'd done that had been sold as originals.

"It sounds amazing. But I don't have a car. I can't afford one."

"Well, you wouldn't start right away. We'd want to get this mess with Wayne out of the way first. I'm fairly certain, with a victim this wealthy, that there's a reward you'll be able to collect for providing information on the crime. Then we could provide transport, put you up in Eugene for a week while you train with one of our artists."

"I'd really like to do that." Sierra bit her lip. She didn't want to come off as dismissive or ungrateful of the massive opportunity Delaney had just handed her. And yet she'd never be able to live with herself if she didn't at least *try* to get her planned future back. True strength was about reaching, striving for something with no guarantees.

Her mouth suddenly felt dry. Her skin too tight. What . . . what if she applied that reasoning to the situation with Flynn? The rest of her life hadn't come with a guarantee. Why on earth did she assume that falling in love would?

Grabbing for the forgotten water, Sierra downed it in three fast gulps. "Could I push my luck and ask for another favor?"

"This job offer isn't a favor, trust me." Delaney beckoned for her to continue with one hand. "But sure, go for it."

"I still want to teach. Without proof of my degrees, though, it'll be impossible for me to get a job anywhere."

"That's it? You want transcripts?"

"Yes. They don't exist for Sierra Williams."

Delaney stood, paced the length of the house. Shook her head when it took less than ten steps, and then returned. "I'll verify your actual transcripts. Making a set under your current name won't be any trouble after that."

It was that simple? After all these months of assuming her dream of teaching was gone for good? Maybe she should've gone to the authorities sooner.

Or maybe everything had happened at the right time, for the right reason. That would take some more pondering once her pulse stopped racing with joy. "Thank you. Thank you so much."

Acting on impulse, she hugged Delaney. The marshal stiffened initially, but she did come around to a few light pats on Sierra's back.

"To be clear, you'll have to testify under your real name. Once we catch Wayne and Rick, the danger to you will be over. Would you like protection until then?"

"No. I've already got protection." Sierra heard the confidence brimming in her words.

It was true that she'd never felt safer than when with Flynn. The problem was that she'd said some harsh things to him. Judged him, in a way he hadn't judged her at *all* when she'd shared her story. Flynn was such a good guy, he'd protect her no matter what. Even if their relationship was over.

But she hoped that wasn't the case.

Chapter Twenty-three

A TAP ON his shoulder had Flynn spinning around, fists raised. Especially dangerous since one held a hammer.

Rafe leapt backward, banging into the workbench before tripping over a pile of wood scraps. His mouth moved, and from the thunderous expression on his face, Flynn wasn't at all sad he couldn't hear the words.

He yanked off his headphones. "I thought we had a rule. No sneaking up on each other. Not so much a safe thing to do with ex-mobsters."

"That's why I tapped you on the shoulder. To *not* sneak up on you. Jesus H, Flynn. There's no danger here. Overreact much?"

Flynn thought about that as he put the hammer down on the grass. "No. Not an overreaction at all. Just because O'Connor's gone doesn't mean there's no danger."

"He's not *just* gone. More importantly, he didn't

come here for us. Our cover's still rock solid. No one from McGinty's crew has any idea we're in Bandon."

Yeah. But . . . "We got lazy, depending on the marshals to keep us safe."

"You got spooked," Rafe corrected.

"Maybe it was a sign that we should keep our guard up."

"No way. I'm not living with one eye over my shoulder and one arm cocked again. Not in this new life we've got. This thing with O'Connor turned out to be a big fat nothing. So quit with the fists as your first go-to."

Rafe was right. Flynn hadn't so much cared before if danger came down the pike and necessitated another move. Now that he did, he'd overreacted. Covering, he said, "You're scared because you know I can take you."

"I'm scared you'd embarrass yourself trying."

Flynn decided to test the normalcy of their brotherly bond. He'd either get an elbow to the face or an answer that would help him sleep at night. "Hey, Rafe? Can I ask you something?"

His older brother tugged at the dark wave of hair atop his head. "Shit. Now what's wrong?"

"You *just* said we shouldn't be living under a Code Red mentality." He wiped his hands on his shorts to get rid of the wood dust. "Why assume anything's wrong?"

"Because I know you. Because the last innocent question you asked me was if I wanted sausage on our last pie at Lou Malnati's."

Son of a bitch. Like Flynn wasn't having a shitty enough day without that reminder of one of the things he missed most about his former life. "Why'd you have to go and mention pizza? Every time I get the craving for some deep-dish under control, you go and bring it up."

"That's the problem with going cold turkey. Cutting off an addiction like that never works."

Not as if they'd had a choice.

Rafe of all people should remember that, seeing as how he was the one who made the unilateral decision to uproot them. But Flynn understood why, and wouldn't be giving his brother grief about it anymore. He'd spent too long already moping about the past.

With a hope in his voice he barely felt, Flynn said, "Think we can split a pie when we go back to testify?"

Rafe shook his head. And had the decency to look damned sad about it. "We can't go to the restaurant. It'd be one of the first places McGinty would send people to look for us. But maybe we could sweet talk Delaney into bringing us takeout."

"I dunno. I'm pretty sure the favor I asked her for this week already pushed the limit." Flynn was, in fact, *positive* he couldn't ask her for another favor and needed to do something nice for her. Over-the-top nice. He'd offer to build her something, but he had no idea if the marshal even had a real home, or just followed her protectees around the country 24/7.

Didn't that just put things into perspective about his six months of bitching about the homes she'd tried to get him to accept?

"You asked for help changing someone's life," Rafe said. "This isn't close to being on the same level. I'll give her the money. I just want a fucking slice."

The ferocity in his tone gave Flynn more than a little satisfaction. It was only right that Rafe should crave it as much as he did. "About the whole danger thing . . ."

"Christ. We're circling back to that? You want to rig up pots and pans hanging from the ceiling like *Home Alone* in case someone tries to break in?"

"Very funny." Flynn twisted his upper body to deliver a high side and back kick combo to the air. "You forget that I know seven ways to completely disable, if not kill, an opponent with my bare hands. I don't need a homemade alarm to keep me safe."

"Then what's with the one-track mind?"

Flynn paced a slow circle around the bookcase he'd almost finished. He'd been too busy having fun with Sierra all these weeks to work on it. That excuse was gone now. It looked solid and normal. Just like them.

One kick and it'd shatter, though. One kick to their family and the Maguires might shatter. They were only strong and solid when they were put together right. Like they were getting back to now. But that didn't mean they couldn't be yanked apart again.

He smoothed a hand over the well-sanded top. "Do you ever feel guilty for getting Mollie involved in all of this? For the danger that might—at some point—come our way? She'd be in the cross fire if that happened."

"There's an image I didn't need in my head." Rafe scrubbed his palms over his eyes.

"Don't stand there and pretend it hasn't occurred to you."

"Fine." Rafe toed out a chair from the glass-topped table and sank into it. "Of course I worry about Mollie. You and I, we can take care of ourselves. But Kellan? Mollie? They don't know our world. They don't know how vicious it can get."

"So how do you live with the guilt of dragging her into it?"

"I don't have any. I still feel guilt for dragging you two into WITSEC, but I've got zero on my conscience about Mollie."

"Why?" Flynn asked as he dropped into the opposite chair.

That was the key question. He'd thought that telling Sierra the truth was the right thing to do. But even though she'd broken up with him, what if she worried every night? Without him around to comfort her? He was fucking racked with guilt for dialing her in to his messed-up life.

"Because Mollie's an adult. I laid out the facts. Staying with me was her decision. I mean, I'm awesome and all that, but she could've walked away."

Flynn knew his brother's ego was big, but that was off the charts. "You think your alleged awesomeness is bigger than the possibility of being gunned down when we walk past that weird-ass red statue into the Dirksen Courthouse in October?"

"Mollie's a doctor. She's more aware than most how quickly a life can end, without any warning. So she focuses on enjoying each day that she gets. Each day that *we* get together. It took some convincing on my part. I didn't think I was being fair to her. It's why I refused to date her when we met."

"You did date her." In fact, Rafe, who'd left a trail of women in his wake in Chicago without so much as a backward glance, had dated Mollie from day one like his life depended on it. Flynn had never seen someone fall so hard, so fast—all while trying to deny it. He and Kellan laughed about it all the time.

Rafe's whole face sort of . . . melted. Melted into a look of love that said he'd follow Mollie anywhere. Even go shopping with her on Black Friday, if that's what it took to get another kiss. "Well, that woman's damned irresistible. The point is that I was worried about the future. She taught me to enjoy the present. Because, yeah, it may be all we get. Might as well live it up."

"I hadn't thought about it like that."

"I'd say you haven't thought about much of anything besides how pissed off you were for a long time. Now that Sierra got you to pull your head out of your ass, you should live it up, too. Do something awesome for the Fourth."

"I tried that. My girlfriend broke up with me. And I have to be at work in three hours to help everyone *else* celebrate the holiday."

Rafe winced. "Mollie and I'll swing by the Gorse

later. Keep you company after the fireworks. How's that?"

"Probably the best offer I'll get. Thanks."

Female laughter floated down the path along the side of the house. He didn't need to look up to know that Sierra was one of them. He'd recognize her laughter, her voice, her scent *anywhere*. When they appeared from the behind the six-foot-tall bush with big red flowers, Flynn white-knuckled the arms of the chair to keep himself from leaping up and running to her.

Karen stopped first, with her hands planted on her hips. "Flynn, where's your sexy brother?"

"I'm right here," Rafe said, sounding plenty put out.

"Very funny. You're not only taken, you're not my type."

Even Mollie looked surprised, along with amused. "You don't go for tall, dark, and muscled?"

"In my fantasies, sure. In real life?" Karen's mouth turned down at the corners. "Your man's too much for me. He has a dangerous swagger about him."

"I know." Mollie wrapped her arms around Rafe's neck and dropped a kiss on the top of his head. "It's super hot."

"I like my men more . . . polished. Suave. Kellan seems like he *knows* things. Like he'd know how to show me a good time."

"We don't know where he is. But you can bet I'll tell him that you're interested. If he's absorbed even half of my charm and talents with women over the years, I guarantee he'll come through on that good time."

Flynn couldn't believe they were standing there talking like everything was normal.

It wasn't. It wasn't fucking normal at all. Because Sierra was across the yard, not looking at him, not touching him. And he didn't have any damn right to go over there.

God, it hurt. Yet he couldn't *stop* looking at her, in her plain white tank and denim shorts, with a red, white, and blue striped bow around her ponytail. He couldn't stop drinking her in like she was the first water he'd been given after a week crawling across the desert. Sierra looked beautiful. She looked like everything he wanted.

Everything he couldn't have.

Mollie tugged Rafe out of his chair. "Hey, Karen and I were hoping you could set us up with some cold ginger ales. We've been on the boardwalk with the sun beating down for too long."

Rafe looked at all three women. Then over at Flynn, confusion pulling his brows together. "Suuuure," he drawled out.

Karen and Mollie hustled him inside. Flynn just kept his grip tight on the arms of the chair. Because he didn't know what Sierra was doing here. She'd made it clear that he wasn't supposed to talk to her. Wasn't supposed to make any move at all in her direction.

So all he could do was sit there, keep his mouth shut, and wait for her to do . . . something.

She set down her sketchpad, the easel from under

her arm, and slid her backpack to the ground. "Hi," she said in a small voice.

It was like gargling with gravel, but he managed to get a return "Hi" out of his bone-dry throat.

"I did sketches on the boardwalk today. For money. It went really well."

God, he was proud of her. Sitting up a little straighter, Flynn said, "Of course it did. Your talent is amazing."

A smile bloomed across Sierra's face, and pink raced across her cheeks. "See? That's why I wanted to come here. When I finished, all I wanted to do was race over and tell you how well it went. Because I knew you'd be supportive. I knew you'd understand what a huge step it was for me."

Cautiously, Flynn asked, "What made you change your mind, decide to make money off your art again?"

"A lot of things." She held up a hand and ticked off points on her fingers. "The girls reminded me that I should make money off of something I love, something I'm good at. The marshal reminded me that pretty soon, they'll close the door on that horrible chapter of my life, and it shouldn't haunt me anymore. And you, Flynn, most of all. Your belief in me gave me the strength to do it."

Her words shocked him. Sierra was acting normal, too. Like they hadn't fought. Like she hadn't dumped him. Like he hadn't broken her heart and trust—even if accidentally. "I'm glad I could help." It was all Flynn let himself say. He didn't dare push at all for more. He didn't deserve it.

As if noticing it for the first time, she did a double take at the bookcase. Walked around it, stepping over the can of whitewash and the paintbrush at its corner. "Is this for me?"

"Yes." God, they were being so careful with each other. Was this what it was going to be like from now on?

"Given how our fight ended on Sunday, I'm shocked that you kept working on it."

Aaaand her surprise shocked him right back. In fact, it propelled Flynn right out of his seat. "Why?"

Still not looking at him, Sierra stood on tiptoe to run her fingertips across the whisper-soft grain of the wood he'd sanded this morning. "What if I don't forgive you?"

As if that made any difference whatsoever. Aside from how it hurt worse than a kick to the balls. She was imprinted on his heart now. Hell, she *was* his whole heart. Even if it made her mad again, Flynn had to speak the truth. "That won't stop me from loving you."

At that, Sierra turned. A fat tear wobbled in the corner of each eye. "That's exactly what I wanted to hear."

"It is?" Flynn hadn't let himself hope she'd change her mind.

He'd given up on hope of getting what *he* wanted out of life years ago, when McGinty laid down the law on every aspect of it. Until WITSEC, weirdly enough.

Until moving here, to a town where the people refused to let you sulk in silence. Where everyone did their own thing and was accepted for it. Where he'd discovered how much he liked doing a job he'd sure as hell never planned for.

Where the gift of Sierra's love made him believe in the future again.

This time, he knew he'd ultimately be okay, with his brothers and his job and his friends.

But the thing was, he wanted more than *okay*. He wanted Sierra. He wanted, as much as it made him sound like a Disney fucking princess, a happily ever after with her.

Sierra knelt on the grass. Then she lifted the cover on her sketchpad, flipped to the back, and tore out a piece of paper. "I brought you something. A peace offering. An *I'm so sorry I was judgmental* gift."

"That's not necessary."

"It is," she insisted. "It took me a little time to come around to it, but the fact is that you didn't do anything that I didn't do first. I lied about my name. So did you. I lied about my past. So did you."

"The past you lied about was a god-awful scam you got bamboozled into. A crime you witnessed, but didn't commit. My past involved being a sworn member of an organization that committed crimes and hurt people. What we did wasn't the same at all."

"It was. You never committed a crime, Flynn. And— what matters the most—you didn't *want* to be bad. You just stood by and watched, like me. I kept my secrets to keep myself safe. You did it to keep your brothers safe. Most importantly, we finally shared them because we cared enough to be honest with each other."

It all sounded too good to be true. It sounded like Sierra wasn't mad at him anymore. But he knew, deep down, that he didn't deserve it. "That sounds a lot like you giving me an out."

"I'm not. Because what you did, lying to me, was wrong. Just like what I did, lying to you, was wrong." Those big blue eyes looked up at him, shining with tears, but also shining with all the care and tenderness he was used to seeing in her gaze. "But I'm forgiving you, Flynn."

"Are you sure that's smart?" He had to be certain she meant it. Certain that Sierra had considered all the facts. Because he couldn't take it if she changed her mind in two days. Or by Labor Day. Or *ever*.

"I thought I was being smart by breaking up with you. To protect myself from the potential of repeating a mistake. To protect my heart. But there's nothing to protect without you. *Everything* is better when I share it with you. I don't want to be with someone with a clean record, an upstanding citizen. I want to be with *you*, Flynn. I need you in my life, by my side. So I forgive you. And I hope that you forgive me, too. For lying to you, and for what I put you through these past couple of days while I worked everything out in my head."

Flynn fell to his knees. Then he gathered her against

his chest and hugged her. Breathed her scent in. Felt her heartbeat against his. Felt how *right* they were together. "God, Sierra, I'm sorry for putting you through that, too."

"We won't talk about it anymore. We both screwed up, and we won't do it again. Let's make it part of those bad pasts we're closing the door on, okay?"

"Okay." And because he wasn't an idiot, Flynn kissed her.

He fell back, pulling Sierra to lie on top of him, and kissed her with fast pecks across her cheek, and long, wet, openmouthed kisses that seared the air around them. Unable to contain his relief and happiness, Flynn tightened his hold at her waist and rolled them across the lawn, kissing and laughing the whole way.

"We both spent a lot of months frozen in place by our old lives. So I wanted to give you something to remind you how good our new lives are." She handed over the thick paper.

It was a drawing of the two of them, from behind. Sitting on the sand at the Coquille River Lighthouse. Sierra's drawing was so good, it was easy to see the intimacy in the tilt of her head against his, the clasped hands visible between their bodies.

"This is just a sketch. I didn't have time to do more, because I didn't want to wait any longer to see you. But I want to do it in oils, with the sunset and the water and your thick black hair I love to touch and—"

Flynn cut her off. "Stop right there. Or I'll need to

take you, right here, in full view of that kitchen window I know damn well Rafe and Mollie and Karen are staring at us through."

Giggling, Sierra peeked over her shoulder. Then stuck out her tongue and wiggled her fingers from her ears at the window. "It'd serve them right."

"Look, I'm happy as hell that you're back. And I think you've got a solid plan in us not talking this thing 'round in circles. Aside from me saying I'm sorry and I was wrong and I'll do anything to make up for hurting you."

"Duly noted. I may cash that in for a foot rub after our shift tonight."

"But we have to finish the conversation." Flynn wanted to get it over with so that he'd never have to feel uncertain about their love ever again. "I love you. You don't need me. You're twenty times stronger than me. You had to start a new life from scratch with no help, no funds, no plan—and you thrived. I did it with the entire government backing me, and acted like an asshole for six months. You amaze me."

Sierra stroked her fingers through the hair right above his ear. "Your strength kept you going in, every day for years, to college classes that didn't interest you, to a job you didn't want. You did all of that to give Kellan a good life. That's a strength that humbles me, because it was all on behalf of someone else. No matter how bad we might have been in the past, we are *definitely* good for each other."

"I don't know what's going to happen at the trial. I

don't know what sort of a future, if any, I'll have after October."

She blew a wet raspberry from between those lips Flynn couldn't wait to take again. "Now that I've met your marshal, I have no doubt that she'll keep you safe. Her biceps are almost as impressive as yours."

No wonder he loved this woman. She brought sunshine to every aspect of life. "I'd love nothing more than to march you down to the jewelers and buy you a ring. But that wouldn't be fair to you. Because the truth is that I can't promise you anything."

The indulgent smile said Sierra thought he'd missed something as obvious as the ocean being blue. "Sure you can. Promise that you love me. That's all I need."

"I do. I will. Forever."

"Then I'm good. Because love is the best thing of all. And being loved by you, Flynn, is as good as it gets."

He'd never been good before. The tattoo on his hip proved it.

But he'd damn well work every day of his life to be good for Sierra.

Kellan Maguire is the only "Good Guy" in his family of mobsters and he's pissed as hell that he had to leave law school to hide out in Witness Protection. But maybe his new life won't be so bad, as long as their gorgeous U.S. Marshal handler sticks around . . .

Don't miss the final fun, sexy novel in Christi's *Bad Boys Gone Good* series . . .

GOT IT BAD

Coming September 2018!

Northwestern University Law School, Chicago
2:30 p.m., November 1

KIERAN MULLANEY PUSHED through the double glass doors of the Northwestern University Law School and sucked in a deep breath. Sure, other people might think he was nuts, what with the exhaust fumes, pollution, general downtown stink of Chicago in the air. But Kieran only smelled *freedom*.

No more notes on his iPad. No more trying to hide his side-eye when that douche canoe Pietro cut off every woman in the class when they tried to answer. Pietro, by the way, who'd gone by Peter for the first two years of school. Until he partied all night in Boytown with a hot Latin lover named Manuel. Suddenly his name changed, he started wearing loafers without socks, and he only bought empanadas and rice at lunch. His general douchiness had, however, always been there.

Law school didn't suck. It was sometimes interesting. It just wasn't fun. Or rewarding. Or, you know, even his choice. Not that he'd get pissy about that now. Nope, Kieran planned to celebrate his freedom, for the next few hours, at least, by finding someone sexy and sassy and talking her into a drink. No talk about tort law. No case law. No law, period.

Flirting. That's what was on the docket. Kieran didn't need his four years of undergrad and now rounding the corner into his third year of law school when it came to his mastery of romancing the fairer sex. He'd been charming women out of their tops, bottoms, and everything underneath since . . . well, since long before his brothers Ryan and Frank actually *thought* he'd lost his virginity.

He looked down Superior Street for a hot prospect. Pretty much any female that he didn't recognize from law school would do. Kieran almost jolted when his gaze connected with two very blue eyes staring right at him. Very blue, long-lashed, and with a single, *I'm interested* raised eyebrow.

"Oh, hey there." And then she added an upward tilt to her mouth that sealed the deal. This girl had *noticed* him.

This was a million times better than trying to stay awake in Criminal Procedures class. Plus, she was unexpected. Kieran fucking *loved* surprises.

"Hi yourself, beautiful. Are you hanging around the law school because you need a lawyer? Or because smart men with enormous earning potential turn you on? Because, either way, I'm your man."

Her smile flipped downward into a disapproving smirk. "Wow. Has that line ever worked? I mean, *ever*? There's four huge problems with the four sentences you just smarmed at me."

Kieran was equal parts pissed that she'd called him out on his lazy come-on . . . and intrigued that she'd called him out on his lazy come-on. "Smarmed isn't a word."

"Didn't you hear? You can make anything a verb these days. The grammar police officially gave up when *squeed* got added to the OED."

Surprise Girl was definitely around his age. Definitely his type, what with the sass and the smarts.

Definitely hot, with those wide, pink-glossed lips that begged to be kissed. Thick blond hair skimmed just below her shoulders. Kieran really wanted to slide his fingers through it, tug just hard enough so that her head tilted back and he could skim his lips along her throat. And he'd glimpsed one hell of a body wrapped up in a cream sweater and jeans before locking his eyes respectfully above her chin once they started talking. Oh, and those knee-high brown leather boots that were the best god-damned thing about autumn in the Midwest.

He crossed his arms over his chest. "So what are your official complaints with what I said?"

A super slo-mo blink indicated that she'd expected an apology, and was surprised by his challenge. Then she shoved up the sleeves of her sweater with a determined squint. Game on.

"You can't assume I'm 'hanging around' the law school. I just saw you come out the door, which means you have zero knowledge of where I'm coming from or going. And I just came from a walk on the lakeside trail, so in fact I know you're wrong."

In Kieran's book, feisty was more fun than overtly flirty any day. He shrugged, just to egg her on. "Okay, that's one."

She tossed her head. The motion sent her hair rippling in the late afternoon sunlight. Exactly the way it'd ripple if Kieran flipped her on top of him in a bed. "If I did need a lawyer, I'd go find an actual lawyer. Not some student who may or may not pass the bar exam on the fifth try."

He held up two fingers, spread in a wide V. "Two." Kieran barely bit back a snort. No way would he be one of those idiots who didn't prep enough to pass on the first try.

"As for that presumed earning potential?" She patted the bulge of her fat, pumpkin-colored purse. Geez, that thing was big enough to hold a gun. Most women he knew stuck a credit card in their iPhone case and called it a day. What could she be lugging around in there?

Kieran widened his stance, tucking his thumbs into the front pockets of his jeans. Arguing with the pretty stranger was a hell of a lot more fun than arguing in mock trials. "It's a well-known fact that even the dumbest lawyer can pull in the big bucks. Why do you think so many people suffer through three years law school hell?"

"What if you become a public defender?" A motorcycle missing its muffler roared by, and the sharp blast it made whipped her head around as fast as if she'd thought it was a sniper. Guess in today's world you couldn't be too careful. Just as fast, she whipped her attention back to Kieran. "Or you took out loans for all seven years of college and won't actually turn a profit on your super fun eighty-hour work weeks until you're pushing forty?"

"Three." He conceded her point with a nod. And wiped a hand across his mouth to hide his grin.

Finally, the woman threw her arms up in the air. "Either way, why on *earth* would you think that *you're* the man I need? You don't know anything about me!"

"Four." Kieran moved closer. So close that he smelled her perfume. Something fresh, like rain in a forest. Close enough that, yeah, he could see straight down her cleavage to a *thank you, God* amount of creamy skin surging against the lace edge of her bra. "And now I've got an answer for you."

"This ought to be good." She tilted her head up, her chin jutted forward in an ongoing challenge. "Go on."

"Yes, apparently all of that does work—because you're still standing here arguing with me." Kieran let his arms swing forward just enough so the backs of his hands brushed the backs of hers. A jolt—tiny, but visibly noticeable—ran through both of them at the touch. So he did it again. "And arguing invariably leads to kissing."

Those pretty pink lips parted. Then they closed again, and she licked them. God, the woman was *killing* him with this non-flirting flirting. "Is that so?"

Kieran spread his fingers to interlace, backwards, with hers. Just the tips. Just to tease both of them a little. "Well, you have two choices. We could skip right to the kissing. Or we could go for a drink first. Do something old-school like—and I'm just spitballing here—learn each other's names."

"Ooh. Looks like I've found an actual gentleman."

Not like he'd had a choice. "Believe me when I say I've had chivalry literally beaten into me."

Her hands flipped over to lace even tighter with his, and she squeezed. "Your mom hit you?"

"Never. Not once," Kieran said emphatically. "But after she died, my big brothers raised me. At that point, we'd been wrestling and beating each other up for years. It was better to get an atomic wedgie as a reminder to hold the door open for a girl than because, oh, they think you looked at them weird when passing the ketchup."

Her whole face softened. Thick, dark brown lashes batted in double time over those wide blue eyes. "I'm sorry to hear she died."

Crap.

Usually Kieran remembered to keep the whole *dead parents* thing under wraps. Women tended to focus on it. To abandon all other topics and be the comforter, the soother. Soothing wasn't sexy, though. If he wanted to share memories, he'd turn to Ryan and Frank. Because those memories weren't something he casually discussed. Ever.

"It was a long time ago." He'd learned to use the technique of deflection on this topic long before officially learning its usefulness in law school. "And wedgies aside, I couldn't ask for better brothers. They both work like dogs so that I can go to law school and just study, instead of also humping it at a job or worrying about loans."

Something in her eyes flickered. "They sound great." Another flicker. A . . . shimmy of her eyes. Like thoughts were racing fast behind them. Kieran didn't know what that was about. Did mystery woman have brothers? That she missed? Maybe off in the armed forces?

All he knew was that he wanted to find out.

"Ryan and Frank are the best guys in the world. I'd lay down my life for them, but they'd move heaven and earth to beat me to it."

Flicker number three. "I'm impressed."

Uh oh. Kieran lifted a hand to brush away a stray leaf the November wind had just gusted into her hair. "Before I ruin my chances and send you running into my not-nearly-as-hot-as-me brothers' arms, how about that drink?"

"I think I'd really enjoy that."

It occurred to Kieran that it was the middle of the afternoon. Luckily, they were in Chicago, so finding an open bar day or night wasn't exactly a problem. "Let's walk to Navy Pier. Hit the Tiny Tavern, soak up the view of the lake and the city?" Because he absolutely wanted to keep talking to this fun, feisty woman.

"How about we drive?" She pointed to a huge black SUV half a block down. The oversized, darkened window kind that usually alerted you to the presence of movie stars in the city. "I rolled my ankle skidding on some leaves piled at the entrance to the tunnel under Lakeshore Drive."

"Then you shouldn't even be standing on it." Kieran lifted her into his arms with a fast but smooth swoop. It did not at all suck to have his forearm squeezed between her calf and thigh. And he wouldn't begin to let himself notice the softness of her breast pressed to his chest.

Okay, he'd *notice*, because he wasn't fucking dead. And this woman snuggled tight against him was the best thing he'd held in a very long time.

Her arms lifted to wrap around his neck. "I'm Delaney Evans."

"Kieran Mullaney."

"I guess that makes this an official date. Now that we know each other's names."

"Nope. Not official yet." Kieran tilted his head to just barely brush her lips with his. At least, that's what he'd intended. But she tasted like coconuts and freedom. Kieran slid his tongue along the crease of her lips, and hell if they didn't part right away. His grip tightened on her, hand splaying wide across her taut stomach.

"You hang on to me while I get the door open."

The big door to his left opened and Kieran twisted at the noise, instinctively tucking Delaney a little bit behind him. Then he gaped when he saw his *brothers* inside.

"Get in, K.," Ryan ordered.

There was someone in the driver's seat. Delaney stepped around him—without any limp—and climbed in to sit next to Frank. Confused as all hell, Kieran followed her, dropping his backpack on the floor. She closed the door. The car merged into traffic, moved down the block and was on Lakeshore Drive before Kieran could do more than squint in confusion at Ryan and Frank as he buckled up.

"What the hell is this? Where are we going?" Then he twisted around to look, *really* looked at Delaney. The residual softness in her expression from their kiss was gone. She'd added a brown blazer before doing her seat belt. And now? She'd just pulled a gun out of the side pocket to her seat and tucked it into the back of her pants.

A *gun*? A freaking gun? He'd hit on a woman who carried a gun? Yeah, that stuck with Kieran a little harder than wondering how she knew his brothers. Or why anybody needed a gun in the middle of the afternoon. Which, as a soon-to-be lawyer, was probably a dumb thought. Criminals didn't punch a time clock. Was she a criminal?

"Who are you—really?" he demanded.

"Delaney Evans. U.S. Marshal."

No shit? Marshals were way hotter than he'd ever imagined. Kieran was also pretty fucking off balance to have that be his first response to whatever the hell was going on right now.

"I'm sorry, Kieran." Ryan shook his head and let his

hands hang off of his knees. His oldest brother hadn't looked that sad and serious since . . . hell, probably since their dad died. "It's a shitty way to do this, but I can't think of a good way."

"To do what?" Because Kieran was fucking *worried* at this point.

"To tell you that we're in the Chicago mob. Both of us." Frank pointed back and forth at his older brother. "Or we were, until this morning.

No. No fucking way. Kieran shook his head, trying to shake Frank's words back out of his ears. "That's one hell of a sick joke."

"Notice how we're not laughing."

Yeah. He'd noticed alright. The pair of them matched head to toe. Kieran catalogued the oddness of all of it. Their mussed dark hair—and they both liked to hog the mirror *a lot* to be ready for any hot women that might cross their paths on a given day. Black jeans and tees, on a week day when they should at least be sporting ties. Most of all, the hangdog downward tilt to their whole faces. This . . . whatever *this* was, it was deadly serious.

He tried to lunge sideways to get to Delaney, but the damned seat belt snapped him back in place. Kieran white-knuckled the arm rest as he torqued his body around. "Holy shit, did you arrest my brothers?"

"No."

"Then why—oh." His brain finally revved past the shock. If what Ryan and Frank alleged was true, there was only one reason there'd be a U.S. Marshal in the car with them. "You fuckers are going into Witness Protection, aren't you?"

"Yeah. I'm so, so sorry, K."

"Cut the apology crap." He didn't have time for it. Because Kieran had the feeling he was already on borrowed time. That any second *Marshal* Evans would kick him out of the car and he'd never seen his brothers again. "You're leaving me? This is you two saying goodbye? Forever?"

Damned if there wasn't a lump in his throat. This couldn't be happening. The Mullaney brothers were tight. Tight in a way that only happened when you lost both your parents before you could shave. He'd never even thought about what life would be like without his brothers.

"No." Ryan fought briefly with his seatbelt before just reaching over and gripping Kieran's upper arm. Squeezing it like a python. "We stay together. Always. Keeping the three of us together is the only thing that matters. It's the reason we're joining WITSEC."

"I don't understand. You're ratting on the mob . . . for us?"

"The head of the mob, Danny McGinty—"

Delaney cut him off with a buzzer-like noise. "Hey. Remember the ground rules. Kieran doesn't need details. The less he knows, the better."

Ryan's eyes burned with blue fire he aimed back at the marshal. "He needs to know the name of the man who fucked us over. The man who was behind the death of our parents."

Kieran's suddenly upside-down world did another one-eighty. Nobody had ever said their parents were *murdered*. What else about the life he thought he knew was a total lie?

The woman he still—unfuckingbelievable—wanted to kiss gave a sharp nod. "Fair enough. But watch yourself."

"McGinty had some deals fall apart. He needed someone to take the rap, do time in prison. He picked Frank to be the fall guy. When he oh-so-generously gave me the heads-up, I decided to take action. No brother of mine would rot behind bars for something he didn't do."

The repeated honk of the taxi in the lane next to them bought Kieran time to figure out how to ask the obvious question. "You're a mobster—but you *didn't* commit a crime?"

"Pretty much no. I really do—" Frank grimaced, "*did* run the construction company you know about. Kept my nose clean. It was the front for the mob, but legit. I sure as hell didn't do what McGinty wants me to cop to."

Ryan held up two fingers. "No prison. And we stay together. Those were my terms when I went to the Feds and asked for protection. They gave their word. It's all going down today. The raid on McGinty's crew. And the three of us disappearing forever."

Forever? Talk about dramatic overkill. Ryan always did like to tell stories. He looked out at the enormous, overwhelming blue of Lake Michigan. The lake that had anchored his whole life. They weren't leaving Chicago. No way.

He pushed off Ryan's hand. "Wait a minute. You mean we'll be holed up in some boring safehouse in the suburbs for a few weeks while you get questioned."

"No." And Delaney actually looked at him with pity—fucking *pity!*—as she continued. "That's only step one. The Irish Mob is bigger than McGinty, bigger than Chicago."

Frank glanced out the window, then deliberately turned his back on the view. "It won't ever be safe for us to come back here. Or ever be Mullaneys again. But that's just a fucking name, right? We'll be together, wherever we end up. *Whoever* we end up."

He was right. Nothing else mattered but sticking with his brothers. The rest was just details. Really fucking weird and impossible details, but still. Practically immaterial compared to the Mullaneys being side by side.

Kieran hadn't, couldn't process any of this. How big of criminals were his brothers? What did they do? What would they do now? Even with traffic at a crawl, he knew they were too far down Lakeshore Drive to see Northwestern any more. Still, he craned his neck out the back window, trying to get one more peek of the law school. Because it was all he knew. All he'd planned and worked toward for years.

Stretching out her arm, Delaney said, "Hand over your wallet."

When a woman with a gun down her pants issued a command, Kieran obeyed. He gave it to her, but kept his hand on top it, so his fingers brushed the inside of her wrist. That electric charge of awareness tingled in him again. Then she pulled out everything but the cash and gave it back. She tucked his ID and credit cards into her bag.

"Right now is the moment your life as Kieran Mullaney ends. Officially."

Well, *shit*.

A Letter from the Editor

Dear Reader,

I hope you liked the latest romance from Avon Impulse! If you're looking for another steamy, fun, emotional read, be sure to check out one of our upcoming titles.

If you like a bit of suspense in your contemporary romance or just love a good Channing Tatum movie, then you do not want to miss STRIPPED by Tara Wyatt! The first book in her new Blue HEAT series is a delicious mash up of 21 Jump Street and Magic Mike, as an elite undercover detective must infiltrate a drug ring operating out of a male strip show. What makes this novel extra steamy? His one-night-stand-turned-new-female-partner is in the audience as back up . . . and watching the whole thing! One-click away!

You can purchase this title by clicking the link above or by visiting our website, www. AvonRomance.com. Thank you for loving romance as much as we do . . . enjoy!

Sincerely,

Nicole Fischer
Editorial Director
Avon Impulse

About the Author

USA Today bestseller **CHRISTI BARTH** earned a master's degree in vocal performance and embarked upon a career on the stage. A love of romance then drew her to wedding planning. Ultimately she succumbed to her lifelong love of books and now writes award-winning contemporary romance.

Christi can always be found either whipping up gourmet meals (for fun, honest!) or with her nose in a book. She lives in Maryland with the best husband in the world.

www.christibarth.com

Discover great authors, exclusive offers, and more at hc.com.